Growing Up Again

Catriona McCloud

First published in Great Britain in 2007 by Orion Books,
an imprint of The Orion Publishing Group Ltd
Orion House, 5 Upper Saint Martin's Lane
London, WC2H 9EA

1 3 5 7 9 10 8 6 4 2

A CIP catalogue record for this book is
available from the British Library.

ISBN-13: 978 0 7528 7488 3 (hardback)
978 0 7528 7489 0 (trade paperback)
ISBN-10: 0 7528 7488 8 (hardback)
0 7528 7489 6 (trade paperback)

Typeset by Deltatype Ltd, Birkenhead, Merseyside

Printed and bound at Mackays of Chatham plc,
Chatham, Kent

The Orion Publishing Group's policy is to use papers that
are natural, renewable and recyclable products and made
from wood grown in sustainable forests. The logging and
manufacturing processes are expected to conform to the
environmental regulations of the country of origin.

In memory of E.A.P.

Acknowledgements

I would like to thank: Lisa Moylett and Nathalie Sfakianos at the agency; Sara O'Keeffe, Thalia Proctor, Jane Wood, Lisa Milton and everyone else at Orion; Cathy Gilligan and Neil McRoberts, my first readers; Jim Hogg and Nancy Balfour of Edinburgh Central Library; Kate from the Corstorphine branch of William Hill; the servitors at Edinburgh School of Art; and all my family and friends for their interest and support.

Chapter 1

4 March 2002

Last night I told Ludo I was leaving him, after seventeen years together, twelve years of marriage.

'After seventeen years?' he said, eyes already filling.

'Well, twelve,' I pointed out.

Seventeen years, almost half my life, since I had seen him across the room at Shona Ward's party in the first year at university, drinking Jim Beam from a bottle while everyone else was on student punch. He had talked to me for hours and, through the punch, I listened.

Twelve years since that day in the ill-advised dress, not enough of a wedding dress to stop the relations tutting but too much like one for me ever to look at the pictures and not cringe. He talked for quite a while then too, in his bridegroom's speech, and this time everyone had to listen. Did I already hate him then? Of course not; I don't even hate him now. And he doesn't hate me. So why am I leaving?

'Why are you leaving?' he said, voice cracking, mouth trembling and wet.

Because you're sitting there crying and you've no idea how ugly it looks. But he's only crying because of what I've told him, so it can't be that. Causes come before effects; we live in linear time. We live in logic, Ludo and me, so there must be another reason. Why am I leaving? Because I'm a heartless cow and he's too good for me, too gentle, too tender, and when a good, gentle, tender person lives with a heartless cow he gets crushed. And when a heartless cow realizes one day that she's married to someone who's crushed, she looks ahead and sees a lot of hard work to uncrush him and she can't summon the effort even to start. It's either that or it's the dizzying possibility – hold on tight to your hats – that between the ages of nineteen and thirty-six at least one of us, possibly both of us, wait for it . . . changed. I don't know which of these versions is closer to being true. Am I flagellating myself with imaginary guilt even though I've done nothing wrong, or am I sloughing off the guilt for the unspeakable thing I am doing before I've even done it? I honestly do not know.

'There's no point going into all that,' I said.

I went upstairs to the spare room and got into bed.

We keep the spare room bed made up. We always did. It used to be for friends too drunk to go home and it was well-used in those days. We were the first couple out of all of our friends to have a proper spare room; we had lamps on our spare room bedside tables before there was even Ikea to buy them from. Then when everyone got cars and stopped drinking, the spare room was kept made up for weekend guests, so that we could lie in a tangle of sheets and Review sections on Saturday morning, knowing that everything was ready and we only had to get up in time to make lunch. And I'm sure we lay in a tangle at least once, but I was always simmering mushrooms for stock, or having to leave enough time to chill the mousse and Ludo was always busy moving the impressive books into the sitting room from the pile beside the bed. That and hiding the compilation CDs. Or perhaps that's unfair; I only saw him do it once and he insisted he was putting it to the back because it was scratched. See? Am I a heartless cow who loathes her husband for no reason at all, or a woman finally worn out by trying to love a pseud and a poser? There's no way to know. And anyway, I don't loathe him. Last night, lying in the spare bed, my heart hammering at the thought of what I had just said, I knew for a fact I didn't loathe him; I knew I still loved him and I was on the point of getting up and going to tell him I didn't mean it, when I heard him coming to me.

'Why now?' he said, in a quavering voice that made me want to scream.

'It's just time,' I told him. 'Let's leave it if you're too upset to talk.'

He took off his shoes and trousers and got in beside me, still crying. There's another thing. He would never have got into a bed with me in his shirt, boxers and socks when we first met, when we first were married. On our honeymoon, he threw my provocative nightie out of the hotel window and roared, 'Never! Never!' and even though it was hand-stitched silk and very expensive I was too embarrassed to go and ask if anyone had found it the next morning and I never got it back. Now: pyjamas. He even irons them. My mother would say I should be happy he irons them himself and doesn't expect me to, and I am. I still am happy that he's so fair and so sensitive. Of course I am. But if I ripped off his ironed pyjamas one night and threw them out of the window shouting 'Never!' would he laugh? Would he remember? If I did it right now, with his shirt and his boxers, would he finally get it? I doubt it, somehow. For someone who studied philosophy for four years, Ludo has a surprisingly literal mind. For every action: a cause. For every question: an answer. He could not comprehend a level of confusion where you might leave your husband and not know why.

'What is it?' he asked, over and over again. 'What's wrong? Tell me what to do and I'll make it right again.'

It's the fact that you're crying and asking me what's wrong. It's the fact that you don't know. It's the fact that you want me to tell you what to do. Some suggestions? Shout 'Bollocks, you're leaving me!' and kiss it better. Shout 'Piss off then!' and go to the pub. Do anything at all except ask me about it in that voice and sound so up for whatever I tell you. You want it in shorthand? Be a man.

Oh God, I sound like his mother. I've definitely heard his mother say that.

Is that what he's done to me? Has he turned me into his mother? Did he turn his mother into his mother? Was she a sweet young woman who just happened to spawn an unlovable child? (That's how over this marriage is, folks. It's one thing to blame your mother-in-law for how your husband turned out, but when you starting blaming *him* for everything that's wrong with *her*, perhaps you've passed the point where things can be rekindled.)

Eventually, because none of the general interrogation was getting him anywhere, he went in for the kill. He asked the question, as I knew he would.

'Is it babies?'

Was it babies? Could we call it babies? Could we call it contempt because he should have known better when I clearly didn't, and instead he listened to me and did something no one would ever believe and, now that I've changed my mind, I've got to choose between staying with him out of guilt, despising him so much he makes me shudder, or doing this. At least it's an answer. If I agree it might shut him up.

'Sort of,' I said.

'Because if it is, I could have it reversed.'

Which is either more proof as though proof were needed that Ludo is an angel and I don't know I'm born, or that Ludo is a world master of manipulative victimhood and I'm a saint to have stood it this long. Has he destroyed me or I him? Or both? Or neither? Do I loathe him? Do I love him? Did I ever?

I must have fallen asleep, because I woke at one point in the dark. He was still there and I knew he was awake; I could hear him breathing carefully so as not to disturb me. I could hear him blinking. If I had told him I could hear him blinking he would have apologized and shut his eyes. He could, in fact, have it reversed. Or we could get a donor. Or we could adopt and that would be my punishment, then we'd be even. Did I just sigh?

'Are you awake?' he said, quiet as breath in case not. I must have sighed.

'Mnmnmnm,' I said, which was a lie of sorts.

4

'Sorry,' he breathed, even quieter.

'I'm sorry too,' I said, but still I made it sound very sleepy so as not to start him.

We lay silent. I could ask him a question and he would answer me. I could slap him and he would forgive me. I could demand anything in the world I wanted and so long as I described it in enough detail he would do it for me. When you get right down to it, compared with the lives that some people, some women, have to lead, is there anything wrong with that?

'I love you.'

I was tired, more than half-asleep, worn out from fighting, and I swear I do not know if he said it to me or I to him.

Awake again. Still dark, but there is traffic now. We are not touching and he makes no sound. I know I'll regret it but I reach out towards him. My hand clunks on the wall. It's floppy from sleep and so I am not really hurt, but the slight pain is still enough to distract me for a moment while I shake out my wrist. Then I stop, my arm up in the air.

What wall?

Of course, I'm in the spare room. But this answer is good for less than a heartbeat because our spare room has a double bed sticking out with a table on either side. No wall. Why would he move the bed against the wall while I was in it? This sign of independent action, pointless as it seems, interests me. What else has he done? I raise myself on my elbows and squint for outlines in the dark. Outside a lorry changes down a gear, and again, as it climbs the hill.

What hill?

I sit up to stretch over the width of the bed towards the lamp, but the arm I slide out to support me flails in the air and I almost fall onto the floor. I wait a moment and then begin to feel around. I'm in a single bed. We don't have any single beds in our house. I start to scrabble for the switch on the lamp on the bedside table, but I don't know where to look for it, because it's not my lamp, nor my table, nor my bed, and outside is a hill that's not any hill I can think of and a lorry that cannot, therefore, be going up it. I find the switch at last and click, but my eyes are screwed tight shut and I can't open them. Where am I? What has he done?

One deep breath and another and finally I am brave enough to look. What I see is both a relief and then, right on its heels, a new worry. I'm in my parents' house in my bedroom with the daisy curtains and I can't remember getting here. The last thing I remember is closing my eyes in the spare room, Ludo beside me in his shirt and socks, and now here I am ninety miles away in Edinburgh, in my parents' house, all on my own in – I look down – a borrowed nightie. Could I have gone back down to the kitchen last night and drunk myself into oblivion? But why would Ludo bring me all the way here to sleep it off?

From downstairs comes the noise of the kitchen tap and a second later, as I knew it would, the pipework gurgles where it's boxed in behind my headboard. I don't have a hangover. Maybe I had a blackout. Maybe Ludo, lying beside me thinking it all over, finally snapped. Maybe he hit me, or even strangled me. Maybe my brain was deprived of oxygen for so long that it was damaged and I'll never be the same again. I sit up. I don't feel brain-damaged, but I don't feel exactly normal either. I feel slightly blurred, slightly out of focus, and so I barely open my eyes as I swing my legs out of bed, put on a dressing gown, faintly familiar, and go downstairs.

The stairway and hall are in darkness, as they always are when only one of my parents is up. Their marriage is full of these little courtesies or, since courtesies sounds so hollow, let's call them tendernesses. There is no light around the edges of the kitchen door. I open it slowly. My mother is standing there in the darkness, the back of her wiry hair hardly flattened from her pillow, her dressing gown snugly belted and her feet in slippers. She stares out of the window into the dark garden, waiting for the kettle to boil.

'Mum? Do you want a light on?'

'There's a mouse on the bird table,' she says to me without

turning. 'It's not a squirrel, and it's too small for a rat, thank goodness. Come and see.'

I go to stand beside her, squinting into the darkness. On the bird table in the middle of the grass, I can almost see a small creature. All I can really see is movement, a kind of huddled busyness. My mother leans over the sink and raps against the windowpane. The 'mouse' turns its head sideways and looks at us along its beak then flits off in three light swoops to sit in a tree. We both laugh.

'Mum,' I say again. 'I don't think I'm well. I think I've had a ... What would you call it? ... a blackout.'

She crosses the kitchen, suddenly alert, and switches on the light.

'Look at me,' she says, as I rub my eyes. I look at her. Then I stare at her. I can't take my eyes off her and so I don't notice anything else, at first.

'What?' she says, putting her hand up to her hair.

'You look fantastic,' I say. 'What have you done to yourself? You look like a million dollars.' She laughs, but is still aquiver with worry.

'It's your eyes, ducky,' she says.

'It must be,' I agree. Have I seen her since Christmas? She must have had something done. Her hair is dark with only a twinkle of grey at the temples, a really subtle job. But her hair is nothing. She has definitely had something done, and yet it is unthinkable that my mother, *my* mother, who has never had more than two lipsticks at once in her life and washes her face with soap and water, can have had something done.

'I'm not well,' I say again and close my eyes, for this must be a hallucination, caused by whatever caused the blackout. She puts the back of her hand against my forehead and then pokes the glands in my throat with the cold tips of her fingers.

'Where's Ludo?' I ask.

'What do you mean?' says my mother, confirming that something somewhere has come adrift. She clearly thinks I should know where Ludo is and how I got here.

'That's what I'm trying to tell you,' I say. 'I can't remember what happened. I can't even remember arriving, and you look strange.'

'It was "fantastic" a minute ago,' she says, putting her arm around me. 'I'd have settled for that. What can't you remember?'

I can hear the tread of my father's footsteps coming down the stairs, his throat-clearing and the rasp of him scratching at his stubble. These sounds are as familiar as my own heartbeat to me and so hearing them, reassuring, comforting, calming, at the same time as my eyes begin to clear, begin to see, is like being caught in an undertow, the water rushing up the beach pushing me to safety while draining away down the beach under my feet pulling me with it, pulling me away.

He stops to pick up the post on his way past the front door and he's looking down at the envelopes as he enters the kitchen. He isn't wearing his glasses. His hair has already been slicked back with a comb at his first stop in the bathroom. He hasn't had enough hair to slick back for years. He sticks the bills in the spice rack. That rack was a sore point. My mother never used the spices much and once the first lot of bottles were past their dates it stayed empty, except for all the brown envelopes my father used to stuff in there every morning, that my mother said made the place look a tip. They got rid of it when they ripped out the breakfast bar and put in a pine kitchen with a round pine table to match. My father, with his doleful morning face, slides onto a stool at the breakfast bar to wait for his tea.

The undertow isn't going up and down the beach any more; it has started spiralling, and I'm dizzy, but it doesn't seem like the ordinary dizziness that's all to do with your blood. This dizziness is coming from somewhere else in me and I've never felt it before.

'What . . . day is it?' I ask.

'Thursday,' says my father. 'All day.'

'I mean what date,' I say. He looks at me and then at my mother.

'She says she's not feeling very well,' my mother explains.

'I'm not,' I say. 'I'm sure it'll pass but I'm really not.'

'It's the fifth of March,' my father says. 'Is it something you ate?'

'Two thousand and . . . ?' They both look at me blankly.

'Two thousand and what, darling?' says my mother.

'It's Thursday the fifth of March,' I say, trying again. I know what I have to ask and I know how to ask it, but to say the words out loud means taking a step I do not want to take, a step away from everything I believe and towards . . . Well, towards insanity, I suppose. This makes me hesitate even more. I can't bring hints of insanity into my parents' kitchen. They just don't go in for that kind of thing. My father especially, who hates any kind of talk first thing in the morning, hates 'loopy talk' most of all. Still, I can hardly just leave it.

'And the year?' I ask, loud to sound brave. 'Nineteen . . . ?'

'It's nineteen eighty-one,' says my father, annoyed. I breathe steadily and try to think it through. He would never play a trick like this on me. If my father says it's nineteen eighty-one, then there is only one possible way to account for it, and that is quite simply to accept that I have, indeed, gone mad. And I do accept it. I take it in my stride; I even manage to smooth the frowns, one anxious and one irritated, from my parents' faces.

'Sorry,' I say. 'I've had a bad dream, I think, and I can't seem to shake it off. It's nothing though. Don't worry.'

Then I go towards the downstairs loo, planning to fold a towel into a pad and hold it against my face so they won't hear me screaming. But when I get there I don't scream after all. I look at myself in the mirror above the basin. If this is madness, then I have a gift for it, because in the mirror I don't look crazed; I look fifteen. My eyebrows haven't seen a pair of tweezers in their life and my hair (God help us) seems to be permed, but I'm fifteen. My face is as smooth and as blank as only my calves were yesterday. I lift my nightie up to my chin and gape, dazzled, at what I see underneath.

At this moment, not only am I almost too impressed by

9

what a great job I've made of my delusion to be properly freaked out, but I'm also feeling pretty lucky. It could have been persecution, the voice of the devil telling me to kill everyone, or snakes and cockroaches climbing the walls. Yes, as delusions go, recaptured youth is a bit of a soft option and some part of my brain even manages to take comfort in the fact that I'm feeling this way. See, I tell myself. If it had *really* happened, I'd be a gibbering wreck. See how calm I am. I've gone mad. I've gone mad and it's lovely.

I still can't wait to get back to reality of course, even with Ludo, his weeping, the vasectomy reversal and then – who knows – IVF and sickly triplets, but this, whatever it is, on the strict understanding that it won't last too long, and even though it's ... weird hardly begins to describe it ... this is okay.

'Hello,' I say to my reflection. 'Hello again.'

Chapter 2

5 March 1981

The first day was a hoot. Exhausting of course and every so often the unanswerable questions would nip at me and I would have to close my eyes and hold on to something until they passed, but I managed to keep myself upright and out of detention and, on balance, I enjoyed it.

Oh, I could have told someone. Of course I could. But there was no one to tell. No one, that is, outside of it. I needed to explain that I was having a hallucination that it was 1981, but nobody who was around to hear me would believe it wasn't. They would think I was deluded, certainly, but they would point to the wrong bit. They would tell me that I'd had a dream in which I grew up, got married and headed for forty, but now I was awake again. So, they would say, no harm done. And if I insisted, they would say I was mad and then they would send me to a doctor, or sign me into a clinic. I thought I was mad too, but I was mad back home with Ludo, not *here*. And if I was going to be dealt with, I wanted it to happen where I could get the good drugs. Besides, this was too interesting to miss; I didn't want to spend my whole visit sitting in waiting rooms. So I kept my head down, said nothing. I'd soon be home, after all. That's what I thought, then. And now? Define 'now'.

I had a shower. The hair I had inherited from my mother (imagine the result of a cairn terrier mating with a clump of gorse) plus the complicating factor of the bubble-perm, meant that post-millennial hair products were sorely missed. I had just squirted on a quarter of a bottle of Silvikrin when my father rattled the door handle and asked what I was doing. I was forgetting the bathroom batting order and using his slot, was the answer. Off with the Silvikrin, back to the bedroom. I opened my wardrobe door.

It didn't look good in there. Nineteen eighty-one, fifteen years old, I was changing from a schoolgirl in Aertex and clogs into a creature of black canvas drainpipes and pixie boots, oversized mohair à la Dennis the Menace. I stood in bra and knickers for longer than it's comfortable to admit to, trying to decide. There was no way I could walk in clogs, but the thought of my bottom in drainpipe jeans was almost enough to make me try, until I remembered. Wonder of wonders! It wouldn't look big in anything for ten years. Drainpipes it was, then. I looked like a Boomtown Rat and the perm added a curious note, but it could have been worse.

My hamster watched me as I searched my schoolbag for a timetable, sitting in his wheel, rocking gently, pink paws under his chin and apple-pip eyes shining. I never played with my hamsters, never cleaned their cages, but that didn't stop the hysterics whenever one of them died and it didn't stop me immediately getting another. I couldn't even remember, if I was honest, what this one was called. Twiglet? Benjy, maybe?

I hoped I *had* a timetable and didn't just carry it around in my head. And I hoped it would show me Thursdays stuffed with bluffable English, art and gym. Found it. Good. Less good was what it told me: double physics, break, maths, Latin, lunch, biology and double German. Not a hope in hell.

I stared at the timetable. It was marked out in eleven different colours of felt-tip pen and, looking closer, I could see that I didn't even have eleven different felt-tip pens, but had made pale green out of dark green and yellow in Seurat-style dots – what were they called again? – and peach out of pink and brown. It must have taken me hours. What a sap I had been.

'What do you call that style of painting that's just tons of wee dots?' I asked my parents back downstairs in the kitchen again.

'What?' said my father, frowning.

'Seurat, you know,' I said. 'That famous picture of the park in Paris on a Sunday? What's it called again?'

'What?' said my mother. Perhaps, now that I came to think about it, we didn't discuss the techniques of the post-impressionists over breakfast on the average Thursday morning.

'Never mind,' I said and added, 'duh!' self-deprecatingly, as you do. Or rather as you do now, but didn't then. I blushed. No one said anything.

Getting to school was fine. Traffic was light, of course, and children were walking. It was different in other ways too, hard to describe. People didn't seem to be carrying so much, for one thing. I saw a couple of men with slim, polished briefcases and all of the women had handbags, but no one had anything like the tonnage that we haul around with us now, the bulging back packs and sports bags and extra carriers. Where was it all? *What* was it all? What did I take to work yesterday in my Gap sack and conference bag that I wasn't taking to school this morning? I had only been gone a day and already I couldn't remember.

At the school gate something was happening, something I had forgotten all about, but which I recognized again in an instant. The pupils, being sucked towards the school like fluff up a Hoover, tangled at the gate and then separated into three strands. A thin thread of good girls and boys in blazers and black shoes went straight through and up the path to the buildings. The bad girls and boys, in denim and leather, clumped into a snarl round the corner, where they smoked and spat and took the first steps towards – Mr Meldrum, the head, used to hint at this without saying it straight – getting each other pregnant.

I loved those kids. I wanted to be one and I almost was one for a while. I learned to smoke and I drank enough vodka at a Valentine's disco to be impressively sick, but I was too much of a swot at heart and most of them left after fourth year anyway, so I had to crawl back to my old friends and put up with them sulking and their mothers sniffing at me to see if they could smell cigarettes. It had ruined fifth year for me, all

13

that sanctimony. I had a good look at the bad kids now, remembering what I knew about how they had turned out, and it occurred to me that Mr Meldrum had had a point.

In between the good kids and the bad kids, at the gate, but not smoking, in canvas and mohair, Aertex and clogs, like a harmless wisp of cobweb that had stopped for a minute, but was surely on its way up the hose in the end, was my lot.

'Janie!' It was Linda, so enthusiastic that I wondered for a moment if she *knew*, until I remembered that she always sounded like that. Linda, Alison and Evelynne: there they were. Linda had become a primary teacher, married another teacher, and had three children, two girls and then a boy (which must have told the second girl she was a failed attempt at a son) and then her husband left her for another teacher. Alison did a law degree and went round the world, getting as far as Australia before she washed up on a beach with some guy who had a funny religion and a pile of kids with different mothers. She left him but she's still got all the kids. Evelynne, standing there with her flute case, looked as pink and white as the others but she turned out surprising. Gay, a revolutionary communist even after all the real communists had called it a day, she was instrumental in setting up the *Big Issue* in the North and she nearly died from a septic piercing.

What could I tell them all?

Even Colin Firth wasn't sexy as a teacher, Linda. Get yourself a life.

Beware beach bums, Alison. Steer clear of the Pacific rim on your gap year.

If you ever feel like decorating your labia, Evie, stick to jelly tots.

'Hi,' I said.

'Hiya, Janie,' said a voice at my shoulder, before they could answer. It was Danny Conway. Danny Conway with his fluffy hair, his grey trousers with the patch on the knee and his big beaming smile. We had sat at the same table in primary seven and even though I rose clear out of his league the first day at high school – he was your classic squirt – he never stopped acting as though we were friends. My real friends used to make kissing noises whenever he trotted up and grinned at me and eventually I shook him off, but it took some doing, I could remember. I had been forced to draw him aside one day in the corridor when we were both late for a class and tell him not to speak to me any more because he was a – what word did I use? I wouldn't have said 'loser', in the eighties. I tried to remember. 'Danny, stop speaking to me, eh? Primary school is over and frankly you're embarrassing both of us because you're a real little . . .'

Something like that. It worked too. God, they're right when they say children can be cruel. Except if he was still bounding up with his tail wagging today, and we were fifteen, then I hadn't been a child, had I? I had been a complete cow who was comfortably old enough to know better. I wondered what had become of him.

'Hiya, Danny,' I said. 'Good to see you.'

His eyes glazed over with joy and he gulped before turning away and walking up the path towards the school with his bouncing, balls-of-the-feet gait even springier than usual. Beside me the chorus began.

'Ooooh!' said Linda. 'Good to see you, Danny.'

'Come up and see me sometime, Danny,' said Evelynne.

'Janie and Tinkie Conway,' said Alison. 'Wooo!'

Let us draw a veil over double physics. Oh all right then, let us not. Mr Watson spoke to us for a while, and we scribbled in our jotters. I concentrated on writing down everything he said, not wanting to leave a gap that would upset the careful revision my fifteen-year-old self would undertake, if she was back in time for the exams. Back from where, though? Where was she? Did she wake up in the spare room with Ludo whimpering at her side?

' . . . Lawson?'

It had happened.

'Miss Lawson?' said Mr Watson again.

'Mr Watson?' I said, and I meant nothing by it, but the class giggled and Mr Watson frowned.

'Do you need to borrow a pencil?' he asked. I looked down at the pen in my hand, then around the lab benches at the twenty-five pencils in the others' hands. Of course! Mr Watson. Mr Watson did not allow the use of pens in lab books or jotters, and everyone in the class complied. I considered pointing out how ludicrous it made him look that he cared, how he should learn to choose his battles, how he really should chill.

'Sorry,' I said, rummaging in my pencil case, 'I forgot.'

'You forgot?' he said, with a forbearing smile beginning to spread over his face.

'Yes,' I said. 'It slipped my mind. I apologize. It won't happen again. I just forgot.'

The class was making a rushing noise like the wind in the trees.

'That doesn't seem at all likely,' said Mr Watson. 'After yesterday.'

'I can only imagine,' I said.

'Well?' said Mr Watson. At that I lost all patience. Twenty-six pupils were sitting here having their education interrupted while this silly man got off on having the power to call the shots between a pen and a pencil.

'Well, Mr Watson,' I said. 'I think the best thing, if you don't believe me and won't accept my apology, would be if you and I discuss the matter later and in the meantime we carry on with the class.'

I had never been sent out of a classroom before. Moreover, I had never spent forty minutes in a corridor with nothing to sit on, drink, or read. Even in low-cost airline check-in queues you have something to read, for God's sake. And it's not as if there was any point to my principled stand. No one was losing out on their education just because, inside my delusion, I couldn't keep my mouth shut. My other self was not going to come back to be grateful or annoyed about the state of her lab book. None of this was *real*, remember. I pinched the piece of skin between my thumb and my finger and squeezed hard, trying to bring my nails together. Crescents sprang up, first white and then slowly filling with red, and my eyes watered.

I had just sat down on the floor and put my head on my knees when the swing doors at the end of the corridor battered open and a pair of crêpe-soled shoes squeaked their way along the polished tiles towards me. They slowed as they drew near and then they stopped. It had to be the headmaster: Sod's Law demanded it.

'Janie?'

I raised my head. It was Mr Matheson, one of the English teachers. We called him Mr Maths, on account of one of the maths teachers being called Mrs English, and he let us.

'What are you doing out here?' he said, and on his face concern and amusement were mingled.

'Stewing in my own juice, I think.'

Mr Matheson laughed. 'What did you do?'

'Used a pen instead of a pencil and was insufficiently sorry.'

He laughed again. Mr Matheson always laughed a lot, and he always treated the pupils like people, so I shouldn't have read anything into it, but when he squatted down in front of me with his crêpe soles screeching and looked at me in that way of his, as though he was trying to understand something very difficult that only I could teach him, I was tempted to blurt the whole thing out. The tussle must have shown on my face because he laid a hand on my arm and shook me gently.

'Be careful, Janie,' he said. 'Choose your battles.'

I had forgotten it was Mr Maths who first said that.

The bell rang and, before anyone could emerge from any of the other classes to witness my shame, Mr Watson opened the door behind me.

'In,' he said. And that was that. No discussion, no exploring what had gone wrong, no fresh starts, obviously no chance of ever finding out what had happened the day before. Just transgression, punishment, the end. It was as I imagine a gulag to be, all control and no rehab. Refreshing.

For the rest of physics, I kept my head down. Three of us

p a pair of trolleys, added ticker tape and made them
ide at different speeds, reading the results of the impact off
ie tape and thus learning useful facts about velocity. Or
rather two other people – Yvonne Litton and Derek somebody – set up trolleys and read results, and I watched the
trolleys collide, saw the dots on the tape and wrote down the
same as Yvonne and Derek, in pencil.

Then break. I had been longing for it. I met Alison and
Linda on the stairs and they led me outside to where Evelynne
was leaning against a wall with a view over the hard
playground and the football field.

'So!' I said, waiting.

Linda took out a packet of gum and offered it round.

'No thanks,' I said, still waiting.

'Has Suzanne's big sister really had streaks?' said Alison.

Finally I stopped waiting, remembering at last that this
was it. There would be no coffee, there was no common room,
not for fourth years (that big room with the beanbags that I
remembered must have been fifth year onwards). We were not
going to do anything. The small girls might skip or mark out
hopscotch beds and the boys of all ages would produce
footballs from their schoolbags, but we would just stand here.

'Look!' said Evelynne.

'Shut up, Eve,' said Linda. 'There's nothing to look at.'

'I wouldn't say that,' said Evelynne. 'Would you say there
was nothing to look at?'

'I would say there was plenty to look at,' said Alison.

'Shut up, Alison,' said Linda.

That was how it was. They talked about nothing. Literally
nothing. They did nothing and they talked about nothing. I
knew they were only fifteen and I wasn't expecting Tony Blair
and house prices, but still. It was quite something to witness
this absolute, pared to the bone, Zen, nothing.

'I'm going to get a drink of water,' I said.

'Where from?' said Evie, and the others looked at me,
puzzled.

It was a good point.

'I mean, I'm going to the loo,' I said. This only started the chorus off again.

'Ooh, the loo!'

'I'm going to the water closet.'

'I'm going to the powder room.'

'All right,' I said, too harshly, then I saved it. 'All right, all right, don't get your knickers in a twist. Is someone going to chum me to the toilets?'

We all went. It was the high point of break.

In maths, we worked on algebraic equations taking home any we didn't manage to finish. I took them all. In Latin, it was seen translation, Latin to English, thank God. I got by. I can string a sentence together, and I remembered quite a bit of the grammar. Also, although Mrs McDowall looked up once or twice at the sound of fluttering pages as I ransacked my glossary for every second word, she said nothing. We read out at the end, five lines each.

'What is more blessed than to lay worries aside?' I said. 'Let the mind relinquish its cares and, exhausted by the toil of a long journey, let us come home and now rest on the bed for which we have pined.' I was getting a lump in my throat. 'This is the only thing that makes these toils worthwhile.' Not that I wasn't still enjoying myself, but bloody Catullus. Who could withstand that?

'Well,' said Mrs McDowall, 'rather a free translation, Janie. And you should know better than to change the mood of the verb. *Cum mens onus reponit*, anyone? *Cum mens onus reponit*? Daniel?'

Danny Conway, in the row behind, said: 'I had "Let the mind relinquish its cares" just like Janie.'

'*When* the mind,' said Mrs McDowall. '*When* the mind *lays by* its *burden*. I'm surprised at you both. You should know by now to stick to the text.'

Well, well, Danny Conway. One kind word at the gate, one act of loyalty in the Latin class. We were square.

Lunch was less of an ordeal than I had imagined. For one

thing I got to sit down in a chair in a room; I wouldn't have been too surprised to find myself expected to eat gruel with a wooden spoon huddled in the playground, but here was warmth and light, hot food and – Glory be! – water. I tucked in with the gusto of women everywhere eating something they haven't had to cook for themselves. Linda, Evie and Alison picked and grumbled through bacon steaks and boiled potatoes, but mooned over their puddings, sucking the mush of crumble-top off their spoons with closed eyes, like cows at a salt-lick.

I had regained a lot of ground in maths and Latin, I suppose, so really I should have tried to build on it and not do anything silly. I couldn't help myself, though. I was craving. I sidled up to the end of the counter near the till, where a friendly-looking dinner lady was collecting coins from the thinning queue of children. The dinners were only 60p each but the coins were like dustbin lids; they must have had to take them to the bank in a barrow.

'Excuse me,' I said, smiling. She pursed her lips and raised her head so that she was looking at me with narrowed eyes down the length of her nose.

'Could I possibly have a cup of coffee?' I said. 'Or even tea? Please?'

Her eyes widened and she slid off her stool and disappeared into the kitchen's nether regions shouting as she went. 'Here, girls, wait till you hear this. Wait till you hear the cheek of this now.'

'Thanks a bunch,' said the boy who was next in the queue with his tray, coins at the ready. 'I'm starving.'

So much for her friendly face. It must have been the mob cap that threw me.

In the afternoon, in biology, were frogs. There's no more to say about that.

Then Double German. *Ach. Mein. Gott.*

But I survived.

*

I bore the brunt of the day all the way home, from Linda, Alison and Evelynne. What was wrong with me? They couldn't make up their minds if I was sucking up or mucking about, but they could tell I wasn't myself. What was going on? They looked searchingly at me, brows drawn up in the middle, lips pinched in at the sides, genuine expressions behind all the spots and cheap make-up.

'Do you really want to know?' I said. I was actually considering telling them. They were my oldest friends, after all.

'I knew it,' screeched Alison.

'*I* knew it. I told you.'

'I said yesterday, I *thought* so.'

Yesterday? What had happened yesterday? Maybe they could tell me something that would help.

'If you really want to know,' I said. 'If you have time to listen . . .'

'Hoooo!' The shriek came from all of them at once, piercing but breathy like a kettle, like a *Good Housekeeping* consumer test finding out that all three models boiled at exactly the same speed.

'Who is it? Is it Ian Tate?'

'Is it Paul? It's Paul, isn't it?'

'But they're not in Latin, and you weren't yourself in Latin.'

'No boys are in Latin, Evie.'

'Except Danny Conway. "Hi Janie!" "Hi Danny, darling." Who is it?'

'Who is it?'

'Who is it?'

Because what else could it be, right? Getting sent out of physics, meddling with the principles of Latin grammar . . . What could any of it mean except that I fancied a boy? Clearly, I was kidding myself here. There was no way I could tell them what was happening. And even if I did, it was so far from having anything to do with fancying boys that they might not be able to hear it, like a dog whistle.

'Forget it,' I said. 'I'm going home. I've got a lot of homework.'

'No you haven't,' said Linda. 'There's only maths.'

'Well, I've got a lot to catch up on before tomorrow,' I said. 'But I'll see you later. I promise.'

I meant it. I would. When I got back home to Ludo I would phone every one of them and suggest we all get together. I might have to go through their mothers, might even have to log on to Panicking Losers Reunited. But that was for tomorrow. When I was home again.

My mother was chopping leeks for a bolognaise sauce (Ah, Mum's cooking before TV chefs!) but she stopped and wiped her hands and went to get mugs.

'Hot juice?'

Christ, I had forgotten about that. Hot orange squash – or juice as we called it – was a daily treat for me throughout childhood. Soften the tooth enamel with the heat and send in the dextrose. I must have frowned, even shuddered.

'Oxo? Cocoa?' said my mother.

'I'd love a cup of coffee, Mum,' I said.

'You're too young for coffee,' she said. My mother's family are Methodists and, while she's given up on the idea as a whole, there's quite a tailback of suspicion about stimulants. She was against sherbet when I was very small.

'Please?' I couldn't tell her that every sinew was screaming for a cup of coffee, that I was desperate. Only coffee, or maybe a huge gin, would do. But I could see her point. From where she was standing, I was too young and actually, thinking about it, I couldn't be desperate for a hit. Not my sinews anyway, because my fifteen-year-old sinews went weeks between cups of coffee. It wasn't as though my real body was in here with me under my young skin like an alien inside an unfortunate redneck who had come across the fields to see what the lights were. There wasn't room. My mind was inhabiting a body with no cellulite, no caffeine cravings, that had never had a hangover, that . . . Jesus Christ. I was a virgin.

If, that is, any of this was real. And I was sure it wasn't.

'Oh, go on then,' said my mother at last, rolling her eyes and jerking her chin up in a shrug. She put a scant half-teaspoon of Mellow Birds into a cup and quickly poured in a glug of milk. Milk in first, to mollify the stuff before it gathered enough force to wreck her baby's nerves. Then she put two tea plates down on the breakfast bar, flipped open the breadbin and took out a paper bag.

'Biscuit?' she said. Only my mother would call them biscuits, these platforms of buttery pastry, with their skirt of chocolate, their pillows of marshmallow, their lattice of glossy jam and their pebbledash of coconut.

'Lovely,' I said, and she slid one towards me with a smile. Only seven hundred and eighty calories of refined sugar and transfats, nothing in that to hurt me.

'How are you?' I asked her, when we were halfway down our coffee cups. 'Did you have a nice day?'

'What have you done?' said my mother.

'Yeah, I got sent out of physics for being cheeky,' I said. 'But I mean it. What did you do today?'

Her face clouded briefly. 'Auntie Mona popped in,' she said. 'So that was nice.' Mona is my father's sister. She's a doctor, like my father's father. Unmarried and unbowed, horse-faced and smug, she only descends on my mother – still does twenty years later – when no one else is likely to be there. She never stays for lunch, much less comes to dinner, just blows in and blows out again. Pops, indeed. I can't stand her, and it occurred to me right now for the first time, that my mother couldn't possibly stand her either. I took a chance.

'What did *she* want?' I said.

'Janie!' said my mother. She doesn't do bitchy; certainly not then before it was fashionable and not even now. She's never had the opportunity to learn, never watched a single episode of *Sex and the City*. The title alone sends both of them scrabbling for the remote.

'Come on, Mum,' I said. 'What did she come to tell you this time? New car? Booked a cruise?'

My mother had her hands over her mouth in shock but her eyes were twinkling.

'She *had* had her hair done, but I'm sure she just wanted to stop in and see how we were all getting on.'

'She's had her mane plaited?' I said. 'Big show this weekend?'

'Janie!' said my mother again. 'That's your auntie you're talking about. Your own flesh and blood. Those genes could come out in your baby one day.'

That stopped me dead.

'My baby?'

'Oh, I know what you say now,' said my mother, 'but you just wait and see. Once you've met the right one and you've settled down, you'll soon change your mind.'

I laughed before I could help myself. The thing was that Ludo was the perfect one. Handsome, affectionate, a well-spoken boy from a very good family – although I don't quite know who I'm quoting when I say that. But I hadn't changed my mind; I'd changed his.

'Oh Mum,' I said and my voice sounded hollow, even to me.

'Are you sure you're all right?' she asked. 'You weren't this morning.'

'I'm fine.'

'You know you can tell me, don't you?'

At that I burst into tears. Or rather tears burst out of me as though a sac of them had been pierced at the base of my throat. I cried myself hoarse. I cried my throat dry. I cried until my mother started crying too, until my eyes, the end of my nose and my top lip were bloated and purple. And that's how my father found us.

'What is it?' he said, stopping in the doorway, holding his briefcase and the evening newspaper up in front of him. 'What's happened?'

'Nothing,' said my mother, immediately beginning to sniff and pat, pulling herself together.

My father frowned and moved his weight once or twice

from the front foot to the back, from the back to the front. Eventually, the call of a cup of tea won and he came into the kitchen. He handed his case to my mother, and she opened it, took out his lunchbox, threw the apple core and banana skin into the pedal bin, then rinsed the box under the hot tap and set it upside down on the rack to drain. All this before the kettle had boiled, before my father had finished the front page.

'Sorry,' I said, to the top of his head.

'Just so long as everything's all right,' he said, looking very hard at me with wide open eyes the way people do when they're lying or, in this case, terrified. Then he lifted one of the marshmallow pastries, abandoned in the flood, and took a bite.

'The library called,' said my mother. 'Your book's in.'

My father looked up, brushing coconut from his mouth. I looked up too; my father had no time for books as a rule.

'I'll walk down and get it,' he said. Then: 'Fancy a walk, Janie? Fresh air, find yourself something nice to read? Best thing really.' This was as close as my father would ever get to talking about it.

'Lovely,' said my mother. 'You do that.' She was back at her chopping board again, dicing carrots now, and her smile was wide, her happiness heartfelt at the thought that the two of us might go together, that the rocky moment of unleashed emotion was past. She looked so young and, with a sudden gulp of realization, it struck me that she *was* young. She was nearly as young as me. And yet here she was, not planning a baby, not joining gyms and going off for weekends with her girlfriends, but standing there in an apron, chopping vegetables, married to a man whose day was lit up by a library book.

'Tell you what,' I said. 'I'll make dinner and you two go.'

I had ruined it again now. They both stared at me.

'I mean it. It's a lovely day, and I've walked home from school already, and I don't need a book to read with all the homework I've got piled up, and when was the last time I cooked a meal for you?'

'You've never cooked a meal for us,' said my mother.

'Unless you count what you used to bring back from Home Economics,' said my father, sounding understandably wary at the memory.

'Well, it's long past time I started,' I said. 'Go on.'

'I don't want it wasted, mind,' said my mother, but she was already taking off her apron and my father was standing. There was no way he was going to be left alone with me if my mother was going out, not with the crying and the apologies and the loopy talk. I remembered how he had looked in the doorway, even before he found out I was crying 'for nothing'. Even when I might have been expelled or my best friend might have killed herself, he had had his paper and briefcase up like a riot shield.

My mother put on some lipstick in the downstairs loo and took, from the coat cupboard under the stairs, not the anorak with the quilted hood but the short coat she wore for shopping in the city centre and she put a silk scarf around her neck with the ends tucked into the lapels. When I looked after them from the porch window they were arm in arm.

They brought a block of ice-cream back with them from the Italian café and with the extra-rich sauce (I browned the mince), the stem glasses of ice-water I had put out and the conviviality – almost larkiness – that arose as much from me not saying anything else to worry them as from their arm-in-arm walk in the softness of a spring afternoon, there was a festive air about it. My mother told my father that Mona had been, and unless it was my imagination, she had a little note in her voice left over from *me* bitching up Mona to *her*, and this seemed to give my father permission for a little lip curl of his own, and my mother and I both saw this and smirked, and he saw us smirking and smirked back. And there it was. We all hated Auntie Mona; a fact which had been held underground and never so much as hinted at was suddenly there between us as plain as the bottle of salad cream on the Castles of Rhineland placemats and nothing more had to be said.

I did the dishes – I wouldn't hear any arguments – and so

my parents took their coffee up the other end of the room to the couch. My mother sat down and read out what was on the television from the back page of the paper, while my father stood beside the set ready to turn it to the right station before he settled down beside her. I had forgotten this too, and I watched them surreptitiously while I cleared the table. By the time I had ferried everything through to the kitchen and come back for the cloth, picking it up by its corners to take to the back door and shake, they were side by side.

'We'll have fifteen minutes of this then,' my father was saying, 'and if it's no good we'll turn over to *Nationwide*.'

'But if it's those poor donkeys again,' my mother replied, 'I'll go and do the ironing.'

'I'll do the ironing,' I said.

'I thought you had piles of homework,' said my mother.

'Yes, well, but it's not even seven o'clock,' I said, wondering what time I was supposed to go to bed.

'Ho!' said my mother. 'You haven't seen the ironing.'

'Anyway, it's Thursday,' said my father. I waited. 'It's *Top of the Pops*,' he said. Our deal that my mother and I sat through *Tomorrow's World*, then they sat through *Top of the Pops*, then my father and I sat through *Hi-de-Hi* and everyone was happy, sitting there. Them on the couch and me in the chair.

They always sat on the couch together. They still do and, when I come to think about it, I don't know of any other couple, sixty-ish and forty years married, who are still side-by-side on the couch. They have all retreated to their own little armchair kingdoms. Ludo and I have. It would be easy to say it's caused by the layout of the room, that the best place for the long sofa is over by the window and you can't see the telly, and the two-seater sofa is a bit of a squash. But isn't that the whole point? The two-seater sofa should feel cosy for you and the one you love and the layout of the room should take as its priority the fact that you and the one you love want to sit together in easy reach for cuddling.

Not that my parents do much cuddling on their couch.

There was always a little buffer down the middle, like the bolster down the bed of betrothed gypsy youths and maidens, this bolster made of folded newspapers, library books, boxes of tissues for my mother's sniffles in the winter and for my father's hayfever in the summer. As the years have gone on, several spectacle cases have been added, then the remote controls for the television and video and now the phone too sits there between them, but still, if in the summer my father sneezes, my mother puts out a hand and touches his arm as she says 'Bless you' and if in the winter my mother coughs too long, my father reaches over and bangs her on the back.

It must be this that makes it okay, mustn't it? My mother is not weighed down by chopping veg and my father does not face each day at his office, sandwich box in briefcase, with leaden gloom, not because they are stoical, or because their life is exactly what they had hoped it would be, but because of the love still there between them, keeping them out of armchairs and making them reach out at coughs and sneezes. It's like they're happy, because of the love.

'You're miles away, Janie,' said my mother. 'Your eyes are crossing.'

It was nine o'clock, and Russell Harty was just finishing. My mother had been watching it and my father had been turning the pages of his book (which turned out to be a coffee-table number, full of black and white photographs of crumbled buildings) since Russell Harty was a bit near the bone for his taste.

'And I thought you had homework,' said my father, looking up.

'Can I do it down here?' I said, thinking if I woke up back home tomorrow I would kick myself for not spending every moment I could with them, but I knew they would say no. Homework was done upstairs in silence, no radio, no distractions. They took it very seriously indeed. They were both shaking their heads now.

'Okay,' I said, cheerfully. 'I need to clean out my hamster too.'

'Just don't forget the homework,' said my father.

I nodded. My hamster. I still couldn't remember.

'Speaking of my hamster?' I said.

'Hmm?' said my mother.

'Yeah,' I said.

'Yes?' said my mother.

'My hamster?' I said.

'What about him?' said my father.

'I'm going to clean him out.'

'Homework first,' said my father again.

'Absolutely,' I told him. 'And thanks.'

'What for?' said my mother.

'For caring about my homework,' I said. 'And for tonight. I've had a lovely time.' I ignored their worried faces and fled.

My mother tapped on my door just as I was finishing the maths. The cheap paper of my jotter was almost worn through from rubbing out, but finally I thought I had cracked it. My hamster was bustling around ungratefully making his little lair foetid again after my efforts, ferrying cheekfuls of seeds into out-of-the-way spots and peeing in corners.

'Bedtime, darling,' she called softly through the door. 'School tomorrow.'

Christ, I thought. I hope not.

Chapter 3

6 March ????

Awake. There's a sliver of a moment, because your body wakes before your mind, when all is feeling. And what I feel, suddenly awake, is peaceful. Then I remember. I start to listen for traffic going up the hill outside my parents' house or for wind in the trees outside our house – Ludo's and mine – but the morning air is still if I'm back and the traffic hasn't started if I'm not. Either way there are no clues and so I lie there, peaceful. Peaceful enough – can you believe it? – to drop back off to sleep. Suddenly a noise snaps my eyes open. A low, hacking growl is coming from somewhere near me. It's my father clearing his throat as he gets up for work.

6 March 1981

So not a blip, not Freaky Thursday, not a day trip the way it is in fairytales with a pumpkin at midnight then business as usual next morning.

'JANIE!'

My father was shouting from the foot of the stairs. I knew what shouting meant because the stages were set in stone: my mother called me first, then again, then my father called and then my father shouted and I don't know what happened after that, because I had never stayed in bed to test it.

'I'm up,' I yelled, getting exactly the right note of querulous affront into my voice, and up I got.

He was still frowning when I joined him in the kitchen and I should have resisted needling him, I know.

'See?' I said. 'I'm up.'

And I wasn't even trying to play the part of a moody teenager. I was just being me, which should have told me something. Put it this way: if you're acting in a play and the scene you're playing is morning, you might pretend to be grumpy, but you wouldn't actually say to yourself: 'Sod the lines, sod the other actors and sod the audience,' then turn over in your bed on the stage, putting your head under the prop blankets and getting orange face make-up all over the prop pillow. This morning, without having changed my mind about any of it, I found myself behaving as if I really was here.

'... might as well be back in bed if you're just going to sit there mooning,' my father was saying. He scowled at me, deeply aggrieved.

'You two,' said my mother, sunny as ever.

We both scowled at her and then at each other again. I loved this; I had forgotten how much I loved it, the way that we could be tired together, or in bad moods, or worried or disappointed, and we all just sat it out. There was never any discussion, no soul-searching, no hand-wringing, no wondering what it might mean, and whether we should do something about it.

Ludo and me, on the other hand, you wouldn't believe. Life

31

was one long therapy session: exploring and sharing, resolving issues and agreeing strategies, identifying problem areas and working towards solutions.

It was because we met as students, I think. When you meet as students, especially in the first year, the things you do to strut your stuff are of a very particular kind. At primary school you get your boy by blowing the biggest bubble. You'll chew yourself sick on five bubblegums at a time, you'll pay the price of having it cut out of your fringe if it goes wrong – all for love. At high school he'll punch the boy who pulled your hair, he'll swear the loudest in front of the teacher, he'll drink the most Coke and burp your name – all for love. But when you meet in the first year at university, he'll tell you all the things he learned the day before and you'll tell him and you'll both listen and try to think that these things, these soft green stems of ideas and sweet green leaves, are wonderful truths and these wonderful truths will be the start of your life together, and they will lengthen and thicken, twisted around your happiest times, growing bark, until you couldn't stand up without them. So we used to sit regaling each other in the library when we should have been finding out more, in the pub on Wednesday afternoons when we should have been building our characters with team sports, in the narrow beds of our student flats on Sunday mornings when we should have been twining our legs and arms instead of our heads.

'We've got to get up,' I used to say.

'Ah,' Ludo teased me one day. 'You can take the girl out of Tyler's Acre Avenue . . .' I pinched him, but he wouldn't stop. 'You're right,' he said. 'It's Sunday. We should get up, clean some gutters and do the ironing. Or we could lie here all day adrift on our bed like shipwrecked mariners abandoned to our fate and even when we're old we'll never forget this once-in-a-lifetime shipwrecked-bed day.' He used to talk like that.

'But we do this every Sunday,' I said. 'Why will we remember today?'

'We'll make ourselves remember it,' he said. 'Tell me

something right now that I'll never forget. And then I'll tell you.'

I couldn't think of anything. Quite often, with Ludo, I felt as if, wading up to my waist, I'd stepped off a shelf of rock and was lost and thrashing.

'I'll start then,' he said. 'Janie, I love you.' He laughed at me again, at the way I was blushing and gaping at him. 'There,' he said. 'You won't forget the day I first said that.'

He was right. That was an unforgettable day. But my point still stands. You can only offer your first declaration of love one time and on all the other days you talk about what you're learning, you share what you know, you pretend you care. So if Ludo and I had done ... I don't know ... Botany and Greek degrees, then we would have talked about Botany and Greek and pretended to care about that. And perhaps all we would have ended up with would have been a really great garden and a taste for the dramatic. At worst we might have had children called Alstromeria and Philemon. As it was, though, as it had been, Ludo was doing a degree in philosophy with some social anthropology thrown in, and I was doing a degree in psychology, with nothing but more psychology thrown in, so it was philosophy and psychology that got regaled and nodded at, that grew bark and twined itself around our life, and you can see where it got us.

'The thing is, Janie,' said my father – he had drunk his first cup of tea now and was like a bear who'd taken a couple of tablets he knew would work – 'the thing is that getting out of bed in the morning without being called half a dozen times is something you'll just have to learn to face. You've got a good brain inside that head of yours, but a good brain isn't enough. You need a good head on your shoulders if you're going to make the most of it.'

My mother started laughing and although I tried very hard I couldn't help myself.

'What?' said my father. His eyebrows were drawn down in an attempt to stay angry but his mouth was twitching.

'I've got a good brain in a bad head on good shoulders?' I said. 'How's my neck?'

'I'm serious,' he said, although he was smiling. 'Listen to what your old dad is telling you. You could go a long way. Or not. And the choice is yours.'

I stared at him. This, all of a sudden, was like Ludo talking, not like my father at all. What was happening? My father never did this. This was a pep talk. This was guidance. My father never gave me guiding pep talks, did he?

Or maybe he did. After all, it was pretty minor; it would hardly have made an impression. But why now? Surely if he was going to start, it would be a few months more down the line, once I had taken my running jump into the bad crowd, when I came in smelling of cigarettes and cider, or after that parents' night when Mr Cordingly the chemistry teacher asked if everything was all right at home. I still couldn't understand why he asked that. Granted, there was the cigarettes and cider, and the bad crowd, but of course everything was all right at home. Unless . . .

Unless it wasn't. Unless there was something far from right at home, something a self-centred fifteen-year-old girl couldn't be expected to notice, something which, nevertheless, made an impression on her subconscious and sent her off to cigarettes, cider and a bad crowd. Something which underlay my father's sudden bout of parenting here this morning to which he was waiting for some kind of response.

'I know, Dad,' I said. 'Don't worry. I'm going a long, long way and I'm going there on the right path. I know exactly what I'm doing.'

'That's my girl.'

Now, I had only been awake ten minutes and trying to think so hard without coffee wasn't easy, but I knew that something was missing from this exchange. So far, all I had said was exactly what I must have said last time. What would I say to him now, if I had the chance? Which I did.

'You know what?' I was looking at him closely and he drew back a little.

34

'What?'

'You might be my old dad, right? But when you think about it, you could still go a long way too. I mean, the world's as much your oyster as it is mine.'

Subtle, huh? My father gave me a look that shrank me like salt on a slug. It wasn't a glare, and there was nothing of the parent to the child in it. It was a look straight from him into me and it was a look of fear.

The question of what my father had to fear occupied me through showering, dressing and taming the perm for the day. This last was easy because, with a whoop of delight, I remembered I was no longer too old for pigtails. It was a vicious perm, mind you, starting right in at the roots, and even with the pigtails so tight that they stuck out from my head like the back legs of dogs at lamp-posts the bit on either side of my parting still had the scrabbled look of unpicked knitting.

'You look pretty, darling,' said my mother as I left, which should have warned me.

Nothing bad was going to happen. I knew that. Nothing happened to either of my parents in the early eighties. No death, disaster, scandal or failure befell them, although it was an eye-opener to see them at my age, looking so young and yet acting so past it. Maybe, while I was here, I could do something to stop them giving up on their dreams. As to what their dreams were, though, how should I know?

Alison and Linda were waiting at the school gate and it began almost before I was in earshot, as soon as they glimpsed me. I could see their mouths opening and shutting when all I could make out was a series of squeaks and chirps.

'Pippi Longstocking!' was the first remark I actually heard.

'Janie? What in the name of—'

'OW!' One of the bad boys from round the corner had swooped in, pulled my pigtail and was loping back to his gang in slow motion, with his hands clasped above his head like a victory salute.

'What have you done to yourself?' said Evie, arriving. Look

who's talking, I thought. But Evie's dreads and cheek rings were far in the future, so I said nothing.

The boy and the rest of his gang swaggered past us, shouldering little kids out of the way.

'That hurt, by the way,' I told him.

He turned towards me, his face in turmoil as genuine surprise that I had spoken fought with his default expression of affectless idiocy.

'That hurt, by the way,' he said in a high voice.

'Do you need a bit of time to think up an answer of your own?' I said. 'D'you want to get back to me at break?'

'D'you need a bit of time to mee-moo-mee-moo-mee,' he said, still in the falsetto which was clearly supposed to be me. The way he drew up his lip to make the noise revealed little patches of blue-grey decay along the gum line of his front teeth. Alison and Linda were looking at their feet, but the gang of bad kids were staring at me and sniggering.

'Was that too long for you to remember?' I asked him, putting on a kind voice. A look that wasn't meant to be seen flashed across his face before he answered.

'Fuckin' lesbo.'

'Good point,' I said, nodding. 'You're great at this, aren't you?'

One of the sneering minions behind him laughed out loud and he wheeled around to them.

'Fuckin' shut up, right.'

'Fuckin' make me.'

'Let's go,' I said to the girls.

The kid hadn't stood a chance. Not only was he twenty years younger than me and as thick as yesterday's custard, but I had the nineties: a whole decade of ironic smart-arsery, complete with six seasons of *Friends* and the collected works of Bart Simpson. It wasn't a fair fight.

So what was it? I asked myself, standing on the hockey pitch ten minutes later trying to secure the orange canvas tabard with the flaking white 9 on the back. What were my parents' dreams? Damn. The tabard only had one tie on each side, but I thought if I knotted them onto the loops inside my gym skirt it would hold.

I had forgotten about the tabards. They were made of a fabric never experienced since; a fabric so coarse, so cheaply dyed, that it made the budget bedspreads in the meanest market in Delhi seem like pashmina. The only other thing in the world made out of this stuff was gym hall beanbags, and I had a sudden vision of ruddy-faced, solid-thighed girls at gym teacher training college, sitting cutting down old tabards into beanbag-sized squares, like convent-school girls turning their sheets sides-to-middle in the war.

The others seemed not to care about getting their tabards on straight and making sure the number could be read. They were more taken up with gym skirt management – futile downward tugs or clamping handfuls between their thighs. The gym skirt didn't worry me. A mini-kilt, that's all, a garment which still had representation in my wardrobe back home, albeit not in navy-blue polycotton, but I was mildly concerned that I couldn't remember any of the rules of hockey. Miss Lindley was shouting and pointing down at the other end of the pitch and I could hear odd words: 'Mark your . . .', 'Keep to your own . . .', 'Don't . . .' Then she blew her whistle, the sticks of the two centres clashed and girls from all sides bore down on them, yelling. I stayed put. Miss Lindley blew her whistle and walked towards the scrum.

'Mark your opponent,' she said. 'Stick to your own zone. Stay still and move the *ball*, girls.' She blew her whistle again. 'Five yards,' she shouted. 'Bully off.'

Back to my parents' dreams. My mother's dreams were obvious enough when I came to think about it, only I had never called them dreams before. Now though, the transparency of them struck me square between the eyebrows, there on the hockey field, as unexpected and hard to ignore as the hockey ball itself would have been.

I had always thought of her as revelling in escapism, or I might have called it 'wallowing' to myself, since it *was* only to myself and no one else heard the unkindness. She visited

37

stately homes and open gardens, dragging my father with her; she pored over *Country Life* in the dentist's; re-read a curious selection of old favourites year after year – Jane Austen, Nancy Mitford, the letters of Joyce Grenfell, and a girl's book about a pony by a double-barrelled someone I couldn't remember. She would in time come to buy *Hello* every week, but every week she would have a different excuse for doing so: a headache that meant she needed a treat; a recipe someone told her was worth a try; even an interesting article about Fiji.

So far, so what? Millions of people did all of these things along with her. But. But. The stately homes my mother visited were not the Chatsworths and Woburns, where you might hope to see a Rembrandt on the stairs and seven hundred pieces of Sevres in a case on the landing. My mother visited modest little mansion houses, Georgian townhouses, pretty castles on small estates in the Highlands. And when she was there she didn't parade around gawping and asking questions, but crept between the rooms, looking at the views out of the windows, poking delicately at things she shouldn't touch, like a fox nosing for scents in winter. She loved any place where you were allowed down into the kitchens and up into the attics, and she railed at the unfairness if the rooms open were only a tiny few out of the whole. Then, she would stand outside on the lawns and frown up at the forbidden windows.

In gardens, she would glance at the woodland walks and the redolent, blowsy borders, but her real interest was the greenhouses, the compost heaps, the row of sheds where the pots were stored. Once, in a garden open for Cancer Relief, she found a dusty summerhouse full of croquet sticks and chipped curling stones and she sat there for over an hour.

As for *Country Life*, she would go early to her appointment to get more time with it, but when I asked her why she didn't buy it, she laughed it off.

'A lot of rubbish,' she said. 'It's all adverts.'

But it was the adverts that drew her. The houses for sale, the paintings coming under the hammer.

'What would you do with that?' I said once, glancing over

her shoulder at an advert for a furniture auction, a photo of an excrescence in gilded bronze and green marble, so ornate it gave you indigestion of the eyes to look at it. It was as though a wicked witch had turned Liberace into a table. 'You'd have to keep it roped off when people came round, like the National Trust.'

'Oh no,' said my mother, quite seriously, still gazing at it. 'That's the thing. You would just have it, in the front hall or whatever and you'd have a bowl of car keys on the top and keep the dog lead hooked on one of those twiddly bits. If it was yours.'

I thought at the time she was laughing at them – 'them', the insouciant rich – because laughing at them, or rather making a scornful noise like a peep of fizz escaping an opened bottle, was what my father would do. But now, thinking about it standing under the shower in the changing room and feeling my pigtails grow fat and soft as the perm reasserted itself in the steam, I saw different.

My mother, while being the least complaining, least dissatisfied, most cheerful woman you could imagine, had a life that was light years from the life she dreamed was hers. She dreamed of elegance. Not glamour, not excitement, not passion – it was Jane Austen after all and not Jackie Collins. Not fame – she didn't care who it was, posed on the velvet chaise in the big colour spread in *Hello*. Not even money, really. She dreamed of elegance, careless and easy, unconcerned with new things and what people thought. She dreamed of a house with heaps of curling stones in a dusty shed, not a single polished one like a trophy on the doorstep. She dreamed of a house with French furniture covered in dogs' leads and oil paintings in the downstairs loo, where nothing was kept for best and nobody cared if it all got broken, because there was plenty more. How then, did she come to be married to my father? Did the dreams only start once her life with him had settled into what it was and was going to be? Or did she think when they met that he was going to take her where she longed to be going? She couldn't have.

Because . . . what about my father? I half-listened to a boy – Michael someone – stumbling over Macbeth. Mr Maths didn't often do this to us, but for some reason this morning he had given out parts and was sitting with his feet up, listening with a pretty convincing look of enjoyment. I felt for the boys, hunched over their desks, their necks sunk down into their blazer collars, gripping the texts with white knuckles. The girls thought they were safe, witches long gone and Lady Macbeth busy with other things, and were rolling their eyes and tittering softly, but I wondered how many of them had read ahead in the script and knew that one of us was going to have to say that she had 'given suck'. That would have wiped their smiles off.

My father. What were my father's dreams? What were *his* black and deep desires? He worked at the job he had always worked at, something in an office in a factory that made prosthetic limbs, lived in the house he had moved to just after it was built, just before I was born, happily married to the woman he had always been married to. What else? I tried to think about my father. I failed. When I attempted to picture him all I could get was the house, my mother, the three of us together. Concentrate: what did my father do? He cut the grass when my mother told him twice; he walked to the shop on Sunday mornings for rolls and papers; he went on holiday every year to Jersey or Holland on the ferry with his wife and his daughter. Does this sound normal? Is it normal to know nothing about your father's job, or his hobbies, his interests? He had no hobbies; that was the plain truth. He played no musical instrument nor any sport, was a member of no clubs. Even the garden shed was full of my mother's things and mine – bicycles and deckchairs, foot spas and rowing machines, but then why would I think that the family deckchairs were mine and hers? There was the garage, I suppose, and the car. There! He washed the car. Nobody told him to do it, but every Saturday, he washed the car. Was that it?

'What does your Dad do?' I asked Linda, in the playground. She was passing around sticks of chewing gum, one each, and we unwrapped them. I, as I always do, held the sweet, powdered folds between my tongue and the roof of my mouth, feeling the gum warming and the texture begin to change from crumbly to smooth.

Mr Maths had told us at the end of the lesson to think about Macbeth during break. I wonder if he really thought we did it, the way he really enjoyed us reading the parts. Imagine if we did. Imagine if all those boys scuffling around a football on the dusty concrete were saying to each other:

'Jamesie! Here! So d'you think the witches were a curse or – no pulling jerseys! – were they his fairy godmothers, only doing what he wanted deep down?'

'I think they were – goa— Awww – were all in his imagination myself. Good save, wee man!'

But I should be thinking about my father.

'Chew!' Alison screamed in my ear. I took a sharp breath in and half-swallowed the gum. There was a panicky moment when it seemed lodged in the back of my throat and I flashed my eyes at them, flapped my hands, trying to tell them to do something, *do something*, then with an unpleasantly deep cough I got it back into my mouth again and stowed it carefully in my cheek before I spoke.

'What is your problem? I nearly choked there.'

'Why don't you chew your gum?' said Alison, unrepentant.

'I nearly choked,' I said again. 'I could have died.'

'You wouldn't have died,' said a voice behind me. Danny Conway was standing on the grassy bank that joined the wall we were leaning against to the playground on the higher level behind us. His knees were at eye height, giving us all a good view of the patch on his grey school trousers.

'She might have!' said Alison, changing her tune like a bird changing course in a breeze. It was part of our code of honour to disagree with the nearest thing to an outsider at any point. It had just been me, the freak who chewed her gum wrong, but now it was Danny and I was back in the fold.

'I was going to do the Heimlich manoeuvre,' he said. The girls looked blank. 'Where you grab the person under the—around the ribs and you squeeze them hard and the thing pops out. I learned it in Scouts.'

'You dirty wee pervert!' Linda shrieked.

'Why are you even talking to us?'

'Get away from us.'

'Creep!'

Danny's face turned red under his freckles.

'It's a real thing,' he said, turning away.

They muttered after him for a while, ruffled as chased chickens, then began to laugh.

'He was going to squeeze you till his thing popped out!'

'Pervert,' said Linda again.

I was watching Danny, back in goals, standing between two bundles of anoraks, still looking in my direction. I gave him a thumbs up. He gave me one back.

'What did he just do?' said Alison. 'Did you see that? He just stuck his fingers up at you, Janie.'

'Okay, first,' I said, 'I was choking and I could have died and you lot were going to stand and watch me, right? And the Heimlich manoeuvre *is* a real thing; it's a first-aid technique. But most of all, you know, a boy wanting to put his arms round a girl is not a pervert. You see what I mean?'

'Hoo, hoo, hoo,' said Linda.

'And what if a girl wants to put her arms round a boy? What does that make her?'

'What if his thing pops out?'

'If the boy's Danny Conway it makes the girl Janie Lawson.'

'It's all right as long as you call it "first aid".'

The bell rang, bringing relief from them all, but also bringing maths, which blotted out everything else for as long as it lasted.

'Sticking to the water today, are we?' said the mob cap on the till at lunchtime. 'Or can I do you a nice liqueur?' I smiled, which was obviously wrong because her smirk immediately snapped off like a flicked switch. Of course, I wasn't supposed to be able to see the funny side. She was supposed to tease me and I was supposed to scowl or fill up with impotent furious tears about the unfairness of it all and the treacherousness of life. Or did that only start with Morrissey?

'So what *does* your dad do?' I asked Linda again. She gave me a screwball look, one eye squeezed up and the other staring under a raised eyebrow.

'You know what he does.'

'I don't mean for a living,' I said. 'I mean when he comes home at night, at the weekend. What does he do? Alison? Evie? What do your dads *do*?'

'They don't do anything,' said Evie. 'What do you mean? Why do you want to know?'

Because according to Shakespeare my father should have been striving after Duncan's crown. Duncan's stethoscope, actually, since his father, Grandpa Jock, had been a doctor. His brother, Uncle David, was an engineer of some kind, something to do with machinery used to calibrate some other kind of machinery that was something to do with eyes. It was one of those jobs that no one really understands but no one ever questions. I think it's the word 'calibrate' that does it. He had been at university for a decade. Auntie Mona, of course, had been eight years at medical school, but my father – Jock Jr – hadn't gone at all and, although his job was just as vague as Uncle David's, this was not because no one understood it but because no one in the family ever talked about it. Why should that be? It wasn't as though he worked in PR for a tobacco company or was in charge of the African division of Nestlé's baby milk sector, or anything. He worked in the offices at Technical Prosthetics as it was then, Limtec now. And, anyway, what he did there, since we never talked about it, could easily be something as wonderful as whatever Uncle David did, only my father was too modest to boast.

The world being what it was, though, this seemed unlikely. Whatever brought my father his 1960s semi, five-year-old

43

Austin Maxi, and a fortnight in the tulip fields each July was unlikely to put in the shade those calibrations and all that they had done for Uncle David in the way of a big, red house and a big, blonde wife and four children with loud voices who played the violin.

Perhaps, I thought, this was why my mother's daydreams took her where they did. She left her semi with its Dralon covers and leapfrogged right over David and Mona's villas, spitting on them as she passed, to land in a place they would have to admit was miles beyond them. But why did she have Dralon in the first place? If you wanted Toile-de-Jouy round your four-poster, why wouldn't you take the nearest you could get? What would make you turn your face against any hint of it and try to keep your longing secret?

I became dimly aware, in that way you do, of life around me. My questions about their fathers had made the only kind of impression on Alison, Evie and Linda that any idea ever did and now, while Mr Cordingly the chemistry teacher tried his hardest to ignore it, the three of them were sniggering and gasping, bent low over their jotters, planning a future for me as *Mrs* Cordingly, their dads – as they pointed out – being taken. They were just about holding it together so far, but I could tell from the reddening cheeks and the whinnying tremor in their voices that any minute they were going to go completely Jonners and lose it.

'What is *wrong* with you girls today?' Mr Cordingly said at last. 'This isn't like you.'

Oh, Mr Cordingly, if only that were true.

'Come on, settle down,' he said.

'. . . with me and start a family,' said Linda, her head bowed to hide her moving lips. Alison snorted, one of those huge snorts that hurt the back of the nose, and Evie's pent-up breath hissed out through her clenched teeth like steam. I started then too and, by the time Mr Cordingly had made his way over to us to stand with his hands on his hips and frown, I was as helpless as the rest of them.

'What are you laughing about?' he said. 'Come on, share the joke.'

This only made it worse. Linda was sobbing; Alison's cheap, pocket-money mascara was spreading down her cheeks.

'I'm sorry, sir,' I managed to say at last. 'You know how it is.'

'I know how what is?' said Mr Cordingly.

'Come off it,' I insisted. 'You've been a teacher how long? How many times must this have happened? And how many times has the joke been worth sharing?'

They had sobered up by now. Alison was wiping her eyes and Linda was blowing her nose. Evie was still uttering little giggles on every breath but the danger was over.

'Well, let's have no more of it,' said Mr Cordingly, looking at me strangely. 'This isn't a pyjama party. It's a chemistry lesson. We all know what we're here to do so let's just do it.'

Oh Mr Cordingly, if only *that* were true.

Anyone who knew what they were here to do was at least one step ahead of me; I wasn't even sure yet that I was *here*. But I had almost completely given up on the madness theory. Being my father's daughter with no time for mumbo-jumbo, I didn't believe in anything much that you couldn't see or hear or at least smell, but I could hear the crackle of the dry, permed ends as I held them near my ears and squeezed them; I could smell the tang of the gravy from one end of the school to another; I could feel the tight ache across the bridges of my feet from walking in clogs, and in the light of so much pounding reality, believing in time travel was no more than a swift, rational update.

So if I really was here, was it possible that I was here *for something*? My father's daughter, the cheerful atheist, didn't usually go in for meaning and portent and purpose, but show me the person whose philosophy could stand unchanged by what had just befallen me. How together were you when it happened in your life? Exactly.

So . . . if it had to be for something, since I was pretty sure it didn't happen every day, that meant it had to be for something quite important. Working out *what* was the logical first step. How was I doing so far?

I stopped dead. I was on my way home by now. I had gone to choir and mouthed the words in the soprano section, not daring to make a sound, and when it was over I had kept my head down and left quickly, unable to face another bout of Linda and the rest of them. Now I stopped outside the newsagent on the corner of Orchard Field Avenue as a shudder of realization, like the tingling wave of disgust when you've just downed soluble aspirin, passed through me from my scalp to my fingers and back. How was I doing? *I was doing abysmally.*

There was no way I was here to make my father do an Open University degree or get my mother a chaise longue, because if everyone who had a twinge of regret got another go at it we'd none of us be in the same year for more than a month at a stretch. Family life would barely exist. There would only be Post-it notes. Post-it notes upon Post-it notes, like layers of droppings in the cage of a neglected budgie. 'Darling, there are three weeks' worth of dinners in the freezer. I've just popped round to not have an affair with him after all. Back yesterday. XX.' And if that was the problem, it would be my parents who'd come back, wouldn't it? Hardly me. So it must be something in my life, my own life. Except no, there I went again! It couldn't be some piddling little nonsense in any one person's life. It had to be something big. I started walking.

It's a funny thing, but Ludo and I often talked about travelling back in time. It was a private joke between us. If someone made a mess of something, that was what we would say. When Ludo, for instance, tried to drill through shower tiles to put up a soap dish and the drill skipped off the spot and danced around on the glazed surface making crackling noises and covering him in powdered porcelain, what I said was: 'Never mind. Switch it off, invent time travel, go back,

46

save Elvis. And then try again with the drill set for masonry.' Or when I got really drunk the night before I was supposed to be a bridesmaid at Linda's wedding and woke up with a bruise across my forehead from smacking it against the back of the toilet seat, Ludo brought me arnica and Alka Seltzer and said: 'Time machine, go back, save Elvis, stick to Appletise.'

So, had it been a few years earlier I would have had an idea what I was here for, and would probably already have been trying to persuade my parents to give up Jersey for Vegas this year. As it was, I was clearly not here to save Elvis, but still, I should have had the sense to be thinking along those lines. I opened the back door, dumped my schoolbag and shouted for my mother.

'I'm through here,' she said. 'Click the kettle on, darling.'

It was unlike my mother to be sitting down in the daytime, and I stuck my head around the door of the dining room to check. Right enough, she was up in the living-room end, ironing in front of the television.

'Mum?'

'Hmm?'

'Elvis Presley – he is dead, isn't he?'

'So they said,' said my mother. 'Although you read things . . .'

I let the door swing shut. You did indeed. You still do. And here I was. And . . . Oh for the love of God, even if I had been forced to accept one or two new ideas, there were limits I would not cross.

I poked around in the breadbin and found the baker's bag. Vanilla slices today coming on for the biscuits. I loaded the tea tray, took it through, carefully nudging past the row of shirts hanging from the lintel of the archway, and set it down on the coffee table amongst the three piles of ironed underwear.

'I'll have a shot now,' I said. 'Unless it's tablecloths.'

My mother wasn't listening. The iron rested on its end hissing gently, and she stood clutching one of my father's vests in both hands, bunched under her chin.

47

'Isn't she lovely?' she said. 'So young.'

I looked at the television and saw Lady Diana Spencer.

'It's just like a fairytale,' said my mother.

I sank down as the last wisp of hope left me. It wasn't a dream; it wasn't a breakdown; it wasn't a jaunt. It *was* for something, but it was too late for Elvis, and there she stood in a garden with a toddler on one hip, the sun shining through her skirt, glancing off her hair, honey-coloured, pre-highlights.

Luckily, my mother couldn't tear her eyes from the screen and so she didn't see me sunk back in my usual armchair, grey-faced, sweating above the lip. While she gazed, I ate my biscuit and drank my tea, but it would take more than a vanilla slice to bring my blood sugar back to normal so I scooped up my pile of ironing and went upstairs to put my head in my hands and shake.

I was terrified. I had read Harry Potter, I had seen Bill and Ted, I knew that the first rule of time travel was that you couldn't change things. But I was being silly: Harry Potter and Bill and Ted were made up. That woman on the telly in the navy-blue jersey and the gold 'D' pendant was real.

Elvis was dead, but if he hadn't been I wouldn't have hesitated for a moment. I would have been straight off to Vegas to save him. By ... doing something that, luckily, I could leave quite vague since it was years too late. But the point was that I would have done it. I wouldn't have hummed and hawed and wondered if maybe I'd best not and asked myself if I had the right. Was this any different?

On the one hand, there was all the glamour – the diamonds, the couture, the palaces, the love of millions. And speaking of millions, there were all the charities raking it in, all the solid good done with the little leprous children and the AIDS victims and the landmines. Who was I to stick a spanner in that?

On the other hand, I knew what it was like to lie beside your husband trying not to breathe in case you woke him and he started speaking to you and I knew the ache of disappointment and hopelessness starting up in your chest again like the boom of a bass drum. And how much fun could bulimia be? And who didn't deserve to see forty?

But if I was talking about her life changing direction that much, I was talking about making people not exist. Two whole people. Wasn't that murder? And anyway, not to be churlish, but I had decided that this journey couldn't be to sort out just one person's problems if that person was my mother or father or me. Was this any different? I've never quite known where I stand on that whole teddy bears tied to the railings thing and we've all got to go sometime.

My mother called me downstairs for dinner. I went, ate, returned to my room and put my head back in my hands until it was time for bed. Then I washed my face, brushed my teeth, freed my pigtails and brushed my hair, tugging on my comb like a sailor on his ropes until the perm filled all the space in the mirror around my head even when I stood right back against the door. I got undressed, put on my nightie, got into bed, lay down, sat up and put my head in my hands. Too much knowledge, too much power, and I felt absolutely corrupted.

By midnight, though, things were looking rather different. I had no power here. Not really. Only one person was going to put on that crumpled dress, walk up the middle of the Abbey and say that yes she did or no she didn't. My job was simply to ensure that she made the decision with all the facts to hand.

I was sure, more sure than not anyway, that this was the right thing to do. Scurrilous gossip is one thing but whistle-blowing is quite another and a noble endeavour at that, if undertaken with good intentions. My intentions were spotless. Granted, I was dealing death to two people who hadn't been born yet, but the way I saw it was that if I did nothing I was just dealing death to a load of other people instead – and probably more than two because surely if she'd been happily married and had more time on her hands, what with less traipsing around the Commonwealth and all that, she would have had a bigger family. And don't try to tell me she wouldn't have got married, nor that there wasn't a fair chance of this other marriage, brought about by my meddling, being happier than the one that was off.

In fact, that was the cruncher. Horrified by the thought of robbing her of her life of good works and sparkly dresses, I tried to have a sensible think about what she would do instead, and my best guess was that she would find some amiable chump with twenty thousand acres of Shropshire and spend her life raising money for good causes in a sparkly dress. All she would miss would be the humiliation of finding out that she was married to the one man in the world who was not, not even a little bit, in love with her. That and having her bikini shots touched up to bring out the cellulite. And anyway, as I say, I wasn't going to make that happen – couldn't make that happen – I was only going to arm her with the full facts and let her make up her mind for herself. Perhaps she would go through with it after all, but with her eyes open.

So far, so slightly over-defensive but good. Now, what was I going to do? Had it been a year ago, I could have found out the address of her flat and written her a letter, but now she would be ringed around with pale men in dark suits talking to their shirt cuffs and I had no chance.

From the cage came the unmistakable sounds of a small nocturnal creature coming to life. He bustled to his dish, cracked open a sunflower seed or two and took a couple of warm-up spins on his wheel, before settling to his night's work of trying to gnaw through the wire to freedom.

I would need to be very careful. I had to get to her somehow, but not in any way that could finish up with me sitting a test for psychological health. I was all right on the Prime Minister (back with Thatcher – the joy) and not bad on my name and address, but I couldn't guarantee not to hesitate if asked the date and I had no clue what my hamster was called. To the sound of his teeth on the bars, at last, I fell asleep.

Chapter 4

4 May 1981

I had a good day at school today. The first time around that meant a day with no spots, one where the right sort of boy acknowledged your existence and the wrong sort of boy didn't trouble you with his, a day when the teachers left you alone, you didn't say anything to make your best friends turn on you and you didn't get homework. A good day at school now has different features: for a start, Linda, Evie and Alison must be too subdued by pressure of work or outbreaks of acne to put in a full shift of flirting and giggling because, no matter what else happens, a day is ruined when it's played out against a backdrop of:

'*You* tell him.'

'Shut up! You were the one who wanted to tell him.'

'I'll tell him you *said* you would.'

'I'll kill you if you tell him. *And* you.'

(I keep an eye out for the first sign that Evie will get married in Amsterdam to a radical midwife called Dolly, but she has just bought a ra-ra skirt to wear to the next school disco in the hope that Lyle 'Lightbulb' Boyd will ask her for a moony, so there is still a way to go.)

Also, today, I didn't humiliate myself by not knowing something straightforward which the class studied just after Christmas but which I've forgotten in the intervening decades. This happens less and less, owing to the hours of extra homework I've put in when I would otherwise be on the phone to Linda telling her that if she dares to tell Evie after promising me she wouldn't then I'm going to tell Alison what Linda told me.

What else? There was a planned class discussion in English on the nature of madness (still Macbeth) and a impromptu class discussion in Chemistry about sexism of all things, sparked by the janitor asking for four strong boys to help him shift some benches. I managed to contribute just enough to both debates to leave me feeling I had been true to myself, but not so much that the teachers stared.

Finally, there was nothing terrible in the paper or on the radio this morning that I should have been able to stop. I know that one day something will come crashing down and I won't remember it until it is too late, but it hasn't happened yet. I mean, when Reagan got shot it rang a faint bell, but I couldn't have told you when it was. And the Brixton riots were bad and Bobby Sands is dying, but what are you going to do about things like that?

I open the back door, dump my schoolbag, fill the kettle, and go through. My mother is sitting in the middle of the couch with her hands pressed to her mouth. The radio is on and the television too. She turns when she hears me.

'Janie! Oh Janie, you'll never guess what.'

How can a cold lump sink right down into your stomach and yet still feel as if it's choking you? What have I forgotten? What the hell happened on the 4th of May 1981 that I've forgotten? When was the Falklands? The newsreader's face disappears and is replaced with a shot of the outside of a grand building seen through the fresh leaves of a beech tree just beginning to unfurl. Is that an embassy? What have I missed? What have I not done?

I can tell you what I *have* done – my Diana plan – and what a good idea it seemed; how I put it together so carefully and how it went wrong in ways I never dreamed of and tangled me up in things I couldn't foresee. Perhaps that's why I've forgotten whatever it is that's been going on today. Life just got complicated is all.

I sent a letter to her first, because you never knew. It was a cryptic letter, I suppose, containing not much more than the three little words. I sent the same three little words – well, medium-sized words, really – to her brother, her sister, her mother and her stepmother. I put small ads in *The Times* and The *Lady*, very small ads, just her first name and the three medium words, and 'from a well-wisher' but it still cost me a month's pocket money and meant I had to wait until the middle of April to book myself into a decent salon and get rid of the perm. (Oh yes, the perm's gone, replaced by a chic little flick-crop that I had to draw for the hairdresser because there were no pictures of it yet. No one gets it, but they'll think back to it in years to come and then they'll see.) Then finally, after the letters and the ads, unable to bear the not knowing, I made my stand.

It was a mighty organizational challenge. No budget airlines, I couldn't drive, I had hardly any money, and until my sixteenth birthday there were two people with a legal duty to know where I was at all times. So I lied. I told my mother and father I was going to Alison's house on a major homework drive, and told Alison I was going to an all-weekend party with a boy whose name I couldn't reveal.

'Why not?' she said.

'I can't tell you that either,' I told her.

'Why not?'

I stared at her, unable to think of a single good reason.

'Because,' I said at last, 'he made me promise not to.'

Alison went red with pleasure. 'He made you promise not to tell *me*?'

Why not, I thought.

'Yes,' I said.

'It's someone I *know*?'

Oh Christ, I thought.

'Yes,' I said.

She was still red, still smiling, but her eyes were darting back and forth. She was quivering to know who it was and if she worked it out she would immediately tell the others and then go to her grave telling me she hadn't. I knew this; it was this combination of deviousness and bottomless dishonesty that made me choose Alison to help me fool my parents in the first place. But I was safe; she wouldn't work out who he was. He didn't, after all, exist.

So, my parents swollen with pride at me taking my homework so seriously and Alison swollen almost to bursting point to think that she was my confidante, I got the overnight bus to London.

I was there for seven hours outside the Goldsmiths' Hall, freezing and starving and increasingly bursting for a pee because, no matter what they say about the Blitz spirit and good old London Town with its pearly kings and whistling costermongers, those royal watchers are the most selfish bunch of hard nuts I have ever encountered in a long, and complicated to measure the length of, life. I thought it would be like queuing for tickets for the big Bowie concert; once you got your pitch you could nip off for a cup of tea, get a sandwich, powder your nose. I couldn't have been more wrong. Those smiling ladies in the anoraks with the flags? They would squash orphans to get nearer the rail and a bigger chance of contact. It was a real hem of the garment affair.

'You on your own, love?' one of them asked me as she and her companion jostled in beside me. I smiled at her.

'Yes, just me.' I waited for her offer, whatever it was she was going to offer me first, whether advice or a nip from her flask, but she just turned to her friend with a thin smirk on her face. The friend smirked back and glanced at her watch.

'First time then, is it?' the friend asked.

I nodded.

They smirked at each other again and settled down to wait for me to crumble. I showed them, though. I was still there in the dark, feeling faint, numb and bloated, when a rising wave of noise along the street and the first flashes of the cameras heralded the arrival of the cars. Instantly, the two gimlet-eyed old pros beside me stubbed out their cigarettes, unrolled their flags and started to cheer. I had been resting on the stick of my placard all day, first like Fred Astaire with his cane and then as the hours rolled by more and more like Tiny Tim clinging to his crutch, and now bracing myself backwards against the press of the crowd behind me I managed to squat down, whip off the black bag from the sign and, ignoring the tutting from all around and apologizing for jabbing it into countless knees and shoulders – you have to try to turn a placard right way up in a space too small for a battery chicken before you can fully understand it – I got ready to raise it high.

The limousine swept up, the door opened, like clowns at a circus more men than seemed possible poured out of it and stood all around, and then finally to a roar from the crowd, there she was. In That Black Dress. I had forgotten about that stupendous black dress.

'You're beautiful!' shouted a voice behind me and everyone who heard it cheered and whistled.

'We love you!' a voice screamed, and she smiled and looked down, her chubby cheeks blushing. So she was. She was beautiful then, she was beautiful when she got her cheekbones and her sad eyes, and you could just tell she would be beautiful when she was ninety-nine. So what? Ugly people are just as precious. So blame the dazzle, the crowd, the lack of food, but at that moment I had no doubt. Fiercely, I shouted her name and jabbed my placard, with the three medium-sized words on it in marker pen, high in the air.

She saw it and I knew she had seen it, or rather I knew she had *clocked* it, which is different. In the middle of a sweeping glance around the crowd, checking for toddlers with posies I suppose, she caught sight of it. Her eyes passed, then stopped and darted back, flared in that unmistakable, undisguisable spark of recognition and connection. She read the words and I saw her lips move as she whispered: *Camilla Parker Bowles.* She glanced at *him*, then turned and gave me a long, hard stare with a big question in it. I stared back, trying to make my eyes wide so that I'd look trustworthy, but at the same time trying to give a look piercing enough to ram the message home. I must have succeeded only in looking mad (I checked out the stare in the bus-station toilets later and it was a little odd, as though I was wearing two monocles at once) because she hurried on and two of the men in the dark suits with the earpieces walked away from me backwards to keep me in view until the whole party was inside.

And that was that. I dropped the placard and waited, exhausted, at the barrier until the crowds behind me had thinned then I trailed back to the bus station, glad it was over. If I had only known. I had been worried about being arrested, questioned, put on a list of rabble-rousers that I wouldn't find out about unless I tried to run for a school board and got turned down, and when none of that happened I felt proud to be British (what do they put in those flags?) and very relieved. But the trouble was coming; the trouble was on its way. In fact, it is from the time of that trip to London that I think I can date the end of me keeping my head down and my nose clean and the start of everything beginning to unravel. Or at least to fray.

I was still drained and pale on Monday morning, and my mother was rumbling about a day in bed, but I knew I had to get to school to fill in some details for Alison. So who was he? This masterful boyfriend of mine who was obeyed when he forbade me to speak to my friends. And what harm was I doing to Alison's blossoming sense of her worth as a woman to be going along with it as unapologetically as this?

Linda and Evie were waiting for me at the gate.

'Have you heard?' Evie shouted when I was still fifty yards away.

'About Alison?' said Linda.

'She's got glandular fever,' said Evie.

'She went to hospital on Saturday night because they thought it was meningitis.' Rising to a squeak.

'But it's glandular fever.'

'And we're going to be told at assembly.'

'Mrs Moir's just been here to tell the headmaster and he's going to tell the school at assembly.'

'Alison's been in hospital since Saturday?' I said, weakly. 'All weekend? You didn't phone me, did you? No, you can't have. Why didn't anyone phone?'

'Nobody phoned you,' said Evie, eyes like saucers, 'because Alison said to her mum when they were waiting for the ambulance – she was nearly unconscious but she whispered it, you know – 'Don't phone Janie.' Over and over again, her mum told us, she kept saying, 'Don't phone Janie, promise me you won't phone Janie.' And she was getting dead upset so her mum promised and she didn't phone you and she made us say we wouldn't either.'

I sank down until I was sitting on my school bag on the pavement. I could feel the spines of my lab books buckling under me.

'She said that? In the ambulance?' What a girl, I thought.

'Oh Janie, what *is* it?'

'We've been so upset.'

'How can you have fallen out so badly?'

'And when?'

'And what about?'

'We're sure it's nothing.'

'But,' said Linda, 'Mrs Moir thinks that it might stop her getting better, you know, if she's all upset about something, so she wants it sorted out.'

'Absolutely,' I said. 'I want it sorted out too. I'll go and see her tonight – is she allowed visitors? – and get her a present to say thank you.'

'Thank you for what?' said Linda.

'I mean "sorry",' I said. 'I'll get her a present to say sorry.'

They beamed at me and made little moues of approval and concern and told me that they would chip in and we'd get one big present between all of us, probably clothes.

'Mrs Moir'll be really chuffed,' said Evie. 'She was worried. She's going round to see your mum to tell her all about it and tell her to tell you not to worry about the argument and all that.'

I stared at her.

'When's this?' I said.

'Right after she came here to tell the headmaster,' said Linda. 'She'll be there by now.'

'Oh,' I said. 'Brilliant. Perfect. Fine.'

The one good thing was that I had all day to think something up, since my mother was not the type to come along to the school and haul me out of class demanding an explanation. I considered telling the truth. 'Well, Mum,' I would say, 'the thing is that I went to London to try to persuade Lady Diana to call off her wedding because if she goes through with it . . .' And then they would ask me how I knew. And I would tell them and . . . I didn't consider this for very long.

You would think I could just have shrugged my shoulders and refused to tell them anything, perfectly normal behaviour for a fifteen-year-old. But I couldn't. For one thing careless-ness like that can only really be born out of a clear conscience; fevered explanations are your temptation and your curse when you have something to hide. I had plenty to hide. Also, I reasoned to myself, I was chafing at the reins as it was without my parents going into a total clampdown to punish me. But most of all, I didn't want to hurt them. I remembered all too clearly the looks on their faces when they smelled the cigarettes and cider and how hard they tried not to be disappointed in me. I couldn't do that to them all over again.

So I needed an alibi, just bad enough to make it believable that I would have lied, but no worse, and certainly not enough to put that look in my father's eyes. What wouldn't I give for the overbearing boyfriend now?

On the way out of French, walking along with my head up and eyes focused on the middle distance, I became aware of something bobbing along beside me. It was Danny Conway, his hair bouncing up and down as he walked. It was always very clean on a Monday morning, hinting at a Sunday bathnight arrangement which made him seem more like Christopher Robin than a real boy of my age and my time (roughly).

'Hiya Janie,' he said, noticing me looking at him.

'Hi Dan,' I said back.

I watched him during Latin, thinking, and when the bell

rang for break I hung back waiting for him to finish packing his bag.

'Danny?' I said following him out of the classroom.

He smiled at me, friendly enough but with enough experience of high school to put some wariness there too.

'Can I ask you a favour?'

'Of course,' he said. 'What's up?'

I steered him away from the sunny side of the playground where the football field was marked out and towards the back drive between the kitchens and the music huts. We walked up and down for a bit before I spoke.

'I'm in trouble, and I wondered if you would help,' I said. 'What did you do this weekend?'

'Nothing much,' he said, looking at his feet.

'And how are things?' I said. 'At home.'

'Same,' he said, quietly.

I took a deep breath to carry on and the smell of overused fat coming from the big dumper bins at the back of the kitchens was almost overwhelming.

'The thing is, Danny, I need an alibi. My mum thought I was at Alison's all weekend but—'

'Alison Moir? She's in hospital.'

'I know, and now my mum knows that too and I don't want her to know where I really was and so I wondered if I could say I was with you.'

'Where—'

'I can't tell you, sorry.'

'No, I was going to say where do you want me to say we were?'

It was as easy as that.

'Well,' I said. 'How about if we said I was at your house, doing Latin homework. Would that be . . . ? I mean would . . . ?'

'Yes,' he said, very quietly.

'Only I don't want to worry them, or make them think that anything's going on. So the story would be . . . innocent, you know? Just homework. I'm sure they'll believe me.'

He stopped and looked at me, half-smiling, understanding and not even blaming me really, and it was such a grown-up look that I wondered if maybe I had misjudged it and my parents would think the worst. He seemed to be taller as well, chin height instead of shoulder height, and for a moment I thought about calling it off. But it was Danny Conway, for God's sake. I relaxed and smiled at him.

'Sure?' he said. 'Sure your mum won't think there's even a tiny, tiny chance something mucky might have happened? Have a good look and make sure.' He really was laughing at me now, and at himself and at the whole thing, even the bits that weren't funny.

'You're a pal, Dan,' I said. 'My dad might come steaming round tonight. I don't think so, but you never know.'

'I'll be ready for him.'

I bought a bunch of flowers for my mother from the greengrocers up on the main road, but by the time I neared the house what had seemed like a sweet gesture now struck me as the worst sort of grovelling – smug and obsequious together – and I looked around wildly for somewhere to shove them. The front door opened before I had the chance. It was my father, home a good hour before usual. He saw me looking at my watch.

'Your mother rang me,' he said and stood aside to let me in. She was sitting at the breakfast bar, looking rather frightened. I have seen this in my mother many times; she gets angry and while it lasts she sets some train of punishment in motion, and then her anger evaporates long before the punishment is finished and she just feels wretched until it's done. It happened first when I was eight and had to clean all the family shoes for a week to make up for tracking in dog mess and trying to wipe it up with a hand towel. By the third day she was buying me little treats for when the shoe-polishing was finished and by the end of the week she was doing it herself while I watched, which she called "teaching me to do it properly". This time, I bet, she had called my father at work as soon as Mrs Moir had left and was now regretting it.

'Well?' said my father, sitting down next to her. I sort of half-brandished the flowers. 'Flowers aren't going to help, Janie,' he told me. 'Where were you?' My mother gave me a despairing look.

'At Daniel Conway's,' I said. 'But it's not what you think.'

'Danielle?' said my mother.

'Daniel,' I said, flushing. 'But it's not what you think. We were— I was helping him with his Latin. And various things.'

My father stood and started to put on his coat.

'Are you coming?' he said to my mother. She turned to me, frantic. I nodded slightly.

'Yes,' she said. 'And Janie too.'

'Oh yes,' said my father. 'Janie too.'

The worst thing was that I couldn't really remember where Danny Conway's house was. I knew roughly – it was somewhere in the warren of bungalows that climbed Corstorphine Hill on the other side of the main road – and I knew I would recognize it when I saw it, but my father got angrier and angrier as we drove across and back on the quiet streets, looping in and out of crescents and nosing around corners while I hummed and hawed.

'It's different in a car,' I said desperately. 'I usually go on the footpath, not on the roads.'

'Usually!' said my father.

'Well then, let's park and walk,' said my mother, trying to help.

Luckily, at that moment I saw it. One of those very trim little thirties bungalows with a pointed roof and a bay window on either side of the door, it sat on the curve of a crescent between two others almost identical in construction although otherwise worlds apart. The houses on either side had painted railings and pocket handkerchief lawns, gleaming windows and polished cars under carports to the sides. Danny Conway's house, in contrast, was half-hidden behind thigh-high grass, teasels and hogweed, both dead stalks from last year and this spring's growth. One bay window was blank and dusty; the other was slightly dewed with condensation and was covered by a pair of orange curtains, too long but bunched up on the windowsill, and with not quite enough curtain rings, so that one edge hung down. A towel had been draped over the rail to fill the gap.

Many people would only have got angrier at the sight of all this, and the two milk crates full of limeade bottles beside the front door, but not my parents. My father deflated as he walked up the path until by the time he rang the bell his chin was on his chest. My mother looked as though she was about to cry.

The door opened with a swishing sound of circulars being swept back against the wall behind it and Danny stood there, clean hair still standing up on the top of his head in fluffy bolls, still in his patched, grey trousers.

'You'd better come in,' he said. My mother and father walked inside and stood, shifting from foot to foot in the hall until Danny pointed them towards the back of the house. The kitchen was bare and uncluttered, but there was a sour smell of unwashed cloths and our feet stuck to the lino as we crossed to the table.

'It's not what you think,' said Danny. 'Janie was helping me with my schoolwork, only I've got a bit behind and it's difficult sometimes, you know, to concentrate, because I've got so many other things to keep on top of.' My mother was looking around her, her hands twitching in her lap.

'Where are your parents?' said my father, in a gentle voice.

'Well, my dad's on the rigs, so he's away a lot of the time,' said Danny.

'Are you all on your own?' said my mother. In answer a door opened at the front of the house and a voice, thick as though speaking through folded cloth, called out.

'Danny?'

'In the kitchen, Mum.' He got to his feet and hovered between us and the door. Mrs Conway appeared and stopped, swaying slightly. Her face was mottled, red from the tiny veins over her cheeks but pale near the eyes with the sallow tint of illness. As we watched, she grew paler still, greying around her mouth and beginning to sweat. She made for the table and sat down opposite us with a groan. On the groan, the smell of her breath, a day's drink and yesterday's drink, and bad teeth too, rolled across the table and my parents drew back their chins in the face of it. Danny looked at his hands.

'Who are you?' she said, in the same thick voice.

'You know Janie,' said Danny. 'And this is her mum and dad.'

'Oh well, then, in that case,' said Mrs Conway, 'what can I get you? Danny love, see what there is, eh?'

'Nothing for me,' said my mother in a small voice.

'We just brought Janie round,' said my father. 'But I've had a better idea. Daniel, why don't you come back and have your tea with us?'

'I better not,' said Danny, looking between his mother and me with equal trepidation. 'Anyway, I've got tea all organized.' My mother and I both stole a look around the kitchen, oven cold, counters bare, nothing on the stove.

'Don't worry about me, son,' said Mrs Conway. 'I'm not hungry, and you can always nip out and get me something later. But you'll stay for a drink? Danny love, see what there is, eh?'

'We'd best get going,' said my father, standing up. 'It was nice to meet you.'

We trooped out, scuttling past the door which was now open on the curtained room, trying not to breathe in.

In the porch, Danny said: 'I'll just go and see that she's . . . got everything she needs.' He sped back to the kitchen and we heard his mother again.

'Just see what there is, eh, Danny love.'

My parents and I reeled out into the garden.

'You're a good girl, Janie,' said my mother. 'But you should have said something.'

I couldn't look at her. Not only had I not said anything last time – not in primary seven when Danny cried and I patted his back and promised not to tell the teacher, not in all the years of high school when it was obvious from the grey trousers mended with green thread or the shirts ironed into puckers, that nothing had changed – but I had ground my heel into his face, telling him not to speak to me, and laughing with the others about the stale biscuit smell of his badly dried clothes, calling him Tinker. But this time! This time, granted, I had been kinder, but once again I had done nothing about it and now I had *used* him.

Danny bounded out with his schoolbag slung over his back, pulled the front door closed behind him, and made for the car.

Nobody spoke much on the way home, although at one point my mother twisted round and said: 'So your dad's on an oil rig? When's his next leave?'

'Em, soon,' said Danny. 'But he doesn't always make it back. It's difficult, you know.' This only deepened the silence.

We had dinner then Danny and I went up to my room and did our homework. I was surprised that my parents shooed us upstairs; I had never invited a boy back to the house before, but I had always been sure that if I did we would have been kept downstairs under the parental eye. No doubt though Danny, all five foot two of him with his grey trousers and his pencil case, seemed perfectly safe. *I* suffered a qualm, if I'm honest, thinking that surely he must harbour some feelings for me – Or why did he seek me out every day to say hello? – and if he made a move, I would have fainted from guilt and revulsion and the sheer weirdness of it. He was a child and I . . . well, I couldn't exactly say what I was, but I knew I wasn't girlfriend material for Danny Conway.

We did our French homework and then I put down my pen and summoned some courage.

'I really am grateful,' I said. 'I'm sorry about them coming round and everything.'

'*I'm* sorry,' he said. 'Sorry you've got to put up with me.' I brushed this off. 'It seems to have worked though. I mean,' he gave a strangled chortle, 'I thought your mum was going to pick me up and carry me to the car.'

'Hm,' I said, too embarrassed to laugh.

'I bet she's down there right now knitting me a shawl,' he said, and at last I giggled too.

'Are you okay?' I asked. 'I mean with your mum and everything. Is *she* okay?'

He blew out his cheeks and shook his head. 'Not really. She'll end up in hospital again soon. I know the signs. But at least when that happens my dad'll come down to see me when he's on his leave.'

'Is there nothing . . . ?' I said. His cheerfulness was unnerving.

'Nope. She's an alcoholic. There's nothing that anyone can do.' I knew that, of course. I've had enough experience of life to know that by now, but how did he know it at fifteen and how did he get to be so fine with it?

'This helps,' he said. 'Your mum and dad are nice, aren't they? And your mum's a great cook.' That did it. My mother had served fishcakes and gravy, boil-in-the-bag rice, spring greens, and butterscotch Angel Delight.

'You're welcome anytime,' I said. 'I really mean it.' And I really did.

So that was the start of my relationship with Danny Conway. I couldn't help it; guilt, pity and that interfering bossiness I tell myself I inherited from my mother but which might just be me are an invincible mix, so even though Linda and the rest of them mounted quite a campaign, it did not the slightest bit of good. At first they didn't believe it, until Alison confirmed that I had spent a whole weekend with him, then they laughed, grew puzzled, interrogated me, advised me in kind voices what I was doing to my social standing, sneered, and eventually gave up, contenting themselves with rolling their eyes and saying his name – when they had to – in heavy quotes.

Danny would have been quite discreet if left to himself, barely speaking to me during classes or in the playground and certainly never referring in front of witnesses to time spent together out of school, but it killed me to see him so accepting of his place in the food chain, so I took delight in upsetting it.

'Did you get soaked?' I would call to him at the gate, the morning after he had scurried home in the face of storm clouds at bedtime.

'My mum says do you want to come for tea on Sunday,' I would shout along the rows between my desk and his in the English class. 'It's her birthday and she wants you there, but I warn you: don't eat anything between now and the weekend, because my mother's cakes, you know? Not light.'

And Danny would go red with pleasure and seem not to notice the smirks around him. Of course, this presumption of mine – that I could sing out invitations across a packed classroom – showed that I too thought myself to be the boss of the thing and if Danny had taken me aside and told me gently that he was quite happy for us to be pals but would I mind not advertising it to the rest of the year, I would have wanted to know who he thought he was.

'Who does he think he is?' said Linda.

'Does he think he's your boyfriend?' said Alison.

'*Is* he your boyfriend?' said Evelynne.

'Evie!' said Linda. 'Tinkie Conway is— Sorreee,' she said, as I bristled, 'Daniel Conway, Esquire, is four foot nothing in his football boots with a face like a baby's bum.'

'Come on, Linda, be fair,' said Evie. 'He has had a bit of a spurt.'

'Oh yuk! A bit of a *spurt*. I'm going to be sick.'

'He's a friend of the family,' I would say, desperately. 'Like a cousin.'

So he was. He tucked in to my mother's cooking while my father and I watched in admiration. (The novelty of not having to cook for myself had worn off pretty quickly and I had reverted to exactly the same heart-sink as in the old days when I opened the back door after school and smelled the suet boiling.) He talked to my father about cars and the lawn-mower. And he did his homework up in my bedroom with me, keeping three feet of space between us and only looking

66

into my face when he was trying to see what I did with my lips to pronounce *œil* ('eye'), *moelleux, -euse* ('velvety'), or the dreaded *aïeul* ('venerable elder').

And gradually, as well as being a friend of the family he became a constant distraction. Danny, his mum, his dad, his mum and dad, him and his dad – but mostly his mum – just took up a lot of attention somehow. He was like a puppy clinging to a stick in the rapids, that hard to ignore, and soon it seemed that I thought about little else. He was a worry to my parents too, naturally; a worry and a fixture.

For instance, that day, sitting there on the couch with a hanky clutched in her fist staring at the television screen, at the shot of the building through the beech leaves that might be an embassy (but I *still* couldn't remember) the next thing my mother said to me was:

'Where's Danny?'

'He's busy,' I said. 'Mum, what is that on the telly? Is it an embassy?'

Before she could answer, the shot changed again to a section of moving film from that dreadful engagement photo-shoot with the bright blue suit, and the artful arrangement on the steps to make him look taller: nine-tenths of a bottle of hairspray on her fringe and the rest on his face. No movement from either. My scalp began to prickle.

'It was Kensington Palace,' said my mother. 'Oh Janie, it's off.'

'It's off?' I shrieked.

'The poor Queen,' my mother said.

'She's jilted him?' I shouted, and without knowing I was doing it, I jumped up onto the couch. 'She's dumped him?'

'And given no reason, the besom,' said my mother. 'She seemed like such a nice girl.'

I started laughing, whooping with hysterical laughter, unable to stop.

'Janie!' said my mother. 'It's not funny. What's wrong with you? And get your shoes off the furniture. What's going on?'

'Oh, Mum,' I said. 'I can't even begin to tell you what's

going on.' I'd done it. I had done it! And now, task completed and outcome successful, I would be going home. I cleared my throat and got down off the couch. I would be going home. My mother nodded solemnly at me, clearly thinking that my hysteria had passed to be replaced by a deep and proper royalist grief.

We watched the coverage for as long as it lasted, then my mother gave her nose a good blow and asked: 'Where is Danny? What's he busy with?'

'Got a meeting with social services. I *did* ask him,' I said, my mother starting to agitate as I had known she would, 'but he wanted to handle it himself. And he's sixteen now.' She knew that; she had made him a cake. She had only done it because his birthday was close to mine and she didn't want him to feel left out of things, but he was pleased enough to make me think, with a lump in my throat, that it might be the first birthday cake he had seen for a long time.

'When's she getting out?' said my mother. 'Is she coming straight back to the house?'

I shrugged my shoulders. I didn't know and now it looked as if I wouldn't be here to find out. I was going home, back to my future at last. But if I was going home what was Danny's future going to be? When the real Janie came back to find that Danny Conway was practically her kid brother, she would grind him to dust in the way that only teenagers can, and he wouldn't only lose Janie; he would lose all three of them.

'Mum,' I began, carefully. 'When couples break up . . . No, not really then, what I mean is when friends fall out . . . Okay, take a hypothetical example. If I got a boyfriend and he didn't want me to see Danny, do you think Danny would still see Dad and you?'

'If any boyfriend ever starts telling you what friends you can have, Janie,' my mother said, 'I hope you would—' I stopped listening. She had changed her tune pretty smartly about off-loading a guy if he didn't come up to scratch.

Besides, maybe it didn't work like that. Maybe when the other Janie, the real one, got back from whatever frozen limbo was holding her, she would accept the world she found herself in, Danny Conway and all. If she was in a frozen limbo, of course. And how should I know?

In the beginning, I had tried to work through some of the – I didn't even know what to call them: technicalities, practicalities, repercussions? – some of the details of what had happened but, every time, I ended up bewildered and gasping and recently I had got better than I would have expected at just not worrying about it, trying instead to believe that those crazy new physicists had got it right. It had always seemed a bit of an understatement to call it unlikely, but maybe there *was* a multiverse, an endless infinity of other worlds, each different from the next and each with a Janie of its own, each of those Janies going through her life just one time, and then in a special wrinkled little corner: me, going round again.

I would miss it, being Roundagain Janie, now that I was going back to being Onetime. And I'd never be able to tell anyone about it. Or would I? Who was fond enough of long, complicated philosophical arguments, with so little common sense and such an appetite for analysis that he could get his head around this? I smiled to myself: this was a job for Ludo if ever I'd seen one.

Ludo. The thought was sonorous in my head as though an old-style Shakespearean actor had boomed it in my ear. Ludo. I was going home. A tidal wave of emotion rushed through me, too fast for me to say with any certainty which emotion it was. Guilt perhaps. Trying not to dwell on all the things that made my head spin, I had barely given home a thought and, after two months, I was returning to all the same questions with no more idea of the answers than when I had left. It could easily be guilt then. Or just regret at losing my youth. Perhaps I had got used to being young again, with everything in life ahead of me and nothing lying behind me to make me wince, and the thought of pushing forty this time tomorrow was weighing me down. If I was honest though, there was something else in there with the guilt and regret. Something to do with the fact that I was going back to Ludo. If only, instead, he could have come here to me.

'Mum?' I said. 'How long till tea?'

My mother sighed, unwilling it seemed to take up the reins of daily life again, but then she looked at her watch and calculated.

'About an hour or so.'

Tight, I thought, but probably just enough time. Ludo couldn't join me here, sixteen and full of the joys; I was going to have to face him (and me) where he was, where we'd got to. But I could do one thing. I could hop on a number fifteen up to Morningside Place, knock on his parents' door, ask if he was in, and just have a look at him. I could remind myself that he was a boy when I was a girl and that whatever had happened to him since, some of it had to be my responsibility and up to me to fix.

I went out to the hall to get my coat. It wasn't the first time it had occurred to me to make this bus trip up through the city to the leafiest of the leafy suburbs to get a look at Ludo. But the idea of it was one of the things that made my head spin and so I had always fought it down. Now, though, it wasn't just nosiness sending me, and my head was just about to stop spinning for good. I put my coat on and was counting out change for the bus from the little pot on the telephone table when the doorbell rang.

On the step stood a middle-aged man in suit trousers with an anorak on top, a diffident look on his face.

'I'm looking for the lady of the house,' he said, smiling. My mother was moving around in the kitchen, but I could hear her still blowing her nose.

'She's indisposed at the moment,' I said. 'Can I take a message?'

'Yes, yes,' he said, stroking his chin. 'Yes, I suppose she is. Can you tell her I was surprised at the news.'

I frowned at him.

'Is that it?'

'That's all. I was surprised – but very impressed – at today's news and I wanted to offer my congratulations for a nicely handled little job.'

He was still smiling and he was quite a small man, so it was hard to say why all of a sudden my scalp prickled. I think perhaps his voice changed, something like that. He didn't start to shout; it was more as though he had tensed all his stomach muscles to speak from the diaphragm, like our drama teacher always told us to do, so his words sounded harder, purer, like something that was passing right through me and out the other side.

'I wanted to say to her,' he went on, his voice making me catch my breath and blink fast, as if to clear away tears before they fell. I thought about those sopranos' top notes that shattered crystal. 'I wanted to say, not to let it go to her head. I wanted . . . to urge caution. To assure her she's not alone. To give her this.' His tone had softened again as he rummaged in the pockets of his anorak and those of the suit jacket underneath and he now produced a small white postcard.

'Who are you?' I asked him, and something made him look up, sharp as a little bird.

'Ah,' he said. 'Maybe *not* the lady of the house, then. Maybe you? Were *you* surprised to hear the news today, I wonder?'

'Who *are* you?' I said again.

He handed me the card with a sideways nod towards it that was almost a bow.

'If you ever need to,' he said, then he turned smartly on his heels and strode off up the path. I looked at the card in my hand. There was no name on it, only a telephone number: Hull 36782.

'Who was that man?' My father's voice made me jump. He had walked down the path while I was staring at the card and he must have seen the whole encounter as he approached along the street.

'Uhhh, just a salesman,' I said.

'Selling what?' said my father, turning to look after him.

'Uhhh, conservatories,' I said, not thinking.

'Conservatories? What do you mean: selling conservatories?' My father put his briefcase down and stood with his hands on his hips, staring. 'He's not going to any of the other houses.'

'Have you heard the news?' I asked him.

He whistled and rolled his eyes. 'How's your mum?' he whispered, not quite laughing. I didn't quite laugh back and we went inside.

During dinner I just about recovered from whatever it was the little man had done to me and I replayed everything he had said. The only sense I could make of it was as confirmation: I had indeed worked out what I had come back to do and now, having done it, I was going home again. My visitor, I decided, had come to leave me his card in case anything went wrong on the return journey. I shuddered to think about the kind of thing that could go wrong on that kind of journey, but the more I tried to put it out of my mind the more gruesome the possibilities became.

So with me at that and my mother still morose – not weeping any more but heaving enormous sighs on every other breath – my father was having a pretty dull time.

'Come on, you two,' he said at last. 'I'm sure it's for the best. Nobody breaks off an engagement lightly, you know.'

'I don't think I've ever known anyone else who did it,' I said.

'Grace Kelly did it,' said my mother. 'In *High Society.*'

'Well then,' said my father. 'She came out of it pretty well, didn't she? With a prince, or Bing Crosby, depending how you look at it.' My mother smiled.

'Anyway, that's not what's on Janie's mind,' she said.

I gulped down a mouthful of pastry that could have done with a bit more chewing and took a drink of water.

'Is he going to get back to you and fill you in?' said my mother. 'It's a worry not knowing.'

I stared at her.

'What's this?' said my father.

'Mrs Conway's getting out,' my mother said. 'Danny was having a meeting with the social service people this afternoon.'

They both shook their heads.

'So they've dried her out again,' said my father. 'And now they'll pack her off home until next time. It's not fair on the boy.'

'But what can anyone do?' said my mother.

'They could make her take that medicine that makes you sick if you drink,' I said.

'What medicine's that?' said my father. 'Is this something Danny's heard of?'

'No,' I said. 'That stuff that George Best took. Takes. Should take. I don't know – Danny told me about it.'

'Knowing her, she'd just take it *and* the drink and be sick and then he'd have that to deal with too,' said my mother. 'What a life!'

But Danny, for once, was the least of my worries. I tried the Hull number as soon as my parents were safely ensconced, sighing and clucking, in front of the news. It was an answering machine; pretty unusual for a start, I thought. The voice – not his voice – spoke slowly, as people used to speak on their answering machines when they first got them, slow as cattle going to the river to drink, so slow that your mind wandered in between the words and you missed what they were trying, so slowly, to tell you.

'It's Janie Lawson,' I whispered, 'from Edinburgh. 031 336 7792. Please ring back tonight if you can, because I may not be here tomorrow. Thanks. And, you know ... who are you? What's going on?'

No one rang back.

I hugged my parents hard before I went upstairs to bed and tried not to think about what a blow it would be to get her back again, the other Janie, the real one, grumpier than ever. Whether she had been stuck in limbo or whether she knew nothing about it at all and was going to wake up on the 5th of May expecting the 5th of March and wondering why Danny Conway was even more of a pest than ever, she was bound to take it out on her parents in teenage sulks. On the other hand if it had been a straight swap, she might have grown up a bit and not be so bad. If she had spent the last two months getting sacked from my job, maxing out my store cards and being scarred for life by the advances of my husb—

I had forgotten to go and see Ludo. That little man with the funny voice had come along and blown it right out of my mind.

'Night, darling,' said my mother. 'Straight to bed now. It's been a long, trying day.' And she didn't know the half of it.

'Straight to bed,' I agreed, although actually I was going to clean out my hamster, a night early, because no matter where the other Janie had been and how much growing up she had done, he was going to have to get used to squalor again.

One thing I was determined to do, as soon as I got back, was to phone my mum and ask her if she could remember the hamster I had had when I was sixteen, the orange one with the black eyes, and if so, what was his name. I had got into the habit of using it as a way to get off to sleep, doing it alphabetically: 'Appleby, Albert, Buttons, Bertie, Bundle, Crunchie . . .' But it was no good, I couldn't remember, and it was driving me nuts.

Chapter 5

7 May 1981

My mother kicked off her slippers to step up on her bed and reach down a suitcase from the hat shelf in her wardrobe.

'You're sure about this?' she said, taking out her two hats in their tissue paper nests and putting them back on the shelf.

'Positive,' I said. 'It's no big deal.'

She wiped her hands around the inside of the case and wrinkled her nose.

'Dusty.'

'Exactly, Mum,' I said. 'There's dust in your suitcase. Precisely.'

She brought it to the end of the bed and shook it out onto her powder rug, the synthetic sheepskin she stands on in the morning while she puts on her talcum powder. My mother must have been the last person in the world to stop using talcum powder.

They were off to London on a last-minute booking for two nights' dinner, bed and breakfast (and a show). One reason – that makes me look good – is that it had occurred to me that my parents hadn't spent a single night away together since the day I was born and if it was to be like last time, where I was too selfish to have thoughts like this, they were not due to for another two years. The other reason – less noble but more pressing – was that I badly needed a stretch of time on my own to reflect, review and make some plans for what appeared to be the future. Because although the deed was done, the wedding was off, the world had shifted course and the little man had come to send me on my way, I couldn't help but notice that I was still here.

'I'll be fine,' I said stoutly, and I wasn't only talking to my mother about the weekend. My father came into the bedroom holding up his ironed shirts by their collars. He never irons them, but he always carries them upstairs, because he thinks my mother re-crumples them on the way. What a nerve he's got, when you think about it.

'Of course you'll be fine,' he said.

'I could still ring Auntie Mona,' said my mother. She had me going for a minute, but she couldn't keep her face straight.

'That's my sister you're talking about,' my father said, twinkling. 'Anyway, she'll be fine, Moira. Stop fussing. Janie's very mature for her age.'

A dry laugh from me.

First thing on Saturday, I got to it. I had done a lot of thinking since waking up, still here, on Tuesday morning, and I had come to a firm decision, but I've always been one of those people who needs to write it down. (I get this from my mother who, one December, wrote a list for herself which read: make shopping list, make present list, make card list, buy stamps. My father laughed so much he had to take off his glasses and wipe his eyes.)

So I needed a list. I also needed a stack of A4, some Post-it notes, a highlighter, a pot of really good coffee and a flipchart and I had none of them. Where did people get paper before they had printers? What did they write on? How did we ever live like this?

Behind the shoe rack under the stairs was a cupboard, and in the cupboard were the roll ends of the wallpaper my father had used in all the rooms of the house. They were sacrosanct, because you never knew. Except, I did, of course. I knew that no flood, singe or scuff would harm any of my parents' walls and that these roll ends would go dry and yellowed into the bin when the new ones arrived.

I cut poster-sized lengths of the green-speckled vinyl from my own bedroom, battling it with the bacon scissors while it sprang up stiffly into curls and scraped my knuckles with its raw edges, until at last I had four sheets of it spread on the dining table trapped under the fruit bowl, the letter rack, half a bottle of sherry and a gift-box of fish knives and I went to make myself a big cup of Mellow Bird's.

Mum, Dad, Ludo, Elvis, I wrote. One page for each.

For the new plan, in essence, was to do it all; to forget what I was there for, forget how to get back again, and just do the right thing. Of course, the new plan was nothing of the sort, really. The new plan, *really*, was to act as if that was the new plan and see if that would get me out of here. They do say, after all, that if you want something you must let it go. Also, there was Sod's Law, which was much more my kind of magic. If I started some long-term projects, I was almost guaranteed to disappear in a puff of smoke and leave a huge mess behind me. Finally, there was the unsettling little voice in my head saying that if I was still here then the thing I had done was clearly not the thing I was here to do. And yet I had wiped two people from history. So I had a lot to make up for, and I was going to make up for it by doing the right thing, by doing it all.

And really, really, doing it all; not just knowing that I should, and keeping saying I would, but ending every day planning to start tomorrow. If the world divides into the people who do things – run marathons, start businesses, detox every January – and the people who put books about detox in their shopping trolleys every January along with the first Creme Eggs of the New Year, then I was just about to cross the line.

I was going to work my butt off to get my mother everything she had ever wanted, same for my father just as soon as I worked out what it was. I was going to meet Ludo again and instead of turning into what we had turned into, so that I would be in the spare room planning to leave him seventeen years later, I was going to make it work and make it good and make both of us happy. And I was going to save Elvis, of course.

Not literally, clearly, but that was what I called it because I

77

always had and also because I couldn't write down 'save the world', not even in blue felt-tip on a piece of wallpaper alone in the house.

All I had on my Elvis sheet so far was: Chernobyl, Fred West, Dunblane, 9/11. I felt bad about all the others I knew I was forgetting – there was something in a burger bar somewhere – but I wasn't going to give myself a hard time. I was just going to keep up with the quality newspapers, watch for things that might jog my memory, and hope for the best.

I didn't have a clue what I was going to *do* about any of it, obviously. In fact, it seemed to me that my Elvis jobs divided horribly neatly into those that one person could make no impression on, like AIDS and global warming, and those that one person, certainly one teenage girl, should make sure to keep well away from. Still, I could write anonymous letters and didn't the police check out every tip sooner or later? Surely. Only it wouldn't be the police in some cases; it would be the men in suits and I couldn't write to the men in suits, because I didn't know who they were. Special Branch? Secret Service? MI5, 6, 10? Imagine the red face if I wrote to a department that Ian Fleming had made up or one that was only on *The Sweeney*.

So, I would write to my MP, and to the Home Secretary and the Foreign Secretary and see what happened. I would definitely spend time trying to firm up some dates, though. That was bound to help.

Now Ludo. It was mucking things up with Ludo that had started all of this, and that made him my priority, but on the other hand, as far as Ludo was concerned there was plenty of time. I had definitely decided against going round to his house; even thinking about it gave me an unaccountable shiver. So I wasn't even going to meet him until Shona Ward's party at first year at university, which wasn't for another three years. I was due a couple of unfortunate attempts at relationships before then, of course, but I didn't think I was going to bother this time around. I was still married for one thing, kind of, and for another those boys – Russell Morton and Keith Farries – were children; it would be sick. It would also be boring. I couldn't see myself sitting through *The Blue Lagoon* waiting for Keith to pluck up the courage to take my hand, or perching on a garden chair in the garage watching Russell and his dad working on their kit car.

I really had decided. Only . . . if I could get my hands on Ludo before his first girlfriend had chewed him up and spat him out and before that manipulative little Hazel had kept him dangling on a string right through his sixth year with her pregnancy scares and her almost-but-not-quite eating disorder, he might be all the better for it. He had had just the two before me and I had had just the two before him; we used to smile at each other and say 'third time lucky' until it started to sound sickening. Then he used to say it and I used to scowl until he too, eventually, stopped.

I was too honest not to admit to myself that the main culprit in screwing up Ludo – with two teenage girlfriends and a wife of twelve years to choose from – had to be me, but the whole point was that I was going to do everything differently this time, and so it made sense to save him the hurt that those two would dish out unless I stopped them. And without their advance guard he would surely be that much less likely to take any of *my* nonsense (which anyway I wasn't going to be making him take) and we'd be halfway to a happy marriage from the word go. And besides, surely it was his mother who started it.

A very unwelcome memory suddenly intruded. A dinner party, pretty drunk, and friends teasing me, saying that every boy married his mother. I tried to shout them down, telling them that Ludo's mother was a controlling cow who would still choose his clothes for him if she had the chance, but then I spoiled it all by laying a hand on his arm to stop him refilling his brandy glass and it cracked everyone up. I laughed along with them, but inside I was boiling with rage and afterwards when they had passed out on the sofa bed, we had one of those whispered fights of ours, where I called him a devious shit for doing that right then to make me look bad and he told

79

me that he loved me for wanting to take such good care of him, and I shoved him out of bed with my feet for being such a creep.

What if it was true, though? Ludo's mother was a monster. What if he really had married another one just like her? What if the only reason he had ever looked twice at me was because being with me felt like home?

Christ! It was all coming back to me now: the time early on in our flat-sharing when I had asked him why he never peed standing up and he said his mother didn't let him, and all I had thought was what a good idea and why did women put up with spills and smells instead of just putting their foot down.

And wasn't I sitting here right now tussling with myself about whether to stop him finding out what it was like to go on a date with someone else? Because I knew best? And this was my idea of doing it all differently! This was me making sure we didn't get over-involved over-early? Jesus Christ, Janie! Hazel of the late periods and Soppy Sarah were neither here nor there: Ludo's mother had started the job and I had finished it for her. She made him pee like a girl and I made him have a vasectomy – we had practically cut off one each and devoured them.

So he could have his first love with Sarah and his fling with Hazel. I would wait until Shona Ward's party. But then – boy oh boy! I was going to put right what his mother had done to him: I would simper, I would look up to him, I would beg for guidance and shriek for help and I wouldn't be satisfied until he had a meaningless affair with a younger woman and fobbed me off with filling station carnations in apology. And – this was key – I would do my damnedest to get him off that philosophy course and into ... I don't know. History, law, something bracing and decisive. Something to make a man of him. I wavered for a minute, at that. If I did try to meet him now, while he was still at school, I could steer him towards science and then we'd be laughing. He would slaughter white mice and be in a five-a-side football team. But, on balance, no.

I would be glad to swerve the philosophizing, but there were limits.

So, there was my plan and I had three years to get ready to put it into action.

Next, my mother. Everything my mother wanted could be bought with money (although it still gave me qualms to admit it) and in the old days, for that reason, she would have been the biggest challenge of all. Now though, I was made.

It was 1981, so they should buy another house, quick. As to whether or not they could afford it, whether they had any savings or what my father's income was . . . Well, there was a strong box, kept in the sock drawer of my mother's dressing table, containing all the important documents of their life; their wills, old bankbooks, passports, all that. And in an excruciatingly solemn little ceremony just after he retired, when I no longer lived in the house, my father had told me the combination of the lock 'in case anything was to happen'. Knowing him, it would have been the same combination from the dawn of time to the end of eternity, and it was up there, in his sock drawer, now. I shook my head to get the idea out before it had a chance to take hold.

Also, for my mother, there was gambling. I could count on the thumb of one hand the number of Grand National winners I knew the name of – Usual Suspect – and I couldn't remember what year *he* won it; in fact I could only remember this much because the barman in the pub where I had a part-time job told me he was a sure thing on long odds and to put my shirt on him (I didn't) and then came round afterwards to gloat. But if it was one of the barmen in The Coopers' then it had to be mid-eighties and so it was worth keeping an eye out in a year or so. Except of course he could have raced more than once, or it could have been the Derby.

There was one thing I could count on, one long shot that could make my fortune: Goran Ivanisevic and his wild card. But it was a long time until then and I didn't want my mother to have to wait. Concentrate.

There was a football match sometime around the millennium when Manchester United got two goals right at the end and won something, when they had already won something else, meaning that they won everything. Again, rather a long way off and since Manchester United did tend to play in football matches and did tend to win some, not really something to sell the farm for.

So much for sport.

I could steal an idea. I could pitch the idea of a sitcom about six young professionals in New York, or I could write a book about a cultured cannibal, but the ideas were probably floating around already. (It takes for ever to get a project off the ground. I knew this from a friend who once had a pilot show broadcast on Radio 4 *six years* after they said they liked it.) And anyway, Hannibal Lecter was in another book which was probably out already, and it was the film that made all the money. I might as well wait for Goran as try to get rich writing books.

Besides, I couldn't steal, not from actual people. And, clearly, I was never going to put Ladbrokes on skid row, but there was another way, where ethics didn't speak their name, where morals had no place, where theft had no meaning because there was no humanity to steal from. It was legal and there was nothing anyone could do to stop me. I would need to do some homework, of course, but even right now off the top of my head I managed to come up with quite a list. Vodaphone, IBM, Microsoft, Intel, M&S (for a while), Smith Kline Tom Dick Harry Jones and Glaxo. Even – hallelujah – Man U. You didn't need to know much about sport to know that.

'Buy *FT*' I wrote on my Mother page. 'Get part-time job/ sell something/sweet-talk parents'. How hard could it be? I could even, I thought, looking at my note to get a part-time job and thinking how half-hearted it was, I could even get a full-time job. Leave school right now, do something lucrative, invest, and go back later.

And now my father. I had tried to draw him out, gently,

quite a few times now, but he had been so reticent that if I hadn't known better I would have thought that Limtec was a front and he was a spy. I stared at the back of the square of wallpaper for long enough for my cup of coffee, still half-full, to grow a disc of scum on top as it cooled and the fat in the milk rose. I saw again the flare in my father's eyes when I had told him the world was his oyster. If it hadn't been for that I could have told myself he was a rare example of complete contentment, a yogi in navy-blue cords and Polyveldts. As it was, I couldn't pretend there wasn't something there worth finding out and getting to work on. But where to start? More coffee seemed like a good idea.

In the kitchen, waiting for the kettle, my eye fell on the spice rack bulging with brown envelopes and a thought occurred. It's hard to defend, but I really was struggling with my plan for my father and needing a toehold, not that I'm saying the ends justify the means necessarily. And also, I've often found this, there was the fact that I had been scrupulous and not gone rummaging in the really secret place, so this was like a reward for good behaviour, like those large women in cafes who spoil their cups of tea with sweetener and allow themselves a doughnut for their willpower.

At first, there didn't seem much of interest in the spice rack anyway. A gas bill – paid, a reminder from the lawnmower service people to bring the machine in for its yearly check-up, a list of bedding plants for sale from the local nursery, a receipt from the council offices for a rates payment, and a . . . bingo! A bank statement.

I did hesitate, but not for long. The first thing that struck me was that bank statements then were nothing like as informative as bank statements now. Nowadays with all the Switch details you can retrace your steps pretty closely. More than once after I've gulped at the bottom line and been on the point of phoning the bank to report a fraud, I've been saved from it by piecing together the point of sale debits – petrol station in Pitlochry? Oh yes, that was when Ludo and I took off 'to save our marriage' that weekend.

My father's bank statement (and it was my father's alone – my mother had a deposit account with a little book, but when a cheque was needed she would fill it all out and then take it to my father to sign and when he did he would say, 'Thank you Miss Moneypenny' every single last time) played its cards pretty close to its chest, just cheque numbers one after the other all down the page and two standing orders for five pounds and seventeen pounds going to Oxfam and the RSPB. Good for them.

I was just about to put the envelope back when it dawned on me that, although there couldn't be quite so much information in here as my father would have gleaned from mine if the tables were turned, there should surely have been a bit more than there was. There should be a salary for one thing, and a mortgage payment. Those two, at least. I unfolded the statement again and took another look. There was nothing paid out, even by cheque, that was big enough to be a mortgage payment; the largest amount was fifteen pounds. And nothing that came in could possibly be my father's salary. Nothing came in at all.

I knew my parents didn't have another bank account. My father had the cheque book and my mother had the passbook for paying in cash. And that was it. The passbook lived in my mother's handbag and the cheque book lived in my father's inside pocket and when they were finished they went to live together in the strong box in the sock drawer until the end of the tax year when they were burnt in a little brazier safely set in the middle of the patio out in the back garden. So now there were two questions: where was my father's salary and where did my mother get the cash she was always paying in every Friday? I had only been entertaining myself when I had pretended that maybe Limtec was a front and my father was really deep undercover, too deep undercover to risk even a hobby that might bust him. Now all of a sudden that was looking slightly less outlandish and, just for good measure, my mother was a money launderer too.

Clearly I needed to get out for a while, take some deep

breaths of air, start thinking straight. I could go and buy the broadsheets, and some Basildon Bond. When I opened the door though, it was to see Danny bobbing down the path, looking very smart and slicked down in the kind of clothes no normal sixteen-year-old boy who dresses himself would ever wear.

'Where are you going like that?' I asked him.

'I've been,' he said. 'Visiting Mum in the Royal Ed.'

'Early.'

'Yeah, well, partly it gets it over with, which sounds bad, I know. But mostly, first thing in the morning is the only time a drunk ever feels grateful for being dried out. They can sometimes be a bit of a pain by the afternoon.'

'You're some kid, Dan,' I said.

'Yeah,' said Danny. 'So where are you off to?'

'Oh, just going to get the papers, but if you'll get them for me I'll stay here and make you some lunch.'

'You sound just like your mum,' said Danny.

'They're away for the weekend and the house seems awful empty.'

'Tell me about it,' said Danny.

He brought back Mars Bars as well as the newspapers and we sat at the breakfast bar and ate them.

'You know your mum?' I said presently, wiping my mouth with a tissue and waving another one at Danny, who needed it badly. 'How come she's ... like she is?'

'How d'you mean?' said Danny.

'Well, did something happen to her? Or did it start when your dad went on the rigs?'

'Other way round,' said Danny. 'Dad took off when he couldn't stand it any more.'

'Only – I'm not just being nosey – but I've been thinking about mine. My parents, I mean. My dad mostly. There's something, not drink, but something ... missing, and I'm trying to see what it might be and where it might have come from or how it could have happened. And I just wondered.

Listen, I'm going to make you a frittata,' I announced and headed for the cooker.

'Is that anything like a poncho?' he asked. 'Because I'm telling you now I won't wear it to school.'

'It's a bacon and egg pie without the pie,' I told him. 'And leftover potatoes instead of bacon.'

'Fair enough,' he said. He spread the newspaper on the breakfast bar and read the headlines. 'Will I set the table? Frittata sounds like you should set a table but leftovers and eggs sounds more like a plate on your knee.'

'I'm putting avocados in the side salad,' I told him.

'I'll set the table.'

He knew where everything was, from the last few months of being the son my father never had and such a wonderful boy that my mother's eyes misted over every time she looked at him, and I smiled as I listened to him gathering cutlery and glasses from the sideboard. This weekend was the least of my parents' good fortune, really, even with the show (I had advised them to go and see *Sleuth* and it was hard to explain how I knew that it was a really good mystery with a twist in the tail without telling them that I had seen the film version with Laurence Olivier and Michael Caine that hadn't been on the telly yet). Even better than London hotels was the fact that they had a daughter who did at least half the housework, had no tantrums, would never smoke, drink, or take drugs, and who had brought into their life the personification of Orville the orphaned duckling that was Danny Conway.

'Do you need this wallpaper for anything?' Orville called from the dining room. My blood ran cold. He had put the sherry bottle and the box of fish knives back in the sideboard, the fruit bowl and the letter rack back on top, and was rolling the sheets up together tightly. 'Cos you're going to need a rubber band or some string,' he said.

I tried to tell from his face whether he had read them and whether, if he had, anything had made any sense, but he just waved the roll of paper at me and made a noise like a light sabre. I went to find an elastic band from the junk drawer in the kitchen, getting there just in time to save the onions from burning. Danny snapped it over the end, rolled it to the middle, laid the paper along the back of the sideboard, and then, apparently, forgot about it. I could see it though, out of the corner of my eye, as though it was glowing, all through lunch.

'So are you going to tell me?' Danny said, just as we were finishing up the salad, picking the good bits out of the bowl with our fingers.

'Are you going to ask me?' I said, matching his tone, which was light and amused. Underneath I was desperately trying to remember what I had written on the sheets.

'Okay. Because the only thing I can think that you'd need a pink paper for is to make pink papier maché. Is that it?'

'Right,' I said. 'The *FT*. Yes. Well, as it turns out I probably don't need it after all, but I had been thinking about maybe getting to grips with the stock market.'

'Really?'

'But like I say, it's looking like a non-starter.'

'Why?'

'Various reasons. Mostly, I haven't got any money. I could get a part-time job and invest my wages, but I'm thinking probably there's a lower limit. God, I can't believe I don't know anything about this stuff.'

'What do you need investments for?' said Danny. 'Is it something to do with that other thing?' My eyes slid over to the roll of wallpaper at the back of the sideboard. 'When you went away that time? Are you going again? Because I don't know how I would feel about lying to your mum and dad again. Not now I know them. Sorry.'

'No, it's not that. It's my mother, but it's hard to explain. It's nothing bad.'

'Your mum too?' said Danny. 'I thought it was your dad that was the problem.'

I said nothing.

'I could give you money,' he went on. He wasn't looking at me, but was peering into the salad bowl as if still looking for

87

tasty bits, although I could see that what he was picking out was just little scraps of iceberg.

'I'm talking about a lot,' I said. 'Enough to . . . I don't know . . . buy a house with, so that's why I was thinking about stocks.'

'What's that thing you always say?' said Danny. 'Duh!' He did a perfect Duh, sounded just like Chandler Bing, but I couldn't really appreciate it for the surprise of finding out I still said it. I should stop that. 'I could give you money to bet on the stock market,' he said, speaking very slowly and clearly as though to a child. Or as though to a drunk, I thought.

'Have you got some?' I said. I tried not to sound too incredulous, but it was hard not to think of his school trousers with the patch and the crate of dusty limeade bottles on the front doorstep.

'Duh!' he said again. 'My dad's been working on an oil rig for four years and I've been in charge of the housekeeping. We could go halfers.'

'Absolutely not,' I said. 'You can stake me and I'll pay you back, but your money's your money.' Truthfully though, I was taken with the idea. If Danny had funds I could stop thinking about that mystifying bank statement. 'Anyway, it's not betting; it's long term; it's totally different.'

'It'll be a laugh,' said Danny. 'Me and my mum do the horses, when she's feeling okay, like when she comes out and for a month or two after. Then she just signs the slips and I do it on my own, but the stock market would be a change. Maybe I'd be more lucky.'

'You're serious, aren't you?' I said. He was on his way to the kitchen to get the newspaper. 'You really have got piles of money lying around? Because . . .' I couldn't think of a nice way to ask about the trousers and the limeade bottles and all the rest of it, so I just smiled at him as he returned. He pushed our plates aside and opened the paper at the centre pages.

'What do you do?' he said, looking at me expectantly.

'I've got no idea,' I answered. 'Look in the Yellow Pages and find a broker, maybe? Or perhaps you just write to the company and ask to buy some shares. I really haven't got a clue. Pathetic, when you think of it.'

'Not that,' said Danny. 'Not all that boring stuff. We can work that out somehow when we have to. I mean here, now. What do we do? How do we pick a winner?'

'Ahh,' I said, twiddling my fingers like a pianist about to buckle down to the Minute Waltz. 'Leave that to me.'

Chapter 6

June 1 1981

A momentous day. I knew it was going to be a bit special anyway, because today was the day that our little raft – Danny's and mine – that we had started building over lunch and the *FT* that morning, was finally going to float. But I couldn't have dreamed the rest of it. Perhaps I should have. Perhaps I should have been able to see that something was brewing. Did my father looked strained? Did my mother look anxious? If they did, I didn't see it; too busy trying to make things right for them to notice what was wrong.

Also it was the day of the last O-grade exam: biology. The last day in my life I would have to think about the innards of the lesser creatures, at least until I passed my driving test again and ran over my first roadkill. I reeled out of the gym hall with Alison, Evie and Linda and threw myself down on the grass beside them.

'Oi!' shouted one of the boys who had just come out of the exam hall with us. 'Get off the pitch!' But none of the girls lying on the grass moved.

'Mickey Docherty's having a party,' said Evie. 'God, I don't feel well.'

'Yeah, I know,' I said, then remembering that I hadn't heard about the party yet and *shouldn't* know, I added: 'When does it start?'

'It's already started. Started at lunchtime and it's on all night and the whole of the fourth year's invited.'

'His mum and dad are away on holiday,' said Alison. 'And he's got forty pounds' worth of beer in a paddling pool in the back garden.'

'In cans?' said Linda. 'Or just in the paddling pool?'

'Like the world's biggest slug trap,' I said, but they all just stared at me. Any of my jokes that depended on them having seen *Gardeners' World* tended to fall quite flat.

'What are you going to wear?' said Linda. My clothes were still a great source of amusement to them.

'Who says I'm going?' There was a chorus of groans and raspberries.

'You never do anything,' said Evie. 'The exams are over, in case you hadn't realized.'

'I'm busy just now,' I said, 'but I might look in later.'

'Well, we're all going. I'm going even though I feel like death,' said Evie, 'and we're not waiting until after whatever it is you've got to do with darling Daniel that's soooo important.'

'Who said it was anything to do with Danny?' I demanded. Danny himself arrived just at that moment, right on cue.

'Hiya, Janie,' he said. He stood over us blocking out the sun, looking – with the light shining through his hair and his ears – like a space alien. 'Linda, Evelynne, Alison,' he added. I wondered if he knew what a loser he made himself sound like or if he ever looked in a mirror before he went out in the morning, and why he couldn't make the tiny bit of effort it would take to get normal. It was only when other people were around that I ever had thoughts like this though, and they were unworthy of both him and me, so I told myself it was academic burnout talking, and made a stab at being nice.

'You all set?' I was sitting up and brushing grass off my back. 'She signed it?'

'Who says it's anything to do with Danny?' whispered Alison, too quiet for him to hear.

'Yup,' said Danny, patting the clipboard folder hugged against his chest. A clipboard, for Christ's sake!

'Are you going to the party?' I asked him, standing and stretching. 'We're all thinking of going to the party.'

'Except I don't feel well,' said Evie. 'God, I really don't feel very well.'

'It's the heat.'

'You're just tired.'

'I feel as if I'm going to explode,' she said, sitting up very gingerly.

'What have you eaten?' said Danny. Alison and Linda glowered at him, but Evie – and this was a testament to how ill she must be feeling – Evie answered him just like one normal person having a conversation with another one.

'Nothing! I was too nervous to eat. All I've had all day is orange juice and mints.'

'It's probably your blood sugars going bananas then,' I said. 'Do you feel faint?'

'No!' said Evie, with a rising note of terror in her voice. 'I feel volcanic! Oh help!'

She clutched at my arm and dug her nails in and the look on her face was exactly the look on Ludo's face on a bus in Delhi when he gave up trying to explain to the driver why he had to stop and turned instead to me in search of a miracle. It sparked an idea.

'What kind of mints?' I asked her. She just shook her head; it was no time for pointless questions.

'Sugar-free mints?' I asked her. She nodded, a faint look of hope lighting up her face. She had been crunching away all morning during the French exam, as well as the three hours of the biology paper.

'How many have you eaten?' I asked her.

'What is it, Janie?' said Alison, crouching over Evie, her eyes wide with fear. 'Is she going to be all right?'

'Eventually,' I said. 'But sugar-free mints! Didn't you read the packet? They're a really, really powerful laxative, Eve!'

On the stressed syllable of '*lax*ative', as though the word itself was imbued with magic, a terrible liquid rasping sound came from under Evie, and the rest of us, unable to help ourselves, recoiled with a harmonized 'Aaah' of disgust.

'Make him go away,' was Evie's first utterance.

I started to laugh. 'Yes, go away, Danny,' I said. 'I'll meet you at the gate.'

'And stop laughing!' said Evie. 'I can't believe you're laughing! How can you be laughing at me?'

'Oh come on!' I said, looking at Linda and Alison for support, but their faces were solemn and Linda had tears in her eyes. This only made me laugh even harder.

'You're such a cow,' Alison said.

'What's going on?' One of the boys had given up on the idea of football and had wandered over to see what the upset was. 'And what's that guff?'

'What's up?' said another one. It was Lightbulb Boyd. The third most fancied boy in the year after Co-co Swain and Mickey himself, and the one Evie had been choosing her clothes for since Christmas.

'What's that smell?' said Lightbulb. 'Tinker, have you farted?'

Danny stared at him. Then he put down his clipboard and faster than you would have believed possible, fast enough to look like a silent film of a vaudeville comic act, he kicked off his shoes, ripped off his trousers and shirt, peeled off his vest, plucked off one sock then the other, took a deep breath, yanked off his underpants and set off towards the far edge of the playing field with all the boys racing after him, whooping.

'Let's go,' I said. I pulled Evie to her feet, grabbed Alison's long cardigan and tied it around Evie's waist. Then the three of us flanked her like bodyguards, one to each side and one – me – at the back, and trying to breathe through our mouths we hustled her to the girls' changing rooms.

Alison and Linda finally started laughing once Evie was in the shower and her clothes were tied up in two layers of bin bags, but it was Danny who got the brunt of it.

'He's mental!' said Alison. 'I can't believe he did that.'

'I can't believe I wasn't looking!' shouted Evie from behind the shower curtain. 'I can't believe I missed it.'

'We didn't have to look!' said Linda. 'It was right at eye level! We couldn't have missed it if we'd tried.'

'And it was all flying about when he started running,' shouted Alison.

It occurred to me that, since neither Alison nor Linda had brothers, this was probably their first sighting. It occurred to me too that since Evie now had a naked male to thank for saving her from such humiliation, her sexuality might just tip the other way and Dolly the radical midwife might stay on the shelf. As though to add weight to this theory Evie stuck her head out of the cubicle.

'Tell Danny he can come to the party,' she said. 'And tell him thanks a million squillion. Have you found me anything to wear?'

'It's a choice between gym kit or trying to get your waist in the neck of a jumper and pretending it's a skirt,' said Linda.

'What colour's the jumper?' Evie said.

'I've got to go,' I told them. 'I really do have something I need to do, with Danny, but I'll see you later. Evie?' I shouted over the sound of the shower. 'Have some eggs for your tea.'

The playground was deserted. Danny's clipboard lay where he had left it and his vest and one sock were still there too, hinting at a hurried re-dressing. Making a shrewd guess, I picked up all three and went around to the front door of the admin block. I could hear the headmaster's voice as soon as I stepped inside. 'Aware of your difficulties' and 'always seemed to be so very' and 'high spirits, but this!' I knocked on the door.

'What?' barked Mr Meldrum.

I pushed open the door and went in.

'Have you told him?' I said, looking at Danny. He shook his head.

'Who?' said Mr Meldrum. 'Told me what? Told who? What?'

'It was a diversion,' I said. 'It was an act of heroism.'

Mr Meldrum's eyes narrowed as though he thought I was making fun of someone and he wanted to be very sure it wasn't him.

'Evelynne Armitage had just had a very unfortunate accident, right there on the grass outside the gym hall,' I said.

My lips were twitching again at the thought, and seeing me trying not to smile, Mr Meldrum's brows lowered further than ever. 'And a crowd was beginning to gather and Danny here, very courageously, lured them away.'

'What kind of accident?' said Mr Meldrum. 'Is she injured? Did you call the nurse?'

'A massive dose of laxatives related accident,' I said.

He blinked once or twice.

'That seems most unlikely.'

'Her clothes are in a bin bag in the girls' showers, sir. I can get them for you.'

He stared at me. 'Evelynne Armitage shit herself in the playground?' he said, and his lips were twitching now too. 'And you?' he turned to Danny. 'You thought the best thing would be to . . .' He threw back his head and laughed, then cut it off short and fixed us with a hard stare. 'Defecated, I mean. Defecated.'

'That's what we heard you say, sir,' said Danny.

'Still,' said Mr Meldrum. 'We can't have it, you know, Daniel. I'll have to punish you or where will it end?'

'Sir?' I put in. 'I absolutely agree – a firm hand and all that – but Danny's got an important piece of business to put through for his mother and he needs to get to the bank before it shuts.' I gave a half-wave of the clipboard folder and Mr Meldrum took it out of my hands.

'For your mother?' he said, opening it. Danny hung his head. I wasn't sure how much the school knew about Mrs Conway. Everything, if she had ever been at a parents' night, I suppose. He read the form, looking over the top of his glasses.

'Playing the stock market, eh?' He was obviously puzzled. 'The longer I'm in this job the less I think I know.'

'Yes,' I said, which didn't sound good, but he seemed to miss it. 'And Mrs Conway has dated her signature, so unless we get there today . . .'

'Oh absolutely, absolutely,' said Mr Meldrum, handing Danny the folder. 'Come and see me tomorrow, Daniel, but . . . absolutely, run along with you now.'

'Thanks, sir,' said Danny.

'Thanks, Mr Meldrum,' I said.

'Tesco?' he said, as we were on our way out of the door. 'The food shop?'

'Take it from me, sir,' I said. 'It's a sure thing.'

'We're not going to make it,' I whined, jogging along the road towards the bank beside him. 'It's twenty past already.'

'Plenty time,' said Danny, puffing along beside me.

'How did you persuade her?'

'I just shoved it under her nose and said, "Mum, sign this",' he panted. 'She didn't read what it was.'

'Isn't that kind of . . .' I ran out of breath. 'Anyway, we're never going to get there. All that research, all that planning, all down the drain because bloody Evie can't keep her arse shut.' I had stopped running now.

'We'll be fine,' said Danny. 'Come on.' He got behind me and pushed until I was jogging again. 'God, imagine if we end up millionaire entrepreneurs and we get asked in an interview about our very first steps as investors,' he said. '"Well, I stripped off and ran round the playground a bit then bought 100 each of Tesco and—" what's that other one again?'

'You were magnificent,' I said. 'I was proud to know you.'

He gave me a look it took me a moment to decipher.

'Behave!' I shoved him with my elbow. 'I mean you were magnificently brave and resourceful. And I promise I'm not going to make you embarrassed about . . . you know what.'

'About seeing me in the scuddy?' he said. 'The only way to stop me feeling embarrassed about that is to even things up, and I'm too much of a gentleman to let you.'

He stopped, held open the bank door and bowed deeply, waiting for me to go in. It was 3.25 on the clock. Five minutes to spare.

The front door was standing open at my house when we got back.

'Mum?' I shouted. 'We're here. We're finished. We're free!' Silence. 'Mum?'

Danny put his head into the living room, then drew back and shrugged, and we trooped towards the kitchen. My mother was sitting on one of the bar stools with her feet wound around its legs and her head back against the wall. My father was standing opposite, leaning against the sink. On the breakfast bar and all around the kitchen work tops, bloodied hunks of meat rested on squares of polythene. A tangle of bones, scraped almost clean, was sitting on the draining board and blood was still running out from under it into the sink. My parents, who had got their first big freezer only a year before, had been to the wholesale butcher's for a forequarter of beef again.

'Jeez, Mum,' I said, blinking around. 'It looks like a party at Dennis Nilsen's house.'

My mother pushed herself up off the wall and did something that started as a sigh and ended as a smile. She unwound her feet from the legs of the bar stool and patted her lap before standing.

'How did it go?' she said.

'Not bad,' I said. 'French was fine. Biology was biology. Are you okay? Dad?'

My father glanced at Danny, then surveyed the kitchen once, held his hand out to my mother and led her through to the living room. They weren't having a row then, I thought. You don't walk around the house hand in hand if it's a row. But then, when do you? Danny and I frowned at each other and followed them through. They were sitting side by side on the couch, as usual, and they both turned and smiled, brightly, bravely, at us. My heart lurched. What did they have to be brave about?

'So what's the plan?' said my father. 'How are you going to celebrate?'

'No plan,' said Danny. 'We can finish off your butcher meat for you if you tell us what to do.'

'Actually, there's a party,' I said. I thought to myself that if

97

I started right now on the list of places I'd rather be than Mickey Docherty's party, everybody would have gone home before I was finished, but it would be an experience for Danny to be in with the in-crowd for a change. And he would certainly be the hero of the hour today. No one knew why he had done it, of course, but Mickey, Lightbulb and all that lot? They'd still be impressed.

'That's nice then,' said my mother. Now I knew something was badly wrong. That's nice, then? What had happened to: whose party, where is it, are there going to be adults, what time does it finish, *why* can't your dad come and get you?

'I'm not fussed about the party,' said Danny. 'Sitting about watching everyone get plastered. I'd rather render bones.'

'Mum, Dad,' I said. 'You're not kidding anyone here. What's going on?'

They said nothing.

'I'll shoot off then,' said Danny, standing. 'I'll see you tomorrow.'

They didn't speak as he left.

When I came back from the kitchen with the tea tray they were still just sitting there.

'Look,' I said. 'Either I can go and you two can talk it over, whatever it is, or you can tell me and we'll all pitch in together. But this is torture.'

My father cleared his throat and took a deep breath, but it came to nothing. It was my mother who spoke.

'I'm going to have a baby,' she said.

'No, you're not.' It was out before I could stop it and they both flinched as though I had hit them. But I was right: my mother didn't have a baby in 1981. My mother didn't have any baby ever, except me. What was she talking about? 'How?' I asked her. 'When?'

'London,' she said.

'What? I meant when's the baby due, actually. But, London? I see!'

My mother giggled, and my father shifted on his seat. I started to grin. Of course my mother could have a baby that she didn't have the last time. If their daughter sent them off to London, unlike the last time, anything could happen.

'That makes up for *Sleuth*, then,' I said.

My mother giggled again. *Sleuth* had not been showing in London when they were there. What had been showing was a play I thought was *Sleuth*, but which was in fact *Endgame*. Confusing titles, I think you will be forced to agree, but one was a twisty thriller that got made into a film with Michael Caine in it, and the other was – for those who haven't seen it – Samuel Becket on rip-roaring form: a blind man dying in an empty room with the ghosts of his parents in dustbins in the background. No wonder they had turned to each other for comfort. I started to laugh out loud.

'That's fantastic news,' I said. 'I'm sorry I said you weren't; it was just such a surprise. But I'm really delighted for you.' It gave me a twinge to think that they might have been worried about telling me. (Why else were they so solemn and silent when I came in?) So I laid it on thick.

'It's great news, isn't it? Isn't it?' My mother was smiling, even if the smile was a bit wobbly, and my father's eyes were shining, but still a little hot nugget of worry began to grow, high up in my chest. 'Is everything okay?' I said. 'Mum? You're going to be all right? I mean, I never really asked you why I was an only one.'

'Ch-ch-ch-ch,' said my mother, using the same noise to shush me that she had used to stop me putting more sugar on my porridge when I was tiny, to stop me trampling into flowerbeds in my baby-walker. 'I'm fine,' she said.

'So what's wrong?' I asked them.

'Nothing,' said my father. 'We're thrilled about the baby.'

'You don't look thrilled,' I said. 'And you sound anything but.'

'Well,' said my father. 'It's just that it's not going to be easy. I've lost my job.' And he put his head in his hands. 'I only heard today.'

'And when did you get the baby news?' I asked my mother.

'This morning,' she told me. I whistled.

'Overload,' I said. 'No wonder you're poleaxed.'

'It's not definite,' said my mother.

'The baby?'

'Your dad's job. It's not for sure.'

'All but,' said my father. He rubbed his face roughly and looked up again. 'They're putting in an automated— I mean, they're going over to a different . . .' My mother put her hand out to him. 'The union are in there now,' he said, 'thrashing out a deal. We'll hear tomorrow.'

'Wait a minute,' I said. 'You mean you're being made redundant?'

His head sank down again. 'Not for certain,' he said. 'They're going to offer it. I don't have to take it, if they offer me a different contract instead.'

'But that's good, Dad! I thought you meant you'd been sacked. Redundancy's totally different! This is great.'

Which was taking optimism to the extreme, where it became crassness. My father sat shaking his head slowly as though to brush off anything I might say, then he stood, kissed my mother's hair and left the room. We heard him going very heavily up the stairs.

It was always easier to work on my mother and I didn't hold back. But first I went to her and put my arms round her.

'A baby,' I said. She hugged me back.

'Your dad's happy too,' she said, as loyal as ever. 'It's just . . .'

'I know,' I told her. 'Just the timing. But Mum, you know I'm right. He's worked there for years; they'll have to be generous and then he can take his time and do something better. Something he really wants to do. Because it's not as if he's exactly bubbling over with this job, is it? He never talks about it.' I didn't add that I knew from looking at their bank statement that it didn't seem as if they paid him either. 'And with the new baby! It looks like Sod's Law, I know, but it's not.' Now she was shaking her head too.

'You're young,' she said. 'All that enthusiasm. The world

just waiting on a plate for you – it can be very convincing. But this is serious now.'

'Okay,' I said. 'But make a promise. Tomorrow, once Dad's heard all the details, we all sit down together and work something out. I've done masses of finance stuff and—'

'Where?' said my mother. 'Where have you done masses of finance stuff?'

'Well, school, you know,' I said involuntarily scratching at my ear and knowing that I must look as though I was lying, which I was. 'And Danny and me have been looking into it. You've seen me reading my *Financial Times*. You know how I get through the batteries on my calculator. You know what the phone bill was like.' The phone bill had shown the effects of me trying to make contact with the postcard man whenever I had a free minute and my mother had complained to British Telecom and they had checked the record and told her it was all the calls to Hull that were mounting up, and she had said she didn't know anyone in Hull, and on it had gone until I admitted it was me and Danny checking a money market phone-in service. She believed me.

My mother put her head on one side and gave me one of those inarguable, maternal smiles.

'Exactly,' she said. 'The phone bill. Leave the budgeting to Dad and me.' She slapped her hands on her lap and sat up straight. 'So! The exams are finished. You go off out and enjoy yourself. Where's this party? Dennis's house, you said. Dennis who?'

'Mickey Docherty,' I told her. 'I'll go, to give you and Dad some peace and quiet, but tomorrow we all talk.'

'Now Janie,' she said to me in a more than half-serious voice. 'Just because you're sixteen and you're going to be a big sister, doesn't mean you're not my little girl. I distinctly heard you say there was a party at Dennis's house and I'm not letting you go off out to some other party at some other house that you don't want to tell me about. Now, for the last time, Dennis who?'

'Mickey Docherty, Mother.'

'You came in, "Daughter", and the first thing you said was something about a party at Dennis . . . ?'

'. . . Nilsen's house,' I finished, quietly. 'You're right. I did. But I'm not invited. And anyway, something's just come up that I need to do. I'll be in my room.'

I stopped on my way out of the door, and tried to look casual as I asked her: 'Mum? Do you know who Charles Manson is?'

She looked at me blankly, then gave a gasp of recognition and put a hand to her stomach.

'I'm sorry!' I blurted. 'It doesn't matter. Forget I mentioned it.'

I could have kicked myself for that. Who mentions Charles Manson to someone who's just found out she's having a baby? But if it was to make myself feel better that I decided to knock on my parents' bedroom door while passing, I shouldn't have bothered.

'Just a minute!' my father called out in a voice too loud and far too bright to be natural. I heard the sound of a drawer closing and then he shouted to me to come in. He was sitting on my mother's dressing stool, a place I had never seen him sit before. He shaved in the bathroom and kept his comb there too, and that was it for my father's grooming.

'Just wondered how you were,' I said.

'I'm fine,' he answered, although his face was the complicated colour that a weatherbeaten face goes when other faces would go pale. 'This is not your problem. And it won't make any difference to your college plans. There's always your grandpa willing to help.' He glanced down at the dressing table as he spoke and then back at me with his mouth thin and grim and his eyes still anguished. I stepped back and let the door shut.

In my own room, resting my head against the cool gloss paint of my door, I tried to forget his face and see the bigger picture. The two low points since I had got here had been killing those princes before they were born and being the insider-trader to end all insider-traders but having absolutely no money to trade with. Danny was a godsend, obviously, but although he assured me over and over again that any profit was a fifty-fifty split, he had every right to change his mind and spend the whole lot on sweets if he wanted to. So today's events, while they left my parents reeling, were manna from heaven to me. The body count was swinging back again and if by some miracle it should turn out that my mother was having twins I'd be all square. And my father's redundancy cheque, if I could only get my hands on it, could start the ball rolling to set my mother up with more ormolu and dusty croquet mallets than she could ever have hoped for.

I could still hear the creak of my mother's dressing stool as my father shifted about on it. What was he doing? I couldn't imagine him, redundancy or no redundancy, sitting staring at himself in the mirror for this long.

With a huge effort of will, pressing the heels of my hands into my eye sockets and taking a deep breath, I put them, and the baby, and Limtec, completely out of my mind. I hadn't done much for Elvis recently and, for all I could remember, there might not be a moment to lose.

Dear Sirs, (which was still standard, I thought)

I am writing to suggest that you investigate someone by the name of Dennis Nilsen, who lives in a house in London. I am afraid I do not have any more details about him but I trust that it is an unusual enough name to allow you to track him down. There is a distinct possibility that this individual has murdered at least once already and unless he is stopped he will kill again. You should dig up his garden and check his cellar (if any).

A Well-wisher.

'I'm going out to the post box,' I shouted at my parents'

bedroom door, and I went downstairs two at a time and out into the brightness of the afternoon. The front door was still standing open, but I shut it behind me.

Chapter 7

2 June 1981

I was far too pumped to sleep that night. It wasn't the letter,
I'm ashamed to admit, and not even my parents' bombshells,
but just a general feeling of skittery not-quite-panic, like when
you paddle in the shallows and those little fish just the colour
of sand suddenly rise up and stream away over your feet. So I
suppose it *was* the letter *and* the startling news, and also the
fact of Danny Conway more than likely having a note about
sexual exhibitionism on his school file, and Mrs Conway now
being a minor shareholder in Tesco's, which she didn't know
about but Mr Meldrum the headmaster did, and it was me not
having gone to the party which made me wonder whether
anyone else would have noticed Janis Prentiss passed out cold
and moved her onto her side just in time for the big spill or
whether without me there she would have choked-on-her-
own and gone the way of Janis Joplin – who must have been
her namesake, because why else would her parents have given
her such a clanging combination, right? – and it would be on
my head and her parents would never recover from the grief
or the irony. And since it was three o'clock and I was still
awake I might as well have *gone* to the party.

I told myself firmly that there were a hundred reasons why
Janis Prentiss wasn't dead – look how Evie had got the runs
yesterday and not last time – and then I made myself translate
the lyrics from *High Society* into German until I finally drifted
off.

When I woke it was still swirling around in my head (with
Grace Kelly sounding just like Marlene Dietrich, given the
language and the fact that both of them were always sliding off

the note in the same direction, like honking geese) and, despite everything I had told myself, the first thing I did was phone Alison to check.

'Good party?'

'No.' Her voice was low and flat, just the way you would sound if you'd been at a party where someone had died.

'What happened?' I said, trying to sound calm.

'Wait a minute till I move the phone. I don't want my wee sister listening.'

'Why not?' I said. 'What *happened*?'

'Nothing. She's just always listening. Get lost, Sonia!' I waited, humming to myself, while Alison manoeuvred the phone into the cloakroom and shut the door.

'Were you just singing "What a swell party this is"?' she demanded, when she put the receiver back to her ear. 'What's wrong with you, Janie? You never used to be so snidey.'

'I was translating to help me get to sleep last night and now I can't get it out of my head. *Hast du gehort? Es ist in den Sternen. Nachste Juli, wie kolliederen mit Mars . . .*'

'*Nächste*,' said Alison.

'What?'

'You're pronouncing it wrong. It's *nächste*. Look, shut up, will you?'

'Tell me what happened at the party,' I said.

'Well, you didn't turn up,' said Alison. 'Evie bagged off with Lightbulb. Linda bagged off with Tony Moley—'

'Tony Moley?'

'Yeah, I know,' said Alison, sounding more animated, then she remembered. 'Shut up. And I sat in the garden with Janis Prentiss, holding her hair back.'

'Great,' I said. 'I mean, good for you. I mean, poor Janis and lucky you were there to help.'

There was a long silence.

'Sorry,' I said at last. 'I meant to come, but the thing is my dad lost his job and my mum found out she's pregnant.'

'And your dog ate your homework, and all the while you were singing in German,' said Alison in the same flat tone.

'I was! *Kleine Eine, Ich ware sie duster. Kleine Eine—*'

'What?'

'How could I have these, to hand, in German, if it wasn't true?' I said. '*Wie Willen sein ein Millionär? Nicht Mich.*'

'If you're going to tell porkies, Janie, you should at least try not to insult people's intelligence.'

She rang off.

I didn't fare much better with the parents. I met my father in the kitchen where he was making weak tea and hunting out plain biscuits to take up to my mother in bed.

'It's all in the mind,' he grumbled, on his knees with his head stuck in the cupboard. 'She was fine yesterday morning before she knew for sure.'

'Probably,' I said, hoping that it was just his usual morning mood and the bad news making him disagreeable, because otherwise – what a pig! It wasn't as though she had knocked *herself* up. 'But later, once she's feeling better, and you've been to work and heard the ins and outs, we're going to sit down and have a summit.' He was resting back on his heels with a packet in his hands at last and he wasn't listening.

He still wasn't really listening later that afternoon when he had come back from the union meeting and I had pushed him, physically pushed him, into a chair at the dining-room table where my mother was already waiting.

'When's it due, Mum?' I said, pen poised over the slab of Basildon Bond.

'Twenty-eighth of January,' said my mother. 'Brrr, poor little thing!'

And Dad? When does the balloon go up at work?'

'End of the month,' he said.

'End of January?'

'The end of this month, Janie,' he said. 'The end of June.' Which stopped me short for a minute.

'Okay,' I said eventually, 'okay, so there's not a lot of time, but on the other hand there's not a lot of hanging about waiting, so that's good. And what's the deal? What's the score? What's the magic number?'

He said nothing for a while, looking at my mother, glancing at me once or twice. Then he spoke.

'I'm going to sign the new contract.' My mother let out a breath, and I let out a howl.

'Dad, you can't! Look, you've worked there for twenty years, right? So the redundancy deal must be pretty stiff. I'll go ahead with an estimated figure if I have to, but I wish you'd just tell me.' I waited. They said nothing. 'Okay, as you know, I've been getting quite interested in finance recently and I've got some absolutely sure things that I've been itching to do something about. I haven't had the wherewithal but you've got to see, Dad, that a lump sum is like an opportunity.'

'We have to live,' said my father.

'You'll get another job,' I said. 'I'll get a job. It's the summer now. Mum can get a job too, we can all pull together and by the time Mum's too far gone and I need to go back to school, the lump sum will have started working for us. And—'

'"Get another job",' said my father, flatly. 'You're not living in the real world, Janie.'

'I don't mean a proper job,' I said, stung. 'I just mean a money job. We can all stack shelves, or we can stand at the door of a shop and look threatening.' They looked up at that. 'Well, maybe not Mum.'

'You think I could that, do you?' said my father. 'Instead of a "proper" job?' I couldn't read the look on his face.

'I didn't mean to insult you,' I said.

'I know you didn't,' said my father. 'You're only trying to help.'

'There must be something you'd rather be doing,' I said.

'There's plenty that everyone would rather be doing,' said my father. 'But life's not like that.'

'It would have been different if it wasn't for the baby,' said my mother.

But the thing was that it wouldn't have been; it wasn't. The last time, he must have signed this new contract without me ever dreaming that anything had happened. He had just stayed at Limtec doing the same job on a new contract for less money no doubt (*bloody* Thatcher), the same job that had turned him practically see-through with boredom before he was even forty. It wasn't going to happen again.

'You'll still get to university, if that's what you're worried about,' said my father.

'Of course it's not.'

'Because your grandpa's willing to help.' His voice was hard. 'He put David and Mona through and would have done the same for me if I'd been . . . interested. I phoned him from work this morning and he's only too happy to help.' They sat looking at me with identical bright smiles and identical brimming eyes. So that was how it was last time then. He had gone cap in hand to my grandfather and because he had never told me I had never even said thanks.

'Can I ask one thing?' I said. They didn't say yes, but they didn't say no, so I ploughed on. 'Promise not to turn down the redundancy until the end of the month? Give me until then to change your mind.'

My father rolled his head from side to side as though my words were scorching his face. At last, to let them talk it out in comfort, I left them.

I needed to pull the biggest ever rabbit out of the hat now. There was no point in thinking long-term investment; I needed to do something flashy, something to make my father cut loose into unemployment with a new baby on the way. This from a man who never changed jobs or houses in his life. I was sure I could come up with the goods but I wished I didn't have to start right then with a cotton wool head from not sleeping and the strains of *Wie willen sein ein Millionär?* booming around my brain. I was still sitting hunched over at my desk, making notes and doing sums when my father called my name what felt like hours later, but all I had written down was: Oscar-winning screenplay, police informant, invent pore strips. And I had crossed them all out.

'We're going for a walk,' he called up the stairs. 'We'll probably go for a pub supper.'

'Good idea,' I called down, hanging over the banisters and

grinning at him. 'Don't let Mum get drunk, mind.' He grinned back at me.

'You can come if you want,' he began, but I was already shaking my head.

'Do you good,' I said. 'And I'm busy. I'm thinking up ways to change your mind.' The grin faded at that.

This time I couldn't pretend I was doing it for them. This time I needed some answers for myself, needed them so badly I didn't even know what the questions were. I had worked out, you see, why my father had spent so long sitting on my mother's dressing stool the day before, the only possible reason. The strong box in the sock drawer. I had no choice.

I waited until they were gone, until they had disappeared round the corner, strolling along so gently, and with my father so solicitously patting my mother's arm as it rested on his, and my mother looking up at my father with such a supportive smile as he stared resolutely ahead, that any of the neighbours who happened to be looking would have known at a glance. Aha! they would say, job loss and unplanned pregnancy at Number Twenty-three. Well, well, well.

I put the chain on the front door, then I locked the back door and left the key in the lock. Now even if they came back or if Mrs Robertson tried to get in with her spare, I would not be discovered.

The key was in the Caithness glass ashtray in the niche on the landing. I scooped it up and took it into their room. Sitting on the dressing stool, I pushed aside pairs of socks, neatly folded into tubes, and took out the strong box. You were only supposed to do this after your parents were dead. It was supposed to be that even if their papers revealed that your father had been in jail or your mother had once run off with a sailor but had it annulled you didn't have to face them afterwards. 1, 6, 4, 4, 3, my mother's birthday, and the padlock sprang open. I turned the key.

On the top of the pile was a birthday card, home-made, to my father from me. *To The Best Dady In The World* was written on the front in thick glue, which must once have had glitter stuck to it. *With lots of love and hugs and kisses to the best dady in the whole wide world from your dauhter Janie*, it said inside. He was, I thought, and look how I repay him. Love, hugs, kisses and spying. I cringed and turned it face down so it couldn't see me.

Birth certificate, marriage certificate, passport – just the one, with my father as head of the household and my mother and I along for the ride, a bank book – I wouldn't open that unless I had to. Underneath, a small sheaf of brown envelopes. A letter from the Ministry of Defence dated 1958, stating that my father was being rejected for National Service. I glanced at it, but I already knew this; it was part of family lore. By 1958, National Service was winding down and the MoD were desperate for excuses to turn away the hordes of gangling boys.

There was a letter from a Mr Purves in the Personnel and Payroll Dept of somewhere called Arnott Bros telling my mother in perfectly proper and yet still withering tones that he accepted her resignation, and that he had been expecting it since learning of her marriage, and that it was very sensible of her, in her condition, to be planning to leave immediately.

Next another letter from this same Mr Purves, congratulating my mother on joining Arnott Bros, but remarking that he was disappointed to hear only now when the appointment was settled that she was engaged to be married. He trusted that the engagement was to be a long one.

The last envelope. It was a fat one, bulging with more than it had originally been meant to hold, and it was taped shut with Sellotape that was just beginning to grow brittle. Taped shut, right at the bottom, in a box with a key and a combination padlock. I fingered it, hooked a nail under the edge of the window to see if I could read anything. This had to be my father's stuff, right? I turned it over and flexed it very gently. The Sellotape gave way at once. When I straightened the envelope again it sprang back into place. He would never know that it hadn't just dried out on its own. I lifted the flap and drew out the contents.

A letter from Technical Prosthetics from the equivalent of Mr Purves, close typed in smudgy ink on a proper typewriter, dated 1962: 'pleased to inform you', 'appointed to the position' and 'list of duties' it said. I breathed out a sigh of relief. What had I been expecting? I started to fold up the letter, but then a word caught my eye. 'Uniforms'. Uniforms? I spread it flat again and kept reading.

'You will be provided with a uniform consisting of one cap, one coat and two pairs of trousers, to be made up at our expense and to this end we would be grateful if you would provide measurements at your earliest convenience. The care and cleaning of these garments is the responsibility of the employee. Three shirts per year will be provided, and again the laundering of these is at the employee's expense. Black shoes must be worn and a yearly allowance is given in February to provide for the purchase of these. An umbrella and a rain cape to be shared by the day and night duty doormen will be kept in the doorman's kiosk at all times.'

It took a minute to sink in. I unfolded another letter and glanced at it, hardly seeing it: a logo for some Edinburgh college; all I noticed was the line that said 'conditional on the completion of remedial classes by September 1960' before I folded it up again.

Then I sat absolutely still, unable to do anything, and yet even then half of me was thinking, How can I be so dumbstruck by this? So what? So he doesn't work in the offices. So what? Still I sat there. Then a noise at the front door had me on my feet, the box and its contents flying off my lap and scattering. I stood on the powder rug, trapped, heart pulsing. Slowly, the noises from downstairs began to make sense. It was the paperboy lifting the letterbox and letting the *Evening News* thunk onto the mat. I heard his footsteps on the path as he walked away and I flinched down into a crouch, heart still hammering, not wanting him to see me standing there in front of the window in the middle of my parents' bedroom floor. With shaking hands, I started to gather the papers together and put them in order again. The

Sellotaped envelope still had the other papers tucked inside. The letter from the National Service Board hadn't been in here and I wondered why not. I read it again now. Grade 4 was filled in in ink on a dotted line and in brackets afterwards it said 'physical or mental incapacitation'. I tried to remember if I had ever known what it was – whether flat feet or dandruff – that was the exact problem. Turning over the page now, I found the answer. 'Educationally subnormal' was written there in the same hand, and 'functionally illiterate'.

I couldn't take it in, just could not take it in. My father wasn't 'educationally subnormal', he was bright, brighter than me, or I wouldn't have been so frustrated by his lack of gumption about leaving Limtec in the first place. He listened to intelligent music – Dvořák, Mahler, spiky stuff you couldn't *understand* if you were stupid, never mind enjoy – and he explained things better than anyone else I knew: the rules of golf, the fermentation process in wine-making, the case against Scottish devolution. He was an intelligent man; how could he be illiterate? I saw him reading all the time: his post, the newspaper … I stopped.

Actually, I didn't see him reading all the time. I saw him glancing through the mail, finding his own and then stuffing it in the spice rack. I saw him glancing at the paper and then switching on the television news. I had been surprised to hear he had ordered a book from the library until I saw it was a big book, full of pictures, about architecture. And what about writing?

I tried to picture my father's writing. I could see my mother's shopping lists and recipes, her letters to old friends on the peach paper with the harvest mouse in the top corner. My birthday cards came with messages from her in her writing plus '& Dad xxxxx' But that was normal; everyone's cards came 'with love and best wishes on your Birthday, darling, and have a wonderful day from Mum' '& Dad'. Hell, *my* cards to them were 'Blah blah blah blah blah from Janie' '& Ludo' and even then half the time I had forged it.

At last, I stuffed the form in beside the job offer from

Limtec and piled the rest of the letters and certificates on top, ending with the birthday card *To The Best Dady In The World*.

I had to recheck the look of the sock drawer three times and move the key twice in the ashtray to make it look natural before I was happy. And it was half an hour later that I sprang to my feet in my own room and galloped across the landing to smooth out the dent where I had sat on my parents' bed.

That was the mystery of the bank statement cleared up then. I had been looking for a salary, but he got his wages in a little envelope and my mother took some of it to the bank and paid it in. I had thought they lived modestly for their means, but it was hard to see how they even had come by their semi if that's what he had been doing since 1962. Since 1962, for God's sake. Since he was twenty. Why in the name of Christ couldn't he have got a job on a building site when he was twenty, learned the trade? You couldn't be a doorman at twenty. But then I remembered Grandpa Jock at a party saying 'Jock Junior's in prosthetics' (the bogus old creep) and I wondered if that was it. You couldn't hide someone working on a building site and coming home covered in brick dust with mashed fingers, but if someone left the house with a briefcase every morning and went to a plastics factory, then it was quite easy to leave the rest of it vague. Perhaps Grandpa Jock helped out with buying the house – there was no mortgage on the go – perhaps he even helped my father get the job and perhaps he wouldn't stand for my father chucking it in. I didn't want to know for sure. I didn't want to know *at all*. I wondered if Uncle David and Auntie Mona knew. Of course they did. It explained everything.

And there I had sat saying what a brilliant deal Limtec would have to cough up after twenty years and how he could get another job, and they had squirmed and smiled at me and squirmed some more and— Jesus Christ, no! I had said that if he couldn't get a proper job he could be a security man, and I had told him I didn't mean it as an insult. I groaned and tried to cover my head with my arms, tried to squeeze the memory out of my brain. And all the time I was thinking, how the hell can my father be illiterate, and how can I be such a snob and so shallow and so *bothered* about it?

I couldn't take any more time alone with my thoughts. I phoned Danny.

'Are you sure they won't mind me being there?' he asked. 'What with everything going on?' Danny had been told about the pregnancy and had sat round-eyed and silent for a while and then told them he would always be happy to babysit.

'They're out,' I said. 'Come round.'

We pored over the *FT* for a while.

'Tesco are at fifty-eight and a half,' said Danny, like he knew what that meant.

I kept looking, but nothing jumped out at me. Danny watched me running my pen up and down the lists, humming under my breath.

'What are you looking for?' he said.

'Hard to say,' I answered him. 'It wouldn't mean anything to you, but I'll know it when I see it.'

'And what in God's name are you singing?' he said.

'Oh, I know. It's "Who wants to be a Millionaire", in German. I can't get it out of my head, but it's annoying me more than it's annoying you, I guarantee.'

'It's what?'

'"Who wants to be a Millionaire".'

'Me,' said Danny. 'But don't change the subject.'

'You must have heard of it. "Who wants to be a Millionaire? I don't." It's a saying. It's part of the popular culture of the land where you were born.' I sang him a couple of lines.

'Liveried flunkeys?' he echoed, inaccurately. 'Flashy chauffeurs? That's not English *or* German.'

I laughed. Danny was great. Danny and the hamster sometimes seemed like the only things that kept me going. I had even started calling the hamster Danny, just to myself, because I had to call him something.

'How's your mum?' I asked, suddenly determined to be a better friend to him.

He rolled his eyes. 'Drinking. Not every day and not early on but ...'

'And there's nothing you can do?'

'There's nothing anyone can do,' he said. 'What a pair we are, eh? Mine are getting drunk and running away from home and yours are getting pregnant and losing their jobs. Who'd have them?'

He didn't know the half of it, I thought.

'Is your mum from a family of big drinkers?' I said. 'I hope you don't mind me asking.'

He shook his head. 'Hardly. None of them speak to her any more. She's a black sheep. I haven't even seen my granny for five years. Haven't even had a birthday card.' It was Orville again. He didn't even know he was doing it. And tonight it was exactly what I needed to hear, to put my stuff in perspective.

'Well, at least that way you don't have to put up with them looking down their noses,' I said.

'They can look down their noses as much as they like,' said Danny, sounding fiercer than I had ever heard him. 'She can't help it.'

'Still,' I said. 'It's surprising the things that can run in families, isn't it? How clever you are, or being bad-tempered or depressed or whatever. If a dad's always getting into fights and his son grows up using his fists, no one's puzzled. Or if you're a bit thick and so's your whole family, nobody's going to keel over from the shock.'

'It's nothing to do with being thick,' said Danny, drawing back from me a little.

'I'm only picking an example,' I said. 'Same deal if your parents are really bright – professors and doctors and whatever – and so are you. Nobody thinks it's weird. That's all I'm saying.'

'Alcoholism is an illness,' said Danny firmly.

'I know. I'm just saying.'

He gave me a serious look.

'What?' I said.

'I wish you *would* "just say". I wish you would talk about what you're trying to talk about, instead of standing three streets over and pointing.'

'You crack me up, Danny,' I told him. 'You're supposed to be a sixteen-year-old boy. You're supposed to only grunt and swear and spit, you know. Where do you get off with this wisdom of Solomon stuff?'

'Look who's talking,' he said. 'Janie Lawson: sixteen going on forty.'

'You never said a truer word.'

I almost told him. Right there, sitting at the dining table looking at the evening sun shining through his ears. For one thing, any boy his age who could not hate his mother after the life he'd had – talk about empathetic. I caught a hold of myself in time, though. I realized that I wouldn't be able to stand it here if I told Danny and it freaked him out and I never saw him again. Then I would be absolutely alone. Because there are limits to what a hamster can give you. I decided to try Hull again instead, bare my soul to the answering machine. From a callbox.

'So,' said Danny. 'What's flashy flunkey in German, then? I can't believe it didn't come up in the exam.'

Later, lying in bed, I cursed him. I had taught him the song and he had re-translated it and managed to get it to scan, managed to get bits of it to rhyme, even, like the swot he was, which meant that now for the second night in a row I couldn't get it out of my head. I comforted myself with the thought that maybe he was lying in bed with it looping round and round too. And if he was, then when the quiz show started up, Danny Conway would think of me every time he looked in the paper and saw it in the schedules.

Is there anyone, I wonder, who didn't get there before me? Hmm? There I was, needing a get-rich-quick scheme, to get my mother her French windows onto the terrace, to get my father (I now knew) out of a job that he was so ashamed of he kept it hidden from his own daughter. I had never read the ingredients on a pore-strips pack and I couldn't remember any race results, but I had been singing 'Who Wants to be a Millionaire?' for almost twenty-four hours and only now did it hit me, like an iron dropped by Jerry, falling on Tom.

Oh please, please, please, please, please, I thought, sitting at the telephone table flipping through the general information pages at the front of the directory. The on-screen graphics could be got round, I was sure – they already had flashing lights on *University Challenge*, and that little box on *Mastermind* looked like it was added later. Even if it wasn't possible, *Countdown* still had Carol doing the grunt work and nobody minded. But the phone lines were make or break.

'Janie?'

My father was halfway down the stairs, wrapped in his dressing gown, blinking.

'Who are you phoning at this time of night?'

'No one, Dad. I'm trying to work out how premium-rate numbers are organized.'

'Premium-rate numbers?' he echoed, coming down for a closer look. 'What for?'

I wasn't ready to start explaining it yet, though. And I wasn't ready to talk to my father face to face. I had been avoiding him all day, sure that I wouldn't be able to look at him without him seeing something in my eyes that would kill him.

'They might not be called that,' I said. 'I've had an idea. To make us some money. For after you're finished up at work. And it won't—' I laid a hand on his arm, stopping him from backing away from me. 'It won't even need any of your redundancy cheque. Well, a tiny little bit, to get a letter professionally printed, make a good impression. I'll tell you about it in the morning.'

His head had drooped as I was speaking and now he shook it without looking up.

'Actually,' I said, 'I'm going to need your help with it. It's the kind of thing you're better at than me. General knowledge, logistics, that kind of thing.' It was myself I was trying to convince, but he *did* know more than me about almost anything you could mention.

'Dad,' I said. 'Listen to me. I'm not trying to wear you down. I'm not just going to convince you. I'm going to *show* you.'

'What's the difference?' said my father. He was looking at me again, at least.

'There's a world of difference,' I said. 'You're worried about money, right?'

'Of course, I—' He stopped and started again in a whisper, trying not to wake my mother. 'A pay cut and a new baby? Of course I'm worried about money. And I'm worried about you. I don't know what's got into you, treating this as if it's a game. Treating your mother and me as if we're—' I was glad he couldn't find a word for it. It was too near the truth even at that.

'Please listen,' I said. 'I know you're worried and I know you think I'm going to do something vague like tell you to take the plunge and reassure you that it's all going to work out. I can even see why that's so annoying. But I promise you, it's going to be real. I'm not going to solve your money worries by saying you shouldn't worry about money.' I took a deep breath and a firm hold of the phone book. I was sure about this. 'I'm going to solve your money worries by showing you a fat cheque and a cast-iron promise of more where it came from. That's the difference. Do you see now?'

He nodded slowly, and just for a moment the cloud lifted off his face as if a sudden gust had got under it and blown it away. Just for a moment, but when it came back there was even more pain than before.

Chapter 8

3 June 1981

Who knows what the future holds? Well, all right, I do. But not really. Less than most people when you think about it, because I don't even know if the future holds the future. For all I know, my future might hold the past, again. One thing I do know is that I hope to God I never have to take another trek through June 1981. And even if I did, I don't think it would be possible – despite my new perspective on the sum of things that are possible – for another June 1981 to be any worse. See what you think.

I phoned British Telecom first thing, while my father was in the shower and my mother was sitting up sipping her ginger tea and nibbling her plain biscuit. (And I had to agree with my father on that one; she looked fine to me.) When I dialled for the operator, it rang twice and then a person said hello. A person, a human being, after two rings, which plunged me into leaden surety that the technology couldn't be up to it. On the other hand Live Aid was pretty soon and I clearly remember phoning up and pledging money for that.

'Hello? Hello?' said the operator again.

'Sorry! I was dreaming.' I cleared my throat and gathered my thoughts. 'What I want to ask is this: would it be possible to set up a system . . .'

It took less than five minutes to find out that yes, it would be. I wasn't transferred to a single other department, I wasn't put on hold, I heard no light classical medleys and nobody asked me when my home insurance was due for renewal. It was almost disappointing that the premium-rate number existed: it was hard not to think of it as the start of the rot.

Pining for Hat Trick and Carlton, I wrote to Tyne Tees, Yorkshire, STV, Anglia, Granada, Thames and, because you never knew, the Beeb. I was just about to send one of them into light entertainment orbit. Whichever one wrote back first. Well, actually, whichever one wrote back second, because the first answer, from Anglia, was an inexplicable 'no'. In the meantime, I made myself forget all about it. Only at night, sitting in my room, did I whisper any of it to my hamster as he ran over and over from hand to hand, pushing himself through the loop of my thumb and finger. 'I'm not even going back to school, you know, fluffy nameless one. I'm going to concentrate full time on Elvis. I've got to really. Well, part time anyway and part time on my stocks and shares. And I'm going to help my mum with the baby – I bet even when she's rich she won't get a nanny – and I can't forget my dad. I'm definitely going to get to the bottom of that. Soon.' My hamster trundled on, hand over hand, busy going nowhere. Why didn't he ever swerve and run up my sleeve for a change? Had he turned psychotic from hours on his wheel? I should let him out more or keep him out longer at least. I felt a sudden hot little patch on the palm of one hand.

'Yeuch!' I shouted and dumped him back in his cage. I shook my hand before I could help myself and drops of reeking rodent urine flew about in all directions.

'What is it, darling?' came my mother's voice.

'He's pissed on me!' I shrieked.

'Who?' said my mother, opening the door. Good question, Mum. I pointed to the hamster.

'Naughty B—,' said my mother and my heart leapt, but she cut herself off. 'Don't say that word, Janie, please. "Pee" if you must.' Then she laughed and rubbed just below her waistband. 'Anyway, you'll have to get used to worse than that, come the New Year.'

Every day I made myself get up before my father left the house and put in some time on him at breakfast. He sat there pale, with a line between his brows and deep lines joining the sides of his nose to his mouth, looking as though he would never smile again. I hardened my heart, knowing it was all for his own good.

'You're not going to sign that new contract today, Dad, are you?' He said nothing, but he slumped a little in his seat and my mother shook her head at me to shut me up. 'Just promise me you won't sign it today. Not before I've had a chance to tell you my good news, when it comes.' He was struggling with himself, determined not to believe me, unable to stop himself from hoping I might be right. 'It'll be here soon,' I finished off.

True, the post had just arrived and brought another rejection, but it couldn't be long now. I knew there would be a slush pile on a little desk in a corner somewhere and a junior reader assigned to wade through it, from there a smaller pile on a bigger desk in a room with a window, and then a meeting round an even bigger table where real decisions got made.

My father had drained his tea and now rubbed his chest and slipped an indigestion tablet into his mouth. An indigestion tablet! My father, who ploughed manfully through my mother's cooking every day of his life; my father who had put away two helpings of my mother's take on a light summer dessert not twelve hours before (steamed pudding and custard, but with coconut on top and the custard straight from the fridge). I told myself that you couldn't nag someone's stomach sore and that it was Limtec's fault, not mine, but still when the phone rang I leapt up to answer it, just to get away.

It was Danny, telling me he had already bought today's *FT* and he needed my advice about something, trying in short to make out he had important business with me, but I think he was just bored and looking for a distraction.

'I'll come round,' I said. 'No, really, I'll come to you. You could cut the atmosphere at this end with a cake slice.' I made sure to raise my voice enough so that they would hear me.

'Who was that?' my father bellowed, as I hung up.

'Danny,' I shouted back. 'I'm going round.'

'Well, don't go blabbing our private business,' came the

response. I went back and opened the kitchen door, open-mouthed in disbelief.

'To Danny?'

'To anyone,' said my father, scowling.

'*Danny?*' I said. 'If anyone knows what it's like to have stuff spread about the world . . .'

They both had the good grace to look sheepish at that.

'You'll look back on this and laugh,' I told them, and the frowns clicked back down in perfect unison. 'Trust me, you will. I mean *if* you trust me, *then* you will. Don't sign anything, Dad. See you tonight.'

Mrs Conway was still asleep. I knew from the way Danny tried to lift up the whole weight of the door as he turned the catch and the way he beckoned me inside. The kitchen was the same as ever, neat but dirty, and when he opened the fridge to get milk for our tea I could see dried spills on the shelves and a layer of onion skins and tomato stalks in the bottom drawer, but not much in the way of food beyond a tub of Stork and half a cabbage face down on a dinner plate.

We took our tea out to the back garden – 'No biscuits, I'm afraid, sorry' – and sat on two stripy nylon chairs in the sunshine watching Danny's school clothes sway back and forward, dripping, on the clothes line above the tufty grass.

'Are you supposed to wash blazers?' I said. 'Aren't you supposed to get them dry-cleaned?'

'It's never done it any harm before,' said Danny. I pictured him at school, crumpled from head to toe, even his shoes crumpled from getting wet and not being stuffed with paper while they dried, even his tie crumpled. I had never been able to understand how a person crumples a polyester tie, but looking at it now, tied to the washing line in a reef knot, I began to understand.

'Anyway, I won't be wearing it next year.'

'You're not going back?' My stomach swooped. Could I face it without him?

'Yeah, I'm going back.'

'Oh right, but fifth year – nobody wears a blazer in fifth year.'

'I meant I'd grown out of it,' said Danny, looking hurt. 'I was going to buy another one. Do you think I shouldn't?'

I shrugged. It was nothing to do with me what he wore.

'I could get something else,' he said. 'I don't suppose you'd be interested in a shopping trip, would you?' I shook my head. I wasn't going to start picking out clothes for Danny Conway. For one thing, it was a bit too much like boyfriend and girlfriend and for another I was still determined to change my ways in time for Ludo and this would be good practice.

'So anyway,' said Danny in a louder voice – maybe he was hurt and hiding it – 'I've got the *FT*. And I've got this: ta-dah!' He dug into the pocket of his jeans and pulled out a huge handful of money, all twenty-pound notes and it looked like about a dozen of them. 'But I'll have to wait to get another order form signed.'

'We can't keep looking every day and sticking a tenner on,' I said. 'It doesn't work like that.'

'You don't need to tell me,' he said. 'I thought it would be a lot more fun than it's turning out.'

'And you should do some shopping,' I said. 'There's bugger-all in your fridge. How come you didn't go yesterday with all that cash?'

'Because yesterday,' he said, 'as you would know if you knew anything, was Derby day. 'Where do you think all this *came* from?' He waved his wad of twenties in my face again.

'Please tell me you didn't put everything you had on the Derby,' I said. 'Not when there's only a tub of margarine in your fridge. Please tell me you weren't that daft.'

'It worked out okay,' he said, not looking at me.

'And what if it hadn't?'

'It did. Anyway, that's the house rule. Nothing comes in and goes out again without going round the track first.' He sounded proud of it.

'This is your mum's idea, right?' I said, speaking very matter-of-factly, thinking that that would be less insulting in the end than trying to be gentle. 'Do you think she's really a great housekeeping role model?'

'Makes life interesting.'

I said nothing, but put my hand out for the newspaper, determined that I would find something for us to buy, hoping this would keep him away from the bookies for one day at least.

'I'll just keep the Sports,' he said, beginning to pluck the pages into two piles.

'What for? Danny, for God's sake, you had a good day yesterday; can't you just coast on that for a while?'

'No way. I had a shit day yesterday. I started with a grand and ended up five hundred down. I've got everything to go for today.'

I stared at him. 'You lost five hundred pounds on the Derby? You *bet* five hundred pounds on the Derby? You— You said— You just said to me a minute ago that you *won* all that.'

'I did,' he said, patiently. 'Side bets. Thank God for side bets, eh?'

I looked at the lists, not trusting myself to speak.

'Well?' said Danny after a bit.

'ABH is a possibility,' I said. 'I think I remember hearing something about them. Of course, I can't remember what I heard. Maybe a rumour that they crashed – I mean that they're going to crash – and the CEOs are going to do time for embezzlement and all the shareholders are going to die in the poorhouse. But if you're feeling lucky we could give it a go and get out quick if it starts to slide.'

'Let's bung a couple on it,' said Danny. I had thought he would see right through me, the way I was talking it up, making it seem as dicey as an outsider at a hundred-to-one. It was more worrying, somehow, that he didn't.

'What time does your mum usually get up?' I said. 'When can we get the form signed?' He glanced over his shoulder into the open kitchen door and lowered his voice before he spoke.

'It's not as easy as that,' he said. 'We need to catch her at the right moment. If she's too sober she'll read the form and ask all sorts of questions, but if she's too far the other way the signature won't pass at the counter. It happened with a phone bill once, dead embarrassing. Sometime just after lunch, I'd say.'

Not for the first time I marvelled. I knew he couldn't really be as breezy as he made out about it all. No matter how many times he repeated his mantra about it being an illness, it had to hurt.

'Okay,' I said, standing and stretching. 'I'll meet you outside the bank at three. Promise me you're going to go shopping.'

'School doesn't start again for another six weeks, Janie. Give me a chance.'

'*Food* shopping,' I answered. 'Get another tub of marge in case the one you've got gets lonely.' I reached out to ruffle his hair but thought better of it. He had seen my hand move towards him though and he gave a big smirk. Oh perfect. Just what I needed. Mixed signals giving Danny Conway the idea that I fancied him. Superb.

He wasn't smirking, however, when he shambled along the street towards the bank that afternoon. I shoved myself up off the wall where I was leaning and went to meet him.

'What's up?'

'She wouldn't sign it,' he said, looking at his feet. I didn't believe him at first. The head-hanging seemed so out of proportion to the mildness of the bad news that I was sure any minute he was going to look up and laugh and brandish the form in my face as he had brandished the fistful of twenties that morning.

'Well, never mind,' I said. 'And in a way, I suppose, that's quite good news. I mean, if she didn't get tipsy enough to sign a form without reading it?'

'Yeah, right,' was all Danny said, and then we stood there not quite looking at each other.

'Okay,' I said at last. 'How about this food shopping?'

'I've been,' he said, even more quietly, still looking at the ground.

I thought I would give it one more chance and then leave him to stew in whatever it was he was stewing in.

'Right, well how about we go back round to yours and make a start on the new biscuits, then?' I said.

'Nah,' said Danny.

'Suit yourself. I would say come to mine, but you've no idea, at the moment.'

We mumbled our goodbyes and turned away from each other. I took a dozen paces and then turned round to look at him again. He was standing half-turned, looking at me.

'What is it?' I asked.

'I lied,' he said, trotting back towards me. 'She *did* sign the form, but I haven't got the money to go with it. Or for shopping.'

'What happened to the five hundred?'

'I stuck it on and lost it.'

'*Five hundred pounds?*' He was squirming, but I still couldn't stop my jaw from hanging open.

'I was trying to make a point. You were so snotty this morning.'

'And how long is it till you get more?'

'End of the month,' he said, grimacing like you do when you're watching someone open a bottle of champagne who you suspect has never done it before. Maybe he thought I was going to hit him. 'But I can ask Dad for an advance.'

'And what are you going to say happened?' I could hear myself turning schoolmarmish, but I had good reason.

'I'm not going to say anything. I never do. I think he must think it's Mum. And don't look at me like that; I know, I know.' I had never thought I would feel sympathy for Mrs Conway, but I didn't know what else the twinge I was feeling could be.

'For Christ's sake, Danny. You need to get this sorted out before . . .'

'Before what?'

What I was thinking was that he needed to get this sorted out before Lottery Instants or he would end up on the streets. I shook my head and said nothing.

'Don't blame me,' he said. 'The horse fell down.'

'Boy oh boy,' I said, shaking my head.

'What are you going to do with me, eh?' he said, grinning.

'Well, for starters,' I began. 'You know your house rule?' He rolled his eyes. 'No, listen, I've been thinking. Your house rule that everything goes round the track? You need another one. You need a daily limit. Say twenty pounds a day, absolute max, no exceptions, not even for the Derby.'

'Sounds great,' said Danny. 'That's probably more than I manage now, but I suppose once the shares start cashing out, I'll be laughing.'

'Do you know what the word "limit" means?' I said, rubbing my hands over my face. 'So, your housekeeping comes out first – you've got to eat if you want to grow up big and strong – after that, you've got a limit of twenty a day unless you're buying a stock, or unless one of your stocks goes up. This is getting a bit involved.'

'You should try an accumulator,' said Danny. 'I can buy a stock any day at all? But then I can't go to the bookies? And if a stock I've got goes up I can't either? But if one goes down, I get to bet twenty?'

'If you've got it, after housekeeping,' I said. 'What d'you think?'

'It'll make the whole markets thing much more fun,' said Danny. 'And, you know, it could do with it.'

It was going to take real commitment, now. I had been planning just to keep an eye out for the big ones I knew were winners, but if any day Danny bought a stock was a day he had to stay out of Ladbroke's I was going to have to shift up a gear. And if any day he showed a profit was another day of no gee-gees I would actually need to try to learn what I was doing. But that was okay. The telly plan was on my mind, but I didn't really have to *do* anything except wait. And although I had to keep at my father and make sure he didn't cave in, that didn't really fill the days up either. I could manage this for Danny too. And meantime Mrs Conway would keep signing the forms, at the right moment, just after lunch. There was that twinge again. For some reason the image that popped into my head was Moby Dick. She was a large woman, right enough, and pale and moved slowly, but it wasn't just that. I thought of Danny and me chugging along beside her, jabbing at her with biros. Still, if it was a choice between betting slips and share orders, there was no choice. Because he could always cash them in. I mean, if I studied hard and learned what I was doing and advised him well, then admin charges aside, it was practically a saving scheme. Money in the bank.

'Agreed, then,' I said.

'Agreed,' said Danny, putting his hand on his heart like an American facing the flag. 'I will do my best to grow up big and strong and solvent. And it's nice to know you care.' He smirked at me again, very annoyingly, but still I invited him back for tea – I couldn't let him starve.

So Danny had a friend, a doting pair of near foster parents and a new (slightly) more wholesome pastime. And four television companies (Yorkshire had dropped out of the running) would soon be falling over themselves to secure my parents' future. I wasn't worried that none of the ones who were interested had been back to me yet; at every stage from slush pile to big meeting, I allowed them time to bristle and beat their chests and bewail the fact that they didn't think of it first. But persuading my father to give up Limtec was only half the story; I had to put some kind of firework under him and make him yearn for . . . something. Or work out what he did yearn for and show him how to grab it.

Whenever I thought about my father I found myself saying some of the worst bits over to myself like a kind of reverse mantra. We all do this, self-destructive as it undoubtedly is. I remember coming home to Ludo after work one day, to one of our flats or another, not sure which so not sure when, but he was sitting slumped in an armchair, still with his coat on.

'A dangerous combination of overconfidence and under-effectiveness,' he said.

'Oh yes,' I said, letting my bag slide off my shoulder to the floor and coming to sit on the arm of his chair. 'Your job appraisal. How did it go?'

'A dangerous combination of overconfidence and under-effectiveness,' he said again, looking at me but not really seeing me.

And it didn't matter how many times I asked what else his boss had said, or pointed out that they hadn't sacked him, or suggested that it was the kind of phoney line that proved the guy had thought it up in advance, which showed that Ludo probably intimidated him, he just kept saying it over and over, tugging at it like a hangnail until he was bleeding to his elbows.

'Maybe it's true,' I said, in the end. 'Isn't it better to know? If you know the worst about yourself, you can fix it.'

Which sounds like about three or four years into the relationship, like the kind of mood I was in when we were thinking about getting married. Any earlier and I wouldn't have, couldn't have, believed for a second that the boss-man had a point. Much later and I wouldn't still have believed that Ludo might take it on the chin and use it to make a difference. Four, maybe five years in, though, I still believed that anything was possible.

Anyway, I was as bad now as Ludo was then. The choice little morsels about my father that played over and over like Bacharach in a lift were 'functionally illiterate', 'educationally subnormal', 'remedial classes' and especially for some reason 'doorman's kiosk'. Tears threatened every time I thought about my father having spent the last twenty years in a kiosk and now that his job was being 'automated', as he had let slip that awful day before my mother shushed him, God knows where he would end up. But finally on the night of Friday 20 June – perhaps because reading markets reports stimulates your brain in useful ways as well as inducing insomnia – I found myself not obsessing on the kiosk for once, but wondering about those remedial classes. The evening I had sat with the strong box open on my knee in my parents' bedroom was a bit of a blur, but when I applied myself I could expand the memory to 'conditional on completion of remedial classes' and I could also recall that my cursory glance at the page where this was written had given me the impression that the letter was from a college. I sat up in bed. Yes! It was some college in Edinburgh; I could tell from the logo. And the only things that came conditionally from colleges were offers of places. This could be it. Once upon a time he had wanted to do something and had tried and this – at last – was the thing I had to persuade him it wasn't too late to try again.

So once my parents were safely off grocery shopping in the morning, with only a week to go, I put the chain on the door and, so to speak, turned the collar of my raincoat up and the rim of my trilby down.

Back through the passports and bankbooks and cards, to the bulging envelope at the bottom. I emptied out the musty sheets and shuffled through them. The thing I couldn't quite understand was why he hadn't persevered at the time. He was always so ready to tell me that Grandpa paid for everyone's education and would cough up for mine if he had to. Why hadn't he stumped up for my father? Details, details. Unimportant. I had been through the pile to the bottom now without spotting it. I should take my time. I flattened out the sheets one by one. National Service, Limtec job offer, various school reports – I didn't look too closely at these – it wasn't there. I shook the bankbooks and flipped through the passport. It was gone. With my eyes closed, I tried to remember exactly what I had done that other morning. I had unfolded it, glanced at it, refolded it and ... ? And then the paperboy had made me jump out of my skin and I had dropped the lot. My eyes flew open. If it had fallen on the floor and I had missed it, my father might not have said anything – my skin crawled at the thought that he knew I knew – but he would certainly have changed the combination. So what else could have happened? I looked about myself now as though it could just have sat on the powder rug for a fortnight.

Just to be on the safe side, though not really expecting anything, I slid off the dressing stool and put my face on the carpet to look under the bed. There it was, where it had been all this time, about halfway up right in the middle, in amongst the fluff and stray feathers. Thank God my mother wasn't houseproud.

I stretched under, couldn't reach it, got her mermaid mirror from the dressing table and stretched under again trying to pin it down and drag it out. As it slid towards me I saw, reflected in the mirror, something I wasn't expecting. A zip. And what looked like very old, very bad, fake leather. I sat up sharply. If my parents had articles in fake leather with zips hidden away in the springs of their bed I was pretty sure I didn't want to know about it.

But maybe I would just take a peek. I put the side of my face back down against the carpet and peered. At first I thought it was a suit bag. Well actually, at the very first, I thought it was a body bag, but I realized it was too flat. *Then* I thought it was a suit bag, but it was too big. The suit that filled it would have fitted Herman Munster. Eventually, I realized that what it was was a portfolio, one of those huge flat cases that artists and architects carry around, second only to double bass players' burdens in awkwardness. I grabbed it by the carrying loop on its short end and pulled. It had obviously not been moved for a very long time, but it slid out from between the springs and the struts without too much trouble and slapped down onto the carpet with a puff of grey dust like a flour bomb. The zip was rusty, but it gave, inch by gritty inch, and at last I got it open all the way round and flipped back the cover.

I know he's my father and I love him and nobody could call me objective, but they were brilliant. There were eight big ones – painted – and sheaves of little studies and sketches besides. The sketches were good, better than I could do, better than people who get money for it in shopping malls, but the paintings were unbelievable. I looked at them, then I read the college offer – Edinburgh School of Art, of course. What else? – then I looked at the pictures some more.

I was scared to touch them; the paper was slightly yellowed and felt dry and I was terrified the paint would flake off as I turned them carefully over to lie face down. But I couldn't stop looking at them. They were obviously old, from the fifties, but modern. There was a dancer, chunky like a robot, or maybe it was a skyscraper, or maybe a bridge with a shed at one end. Anyway it was black with a blue tummy, and it looked like it was painted with a wallpaper-paste brush, but it was brilliant. The way that it turned into a bridge when you looked at her legs, or into a tower block when you looked at the shed.

Not that he couldn't do colour. There was one of people (maybe ducklings) that was bright yellow and thick like half-cooked egg yolk, or like the way that the bad kids in primary one used to waste the poster paint, slopping it on until the teacher noticed them. This one made you feel a bit sick, but still you could see it was amazing. And there was some real sixties stuff that looked like a Mary Quant dress – just to show he could colour in neatly when he had to – and one of people with long spindly necks and mouths like mantraps, and a weird one that looked like Arabic script that gave you a headache. But my favourite was another black and white one, just a circle, a kind of Polo-mint shape, black on white paper, but fuzzy, out of focus, so that I thought it must be done with a spray can until I looked really closely and saw the brush strokes. It was like a painting of a cuddle. I loved it.

And they all had J.M. Lawson printed on the back. J. M. Lawson. My father. The genius.

Chapter 9

23 June 1981

It had only taken me a minute to decide what to do. Thinking it would be gauche to roll up with them like a travelling salesman, I had tucked the portfolio back into the bed frame, bundled the papers into the strong box again, tried my best to spread the dust around and bat the worst of the fluff balls back under the hem of the bedspread, then I had made my plan.

Sod's Law, however, was firing on all cylinders by Monday morning. At the art school it was the quiet period after the end of classes and before the exams, when the students are all busy but the staff are at a loose end, the time they use to hold their open days. In other words, it was one of the handful of days in the year when turning up lugging a portfolio and looking hopeful would have been exactly the right thing to do.

'Can you tell me where the admissions tutor is?' I asked a porter in the foyer.

'The who?'

'The undergraduate director? The UCAS administrator? The chair of the selection committee?'

'Have you got your paperwork?' he said. 'What time's your appointment?'

I shrugged and got ready to be frogmarched out, but he had clearly seen it all before.

'Students,' he said under his breath as he punched a number into his telephone.

'Another lost lamb for you, Dr Pitcairn,' he said, rolling his eyes at me.

Dr Pitcairn, a rangy woman of fortyish in black canvas jeans and a black string vest, with those wonderful rough, strong hands that woman artists get, nodded to me genially and waved me into a seat.

'It's not what you think,' I began. 'It's not me. I mean, it's not next year's intake. I mean, can I ask you a question?'

'Have we seen your portfolio?' she said.

'No. I could go and get it . . .'

'It should have been here in April.'

'I'm sorry,' I said. 'But can I just ask, once you've made an offer, how long does it stand for? How long can you defer entry and still have your place?'

'I would advise you to come straight from school,' she said. 'You might think you need to see Morocco first, but you'll find, if you check, that Art School isn't completely hopeless, for Art.' I liked her.

'It's not me,' I said. 'It's my father. I'm just wondering whether he's left it too long.'

'We're full for next year,' she said. 'Oversubscribed.'

'Of course. But there must be dropouts.'

She sighed and said nothing for a moment.

'What was the name?' she said at last. 'When was the offer?'

'Umm, 1960-ish,' I said, trying to make it sound normal. 'And also, do you still do the remedial classes?' This wasn't sounding good.

'The . . . ?'

'Yes, you see, my father is a genius. I only wish I had the portfolio with me to show you. But he isn't exactly bookish.'

'There's a great deal of theoretical study in our Fine Art Masters,' said Dr Pitcairn. 'Less in the BAs. What do you mean, exactly, by not bookish?'

'He . . .' I began. I took a deep breath and tried again, not looking at her. 'He can't read and write. Tell you what, I'll try not to let the door hit me.' I stood and hurried across the carpet to my escape.

'1960,' she said kindly, 'wouldn't have been completely out of the question. But a degree's a degree and if he can't read and write at all . . .'

135

'But you offered him a place before,' I said. 'Look, let me go and get the portfolio.'

'The candidate would have to apply in person,' said Dr Pitcairn. 'It can't be done by proxy. We need to speak to the prospective students, get a sense of them.'

'But if you would just look at the pictures . . . I could tell him that you love them and then he might be able to face you. If I make him believe first, and then he walks in here and you turn him down . . .'

'A robust self-belief is not the least of the talents required for a career in art,' said Dr Pitcairn.

I said nothing for a moment, sizing her up. I knew – I just knew, the same way I knew about *Millionaire* – that if she could see them she would change her mind.

'I'll be back,' I told her and left.

But it was easier said than done. Saturday morning was the only scheduled time that both parents could be guaranteed to be absent together. Shopping for groceries every Saturday, clothes on the first Thursday of the month, household items on odd Sundays to B&Q, if it was raining or if the afternoon film was a Western. To spring the portfolio from under the bed in business hours on a weekday and get it to Dr Pitcairn was no mean feat. Ordinarily, my mother would go shopping, out for coffee, up to see Grandpa, any number of useful timely outings, but the morning sickness (imagined) and the anxiety (real) were keeping her close to home. I went in to sit on her bed, more than once.

'Still feeling dodgy?' I asked.

She nodded faintly and pressed her hand to her throat. This from a woman who, after her chop the night before, had fried a piece of bread in the pork fat left in the pan and eaten it with Branston pickle.

'Maybe some fresh air would do you good,' I said. 'You've been hanging around the house too much lately.' I leaned forward to brush her hair back and I was sure I could hear the creak of the portfolio case moving in the bed frame.

'That's a nice idea,' my mother said. 'I'll go for a walk this afternoon.'

Only Danny phoned me first thing, champing for a share tip and by the time I got back at noon, she'd been. She said she'd thought it would rain later and she'd had a notion to go to the baker's and get hot pies for our lunch. She ate all of hers and half of mine since, after reading the rejection from Tyne Tees that had come in the second post, I was too sick at heart to face it.

And somehow all of a sudden it was the last Monday of the month.

'Post for you, Janie,' my father bellowed up the stairs at six thirty. I humped over on my shoulder cursing him, but then thinking that there was only one thing it could be I threw back the blankets and hurried downstairs, shrugging into my dressing gown. I sat on the telephone table in the hall and ripped the envelope open.

Granada had turned me down. No reason given, just a bald letter thanking me and wishing me luck. A lot of people in a lot of companies would be getting the sack when it hit the airwaves. Was what I told myself. But a cold hand seemed to take a sudden grip of some small but important organ in my middle and twist.

As I sat gulping, the phone rang at my elbow, making me shriek, and my father stuck his head round the kitchen door and hissed at me: 'Your poor mother's trying to sleep! Shut up and answer that.' For all the world as though he hadn't just roared up the stairs himself.

'Janie?' said Danny's voice. 'Monday. Bank's open. What time you coming round?'

'Oh for God's sake, Danny, it's not even seven o'clock. We don't have to buy something every day.'

'Okay,' said Danny, sounding cheerful. Of course he sounded bloody cheerful: if I didn't buy a stock for him he got to go to the bookies.

'I'll slip round after lunch,' I told him. 'But how can you? How much money did your dad send you anyway?'

'Well,' he said in that arch voice that people put on to tell you how naughty they've been, eating three cream cakes or getting another credit card, when secretly they think it makes them look dashing. 'That's long gone, but I had a good day on Friday.'

'Wait a minute, wait a minute,' I began.

'Benson dropped two points,' said Danny. 'You made the rules.'

I was awake now, no point going back up to bed, so I joined my father in the kitchen.

'Anything interesting?' he said. I shook my head as I filled the kettle.

'It was Danny,' I told him.

'Ah,' said my father and paused. 'Actually, though, I meant your post.'

He was striking up a conversation first thing in the morning. I knew what that meant. He thought the envelope might be the great news that I had promised he would find so convincing. Sod's Law in action again. I wondered if my face showed any fear.

'That's me off, sweetheart,' he said, later, standing in the doorway with his briefcase. I was still at the breakfast bar in my dressing gown. He waited.

'Right,' I said. 'Well, have a good day.'

He nodded, and waited.

'Don't sign anything, will you?' I said, dutifully, at last.

'Two days to go,' he told me, sounding almost cheerful. 'Plenty of time yet.'

I gave myself a pep talk once he had gone. The Beatles got rejections, J.K. Rowling got rejections. It only took one to accept, and I had two left in the bag. So what if my genius father got turned down by the other five, five tinpot telly stations who wouldn't know a ratings topper if it put on slingbacks and took them dancing. *I* knew. I knew about *Millionaire*. And I knew about my father, the genius. And Dr Pitcairn would know too if I could only winkle my mother out of the house.

'Mum,' I said, going into her room. 'What are your plans for the day?'

She had nibbled away most of her digestive biscuit, but hadn't quite managed all of it. Quite a contrast to the evening before when she had made herself a triple-decker digestive biscuit wafer with raspberry ripple ice-cream. As soon as I spoke, the room darkened, low, purple clouds descended and a drumming rain began to fall. My mother shivered.

'Well,' she said. 'I'll need to think about maternity clothes soon enough, and I've been meaning to make space for them. So I think I'll spend the day right here in my room having a clear-out.' She smiled. 'It's hardly the weather for anything else.'

Tuesday morning began for me with the sound of the letterbox banging shut, and my father sneezing his early-summer, peacock-cry sneeze as he went to pick up the post. That's how I knew it was a different day. Other than that it went like this:

'Post, Janie,' bellowed my father from the hallway. Up, dressing gown, down the stairs, an envelope – Thames TV: thanks and best wishes – and then the phone rang beside me.

'For God's sake, Danny,' I said. 'I've got more to do than this. Just, for crying out loud, just for today, blow your twenty on a horse, eh? And I'll catch you tomorrow.'

'My mum's not well,' said Danny.

My first thought was: good. If she's not well she won't drink and she won't sign any little slips of paper that are shoved under her nose. That was my thought. Thank Christ I didn't say it.

'What's up with her?' was what I did say, not exactly gracious.

'I don't know.'

'Well, we can guess,' I said. 'Can't we?'

'It seems different this time,' said Danny. 'And they won't tell me anything.'

'Who's they?'

139

'The ambulance men.' He spoke quietly. 'There's never been an ambulance before.'

I offered to go with him and my father offered to go with both of us, but Danny was adamant. His dad was getting lifted off the rig and there was nothing anyone could do.

'It could be her heart,' said my father.

'More likely her liver,' I said. 'It's not as if it's the first time.' I was trying very hard not to think about how she always signed the forms for us just after lunch, once she was just far enough gone and no further.

'How old is she?' said my father. 'What a waste of a life.'

A week ago that would have been my cue to get in a few jabs, but I said nothing. There were six rejections now, seven counting Dr Pitcairn, only the BBC to go. And today was the last day of June. Tomorrow he had to take the money or sign the contract, and I just knew that if he had to sign the contract, especially after I raised his hopes, the boy who had painted those pictures would fold himself away for good.

'Talk about a blink of sunshine,' said my father.

'What?'

'We're a million years dead, then we get a blink of sunshine and back to the dark for ever.'

'For God's sake, Dad,' I moaned. 'She'll get better. She always does. Nobody's going to eternal darkness.'

'You're wrong, Janie,' he said. 'That's the whole point. We all are.'

'Dad,' I said. 'For a man who doesn't speak much in the mornings, you certainly pick your subjects when you do. Talk about morbid.'

'It's not morbid,' said my father. 'It's illuminating.' I was thinking about Danny and so it didn't really go in. He gave me a hard squeeze and a ringing smack of a kiss on the top of my head before he picked up my mother's ginger tea and went upstairs.

I went to the hospital as soon as I was dressed, no matter what Danny said. He was sitting in the main foyer, in the only chair not taken over by a large family who, whatever they were here for, were treating it like a trip to the seaside, with bags of crisps and big smokers' belly laughs at nothing much.

'She's in admissions,' he said to me, his eyes round and red-rimmed. 'They said they're not sure where they're putting her, but it might be intensive care.' One of the children from the large family, having gulped Coke, now burped explosively and everyone laughed. We went to sit on the stairs.

'My dad's going to kill me,' was the first thing Danny said.

I put my arm around him and squeezed. I almost kissed the top of his head as my father had done to me.

'Of course he won't,' I told him. 'And even if he did, it would just be worry and upset; he wouldn't mean it. Don't blame yourself.'

'What for?' said Danny.

'For your mum,' I said, thinking, what else?

'You still don't get this, do you?' Danny said. 'I don't blame myself for my mum. She doesn't drink because I buy her drink. She drinks because she's an alcoholic. I buy her drink so that she doesn't drink in the park, so that when she falls asleep, she falls asleep in her own house. If I was to pour away—' I stopped him with a hand on his arm.

'I know that's what you believe,' I said.

'What's that supposed to mean?' he said.

'Danny, I feel just as bad as you do about it.'

'You feel as bad as I do about my mum being in hospital?' he said. 'Thanks, but I don't think so.'

'I don't mean that,' I said. 'I mean I feel bad about what we did. God, I hope she's going to be okay.'

'I don't know what you're talking about,' said Danny. 'What did we do?'

'Oh come off it!' I began, but he stood up and went to sit halfway up the flight of stairs to get away from me, and that alone showed me that he did know, deep down.

'Why did you come if all you were going to do was have a go at me?' he said, sounding as if he was going to start crying again.

'I wanted to help,' I said.

'What's stopping you?' he asked, with his head on his arms.

'Look, Danny, I'm sorry. I'm in a pretty bad spot just right at the moment. I've made a mess of something I thought I could handle and I know I'm not being much good, but you know what? You called me because I'm all you've got, and I'm here because I know that, and if I'm crabby and useless and I'm not saying the right things, well tough. Life doesn't happen one thing after the other, it happens all at once, shit on shit on shit, and there's nothing anyone can do about it.'

'Jesus,' said Danny. 'My mum's maybe going to intensive care, my dad's getting airlifted in and he knows nothing about any of it. And *you're* having a bad time?'

'As it happens.'

'And did I do it? Whatever it is that's wrong? What are you so angry with *me* for?'

'It's not only you,' I said. 'It's lots of things.'

'Some of it's me, then,' said Danny. 'What did I do wrong?'

'You're just driving me nuts with it,' I said. 'You keep saying she's ill, she's ill, she's ill, and you never stop to think that if she is, then—' I was going to say 'then you are too' but I stopped myself. 'Then she's not the only one.'

'What?' he said. 'Are you ill? Is your dad ill? Is everything okay with your mum and the baby?'

'No, Danny. For God's sake, just leave it. It's not the time. I'm really sorry.'

'Who else is ill?' he demanded. 'What is it with you and all the secrets always?'

My face felt numb with the misery of how badly wrong I was getting this. He was right; his mum was ill, maybe seriously ill, and I was haranguing him, business as usual.

'Who is ill?' he said again, and because his anger and fear were all about his mum and I knew that and I also knew it was my job to soak them up, I answered:

'No one.'

He frowned at me.

'You just said it for no reason?'

'Sorry.'

'Well, it was nice of you to stop by,' he said.

'Tell me one thing.' I couldn't help myself. 'What's your dad going to kill you for? What is it he knows nothing about?'

'Fuck off,' said Danny. 'I mean it.'

'I know,' I said. I went to the bottom of the stairs and stopped with my hand on the door to the foyer. 'You better come back out. Your dad'll never find you in here.'

I waited in at home all the rest of that day and kept phoning, but there was no answer from their place. And the hospital wouldn't tell me anything, since I wasn't a relation. Eventually I tried telling them I was a niece, but the nurse recognized my voice and told me not to phone back. At ten o'clock, my mother came out into the hallway and took the phone out of my hand.

'If they come home now to get some rest and the phone goes, they're going to think the worst,' she said. 'Danny knows how much you care about him, darling.' She laughed and chucked me under the chin. '*I* didn't know you cared about him this much, I must say. You're a cool customer with your "just good friends".'

'What's Dad going to do tomorrow?' I asked her. 'It's the big day.'

'He's going to work,' she said, brightly. 'Of course.'

That wasn't what I meant and she knew it, but I was glad not to have to think of something to say about Dad and his contract tonight. I just told myself it would all look better in the morning.

It didn't. Nothing came first post and I stayed up in my room trying to avoid him, but he knocked on my door and looked around it.

'Still no news of Mrs Conway?' he said. I shook my head.

'Well, no news is good news. Don't look so glum, Janie. Sometimes we all need a little unpleasantness to bring us to our senses.' He smiled at me. 'It can be a blessing in disguise.'

By the time I was dressed and down in the kitchen my

mother was sitting at the breakfast bar, trying a little fried egg and ketchup sandwich this morning, with a napkin tied round her neck over one of her best blouses. I wiggled my eyebrows at it.

'Hmph!' she said through a mouthful of bread. 'Dad said he wants me to meet him for lunch.'

'What?' (Do I need to make it clear how far from normal this was?)

'Yes, at first he said to phone him if we heard any news about Mrs Conway, and then just before he left he said come and meet him for lunch. He's worried about her. Well, we all are.'

I suppose we all were, only I was trying not to think about it. Because you don't end up in hospital from being an alcoholic. You end up in hospital from being an alcoholic who drinks, and it was my brilliant idea to say to Danny he needed a betting slip signed every day the market dropped.

My mother left at eleven, as I was waiting in the hall, trying to look as if I wasn't, for the second post, and calling Danny's house every ten minutes or so. I heard the postman go down Mrs Robertson's path, heard the snap of the letterbox, heard him return to the pavement. Then I saw him through the pebbled glass of our front door, turning onto the path, rummaging in his bag. The flap lifted, the stiff white envelope that was my last chance hit the mat inside with a crisp smack, and the postman walked away.

I sat at the telephone table and looked at it for a while, dusting the rubber plant with my socks, reading the BBC logo upside down.

It was a long letter. I noticed that at once, when I finally made myself open it. And it was kind, very encouraging; good of them to take the time. They pointed out that the title was a line from a song and that they would have to pay royalties to use it. That was the first problem. Then they assured me that I would get a feel for what works and what doesn't eventually, but that it took time to learn the market, that quizzes were not about prizes, never mind about money prizes, that viewers spending hard-earned cash on premium-rate phone lines didn't say 'light entertainment'. It said 'gambling'. It said 'lottery' and it would never catch on here. In the kitchen, on the breakfast bar where my mother had left it, the morning paper lay open. Mrs Thatcher looked up at me like a starlet from under her candyfloss hair.

'What did you do to us?' I asked her.

I tried Danny one last time, while struggling into my shoes, running over the possible lunch venues where I might intercept my father and tell him I'd failed, tell him to sign the contract and buy us all some more time, but there was no answer from the Conway house. Just as I gave up and put down the phone, however, the doorbell rang behind me, making me jump.

'Danny?' I called, squinting through the glass. There were two figures standing there and so, thinking he must have brought his father with him, I galloped along the hall.

'Dan?' I said again, opening the door.

'Miss Lawson,' said one of the men, with a broad smile revealing gleaming teeth, with that aggressive all-over whiteness that you only get from flossing and special toothpaste. His friend stood side-on, staring all around.

I looked from one to the other. They were both wearing suits, white shirts and sober ties, and carried nothing in their hands.

'Are you from a television company?' I said. 'Have you changed your mind?'

'Can we come in?' said the one with the teeth again.

'Are you from Limtec? He's at work. Are you from the union?'

'We really can't go into it on the doorstep, Miss Lawson,' he said. I glanced at his silent companion.

'Are you friends of Danny's? Have you come from the hospital?'

'Can we talk inside?'

'Wait. You're not— Are you from the Art college? Does Dr Pitcairn want to see them after all?'

145

'It won't take long,' he said. 'But we must insist.'

'You're not bookies, are you?' I said. 'Or bailiffs? You're not from the bank?'

'My, my, my,' said the smiling man. 'Bookies, bailiffs, bankers? The union, the hospital, the college, television? You *have* been busy, haven't you?'

'Wait a minute,' I said, their words ringing a very faint bell. 'Is this anything to do with Hull?'

The other one turned to face me at that and without even touching me, much less hustling me, but still somehow completely unstoppably they were past me and into the house.

They sat down in the living room, side by side on the couch with the *Radio Times* and my father's box of hankies between them; I faced them in an armchair.

The silent one reached into his jacket and drew out a sheet of paper, unfolded and in a plastic cover, as though his inside pocket was Mary Poppins' carpet bag. He put it on the coffee table facing me and pushed it across. It was, as I saw, as I should have guessed, my Dennis Nilsen letter.

What can you tell us?' said the teeth.

'I've got nothing to add,' I said. 'That there is all I know. Did it work? Have you got him?'

'All you know how, exactly?' he said. 'Tell us about Hull.'

Which was the first indication that all was not quite as I thought.

'Wait,' I said. 'You haven't come from Hull?' I was trying to sound as girlish and unthreatening as possible, remembering what had happened to Thatcher when they stopped taking her picture from the starlet angle and started snapping her from underneath like she was the fifth face on Mount Rushmore.

'Mr Nilsen is dead. Murdered,' said the flossing man. My entreating smile must have wavered. Certainly the hair on the back of my neck did something. 'His body washed up, five years ago. On the Moray Firth, so not too far from here. The file's still open.'

I tried to get enough breath in through my nose to stop my head from swimming. I didn't want them to see me panting.

The other one did his Mary Poppins routine again, brought out a photograph and put it on top of the letter. It was me, in London, with my perm and my *Camilla Parker Bowles* placard. Now my scalp really started to crawl.

'Who are you?' I said again.

'We're the police,' said the teeth. The other one cleared his throat and spoke at last.

'More or less,' he said.

'S-so . . . can I make a phone call?' I said, trying to keep my voice steady. I was sure that the answer would be no.

'Please do,' came back with a grin. 'I wish you would.' It should have warned me.

I scurried out and shut the door firmly on them but still, after I had dialled the Hull number, which by this time I knew off by heart, and after the answering machine had sung its infuriating little party piece, I made sure to speak in a whisper.

'I've got visitors,' I said. 'I thought it was you, so I let them in, but now I don't think it is. Call me back, for God's sake, and tell me something this time. I don't like this.' I stayed where I was, feeling my scalp prickle tighter and tighter as though it was shrinking, looking at how far away the front door was and wondering if I could get out and into Mrs Robertson's before they caught me.

The phone rang and I snatched it up.

'At last,' I said. 'Start talking.'

'It's me,' said Danny.

'Jesus, Danny, you pick your moments,' I told him. 'I'm kind of in the middle of something here.' There was a long silence.

'Aren't you going to ask me how my mum is?' he said at last.

I didn't need to. The silence stretched and thinned between us.

'Can you come round?' he said eventually, in a very small voice. I looked at the living-room door, which was opening. The smiling man stood there, watching me. 'Please,' said Danny.

'Oh, Christ, Danny. I really hope so. I'll try my level best.'

'You *hope* so?' he said. 'You'll *try*?'

The silent man joined his friend in the doorway.

'I mean, if there's anything I can do, just ask,' I said into the phone. 'I could take the dog for a few days. That would be something.'

'What dog?' said Danny. 'What are you ...'

What he said next changed everything between us for ever. He wasn't Orville any more after that, and he wasn't a kid brother or a friend of the family or just one thing on the ever longer list of things that were totally up to me and totally screwed. What Danny said next showed me that he was one of the people who 'get it', no matter what it is. Even when he didn't know what the hell was going on, he got it.

'Are you in danger?' he said. 'I mean right now?'

'I don't know.'

'Okay, hang up, but I'll keep the phone in my hand, so if you pick up again I'm still here, right? If you don't get back to me in five minutes, I'll call the police.'

I replaced the receiver.

'Bad news about Mrs Conway?' said the grinner. 'Poor Danny.'

'How do you know Danny?' I said.

'We watch,' he answered. 'We listen.'

Of course, that's why they were so keen for me to make a call. Someone, somewhere, was listening to every word.

'Now, Miss Lawson ...' He spoke comfortably, luxuriously, like someone about to slide into a deep, hot bath and it was much worse than if he'd been threatening. This way it sounded as if whatever was coming, he was going to enjoy it. I closed my eyes. I heard the front door open. I heard swift movement from beside me.

'Janie?'

It was my mother and father, red-cheeked and a bit giggly. The two men had ducked back into the living room, but now they reappeared again. My mother noticed them first and nudged my father.

'They're—' I said, but the quiet one gave me a hard stare and made a pressing-down movement with his hand to shush me.

'We're just leaving,' said his friend, flashing a smile. 'God bless you and keep you.' They edged past my parents, smiling and nodding, almost bowing. 'The Lord is watching over you,' was his parting shot.

My parents, making whickering noises like litter blowing around an underpass, went into the sitting room to look after them out of the front window.

'I know you were only being polite,' said my mother, coming back to where I was stranded, my legs feeling as though they'd never hold me up again, in the hallway. 'But they're still two strange men, Janie, and you never can tell.' I couldn't speak. The Lord was watching over me? I was pretty sure I knew what that meant.

'Two very strange men,' said my father, looking down at the coffee table where the plastic folders had been. He picked up a little book and came to join us.

'Pamphlets you can file in the bin,' said my mother. 'But I wish they wouldn't give you bibles.' My father stood with the pocket New Testament in his hand, looking undecided.

'Anyway,' he said. 'The Jehovah's Weirdos spoiled my big moment there.' He beamed at me. I tried very hard to beam back. 'I've done it,' he told me. 'You convinced me. Life is short, and it should be sweet. Now, you owe me some details, young lady. What's this amazing plan all about?'

'I'm so proud of you,' said my mother, squeezing his arm. Then she turned to me. 'What's wrong, Janie?'

What's wrong? Where do I start?

'Janie?' said my mother again. 'What is it?'

God and Danny forgive me, I thought.

'Mrs Conway died,' I said, and I managed to pick up the receiver from behind me without them noticing where it had been. 'Danny's on the phone right now.' I could hear him breathing very heavily when I put it to my ear. 'Danny, sorry to keep you. Is it okay with your dad if we all come?'

Chapter 10

4 July 1981

The funeral was grim, and not for the reasons you'd think. We three were there and Danny and his father, who was a taller and slightly broader version of Danny himself, with a bouncing walk and translucent ears. Both of them, I could see when they sat down in front of us in the crematorium, had a band of untanned skin on their necks revealed by new haircuts, and the stiff collars of their hastily bought white shirts still had sharp corners from the cardboard wrapping.

There was a woman in a rumpled navy suit and dusty shoes, carrying her car keys, who I thought must be Mrs Conway's doctor, and that was it. No other family, no school friends, not even any neighbours, and you have to go some in Corstorphine to keep the old ladies in hats away from a funeral if there's one on offer.

'Come back to the house,' said Danny when we got outside. We were trying to force our way through the incoming hordes for the next service. It's always an awkward moment, this log-jam on a busy day at the crematorium, but when the numbers are better balanced at least it's done with a bit of decorum; the Conways and the Lawsons on their way out versus a hundred determined mourners on their way in was just like trying to go backwards on a Saturday morning in Ikea.

'Are you sure?' I asked when we had got a patch of car park to ourselves.

'Please,' he said, including my parents in it too.

'There's still a lot to do, son,' said Mr Conway, 'and I'm off again tonight.'

All of us boggled at that.

'Or come round to ours,' said my mother, 'since—' she hesitated and I thought she must have been going to say 'since there's only us here' and caught herself in time. '—if you're in a guddle at home. We don't mind.'

'I insist,' said Danny, and Mr Conway said no more, although it looked as though it cost him.

There were six bin bags at the kerb at Danny's house.

'Dear God,' said my mother under her breath. 'And it's not even bucket day till Wednesday. Could he not have kept them round the back till then?'

The crate of bottles was gone and the window with the sagging curtains was bare and open at the top, looking as if it had been cleaned. Certainly, when we stepped inside and braced ourselves against the expected wave of stale air, it didn't come.

The kitchen was much the same as ever – it had always been Danny's domain – but when he opened the fridge to get the milk I could see food in there. That wasn't enough for my mother, however. I think tea in mugs, biscuits from the packet and a milk bottle on the table started it; everyone knew that the tea after a funeral came in cups with saucers, the biscuits on a plate and the milk in a jug, and anyone who didn't know it clearly wasn't up to looking after himself long-term.

'What are you going to do, Danny?' she said. 'If you don't mind me asking.'

Mr Conway drew back in surprise, but began to answer soon enough. 'I need to get back to Aberdeen tonight,' he said. 'And if it was up to me—'

'I think she meant Danny Junior, Dad,' said Danny. 'Much the same as I have been, I suppose.'

'If it was up to me,' said Mr Conway again, 'Danny would be coming to Aberdeen where I can keep an eye on him. We've plenty room and it's the end of the school year, perfect time to make a change.'

'But it's not up to you,' said Danny.

'Only I was thinking,' said my mother, 'that we'd love to have you – wouldn't we, Janie? – when your dad's away. Is it four weeks on four weeks off, Mr Conway? I think we could all just about face four weeks of him at a time.' She wrinkled her nose at Danny, who almost managed to smile back. 'The spare room's tiny, mind you.'

Mr Conway said nothing. Danny only looked between him and my mother with a kind of grim amusement. My father inspected his shoes for a while and then looked up and spoke.

'Plenty of room?' he said.

'Come outside, Janie,' said Danny. 'I want to show you something.'

He led me down the garden, stopping at the washing rope to take off his jacket and tie and hook them over it, then kept going to the end to the small shed whose wooden walls were bleaching for want of creosote and whose door was buckled with damp.

He went round the side where we couldn't be seen from the house and then stopped, sitting down and leaning back against the grey wood, closing his eyes.

'You didn't really have something to show me, did you?' I said. 'What's going on?'

'Well, my mum's just died,' said Danny. 'What's going on with you?' I waited. 'Okay, okay,' he said, after half-opening his eyes and seeing my face; I was trying to glare and look sympathetic at the same time. 'Yeah, I might not have made it absolutely clear that they were divorced. My dad lives in Aberdeen with . . . Ah, what's her name – Gemma – and two wee girls.'

'You've got sisters?'

'Nah, they're Gemma's. Anyway, yeah, Mum left me the house, so that's okay, but Dad's still her executor and he's pretty pissed off about the state of things, really mad about all the shares. And he's putting the thumbscrews on to make me sell the house and go to live with them.'

I felt a flare of something like vertigo, like an extra step in the dark, but when I thought about it I knew what I had to say.

'Might be best if you went.'

'Well, ta very much,' said Danny. 'I *could* stay in Edinburgh since you begged me.'

'You shouldn't be on your own,' I said. 'I mean, you've got a problem with this gambling thing and you need someone to look out for you.'

Danny's face closed and hardened. 'I don't have a problem,' he said. 'I have a hobby. One that you don't approve of and never shut up about.'

'Think about it for a minute, Danny. You loved your mum. You knew she shouldn't drink, but you had to get your betting slips signed. Would you do that if it was just a hobby?'

'Let me get this straight,' said Danny. 'Are you telling me you think I killed my mother?'

'No,' I said, out of cowardice.

'Because she would sign betting slips, drunk, sober and all points in between. She loved the horses. It was our hobby. It was those share orders that took all the careful handling. And anyway, how many times do I have to tell you it's an illness.'

'I know,' I said. 'Let's just leave it. Now is not the time.'

'That's what you said at the hospital.'

'I was right then. And I'm right now.'

'It's not up to me what we talk about on the day of my mother's funeral?' said Danny. 'Even today, it's still your call?' He was shouting now. 'Because I'd like to hear what you've got to say. I think now is the perfect time.'

'Okay,' I said, thinking that maybe if he got angry with me, which he would, it might help him in the end. 'If she was ill, you're ill too. That's all. You can't have it both ways. You can't pick and choose, and you can't just say things because it makes it easier. I'd love to be able to say all my family's problems were "an illness" and everything I do wrong is a hobby. You just can't have it all ways.'

'What problems?' said Danny.

'Tell me one thing,' I said. 'Did your mum think she was ill? Did your mum think she had a problem? Or did she think drinking was just a hobby?'

'That's well known,' said Danny, sticking his chin out and

not quite looking me in the eye. 'That's a part of it, not admitting there's anything wrong. What problems?'

'My dad—' I stopped. 'Can't you see? Can't you see even now?'

'There's no such thing as a bet-aholic, Janie. If there was, don't you think there would be a word for it? What's wrong with your dad?'

'Nothing, it was just an example.' We stared at each other.

'Of course,' said Danny. 'You get to rake around in all the mess of my family but nobody ever gets to hear anything about yours.'

'He can't read,' I said. 'There. He can't read and write. He's illiterate. And I love him and it hurts and I'm ashamed of it and that hurts too. And I'd love to be able to say "it's an illness" but it's just not.' Tears were pouring down my face now, but still he tried to out-argue me.

'It might be,' he said. 'It might be dyslexia.'

I knew he was just fighting with me out of stubbornness and I couldn't even make my brain think about it, to see if it made sense, because there was another thought that kept bulging in front of everything else. She would do betting slips drunk, sober and all points in between; it was only the share orders that needed her gently sozzled by lunchtime. So it wasn't Danny, and it wasn't just me too, or even just mostly me. It was me, plain and simple. It was me.

He thought, because I didn't say anything, that he had scored a point. He even smiled. Then I think he remembered, suddenly, why he was here behind the shed in a black suit, hiding from his father, shouting at me to see if he could get me to feel the hurt instead of himself. He pressed his lips together hard so that his face sprang into little puckers all over. He held his breath but still his eyes began to swim and, when he finally breathed out, a bubble of snot appeared under one nostril and burst.

'Janie,' he said. 'My mum's dead.'

I pulled his head down onto my shoulder and put my arm around him, rocking him back and forward, trying to ignore the hard lumps of earth under me. He was still gulping ugly sobs and shaking when my mother appeared around the corner of the shed. Her mouth was set and her face very pale. I rarely saw this look on my mother's face, but I remembered it from just once before, when something had happened with Grandpa that I didn't understand. She was fuming.

'You're coming home with us, Danny,' she said. 'No arguments.'

Danny sat up and wiped his nose with the heel of his hand. 'Just for a bit,' he said.

'Just for a bit,' she agreed.

'Till after Christmas,' I said firmly. No way was I going to let Danny get used to a family and then turf him out after a fortnight with all his grieving ahead of him. My mother's eyes flared and I glared back at her, ready for a fight. But I had misunderstood the problem.

'Janie, you are not in charge of absolutely everything all the time,' she said. Danny, for some reason, gave a tiny giggle. 'The baby isn't due until the end of January and then it'll be in our room for a bit, so we won't need to chuck Danny out into the snow.'

'I can't just move in,' said Danny. He went as though to wipe his nose on his cuff and then realized he had rolled up his shirtsleeves and stopped. I stuck the arm of my jacket out in front of his face, and he smiled. Then, I think, he realized that he was sitting with his arm around me and my arm around him, wet from tears, while my mother watched him. He struggled upright, away from me, and sat back on his heels.

'I'll stay overnight tonight though,' he said. My mother and I exchanged a look but we said nothing.

He came with me to the Art College, the first day my parents left us alone. I marched straight past the porter's desk trying to look as if I had every right to be there, and Danny was still too low to look around and show us up as interlopers so we got away with it. I knocked on Dr Pitcairn's door, with my fingers crossed.

'Yup,' came her voice. And then: 'You again!'

'What if he was dyslexic?' I said. 'What if this student – whom you accepted, remember – was dyslexic and undiagnosed and that was why he failed his remedial class or was too scared to take it. And what if he was a genius, and you passed him up because he was dyslexic? How would you feel then?' I slapped the crumbling portfolio case down on her floor and unzipped it.

Dr Pitcairn squatted down and stared at the top picture. It was the fuzzy cuddle.

'It's called "Cashmere Doughnut",' I told her. I had invented titles for all of them, trying to help. She looked at it for a long time. Then she slid it out of the way and studied the next, 'Omelette of Life', the melted yellow people swimming around in the gobs of blue. When she got to the black one that looked like it had been painted with a wallpaper brush – I called it 'Legoman' – she said 'Crikey!'

At last, after five minutes that felt like an hour, she stood, groaning and knuckling the small of her back.

'Well, several are clearly derivative, one at least I'd say is a direct pastiche of an Ensor. Although competent.' My jaw, which I only now realized was clamped shut, prickled with pain as I clenched it even tighter.

'They're copies?' said Danny.

'But others,' she went on, 'these two,' – she put the Cashmere Doughnut and the Legoman side by side – 'these are very interesting. *Very* interesting. Terrible titles, of course. He really isn't verbal at all, is he?' I gazed at her. Never in my life had I expected solid proof that a modern art critic knew what she was talking about. 'And the dyslexia painting,' – she hauled out the one with the Arabic writing that made my head throb when I looked at it – 'very effective. Really quite uncomfortable.'

'You mean it's *meant* to hurt?'

'I would have thought so,' said Dr Pitcairn. 'Dyslexia has been compared to migraine in its effects, after all.'

'Are you some kind of expert?' said Danny.

'We get a lot of them,' she said. 'An eye that sees what others can't and all that. It's a head start for an artist.'

'So . . . ?' I didn't quite dare to ask.

'Oh absolutely, absolutely, absolutely,' said Dr Pitcairn. 'These are wonderful. Absolutely. No question. I would buy these two if I saw them in a show. Quite.'

'Well,' I said, 'how would you feel about coming to meet the artist?'

It took a lot of explaining, but Dr Pitcairn turned out to have the heart of a Patience Strong underneath the black polo-neck and the savage hair-do. When I told her about the doorman's job and my mother's late arrival and David and Mona, and Danny chipped in with his tuppenceworth about his mum, which wasn't really relevant when you think about it, she misted over and ended up hugging both of us.

I couldn't resist stopping in at Grandpa's on the way home. He was sitting in what he called his library in a winged armchair with the *Telegraph* and a glass of sherry, looking as though he had been installed by a set-dresser to finish the room.

'It's an illness,' I said, and tried to ignore Danny snorting at my side. 'You're supposed to be a *doctor*. And you're his *father*. He's your *son*. Christ!'

'Language,' said my grandfather. 'Dyslexia? Lot of mumbo-jumbo.'

'Do you believe in cancer?' said Danny. My grandfather glared at him over his half-spectacles. Danny stared back unbowed. It would take more than a few fake walnut bookcases full of bound volumes of the *Lancet* to get him to hang his head.

'He's a genius,' I said. 'If you had let him, if you had supported him, he would have been famous. His pictures—'

'I've seen his so-called pictures,' said my grandfather. 'A child of seven would be smacked for wasting paint. Artists! Drugs!'

He sounded just like Father Jack.

'Anyway, it's all water under the bridge now,' he said comfortably. And the smarmy voice, thick with sherry, finally got through all my indignation and just, in the end, sickened me.

'Come on, Danny,' I said. 'Let's go.'

'Yeah,' said Danny. 'I don't know anything about art either, Dr Lawson, but I know what I like. And I don't like you.'

And my father was surprisingly all right. He wasn't *actually* all right; he was livid, but he was surprisingly less livid than you would think. Possibly he was just beyond caring, what with the job and the baby and the news that my grand plans had fallen through and Mrs Conway dying and then Danny moving in, but when Dr Pitcairn turned up, as my mother was washing the dishes after tea, and started manhandling the portfolio out of the back of her Volvo he caught up pretty fast. I didn't tell him I'd been in his strong box and I think he got the idea, in all the confusion and discussion, that I had found the pictures and just happened to take them to the college and it was them who told me about his application all those years ago and about the dyslexia and everything. Lucky.

'There's a full grant,' said Dr Pitcairn and named a sum that I think must have been more than he was getting from Limtec at the best of times.

'And housing benefit and all sorts,' Danny shouted from the kitchen. He was under the sink getting the toolbox to start banging in nails and hanging the pictures. 'I looked into it all for myself, you know, before, and if you've got dependants as well you'll be coining it in.'

'But Grandpa's probably a bust,' I said, wanting to get this straight as soon as I could. 'I went to see him today and I think I might have blown any chance of support for either of us.'

'Good,' said my father. 'Good girl. Good for you. We'll do without Grandpa from now on.'

'I'll get a job,' said my mother.

'I'll take the baby to college with me,' said my father.

'On your back in a sling,' I said, clapping my hands. 'It'll be so bohemian.'

Dr Pitcairn and my father both frowned at me. I was going to have to watch the stereotyping from now on. And maybe it was only stereotyping; after all, she *had* driven up in a Volvo.

'There's a crèche,' said Dr Pitcairn.

'You won't need a crèche,' I said. 'Mum won't need to work. *I'll* be working.'

'No,' said my father, very loud all of a sudden. 'You will be at school and then at university, getting your psychology degree, because if you think for one minute, for one minute, I would do anything to hold back my child after what was done to me . . .'

I could imagine that there would be no moving him on this, and fair enough, I suppose. Anyway, I needed to go to university to meet Ludo at Shona Ward's party in first year, and I was quite looking forward to the free gym for four years as well, but psychology? I would do a lot to keep my father happy, but I wasn't going to sit through four years of early eighties psychology from people who didn't know the half of it.

'Mind your head,' said Danny. He was kicking off his shoes and clambering up on the couch to put a nail in the long wall. 'Which one here, Mr Lawson?' he said.

'Jock,' said my father. 'Or Uncle Jock. Call me Uncle Jock.'

'I'd go for the cashmere doughnut,' I said, thinking that it wouldn't clash or make guests feel seasick.

'Oh no,' said my mother, 'not in the middle of the living room.' She looked a bit pink in the cheeks. My father grinned, but he also shook his head.

'No,' he said. 'Perhaps not.'

'I was going to ask for that one for a summer show anyway,' said Dr Pitcairn, grinning. 'Unless you'd rather not. It is very . . .'

'What's the problem?' I said. I stared at it. It still looked to me like a cashmere doughnut, or maybe a really hairy curled up caterpillar, or a mink Polo. 'I know this is probably crass, Dad,' I said. 'But what is it?'

'It's your mum,' said my father. 'Ah, young love!'

'My mother shrieked and hit my father's back with a tea towel. Danny didn't shriek but he hit his thumb with the hammer and swore. Dr Pitcairn laughed. I just stared at all of them. If it was true in real life that you shouldn't meddle with the past, like it was true in *Back to the Future* and *Our Town*, then I was in trouble.

A woman with dyed black hair and a Gauloise laugh was standing in our living room asking my father to borrow a painting of his for the summer show, a rude painting of my mother, my pregnant mother. My art student father. Already I thought he was looking less buttoned, less trim, than he used to; he had put on workboots to cut the grass with the rotary mower and hadn't changed into his slippers to come inside and eat. His shirt wasn't ironed since it was only an old one to garden in, and with his hair wild from him fussing the flies out of it while he worked, he looked like one of those butch, worker artists like Eduardo Paolozzi, one that stumped about headlands and grappled with hunks of marble, one that knew how to weld. And a sixteen-year-old boy had just said 'fuck' in his living room and he wasn't bothered. We weren't in Kansas any more.

Chapter 11

14 September 1981

How to account for it? Mostly it was Danny, taking up all the time and imagination I had to spare. We were always going to get a bit closer that summer, living in the same house. But as well as that, I felt close to him because I came very near to telling him everything, near enough to feel what a relief it would be if one day I really did. He felt close to me, on the other hand, because he got the idea that I was more like him than I had ever let on. It started a few days after the funeral.

'Can we please talk about it now?' he said.

'Talk about what?'

'Oh, for fuck's sake,' said Danny. 'About what happened. Why were you in danger on Wednesday when I called you?'

I opened and shut my mouth a couple of times, then took a deep breath and gave it a go. 'Do you believe in ghosts?' I said.

'No,' said Danny. 'What . . . ?'

'Horoscopes?'

'Nope.'

'UFOs, time travel, ESP?'

'Nope. Nope. Nope. Why?'

'So you'd think anyone who did was probably . . . ?'

'A loony, yes. Why?'

'Because,' I was talking very slowly and carefully. I didn't have a Plan B in case this didn't go down. 'Because I persuaded my dad to pack in his job, on account of a brilliant plan that went totally wrong and I only did it because I thought I could tell the future.' I waited for him to say something. Eventually he spoke.

'Why would you think that?' he said, carefully.

'Because of a prediction,' I said. 'And I owe money. And last Wednesday the tarot reader sent two great big hairy guys round to get it.'

'Jesus!' Danny said. 'That's who was there when I phoned? Bailiffs?'

I nodded.

'From a *tarot reader*?'

I nodded again.

'And you told me I wasn't fit to live on my own,' he said. He was smiling. 'So do you need some money?'

'No.'

'How come?'

'I pawned my granny's pearls,' I said. His smile broadened into a grin, and even though I wanted to kick him it was good to see him looking happy.

It didn't happen too often, but so long as he was near me he seemed okay. He took to following me around, which came in useful: there were quite a few telephone calls between our house and Aberdeen and when my father's voice rose I would go upstairs to my room, knowing that he would come too, and we would sit together training the hamster (Bubble? Biscuit?) to run over our shoulders and back like a basketball until we heard the chirp of my father putting down the phone.

And somehow, with Danny always there and with the thought of the part I had played in his mother's death waiting if I let my mind stray away from the daily task of helping him get over her, the summer passed and I did nothing.

At first I thought Hull would be in touch without another prompting – of course they would, after I had said to them straight out that there were threatening men in the house – but they took their time and before I knew it my mother was talking about clothes for school. I slipped out to the phone box and did my best.

'Listen,' I told the answering machine. 'I'm sick of waiting for you lot. What's going on? Who were those guys and what will I do if they come back? Tell me something.'

The next day, the first day of the new term at school, a

postcard arrived in a small brown envelope, Sellotaped shut. I opened it at the breakfast bar, sitting munching cornflakes side by side with Danny. My parents were upstairs. My father had been trying to paint my mother in the bath, her belly and breasts looming up out of the water like a hippo at wallow, but it wasn't going well; it was a fine line between getting the water hot enough to let her lie there for a good long session and having it so hot that her face went red and the paint ran. I read the postcard. 'Call us and describe your visitors. From now on, do nothing. Speak only to us. Trust us.' I frowned at it.

'Trouble?' said Danny, attuned as ever to my slightest expression.

'Ah . . . library fine,' I said. Danny gave me a look out of narrowed eyes – he knew I hadn't been to the library in months – but said nothing.

'I'll . . . ah . . . I'll have to stop in on my way to school so I'll leave early and see you there, okay?'

'Fine,' said Danny. 'The library doesn't open until ten, but I know you'd tell me if you could.' He looked calm, almost smug.

'I would,' I said. 'I will. Someday.'

He had finished his cornflakes and he lifted the bowl to his lips to finish the milk. When he had drunk it, he would burp, as he did every morning, and then he would complain or at least rub his chest. And yet he didn't annoy me. Ludo's habit of sucking in the stray ends of spaghetti turned me vicious enough to kick him and the way my mother drank water, a special way she has that lets you see a lot of her teeth and tongue through the bottom of the glass and reminds you of a sea-life centre, always made me want to rap her on the head with a spoon, but Danny's morning slurp'n'burp, for some reason, never troubled me.

He opened his mouth and waited and in a moment a rasping belch erupted richly from deep inside him. He rubbed his chest and scowled.

'I hate cornflakes burps in the morning,' he said. 'They're cold.'

'I know,' I said. 'You told me yesterday. So, I'll see you at school then.'

'Yup. Can I just ask you one thing, though, Janie?' I stopped in the doorway for him to go on. 'This "library fine". Why didn't you just say it was something to do with "the bailiffs"?'

'The bailiffs?' I echoed.

'You know, the tarot reader's bailiffs?'

I felt my face warming. 'Sorry?' I said, trying to buy time.

'Apology accepted,' said Danny. 'You'll tell me when you can.'

Now he was annoying me. *That* was annoying.

'It's Janie Lawson,' I whispered into the telephone in the callbox by the shops, 'from Edinburgh.' I shovelled in as many 10p pieces as it would take and started talking. I told the machine about the men, their suits, their teeth, their hair, the photograph, the letter, the plastic folders, the capacious pocket, the pamphlets, the bible, the veiled threat delivered in the name of God. 'And then they left. They definitely didn't want my mum and dad to know who they were – ballpark, I mean, because who knows who they were, right? Oh sorry, my mistake, you probably know who they were; you just don't want to tell me. Well, I'm getting pretty hacked off with it all.'

I hung up without saying goodbye, and stood staring at the phone. I'd never make a nuisance caller; I got no frisson from talking to that machine and I clearly didn't have whatever it takes to make people pick up the phone and talk back. So, if force of personality alone wasn't going to make someone tell me something, what cards were in my hand?

I groaned and knocked my head against the change shelf. I had just *had* cards in my hand – all the details about the men in suits – and I'd blurted them. 'Describe your visitors', the postcard had said, and so I had, like a good girl. Where did they get the nerve? 'Speak only to us' indeed! 'Trust us!' And yet, I knew I would – speak only to them, that is. They knew where I was and they had sent a nice little man in an anorak to give me a contact number, while the other lot had sent two spooks from Central Casting. Annoying as it was, I knew already that there was no contest. I was scrabbling the unused 10p pieces out of the cup, still mouthing the words of the postcard over to myself in a sarcastic voice, when I seemed to hear them properly for the first time. 'From now on, do nothing?' 'Speak only to us?' What did they mean, 'do nothing'? What did they think I was going to do? And as soon as I had thought that, the answer was clear: they thought I was going to do something like go to London with a placard or send an anonymous tip-off to Her Majesty's Unmentionables. And they wanted me to speak to them instead. There was my lever. I shovelled the coins back in and dialled again.

'However,' I began, 'I do want to tell you a few things. There's a couple who kill girls. I know their name and the street address and I can tell you it. Also there's a nuclear power station that's going to blow and sod things up for decades. And a massacre in . . . Asia. At a demonstration. I can tell you where it is. When they start the big demonstration, someone has to make them give it up, because thousands get shot and it doesn't make a blind bit of difference.' Now for the clever bit. I let the pause lengthen, then went on: 'But you might already know all this. Or you might not want to help. How do I know you're not going to make things worse? Here's the deal. Tell me who you are, and prove that I can trust you or I'll have no choice but go back to the other— *Jesus!*'

I dropped the receiver and crouched into a ball as a barrage of blows hammered against the windows. On all three sides the thumps hit the panes hard enough to make the edges of the glass grate against the putty. *On all three sides.* Three of them out there. There was no point even trying to get away. I squeezed myself into the smallest shape I could, breathing in the terrible, bottom-of-the-callbox stink, with my arms over my head, waiting for the door to open. Finally the hammering stopped and I could hear voices.

'Janie?'

I lifted my head. Alison, Linda and Evie were standing one on each side looking in, blinking their bewilderment, lashes heavy with bright blue mascara and open mouths greasy with peachy lipgloss.

I rose unsteadily to my feet and caught the swinging receiver, trying to mime laughing it off.

'That was my friends tapping on the window of the phone box,' I hissed down the line, 'and I jumped as if I'd been shot. Also, I think I might have – just slightly but slightly is bad enough – peed myself. So I'm not joking here. Tell me something!'

I shouldered open the door and gave Alison, Linda and Evie an attempt at an innocent smile.

'Hi!'

They looked at me with the soulful expressions of people loving every minute of someone else's misfortune and trying to hide the fact.

'Has your phone been cut off?'

'Cos we heard your dad lost his job.'

'And your mum's started fostering, hasn't she?'

'Is that why you haven't been round?'

'Did you think we would be funny about it?'

'Because we won't. You're a pal.'

'Anything we can do to help, just ask.'

'D'you want to look through my clothes and see if there's anything that fits you?' This was from Evie, who was wearing a glazed-cotton flying suit in cherry red. School policy was that we didn't have to wear uniform in fifth year, but this flying suit would have Mr Meldrum dictating exceptions and amendments before the first bell went.

'And I can do your hair if you can't afford a salon,' said Linda, who had swept up and made coffee in a posh hairdresser's for a month in the holidays and now thought she was Vidal Sassoon.

'And you can come round and stay at mine whenever you want to get away from them,' said Alison. 'On the inflatable bed, only we've lost the foot pump so you need to tell me the night before and my dad'll take it to the garage.'

'Nobody's fostering anyone,' I said. 'Danny's been staying since his mum died.'

'Danny Conway?' said Alison and Linda in chorus, with their lips giving little fish-hook curls at the sound of his name.

'Yes, Danny Conway,' I said. 'And I'm sure he would want to say thanks for the cards and flowers.'

'We didn't send any cards and flowers,' said Evie.

'I know,' I said. 'But I'm sure he would have wanted to say thanks if you had, though. Especially you, Evelynne. After what he did for you at the end of term. But I see you've got a very short memory, or you wouldn't be wearing something that's so hard to get out of in a hurry. And Linda, I want my hair like this – it's a razored bob – and if I didn't I wouldn't come to the only teenager in the world with a shampoo and set to get a restyle.'

'It's a root perm,' said Linda.

'Well, it looks like a shampoo and set,' I said.

'God, Janie,' said Alison. 'We're only trying to help. What's wrong with you?'

'Nothing,' I said. It was true. I suddenly felt a lot better. The mark of a true bitch. They were scowling at me. 'Sorry,' I said. 'It has been hard. With my dad, and helping Danny and everything.'

'No reason to take it out on us,' said Evie.

I thought about asking them what had happened to me being a pal and them understanding and doing whatever they could, but in the end I settled on: 'I'm glad to see you all. I should have come round. I won't be so silly again.'

'Let's go up town after school,' said Linda. 'All of us together.'

'Can I bring Danny?' I said. 'He's still pretty low sometimes and the first day back won't be easy.'

They looked up at the sky and down at the ground and explored their cheeks with their tongues.

'Maybe tomorrow, eh?' said Linda, which I suppose was a start.

There was another postcard the next day. Danny dropped the envelope in front of me at the breakfast bar with a wiggle of his eyebrows. I unpeeled the little piece of Sellotape holding the flap shut and slid it out:

'Fred and Rose are covered. We're on to C. too. Tell us what you know about the massacre. We are the good guys. Don't play games. Trust us.'

'Bloody hell' I said before I could stop myself.

'Can you give any details?' said Danny. 'Is it time to tell me what's going on yet?'

'Okay, you've finally worn me down,' I said. 'I'm a time traveller. I came back from the future to save El– to do good work, and these postcards are either instructions from central control or they're a trap sent by an evil genius. I can't decide which.'

'Thanks,' said Danny. 'I'm glad we've cleared that up, then.' He twitched the newspaper towards him and opened it at the sports pages. 'Can you look into your crystal ball and tell me who you fancy at Newmarket?'

This was said lightly, but still my heart lurched. He hadn't mentioned horses once all summer, not since Derby day, and I was pretty sure he wasn't just keeping it to himself. There was no mistaking the ebullience after a win and it had been so long since I'd seen it that I had almost stopped checking. I hoped maybe he had kicked it, out of his routine, away from all the triggers. I hoped maybe with his mother gone, if it was something that was theirs together, he had kicked it for good.

'You know the ironic thing, Dan?' I said, dead serious. 'I've probably heard the name of every Grand National winner for the next fifteen years and I can't remember a single one.'

'Criminal,' said Danny.

'Except . . .' I was remembering that job in the Coopers'

first time around, the barman pumping a glass up and down under the optic, making himself a double, a triple, and grinning like a maniac. What was it he was telling me I should have put my shirt on? 'Except ... it was the name of a film too ...'

Danny grabbed the paper and started to run his finger down the lists of starters. 'Remembrance?' he said.

'Is that the name of a film?'

'Maybe I'm thinking about *Deliverance*,' he said.

'Anyway,' I reminded him, 'you're too young to gamble and there's no way my mum and dad would get involved so you've had it.'

'You're right,' he told me, nodding solemnly. 'There's no chance that there would be a bookies anywhere in the city who would be unscrupulous enough to take an underage bet. It's hopeless.'

'Be serious for a minute, Dan,' I said. 'How is it?'

'The monkey on my back?'

'Seriously.'

'Sedated,' said Danny. 'But, if I'm honest, and you know I do want to tell you everything after all you've done for me – I'd hate there to be secrets between us ...'

'Oh shut up,' I said.

'Sorry. If I'm honest, it's beginning to stir.'

But I was ready for it. Elvis was delegated to the postcard people. Clearly they were testing me, giving me proof and asking for proof in return, so I would play along. I would phone and tell them all I knew about Tiananmen Square, show them that I trusted them and that they could trust me. But I would call from a different phone box every time, just in case anyone else was listening.

Ludo could wait, my father was ticking over nicely but, although my mother looked happier than I had ever seen her, it was wifely happiness and so it didn't count. I still had a job to do to get her what she wanted for herself. Which summer vacation had I worked in the Coopers'? Some people can begin their anecdotes by telling you it was the spring of '67 when their mother took ill or it was the week before Christmas ten years past when the tree fell on the house, but I've never had the knack, even before the big reshuffle that ended my chances for good. Every year I have to add my own age to the age my mother was when she had me to know how old she'll be on her birthday, and although I knew that I got my hamster for Christmas (Brandy? Bauble? Blitzen?) I couldn't remember whether it was the Christmas just past and so he was good for a year or two yet, or whether it had already *been* a year or two and so I should be bracing myself for the day I would reach into his nest and feel him rock stiffly on his cold little haunches instead of uncurling into my palm.

So which summer vacation had I worked at the Coopers'? What momentous events happened that summer which could help me pin it down? I remembered being picked up outside to go to a concert, the manager grumbling even though it was the first extra night off I had had. Ludo was in the back seat of the car and those friends of his – Vicky and Matt – were in the front and it was at Coasters and it was . . . Nick Cave. Bingo. Now all I had to do was keep an eye on the papers come the mid-eighties and watch for Nick Cave coming to Coasters. But what if the tour wasn't advertised until after the Grand National? I froze. Of course, the tour wasn't advertised until after the National. The Grand National was in the spring. So if the barman in The Coopers' was lording it over me in the middle of the summer vacation, it must have been the Derby.

Okay, that was close, but okay. It was the Derby. But what if Nick Cave came to Coasters every year? Some people can do it with clothes, but I only remember what I wore on first dates – I'll never forget the black dress and granny boots I bought to go to Shona Ward's party in first year, when I looked over and saw a boy drinking Jim Beam from the bottle and watching me – and by the time of the Nick Cave concert there were no first dates ever again.

So maybe my best bet was to try to remember the name of the damn horse. It was the name of a film. A boy's film, I thought, otherwise I would probably remember it more clearly. Fight Club? Lock, Stock and Some Barrels? Ocean's Eleven? Ocean's Eleven sounded like a racehorse. Pulp Fiction? Natural Born Killer? I could hear the barman's voice saying all of them.

I was getting nowhere. But, I told myself, I had ages to work on it. Typical for me to be obsessing about the one thing on my mind that wouldn't matter for years yet and wouldn't matter at all if Tesco and IBM worked out. Which they would, because how could they not? I didn't know for sure; Danny never showed me the statements, never even brought them round from his house. I certainly never mentioned them. The memory was too raw, that memory of him sitting in the long grass at the back of the shed asking me if I thought he had killed his mother, telling me it was those share orders that took all the careful timing.

God, what was wrong with me? Never mind the horse, and never mind my mother. I was supposed to be concentrating on Danny and his stirring monkey. Textbook grief, as any psychology graduate will tell you, shows up as a loss of interest in life and in Danny's case that meant a loss of interest in gambling. Now he was getting over his mother and it was coming back.

Well, I certainly wasn't going to stand by and watch him end up where she had, with horses coming on for the drink. Grey-faced and brown-fingered from chain-smoking in the bookies and living in a hostel counting the races until next giro day. But what could I do about it? I didn't know anything about addiction, not even anything modern and new that I could bring to Danny years ahead of its time. All I knew was the bits of AA you pick up from the movies – surrendering to a higher power and all that – and it had always struck me as twaddle. I'm not saying you can't be addicted. Heroin, sure. Barbiturates, yup. Coffee, absolutely: I could still remember the pounding headache of a holiday in rural India without a coffee bean in sight for a fortnight. But still, so what? I didn't get straight on the plane and come home early. I didn't throw myself on the embassy steps in Delhi screaming for an espresso. I put up with the headache and it went away and when we touched down again in Manchester airport I knew if I stayed off it the headache would never come back again. But it was coffee, for God's sake, not crack cocaine, and I didn't want to turn into one of those women who are always double-checking that it's decaff or fussing after peppermint tea, so when we landed I went straight to Starbucks and buzzed all the way home on the train.

Chapter 12

20 December 1981

Christmastime. My mother was the size of Brazil, Danny was still in the spare room, my father was wearing workboots every day because the studios at the art college were so cold that the boots were the only way he could get enough pairs of socks on. And – oh yes – I was still here.

I had phoned Hull from every phone box in a three-mile radius of home and had told them everything I knew about everything I could think of: the Rainbow Warrior, *The Satanic Verses,* Dunblane, Hillsborough. I told them that Mandela, McCarthy and Keenan would all get out, that Clinton should be told to keep his zip shut. I told them, of course, about September the eleventh. And after every phone call, the postcard came, in its little brown envelope, with its little piece of Sellotape. 'Thank you,' was the basic message, and 'We already know.' Eventually, when I had run out of disasters and hadn't called for a while, a postcard came which said, 'Anything else?' and I rang them back and said 'No.' Literally, I mean. I dialled the number, put in 10p, listened to the message, said 'No,' and hung up again. Another postcard arrived the next day. 'What about the tank?'

I sat on this one for a while. Tank? Was the stuff in Chernobyl kept in a tank? It was a reactor that went wrong, but a reactor was something that did something – like an engine, right? – and engines had tanks. That didn't make any sense. So what tank? I dialled the number. 'What tank?' I said. To which the answer came, neatly typed: 'We'll be in touch. Trust us.'

They hadn't 'been in touch' though, by the time we were

putting up the tree. My parents still had the funky glass baubles, caved in on one side and painted in lurid colours, which would very soon be replaced by fake Dickensian balls with red bows on top and fairy lights like strings of carriage lamps. Except maybe they wouldn't now. It had started with the painting hanging in the living room, slightly squint on Danny's banged-in nail. Next, the dining table was moved up to the front window so that my father had good light for sketching, and my mother started leaving the ironing board set up in the dining-room end so that she wouldn't have to manhandle it out of the cupboard with so little arm sticking out beyond her stomach. And then one day she came home from a shopping trip and showed me the baby clothes she had got in Oxfam – a red and blue striped jersey with little buttons shaped like lions' heads on the shoulder and a pair of denim dungarees – and I hadn't been able to help staring at her. Oxfam? Babies not in pastels? Sometimes I thought I had done no better a job of paying attention this time than last: what was happening to my parents?

'Does it bother you?' I said to my mother. 'Second-hand baby clothes?'

She laughed and ruffled my hair. 'Not at all,' she said. 'It's honest. It's who we are. Your father's a penniless art student. It's what I always thought—' She stopped herself, but I knew what she meant. This was what she was signing up for when she married him, before he failed the remedial test and Grandpa pulled the plug on him, and she was happy to be here, even twenty years late.

So maybe they would keep their Festival of Britain Christmas baubles after all. Maybe they would stand in front of the tree with their arms folded like Dr Pitcairn and nod approvingly at the classic design and the slightly ironic kitsch. Still, I thought I should make sure and enthuse anyway.

'I love this tree stuff, Mum,' I said. 'Promise you won't chuck it out and go all modern. Mum?'

She was sitting on the floor with her legs stuck out to the sides, resting the fairy lights on the top of the bump while she tried to untangle them, but she had stopped moving and was staring into space.

'Mum?'

She turned slowly and gazed towards me but not quite at me, then after a minute she came back to herself.

'I don't want to worry you,' she said, 'but I think I might just have had a contraction.'

'A real one?' I had been reading up and I knew all about what Danny called the Hinge and Bracket pains.

'Hard to say,' she said. 'I can't really remember. Tell you what though, I'm going to have a couple of rounds of sandwiches in case it is. That's one thing I do remember: even if it takes for ever they never give you anything to eat.'

My father, Danny and I sat in a tense row on the other side of the breakfast bar watching her eat two roast beef and mustard sandwiches and drink a pint of milk. She stopped twice to puff and pant, and both times she got that faraway look in her eyes like a drunk trying to use a cash machine. When she finished, she wiped her lips on a napkin and smiled at us.

'I think I was just hungry,' she said. 'Or maybe it was wind.'

So of course it was no surprise at all to find ourselves careering through the streets an hour and a half later in the Maxi, bound for Simpson's Memorial Maternity Wing, my father gripping the steering wheel so hard that the whole car quivered, Danny beside him, saying: 'Careful, Jock, slow down, it's icy' and: 'For God's sake, Jock, speed up, she's dying,' and my mother in the back with me, bellowing and thrashing her head back and forward, pistoning her legs into the back of Danny's seat and crushing my knuckles so that I gasped almost as much as she did. Then she would stop, suddenly, like a badly placed break taking us from *Apocalypse Now* to an Oxo advert, and say: 'Isn't it exciting! But there's really no need for you two to be here. It could be all night, and we'd ring you straight away.'

'Okay,' I would agree. 'We'll just wait till you're settled and get a taxi back.' Then I would catch my father's wild eye in the rear-view mirror and smile to reassure him that we weren't going anywhere.

The nurses wouldn't even let Danny and me see her onto the ward, but rebuffed us at the desk and told us where the canteen was. My father had the look of a man with the waters closing over his head as the flap doors drew together, but my mother waved from her wheelchair and I gave her the thumbs up.

It was a brisk night at the Infirmary. The last Monday before Christmas, it would be a day or two yet before the office parties really flooded the emergency wards, but the sudden sharp frost had tipped a few people over, even sober, and so the canteen was dotted with the slightly dishevelled and sheepish in new plaster and slings, restoring themselves with cups of tea and waiting for their lifts home. Danny and I slid into a booth and stared at each other.

'Are you okay?' I asked him. I hadn't forgotten that Danny was back in the hospital where his mother had died

He nodded and smiled.

'I'm sorry about your mum,' I said.

'Let's just think about your mum tonight, Janie,' he said. Then he grinned.

'And the baby. I'm going to make it call me Uncle Danny. But you know, I've never seen a newborn baby in real life. And I'm worried I'll offend your mum, cos they're really ugly, and you've got to go right up close and say how beautiful they are, without gagging.'

'Let's practise,' I said, laughing. Danny took the squeezy bottle of ketchup and drew a face on an empty plate: crossed eyes, and a leering mouth with one tooth sticking up from the bottom gum.

'It won't have teeth,' I said. 'Otherwise that's pretty close.'

He leaned over the plate and sighed. 'Awww!' he said. 'What a lovely baby! What an absolute— No! I can't do it. It's hideous. Take it away before I puke.'

'See?' I said. 'You'll be fine. Only don't call it "it".'

176

I wiped the plate with my napkin and was taking the whole revolting mess to the bin when my father appeared and moved swiftly towards me. He looked stunned, pale and blinking.

'That was quick!' I said. 'What is it? How are they?'

'It's not going very well,' said my father, trying to talk calmly for Danny and me, I think, but shaking. 'They're going to do a Caesarean section. It's nothing to worry about, shush now, shush now.' He pulled me towards him, and I could smell a rank smell of sweat, a smell I had never smelt on my father before. 'The cord's not where it should be or something and the baby's getting distressed, so it's best all round if they go straight in.'

'Can you stay with her?' I said. 'Is she in already? Is she on her own?'

'They're knocking her out,' said my father. 'I'm not allowed in. But I'm going back over to wait right outside and as soon as it's done I'll come back and tell you. Danny: take care of Janie for me. I've got to go.'

I've seen tricksy film effects where all of a sudden everything slides out of focus except for our hero standing in the middle of it, sharp and panting, or where the sounds drop to a muffle and we hear only his breath and a thump suggesting his heartbeat. All true, I found out, not actually tricksy at all. By the time the rest of the canteen around me came back to life and colour and my ears once again let in the clunk of the thick china and the distant drone of someone out in the corridor polishing the floor, I was back in the booth with Danny's arm around me and his other hand holding both of mine, three hands clenched together in a sweating lump.

'This can't be happening,' I said. It couldn't be happening. Not my mother, as well as Danny's mother and those poor princes. I couldn't, couldn't, have done this. Not my mother.

'It isn't happening,' said Danny. 'Nothing bad is happening.'

'Placenta praevia,' I said. 'That's what it means when the cord's in the wrong place. That's why it's early and why she was in such pain. It's not nothing. Even now – I mean even in years' and years' time – I mean, it's just not nothing.'

'The baby's probably just a bit tangled up,' said Danny. 'That happens. I saw it in the book.' I felt the heat of his blush, but I knew he had read all the books and I could guess why. He was sixteen after all. And a boy.

'My dad would have said that, though, wouldn't he? He would have said the cord's wrapped round the baby. But he said the cord's in the wrong place. It's blocking the way out. Placenta praevia. She might die.'

'If he had meant the placenta, he would have said the placenta, Janie,' Danny said, murmuring into my hair as he rocked me gently back and forward.

'If anything happens to her . . .' I said.

'Nothing will.'

If anything happened to her I would have killed my mother and then I would be where Danny was now and that was my fault too and when he went through it I stood over him and nagged him and yet here he was, rocking me and shushing me. I struggled away from him, fought with my elbows to get out of his arms.

'Don't touch me,' I said, feeling a cold slab of guilt and grief low in my belly.

'Sorry,' said Danny, red and looking down. 'I was only trying to comfort you.'

'No!' I said, and put my head in my hands. 'I didn't mean it like that. I mean, because I should be helping you. If you ever need to talk about your mother . . . Why don't you ever talk about her?'

'You're unbelievable,' said Danny, gently. 'That started out like an offer of help, but it turned into another nag by the end of the sentence. You crack me up.'

'I'm sor—'

'It's not that I don't miss her,' he said suddenly, cutting through me. 'But whenever I'm round at your house – which is basically all the time – it's as if she's round at my house, sleeping or watching *Crossroads*. And when I am round at my house, getting the post or checking up, it's as if she's in the Royal Ed again and I'm just taking care of the place till she's back.'

'You mean, it hasn't hit you yet?' I knew enough to know that this wasn't good, six months later.

'Not exactly,' said Danny. 'It's more like she was gone anyway, you know. She was long gone. I've been missing her for years.'

I couldn't look at him and I couldn't bear to have him look at me, so I put my head down on my arms and stayed there, letting fear and shame consume me. After a while Danny started stroking my head.

'Here's your dad,' he said at last. I think I had been drifting off to sleep. Certainly the room took a sickly lurch when I lifted my head. I stood up, catching the fronts of my thighs against the edge of the table, but my father slid in opposite us, so I sank down again and took his hands.

'Mum's fine,' he said. 'She's fine. She's going to be fine. And the baby ... it's a boy. And the cord didn't choke him. He survived. He's going to survive.' His face was a greyish yellow and his breath was sour.

'What is it, Dad?' I said.

'There's something wrong with him,' he said. 'He's a ... you know. He's got that ...'

'What?' I said. 'D'you mean Down's Syndrome?' My father's lip wobbled as he nodded but he didn't cry.

'Your mum's still sleeping,' he said. 'She doesn't even know. I'll have to tell her when she wakes up.'

'Can we see him?' I asked.

I didn't know what time it was but the hospital was deserted, the stark corridors ringing empty, the lights low in the silent wards. As we crossed between the main block and the maternity wing, the cold struck high and thin and our feet crushed tiny shards of frost with every step. Near the nursery, though, the place came back to life. Two babies were crying; we could see their legs and arms waving through the clear sides of the cots, and a burly nurse in a plastic apron was threading between them, swishing her rump this way and that to squeeze into the gaps and keeping up a light accompaniment of good-natured shushing and tutting as she passed.

When she saw us, she cleared her throat and assumed a serious face.

'Are they family?' she said to my father.

'Ah, yes,' he said. 'My daughter and my son. In-law.' She appraised Danny and me for a frowning moment, and then turned away and walked through a doorway. 'Step-son, I meant,' said my father quietly. 'They won't let you in unless I say something.' Danny patted his arm and led the way after the nurse.

There was only one cot in here. It seemed to be a side-room for preparing bottles but there was room for just one cot by the door. In it was a lozenge of tightly bundled white blanket. My father stayed in the doorway, but Danny and I advanced almost on tiptoe. The burly nurse stood on the other side looking down without expression. The shawl was pulled right up over his head, and his face was the size of my palm. He looked very smooth, fast asleep, the wide shallow sweep of his eyelashes curling off his cheeks. His mouth was pursed, drawn down with two haughty lines on either side. He looked like a carving of an Aboriginal god. Except pink.

'He's beautiful,' said Danny at my side. 'I didn't think he'd be beautiful. I thought new babies were all squashed.'

'Well, he's a C-section,' said the nurse, looking at Danny and frowning. 'They are very smooth. Even this one.'

'Can I pick him up?' I said, not sure who I was asking.

'If you want to,' said the nurse, with just the faintest odd emphasis.

I wriggled my fingers in under the shawl and lifted him up against my shoulder, then turned towards my father.

'I'll tell her, if you like, Dad,' I said. 'When she wakes up. I think I'm less stunned than you. Or you tell her the good news and I'll tell her the rest.'

'What good news?' said my father. The tears had started at last and he let them fall and make dark splashes on his anorak.

'That she's got a son and he's beautiful and he's healthy. And then I'll come in and tell her he's going to be even more trouble than me.'

'You've decided you're taking him home, then?' said the nurse. 'Shouldn't you wait and see?' Danny was frowning at her. I took a long moment to get her drift. I thought she meant taking him home tonight, before my mother got out, and I was going to say that of course he would be staying with her; she had planned to feed him herself, and anyway it was freezing outside. My father looked between the three of us, tears still splashing, the dark splotches on his anorak beginning to join up to make stains.

'Is that why he's in here with the kettle instead of out there?' said Danny at last. The nurse bristled.

'It's best,' she said. 'The other babies . . .'

'Jesus H. Christ,' said Danny, grabbing the cot and starting to wheel it out into the nursery. 'What about *this* baby? He'll wake up and look around and spend the rest of his life thinking he's a tin of milk powder.'

'He's not a gosling, Dan,' I said, starting to laugh and making the baby stir against my shoulder.

'I'm only trying to be kind,' said the nurse. 'It's sometimes even harder for mum and dad when they see them side-by-side with perfect babies. I've seen it a mill—'

'Nobody's perfect,' said my father suddenly.

'Dead right,' said Danny. 'You, for instance,' he turned to the nurse, 'are fat. And nobody tells you to go and stand in a cupboard if there's thin people around, do they?'

When my mother came slowly awake, I was on one side of her holding her hand and my father was on the other, with the baby in his lap. They had been staring at each other, father and son, for twenty minutes. Danny was perched on the foot of the bed and he was the first to see movement.

'Here she comes,' he said.

My mother groaned and said, 'Baby', in a thick voice.

'Give us ten minutes,' said my father, bending over and

laying the bundle beside her on the pillow. We went back outside into the crystal cold night again and looked up at the stars.

'You were a pig to that nurse,' I said.

'Pff!' said Danny. 'Do you think there's a chance they won't take him home?'

'No. I'd give you a hundred to one.'

'Janie!' he said, his eyes round with shock. 'Are you seriously suggesting a bet?'

'Of course not, you bampot,' I told him. 'It's just an expression. But I'm glad to see you were freaked.'

When we went back, my mother had the same look on her face that my father had had in the canteen, and he had turned doleful again, telling her. She gave a dry sob when she saw me, and held me fiercely in the crook of her elbow, cheek to cheek, when I bent over the bed.

'I know, I know,' I said. 'It's so sad. It's not what we thought. But it's going to be okay.'

'There's no cure,' said my mother.

'I know,' I said. 'But it's going to be okay.'

My father was wiping his eyes and sniffing, trying to gather himself together.

'These nurses don't know anything,' I went on.

'Fascists,' said Danny.

'But we've done masses on it at school.' I tried to ignore Danny shifting beside me. I had shared a student flat with a girl who volunteered and I knew about this. 'He's going to be fine.'

'No, he's not,' said my mother.

'He'll walk and talk and read and write . . .'

'Janie!' said my father. 'Don't. I know you mean well, but—'

'Honestly,' I said. 'They've totally changed what they think about it, Mum. We've done all this stuff on it. We just need to start early, try really hard to get him going and keep him going. The wee soul won't have a minute to call his own. He'll go to school and college and—'

'Janie, please,' said my father, his voice cracking.

'He could be an artist,' I said. 'Just like his dad. He could get his own house and get married. He might not have children of his own, but I'll have loads.'

'You're a good girl,' said my mother.

'For God's sake,' said my father.

'I mean it, Mum. I've read about it.'

'Me too,' said my mother. 'It was in the *Woman's World*. It all sounds so tiring.' Her eyes closed.

'Well, you don't need to start tonight,' I said, brushing her hair back.

'I'm supposed to go to work,' she said softly. 'And . . .'

'*I'll* work,' I said.

'You're going to college,' said my father.

'It's different now,' I said. 'And he's as much my responsibility as he is yours. As far as I'm concerned. He's a full-time job, Dad. At least if we treat him like a full-time job the sky's the limit. But if you just plonk him in front of the telly, he'll turn to mush.'

'You're going to college,' said my father again.

'And so are you,' I said. 'And so is he when the time comes.'

I suddenly thought of something and turned to Danny. I flashed my eyes at him, but he didn't understand. 'Tesco,' I said.

'No way,' said my father. 'You're not taking some dead-end job.'

'Or IBM,' I said to Danny. 'Dad, I'll explain later, but there is a way we can manage this. Isn't there? Danny?'

'Tonight's no time to discuss it,' said Danny suddenly, which was true. 'Only . . . Jock, have you got a mortgage?'

'No,' said my father.

'So you can sell your house and move into mine,' said Danny. 'And Moira can look after the nipper, you and Janie and me can all go to school and you can live off the interest . . . think about it. Big bay windows facing north. Think it over.'

My father's eyes were crossing with tiredness and talk.

'You're right,' I said. 'Tonight's no time for this. We need some sleep. All five of us.'

I looked again at the baby. His head had flopped sideways into my father's elbow and his crumpled little hand was hanging out of his shawl, his arm waving just slightly as he breathed in and out.

'What are you going to call him?' I said. 'Have you decided?'

'Well,' said my father looking down at him and tucking his hand back inside the shawl. 'We did have two names all ready. For a girl or a boy, but ... maybe we should rethink.'

'Oh, Dad!' I said. 'Don't give him a special cutesy baby name, just because he's Down's. I hate that. Don't call him Benjy or Tommy. God, I used to have a hamster called Benjy. What was the boy's name you picked?'

'Lawrence,' said my father, still looking down at him.

'Perfect,' said Danny. 'Dignified but approachable. Lawrence.'

My mother stirred and gave me a sleepy look. 'What do you mean you *used* to have a hamster called Benjy?' she said. 'What's happened to him?'

Hallelujah! Quite a night.

Chapter 13

1 April 1984

The camera panned along the front row of men, bunching and swelling with their uniformed arms linked, as the crowd behind them surged forward. Their faces were twisted and slick with sweat, lips drawn into snarls. I lay slumped on the couch with my Dr Martens on the coffee table, listless, half-watching them, half-looking through the sports pages for the name of the horse.

The door opened and my mother edged into the room with a lunch tray, Danny right behind her holding it open.

'Don't let him watch those miners, Janie,' said my mother. 'Turn it off!'

'Lolly do it,' shouted Lawrence. He had been standing, mesmerized, just in front of the television but he burst into action at the chance to twiddle the knobs without getting scolded.

'Cheers, Lollipop,' I said.

Danny groaned. 'God Almighty,' he said. 'You were the one who put the ban on Benjy and now you call him Lollipop? Give the man some respect.'

'But he is,' I said, stretching out my hands and grabbing Lawrence's. 'You're my boy...'

'Lollipop,' said Lawrence, twisting and jiving like the Duracell bunny, with his nappy rustling.

'You make my heart go...'

'Diddy-up,' said Lawrence.

Danny rolled his eyes and left the room. We sang it right through three and a half times and I would have carried on, but Lawrence got bored and went to find his bike.

'Don't let him watch the news,' said my mother again mildly when he was gone. 'They don't think twice what they show these days.'

'You ain't seen nothing yet,' I told her.

'They had Africans on the other night – there's a famine – and it broke his heart. He kept saying, 'What wrong that man? What wrong that baby?' and what was I supposed to tell him?'

'You sound tired, Mum,' I said. I hadn't seen much of her this spring. I was still living there to save money on accommodation fees, but I left in the morning when she was busy with Lawrence and by the time the university library shut at night and I cycled back, she was usually flat out. Taking a good look now, I was surprised to see the purple smudges under her eyes and the downward pull of her mouth. 'You look tired too. You look worse than your portrait.'

This was an old joke. The famous picture of my mother pregnant in the bath, which my father had worked on day after day for all the months leading up to Lawrence, which now hung in pride of place opposite the fireplace in the big sitting room where Danny's mother had had her faded reproduction of the Ascension, was a huge splurge of purple and black bulges, unexpected details here and there. As Danny had said when he saw it: 'You've got windows, Moira.'

'I love it,' my mother had said, loyally.

'Oh, I love it,' I had assured her. 'But did you really need to lie in the bath?'

She looked up at it now, hanging behind her, and grinned. 'I am tired,' she said. 'I'm exhausted. And worried.'

'About Lawrence?' I said, sitting up straight and putting my feet down with a thump. 'What happened at his assessment?'

'Nothing. He's fine,' said my mother. 'In the ninetieth percentile again. But I'm worried about ... Well, money, if I'm honest. And I'm not having any luck with the schools.'

I bowed my head. It had been my idea to approach the local primary schools. It was commonplace by the end of the century and, I had reasoned, it must have started somewhere, sometime, so why not here and now? My master plan had been to ask them not to take him straight into primary one, but to get him into the nursery class where nobody would be so worried about it, and then by the time real school came round, they'd be so used to him they wouldn't give it a thought. Go in with your head up and the expectation that they're going to say yes, I had told my parents, and I bet you'll be surprised. But it hadn't worked. It wasn't working.

'Did you take a copy of the Act?' I said.

My mother shook her head. 'There's no point putting their backs up,' she told me.

'The 1981 Education Act clearly states that integration is the goal,' I said as though she didn't know. 'And they have a duty to provide appropriate—'

'Yes,' said my mother. 'Appropriate. I could scream when I hear that word. That and "efficient use of resources". The consensus seems to be that the most appropriate place for him, the most efficient use of resources, is Gray Park.'

We didn't look at each other. Gray Park. There was a clue in the name. We had visited Gray Park when they offered Lawrence a place at the playgroup. Flotsam Academy, Danny had called it, after the way the children lay about on mats on the floor, like little seals washed up on a beach. My mother had put her hand over her nose at the smell in the lunch room.

'Yes, it gets a bit ripe,' the head teacher had brayed, with dreadful heartiness. 'Between the ones who can't keep it down and the ones who can't keep it in at the other end, but we change them all before we send them home.'

'Did you ask about the Steiner school?'

'It's three hundred and fifty pounds a term,' said my mother. 'And that's with no extras at all. And no chance of a grant. That wouldn't be an efficient use of resources. Not when Gray Park is right there and it's so appropriate.'

'There might be a way we can manage it,' I said. I was thinking about the shares again. We rarely spoke about them, Danny and me. Any time I edged the conversation near them he seemed to disappear from behind his eyes and I couldn't go on.

'Well, if we're letting ourselves dream,' said my mother. 'There's a Montessori school in the Borders . . .'

'What are they all about?'

'Kind of like Steiner but even more . . .' She laughed and came to sit next to me on the couch. 'Not so into the phases of the moon, though, I don't think. Anyway, there's still at least one more to try, so don't you worry about it. And now, it's the Easter holidays, and I'm expecting tip-top big sistering in the next four weeks. I'm going to sleep for ten hours a night until the start of next term. Beginning tonight.'

'Sure thing,' I said. 'And when Dad gets finished' – even though it was the holiday now my father was still working on his 'big piece' for the end of third year exam. It was Lawrence, predictably since he rarely painted anyone else now – 'why don't you go away for a weekend? We'll take care of Lawrence, Danny and me . . . but can it all start tomorrow? I'm going to a party tonight.'

I certainly was. Tonight was the night. It had come around at last. Tonight, on Sunday the 1ˢᵗ of April 1984, Shona Ward was having a party.

'Money's too tight for a weekend,' said my mother. 'I keep waking up in the middle of the night, Janie. I think, we can't stay here for ever. Then I think, if we can just keep managing until Lawrence is at school, then I can go back to work, unless he does end up in Gray Park because they're not really full time.'

'Would it make more sense for me to work the Easter holiday?' I said. 'I'd happily babysit and let you rest, but I'm sure I could get a job, barmaiding or waitressing or whatever. Just say whether you're more skint than knackered or more knackered than skint.'

I had always worked the Easter holiday last time, but I couldn't remember how I got it past my mother, because this time around she would have none of it. It had been the same the year before.

'No, no, no, no, no,' she said. 'You've got too much studying to do. No way.'

I suppose last time I just ignored her, or maybe last time she had assumed it was none of her business and said nothing, or cared less. Whatever, this time I was certainly wasting my time.

'And don't say knackered,' she said. 'And don't tell me he can't hear you, because for one thing unless you practise decent language when he isn't here it'll slip out when he is, and for another it's not only for Lawrence. We never used to have language like that in our house.'

'It's that Conway boy,' I said. 'He's a bad influence.'

'Yes,' said my mother. 'He's a bugger.'

It was only lunchtime and the party didn't start until ten. Besides, I was going to try hard not to get there before midnight, fashionably late, make an entrance, but already I thought I might not be able to wait that long and I had deliberately left everything – nails, toenails, Immac, eyebrows, hair, ironing – in the hope that it would all take much longer than I expected and I wouldn't have time to sit on my bed making rings under the arms of my dress.

I was going to wear a second-hand, black lace frock from a shop in Stockbridge, a mourning dress from the thirties the assistant had said. Ludo and I had seen it in the window on our second date and he had said to me that I should buy it, that I'd look great in it, but when I had suggested going in to try it on, he had puffed out his cheeks and said he didn't do shopping, and when I went back on my own it was gone.

This time, fingers crossed that it would be there, I had taken the bus with Lawrence and Danny, Lawrence because he helped with the haggling (each toothy grin took a pound off the price at the Crichton Street Sunday market and once when he had hugged a junk shop owner round the knees and told her he loved her she had given us free delivery on a set of bunk beds). Danny came to pin Lawrence's arms to his sides when he clapped eyes on all the feather boas and fox furs.

The dress fitted me. A bit tighter than it would have been worn in the thirties, probably, but it was beautiful, and if only the assistant would ask Lawrence his name, and give him a chance to say, 'Lolly, please ta meetcha' the way he did, she might knock enough off for me to get some extra lace for my hair.

'Tah-dah!' I said, sweeping open the curtain and twirling in front of them.

Lawrence clapped, and Danny nodded appraisingly with his mouth drawn down into a connoisseur's pout.

'Not bad, not bad,' he said. 'Bit funereal, maybe? How about this one?'

He held out what looked like basically the same dress, twenties or thirties anyway, in ballet-slipper pink with coffee lace and cream ribbon.

'It's a bit Daisy Fay,' I said. 'I'll try it on, though.' I would try it on, but I was going to buy the black one.

'Daisy Faisy,' said Lawrence, as I shut the curtain.

This dress, when I slipped it over my head and let it drop, was just quite unbelievably beautiful. It was longer and looser than the black one and made me look languid and . . . rich. I opened the curtain again and stood there, shyly.

'Fairy Dobmodder!' said Lawrence. 'Cinderella. Snow White an sendorf!'

'God almighty, Lawrence,' said Danny. 'Somebody needs to get you a Thomas the Tank Engine book fast.' He was staring at me.

'Dalmighty!' said Lawrence. 'Dalmighty!'

'Oh, nice one, Dan,' I said. 'Mum's going to love that.' I waited for him to say something about the dress.

'You look great,' he came up with at last. 'I'd go for that one if I was you.'

I looked at myself again in the spotted mirror at the back of the cubicle, twisted around and looked at the rear view.

'Perfect fit,' said the assistant.

'Still,' I said, 'I think I'll go with the black. More practical. More . . .'

'Morticia Adams,' said Danny. 'Suit yourself.'

As I struggled back into my jeans, I wondered. Ludo hadn't

seen the pink one; it hadn't been in the window. But I always wore black and so did Ludo, so did everyone, except Danny. Christ, even my father was in black cords and anorak now instead of navy-blue, and black comfortable shoes from Clarks instead of beige. Only Danny, always on his way between football and rowing and fencing, still stuck to the sparkling white T-shirts and crisp blue jeans. And they were sparkling. My mother's housekeeping had never been up to much when it came to dust and cobwebs and it had taken a further nosedive since Lawrence, but she had always prided herself on her laundry and she still, as the phrase had it, 'put out a lovely washing'. So even if Danny did look like one of the jocks from *Grease*, it was good to have seen the back of his bobbly grey jerseys and murky vests.

On the day of the party, I looked at the dress on its padded hanger hooked over the bunk-bed ladder and felt a prickle of heat, almost of pain. At a stretch you could call it 'a stirring in the loins' but actually it felt more like the sudden twinge you get in your bladder when you see someone you love slice their finger open with a bread knife. My mother and I suffer badly from this; when Lawrence, two years old, fell out of the back door with a fork in his hand we both, standing on the washing green, crossed our legs and doubled over with a gasp. That is what I felt when I looked at the dress. And an idea came, as clear and unexpected as if some demon had whispered it in my ear. What if I didn't go?

The demon whispered it but I didn't listen. I was going and I was taking my own bottle of Jim Beam to clink against his. I was going to tell him I loved him first, in my student bed that Sunday. I was going to make sure his boss never told him he was overconfident and undereffective. I was going to lie tangled in sheets with him all morning and let my friends eat frozen pizza for lunch. I was going to get married in a big white dress with six bridesmaids, and not take a nightie on honeymoon. I was going to have nine children and then adopt one to make an even number. And on the 4th of March 2002, I was going to buy the most expensive bottle of champagne I could find and toast him, and me, and our perfect life and never tell him why.

Wrapped in a bathrobe and with cotton balls wedged between my toes, I hitched myself onto the broad sill of the dormer window to get the best light. I was planning to wear my Docs, but you never knew, I thought, unscrewing the top of the varnish. The little brush came out of the purple bottle with a plop and I stared. It was lumpy, varnish over fluff over varnish, like a well-coated herring, and there were flakes of glitter stuck to it in gobs. (It would be years before glitter polish.)

'Lawrence!' I bellowed. 'Get up here, boy. You're in deep, deep trouble.'

'What's he done?' shouted my mother from the bottom of the stairs. I thundered out onto the landing and glared down. The upstairs in Danny's house was an afterthought, two bedrooms tucked into the roof with an open-tread staircase rising awkwardly out of the dining room for access. Danny poked his head out of the other attic door. I could see Lawrence through the treads, standing at the bottom, his beaming face turned up to me.

'He's knackered another nail varnish,' I shouted down, shaking my fist at him. He shook his fist back and giggled. 'God knows where it ended up this time.'

'No, no, no,' said my mother. 'It was for a picture. He sat at the table and did it. It nearly all went on the paper. Oh my God!' she said suddenly.

'What?' said Danny.

'Dod!' said Lawrence.

'He said you gave it to him,' said my mother. 'I asked him where he got it and he said you gave it to him.'

I came slowly down the stairs with the bottle balanced in my outstretched hand.

'Lawrence?' I said. 'Did you make a picture with this?'

'Yup,' he said.

'Where did you get it?' said my mother.

'Janie give,' he said, giggling helplessly and jumping up and down. 'Janie give me! Janie give me!'

My mother swept him up into her arms and whirled him round and round, whooping. Danny clattered down the stairs and caught his feet and together they swung him almost as high as the lampshade. My father banged open his studio door and rushed across the hallway.

'What is it?' he said, with that look he gets when he's been deep in a picture and gets hauled back to reality, like someone just lifted a rock off him in the noonday sun.

'Lawrence told a fib!' said my mother, stopping swinging at last and clutching Lawrence to her again, planting a big kiss on his mouth.

'A whopper!' said Danny. 'A corker!'

'Janie give me!' screamed Lawrence.

'Right,' said my father. 'Oh! Right! That's my boy.' He ruffled Lawrence's hair and wandered back across to his room.

'So, big party then?' said Danny as we trailed upstairs and left my mother to balance the jubilation with a bit of belated moral guidance. 'New dress and toe polish inside your boots – must be serious.'

I said nothing.

'I'm not busy tonight,' he went on, coming to lean in my doorway as I started to rummage in my top drawer for another bottle. 'At least, I've been invited to a party but it's themed and it could be nasty.'

'What's the theme?' I said, shaking the new polish and hearing the little bead rattle. I hopped back up onto the windowsill.

'Kinky Pink,' said Danny.

'Well, you can borrow anything you like of mine,' I said, waving around at my wardrobe and drawers.

'What, and bleach out the black then dye it?' said Danny. 'I don't think there's time. Easier just to come with you to yours.' Any other night we would have gone out as a pair, picked a party – probably the Kinky Pink – and demolished it together from a base in the kitchen.

'I'm not really ... it's not open house, really. It's all ...'

'Girls?' said Danny. 'Black clothes? Philosophers?'

Oh yes, I should have said. I had stuck to my guns and side-stepped the psychology degree. I'd flirted with the idea of something lucrative, law, business studies, computer science, but who was I trying to kid? Anyway, my new beatnik father with his paint-flecked hair and his anarchic way of not cutting the grass every week if he was especially busy and it wasn't that long would have been sorely disappointed in me. And besides, I didn't need lucrative: there was still Tesco et al, and the horse with the long odds in the Derby, with the name like the film, in same year as the Nick Cave concert.

So in the end I decided to use my time at university trying to learn something I actually needed to know and hadn't learned already and forgotten. Philosophy. To try to make sense of this thing. And, I had thought, a bit of physics would help too. It wasn't working, though. The physics was useless; all magnets and day length and really, really hard, and when I had asked my tutor about quantum theory because I couldn't see anything in the options timetable that even mentioned it, he had just stared at me and laughed and reminded me that I had failed the class exam at Christmas. He had a point. I was years out. But even the philosophy was proving a bit of a let-down. Half the course wasn't philosophy at all, but just an endless round of snitty little arguments about the meaning of 'and' and the meaning of 'or' that you had to solve with equations. There was one class on metaphysics where the tutor asked us how we knew there was a table in front of us and it looked hopeful at first; I imagined a group of the best and the brightest hard at work on my problem night after night in the library and not even suspicious because they'd think I was just asking it to be awkward like everyone else. But whenever I tried to steer the discussion somewhere fruitful the other five in my seminar group groaned, and at the end of the first term my tutor wrote on my feedback sheet that unless I got past my 'tedious and unproductive obsession with cyclical time' I would 'find philosophy ultimately unsatisfying'. I'm way ahead of you, mate, I thought to myself. I'm there already. Unsatisfied to the back teeth.

The silver lining to all of this might have been, of course, a sneak preview of Ludo. He was a year ahead of me, but still I thought I might see him in the corridor or in the Pear Tree. It hadn't happened, though. Not in the union, in the queue for the Cashline, in the Pear Tree garden on a Wednesday afternoon, not in front of the notice boards in the department. But perhaps that was for the best; perhaps the first look across the crowded room was how it was meant to be. And anyway, unless we met on the 1st of April 1984, then when we got married on the 1st of April 1990, it wouldn't be our anniversary. And as Ludo always said, everyone gets married on their anniversary; it's tradition.

So there was no way I was going to ruin the happiest moment of my life by having Danny standing beside me, whispering, 'Who's the gimp with the Jim Beam bottle? Bet you it's Irn Bru.'

'I'm meeting up with someone, if you must know,' I told him, carefully dipping a cotton bud into the remover and wiping around my toes where I had smudged. 'I've got a date.'

'Verry inter-resting,' said Danny in his Freud voice. 'And why do you sink you feel da reluctance to tell me ziz? Is he an ugly moron viss halitosis und a bald schpot, hmm?'

Danny was at Edinburgh with me (I had no idea where he had ended up last time without my mother to make him do his homework) taking, if you can believe it, psychology. And the Freud voice wasn't the half of what we all had to put up with. For instance, between Grandpa Jock, the art, the dyslexia, and Lawrence, he wouldn't be happy until he had my father cut up into inch-square pieces and stored in tubes. 'It's just all so interesting,' he would say, when I told him I didn't *know* what my father thought about *his* father, or about himself as a father, or about the fact that Lawrence would never *be* a father, or about whether he thought he was *Danny's* father or what he thought about Danny's father. 'I don't fucking know,' I would tell him. 'Leave me alone.'

'Sorry,' I said to him now, lobbing the cotton bud towards the bucket.

'No skin off my nose,' said Danny. 'Kinky Pink it is.'

'Can you go away, then?' I said. 'And let me get dressed?'

'Sure,' he said. 'But can I ask you a question? Why are you in such a bad mood? If you've got this hot date with the love of your life, why aren't you happy?'

I had no answer for that.

The party was heating to a simmer when I got there just after twelve. The smell of student punch was rolling down the tenement stairs and the flat was packed from the front door on in, but no one was crying on the landing yet and everyone in the queue for the only toilet looked as though they needed to pee, nothing worse.

'Janie!' a voice screeched and a hand with black nails and brass snake-bracelets turning its wrist green waved above the heads in front of me. I climbed up on the arm of a sofa which must have been trundled out of the living room to make space for dancing. Natalie, a girl in my physics class, the only other girl in my physics class, who was therefore automatically my bosom pal even though she understood everything and thought the magnets and day-length were 'ace', was standing with her arm around her boyfriend bouncing up and down on her Airwear soles and beckoning me over. I put my head down and barrelled through the crowds, stopping to kiss a boy I knew and take a swig of his wine. I was boiling hot already, and could feel my thighs sticking together in between the mesh of my fishnets.

'Garry's going to let me shave his head,' squealed Natalie when I got there. Garry nodded glassily and put his thumb up. Natalie got the urge to shave someone's head every time she drank, like other people need curry, and although her boyfriend was always there attached to one side of her, drinking silently until he slid down the wall and she took him home, she was so pretty that there was always at least one willing to let her.

'Clippers?' I said, anxiously. Sometimes there were clippers, in big flats full of boys. We were still well ahead of the ubiquitous Picard buzz-cut but lots of the boys had clippers to neaten the back of their flat-tops, and although Natty was surprisingly deft with a ordinary razor, even when quite profoundly drunk, I was always relieved to hear that there were clippers.

'Clippers are for wimps,' said Garry.

'Yeay!' said Natalie, very excited. Garry's chest swelled with pride and hopeful lust.

'I'm just going to go and em . . .' I said and struggled away from them into the crowd. Go and what? There wouldn't be any food to go and fetch. I still remember the first party I went to where there was food. It was only French bread and hummus but it made me feel depressed just the same. Made me feel old. There was no chance that there would be a buffet here. And there would be no drinks table. We kept our bottles in our pockets, and anyone fool enough to lay theirs down and glance away expecting to be able to pick it up again would have a long, dry night to think again. So there were only two reasons to battle your way away from your friends once you had found them at a party. Going to the loo – far too early for that since I had just arrived – and going on the prowl, either for someone you expected to be there or just for anyone decent you could find.

'Woo-hooo!' said Natalie, eyes glittering, reminding me for a moment of Linda from school.

'Yeah, yeah, yeah,' I said. 'I'll bring him over to meet you. Careful with the razor, eh? And remember to use soap this time.'

'Soap is for wimps,' said Garry.

He wasn't dancing in the living room – well, he wouldn't be. *Dancing*.

He hadn't been in the toilet queue, he wasn't smoking dope in the big bedroom with the guys who had brought their guitars, and he wasn't, surprisingly, standing in the kitchen. I started on the other bedrooms.

'Sorry!' I muttered, backing out of the first one after a flash of hairy thigh. 'Have a nice time.'

There were five girls sitting on top of all the coats in another bedroom, as though adrift on a raft. They were passing a bottle of brandy around in one direction and a packet of Embassy Regal around in the other and they greeted me exultantly.

'Sister!' they shouted. 'Come on, there's loads of room.'

'Everybody's welcome!'

'So long as you hate Simon!'

'And you're not Karen!'

'I *hate* Simon!' said one of them, tearfully.

'He's a pig's anus,' said another. 'Not worth crying over.'

More thighs and grunting in the next bedroom, two smooth ones and two hairy ones – probably Simon and Karen, I thought – and then I was out of rooms. I took a swig from my bottle to give me strength and went round again, paying more attention to the crush in the hallway and skirting round behind the dancers in the living room in case he was sitting against the window wall. I couldn't find him. Unless he was under the coats being crushed to a coma by the bitter sisterhood, I didn't know where he was. I had a small flip of panic at the thought of the hairy thighs, but it only lasted a minute. They weren't Ludo's thighs – not one of the six thighs I'd seen was Ludo's thigh. I had seen Ludo's legs every day, walking away along the corridor from the bedroom to go to the loo in his boxers and standing dripping on the bathmat after his shower waiting for me to hand him his towel and I've never been able to understand why dead people can't be identified even if their faces are not in the greatest shape. Not if they're married, that is. I could identify any part of Ludo that would fill a suitcase, I was sure.

I went back to the living room and scanned the heads for Shona. Chaka Khan was finished for the moment and someone had put on Tom Waits – his growly stoner stage –

so, understandably, few people were dancing. Shona Ward, though, as you would expect from a dancer die-hard enough to have dragged all her living-room furniture out into the hall, was still up on the floor swaying her hippy skirt and nodding her head, in complete agreement with Tom. I grabbed her arm.

'Shona, hi.'

'Janieee,' she said dreamily and laid her arms around my neck. She kept dancing and was leaning quite heavily, so that I had to grunt to push her back far enough to talk to.

'Where's Ludo?' I shouted, over the noise of the tape machine.

'What?' said Shona, still swaying and with her eyes half-shut.

'Where is Ludo?' I screamed. 'Ludovic. Ludovic Masterton. Where is he?'

'I don't know what you're asking me,' said Shona, opening her eyes. One look into them told me that she had managed to drag herself away from the dance floor at some point and spend some time in the room with the guitars.

'Dance with me, Janie,' she said and draped her arms around me again. I mooched about with her for a while, bewildered. Then I thought I'd better just check. Maybe she was so far gone that any question at all was beyond her.

'Where's Garry?' I said loudly into her hair. She giggled.

'He's in the kitchen. Nat's shaving his head.'

I walked back. Not only were there no taxis, but even if there had been I didn't have the fare, and besides, I needed to think. It wasn't just that he wasn't at the party, although that had knocked the wind out of me like a fist in bread dough, but more that Shona didn't seem to know him at all, and she was in his year and they had been friends since freshers' week. It might sound unlikely after all that had happened, but this was the first thing, well, the second thing, which had – third if you count Mrs Conway and fourth if you count Lawrence – but this was the only thing for a long time to really shake me, and it shook me worse than anything since the day I had arrived, because this was the whole point; this was what I was here for. Which sounds selfish, I know, and obviously I was glad to have the chance to do the Elvis thing and didn't grudge it, but *this* was what I had come back for. To do this, and do it right, and now it had gone wrong in a way I didn't understand, before I had even started.

I trudged up the hill from the main road and turned into the crescent. All the lights were out in Danny's house. Good. I couldn't face the inquisition from my parents about whether I had had a nice time and who had walked me home. As I advanced along the street, though, I saw I wasn't to get off so lightly after all. Nothing like it. Outside the gate, a hulking lump broke into two parts and revealed itself to be Danny and a girl.

'Janie,' whispered Danny in a theatrical hiss as I drew near them. 'This is Pam. Pam, this is Janie, my . . . foster sister?'

'Lodger,' I said, and took a good look at Pam. She was dressed in drainpipes and trainers, with one of those denim jackets lined with Liberty print, and she had pulled out all the stops for the party with a pink T-shirt and pink combs holding back her curls. At least, I assumed they were pink, since under the streetlamps they looked the same colour as Danny's ensemble – an outsize shirt and a pair of suit trousers held up by braces. Where had he got a pair of pink suit trousers since lunchtime on a Sunday?

'Very gallant of you to see him home, Pam,' I said. Even I could hear the drawl in my voice and even to me it sounded surly. What was wrong with me?

Pam giggled.

'I only live round the corner,' she said.

'She only lives round the corner,' said Danny.

'Not right next door?' I said and left them to it.

I was sitting at the kitchen table furiously buttering too-hot toast with too-cold butter when he finally came in and threw himself down opposite me.

'Ssh!' I said. 'You'll wake everyone up, you drunken pig.'

He lunged across the table and swiped a piece of buttered

toast. I glared at him as he folded it into his mouth in one piece. Then I blinked and glared again.

'What the hell happened?' I said. He was, as I had thought, wearing a shirt of my father's and a pair of my father's old trousers, but he looked as though he had been dipped head to toe in calamine lotion.

'Yeah,' he said, still pretty loud. 'Well, there weren't any pink clothes so your dad mixed me up some emulsion and I painted myself. I looked brilliant when I set off, but it hasn't worn well. I thought there had to be a reason people didn't paint their clothes.'

I shook my head at him. 'And you went to a party like that? What is wrong with you, Danny? You're almost twenty.'

'It didn't do me any harm,' he said. 'Pam thought it was funny. Pam came over to talk to me. And then it turns out she lives right round the corner.'

'How come we don't know her from school then?' I said. 'Is she twelve?'

Danny gave one of those drunken half-burp half-hiccups that always sound so painful and said: 'Mary Erskine's.' It had to be some kind of sacrilege to speak the name on a wave of beer-burp. I shuddered.

'Well, golly gosh,' I said. 'Mary Erskine's Ladies College, no less. I hope you didn't get pink paint all over her lovely jacket. I hope you haven't *stained* her.'

'What is wrong with you?' said Danny. 'Think about it while you make some tea.' He looked at me with a benign smile on his face for a moment and then his eyes snapped into alertness. 'Oh my God! I'm sorry. What happened?'

'Nothing happened,' I said, turning on the tap at a trickle and filling the kettle, and I couldn't keep the bewilderment out of my voice.

'Well, where is he?' said Danny. 'Did you fall out? Was he a pig to you? Because if he was I'll string him up.' Except he pronounced 'string' without the 't'.

'He wasn't there,' I said, and I knew I sounded as though I

was going to cry. I was tired and drunk and I didn't understand it.

'He stood you *up*?' said Danny. 'He had the *nerve* to stand you up? After you bought a vintage dress for him?' I was shushing him frantically. My mother and father would sleep through anything, but Lawrence woke if you even thought about him, and I was too confused to deal with Lawrence now.

'He didn't stand me up,' I said. 'He just wasn't there. It was nothing definite.'

Only my destiny, I thought. Danny was staring at me, owlishly.

'You told me it was a date,' he said.

'Yeah, well, I was wrong,' I said, knowing that I sounded exactly like someone who had been stood up.

So, fuck 'im,' said Danny. 'He's not worth it. I hate him.' He sounded like a girl on a raft of coats.

I smiled at him and gave him a quick squeeze on my way to pour the tea.

'Janie?' he said.

'Hm?'

'Pam's nice, isn't she?' I felt a spike of jealousy and hatred stab me in the gut. But it was probably the Jim Beam. I should have stuck to punch. 'Just think, she's lived right round the corner for ten years and I had to go all the way to Tollcross to meet her. She's nice. She's got a really nice smile.'

'Excellent gums,' I snapped, but he wasn't listening.

Chapter 14

2 April 1984

When I woke the next day the answer to my problem was staring me in the face: I knew exactly where Ludo would be at eight o'clock in the morning in the vacation, and it was only a number fifteen bus ride away. I hopped off at the corner of Morningside Place, breezed along the street, opened the gate with a flourish and let it crash behind me, then rang the doorbell firmly. After a moment a flurried-looking woman in a rugby shirt appeared with a half-dressed toddler on one hip.

'Yes?' she said.

I peered at her. She must be a relation or a friend of the family; she had probably been at my wedding, but I couldn't place her.

'I'm looking for Ludo,' I said. 'I was supposed to meet him last night but we missed each other.'

'Ludo?' she said, frowning. This couldn't, I told myself, couldn't possibly be his girlfriend, could it? That baby couldn't be his? Nonsense, she looked thirty if a day and he had never had a thirty-year-old girlfriend. So why was she frowning? Why shouldn't I be looking for Ludo?

'I think you've made a mistake,' she said. 'There's no Ludo here.'

I said nothing for a minute. Maybe she knew him as Vic.

'Ludovic Masterton,' I said. She didn't flicker.

'Ludo and his sister Katie and their parents Tom and Margrite Masterton,' I said. 'This is their house.' At last some light began to dawn on her features. The toddler continued to regard me coldly but its mother nodded.

'Yes, you're right, Masterton,' she said. 'I had forgotten. But we bought it – oh – three years ago? We did have their address, but . . .' she gestured behind her into the hall where instead of the polished half-moon table with the claw feet and the wilfully ugly flower arrangement, there was a jumble of coats, cycle helmets and newspapers filling the hallway and swamping the bottom of the stairs, and a Little Tykes bubble car with a half-eaten bowl of dried-up cereal on its bonnet crashed into the mahogany skirting. I turned to go.

Three years ago was when I came back. Were they already gone by then? Or if that funny little man from Hull hadn't distracted me on Diana day, would I have found him? There was no answering that. The question was, how was I going to find him now?

When I got home, Lawrence and my mother were pegging out washing. The washing line was slack and bowed down to waist height so that he could reach it and my mother was standing waiting with each vest, each sock, until he located a peg and snapped it into place. 'A springy plastic one, darling,' she was saying as I waved and went in the back door. 'Not a wooden dolly peg this time. A plastic peg for mummy's tights, remember.' Lawrence rummaged in the peg bag. No wonder she was knackered.

I went to sit in the front room to watch my father, taking him a mug of tea.

'It's looking good,' I said. He was standing in front of it with his brush up in the air like a lighter at a Queen concert, not moving. It would be a toss-up who moved first, probably, him in here waiting for inspiration or my mother out there waiting for the right kind of peg.

'Not happy with this section,' he said, slurping his tea and waving his brush hand at the top right corner. 'It's pulling the whole thing too close.' I looked hard at it, and could almost see what he meant.

'How's life with you?' he said, unexpectedly, after a while. I thought about how to answer, whether to answer.

'Confusing,' was what I settled for, in the end. My father

snuffed a sort of laugh, but half his mind was back on the picture. 'Where's Danny?' I said.

'Well, there now,' said my father, turning right round to face me for the first time. 'He dragged himself up an hour ago at last – Lawrence jumping on him did it – and took himself straight round to this Pamela's. They're going to the zoo, Mum says.'

'For God's sake.' This was out before I could help myself. 'The zoo?' And then having to think quickly before my father asked me what was wrong with the zoo – what was wrong with it? They could stroll hand-in-hand and pick flecks of pink paint off her floral-lined jacket together – I said at last: 'Well, they might have taken Lawrence. He loves the zoo.'

'Yes, so we've not to mention it,' said my father. 'They'll take him next time, but not today, not on their first date.' He waggled his eyebrows at me with innocently gossipy relish and turned back to his painting to stare some more. I left and went to sit in my room.

How? How could this have happened? How could I have just sat there and let it happen right under my nose? And where were they? There was no point going through the phone books calling every Masterton; Ludo's parents were ex-directory, always had been.

And I couldn't afford a private detective. I'm not being defeatist; I knew I couldn't. I checked.

There was one more thing to try. Hull. After all, I had never asked them for anything, unless you count answers, an explanation, a human being to lift the receiver, that kind of thing. But I had never asked them for any favours. And they had found me, so presumably they could find anyone. I called the number and took a deep breath to begin pleading after the beep at the end of the message. But there was no message, just a steady note humming down the line. I listened to it for a moment then hung up and tried again. The same sound started up, the same note, as though it had been going all the while. I tried the operator and she explained what it was. Disconnected. I explained to her how that wasn't possible. I asked her if it was a fault, if it was temporary, and she told me, patiently, no and then less patiently that there was nothing she could do to help me.

I tried to remember when I had called them last. Not since they had asked me if I knew about the tank thing. They had said to leave everything in their hands and I had agreed. But when was that? Was it possible that it was as long ago as it now seemed? I had had my mind on other things, but could it possibly be that long? They had said they would be in touch with me, and I had believed them, but they hadn't made it clear, not clear at all, that from then on until they *did* get in touch with me I was on my own. They had asked me, over and over again, to trust them. They should have told me. I said this to the operator. I pointed out to her, through tears, that they should have told me, and she, patient again, kind really, agreed.

I gave up trying to find him after that. What choice did I have? And for the first time since I had got back, I really began to feel . . . what? Depressed, maybe. Glum, at least. And lonely. That was probably the best way to describe it. I was lonely. I had friends; Natalie was a laugh and there was a boy called Milton who kept sitting beside me and had asked what I was doing in the summer because some of them were getting a house in Cork. But I had to work. I had a job lined up in the stock room in the big branch of Boot's, and I would be looking for a pub job at night too, but when I told him that, Milton only said, 'Fantastic! Come and join us in September and bring all the money.' I tried to explain that my father was a student and my mother was looking after a disabled child and we were lodging with a friend and the money was earmarked for things like coats and shoes no matter how great the Guinness was in Cork, and I could feel him drifting away as if I was trying to sell him a pension.

So much for Milton.

Danny was still hooked up with the unspeakable Pamela. She really did make me shudder. She was thin but had soft, sloping pale shoulders and mournful little low-slung tits, long feet sticking out of the bottom of her jeans. I didn't know how he could bear to touch her, but judging by the giggling and scampering noises that came across the landing from his room when they were there together, he seemed to be managing. I would turn up my tape machine, or go downstairs and find Lawrence, intending to play with him but sometimes succumbing to the urge to tell him to go and say hello to Danny. Even more annoying than that, Pamela started going with him to the track, even to the dog track. She said she thought it was fun. I kept out of it, mostly. Only one time, trying to do the right thing, I said to him that I hoped he was using a condom.

'Jesus H. Christ, Janie,' he said. 'I know she's not your favourite person. But for God's sake, you're better than that.'

'I'm not casting any aspe—'

'Oh no, of course you're not,' said Danny. 'Some of your best friends are riddled with syphilis, eh?'

'Have you ever heard of AIDS, Danny?' He shook his head, then thought harder.

'Except . . . Is this that GRID thing you were on about?'

'It's not gay related,' I said. 'I told you. I wrote to the papers and told them.'

'Yeah, I remember,' said Danny. 'Drug users, hookers, and multiple partners. And so you're worried about Pam? You are such a cow sometimes.'

After that I kept out of it all the way.

Danny and I were still pals, don't get me wrong. Pamela was far too sensible a girl to be clingy and her Queen's Guiding and dressage practice took up a lot of time, so it's not as though we never saw him. And the two of us still had breakfast together every morning. We huddled side by side in front of the racing pages, Danny looking for a sure thing and me looking for a horse with a film title for a name.

'What are you looking for?' Danny would say. 'You have no idea what any of it means.'

I was looking for a way not to take Lawrence's school money from him after all, when the time came.

'I'm just looking at the names,' I would tell him. 'It's good, clean, risk-free fun.' What are *you* looking for?' He would never answer that directly. We didn't talk about it; he would just roll his eyes at me and say 'names'.

'I like the names,' I would say. 'So what? It's amazing how many of them have names that are film titles, you know. There's even a film called *The Sure Thing*.'

'No one would ever call a horse Sure Thing,' said Danny. 'It would be like calling a baby Jesus.' Then he would shake his head at me again. 'You like the names!'

'What? Why does it bother you?'

'It's just dumb. It's so . . . dumb. It's like playing drafts with your chess set.'

Then I would lift the edge of the sports section and slide the middle pages to see what was on at Coasters.

'And that's another thing,' Danny would say. 'You look every day at what's on and you never go anywhere.'

'I'm waiting for just the right thing,' I would say. 'What harm's it doing you?'

'You sound like an old married couple,' my mother would tell us, and we would both stop with cereal spoons halfway to mouths and glare at her.

'Speaking of what's on, Danny,' she said one day. 'If she tells you there's a really great mystery play with a twist in the tail, she's lying. Remember London?'

So Danny and I were like an old married couple, me as the understanding wife who smiled upon his antics with Pamela. Almost. As for my parents, my father was in the Land of Turpentine pretty much full-time now, working for his degree show, and my mother was still the all-singing all-dancing one-woman Corporation for the Advancement of Lawrence. It was working. He was potty-trained, he could almost dress himself, except for buttons and zips – he put together some stupendous outfits, puffing away in front of his open dresser in the mornings – and he could count to four. My mother would laugh and run her hands through her hair and say that she could just about manage to dress herself too and she could still count to five. My father would hang his head then, say he would take a day off and give her a rest, and she would say not to be silly, she was fine, she was joking, they were okay.

They were okay. I heard them talking to each other in their room at night, murmuring softly together, and although I couldn't hear what they were saying, there was a mildness to the lift and swoop of their voices and an ease about the overlaps as one finished what the other had started. Every so often one of them would laugh or my mother would give that half-joking high-pitched sigh that escaped her after she'd said that things weren't so bad, and everything was going to be fine. Somehow.

Lawrence was great, of course. Nobody could really be low when there was Lawrence. Danny had a new name for him. We sang 'Satellite of Love', only we called it Juggernaut. 'Woah, woah, woah, Juggernaut of Love,' we would sing to him, and it ended up eventually as Jugsie, which was rich coming from Danny with his ears, but Lawrence didn't mind.

Still, I was lonely and I'll blame the loneliness for deciding, in the spring of 1985, that what I would do was go out and get drunk. Not as a lifestyle, you understand, but just once, spectacularly drunk, absolutely out of my head. That was the key point: I needed to get outside of this head, just for one night. So on the last day of term I went to the Preservation Hall with Milton and a crowd of others from the department and ordered a tequila.

When I woke up the next morning, I had a split second of calm and in it I felt a feeling I could not easily describe, but which I thought – immediately, irresistibly – was the feeling of being home again. Half-familiar but long-buried scents or tiny sounds . . . no, not even as tangible as that . . . but something and achingly close. I opened my eyes, ready to see Ludo's and my bedroom, my own old groggy face and bed-head in the mirrors on the wardrobe door, and then it hit me. My head and stomach, in unison, rolled over and the room began to spin. Yes, indeed, it was a familiar feeling I had not felt for quite some time. My mouth watered and my ears rang as though a tuning fork had been struck on the back of my neck and then dug in between my eyes to hum for ever. I thought I could feel a space, a space as cold as the empty whistling caves of my nostrils, a new space all around my head where my brain had dried out and shrunk away from my skull and if I moved my head even an inch, the crust of my dried-out brain would grate against the rough bone and I would die.

There was a soft tap at the door and it opened slowly. Danny appeared and slid quietly into the room. He held out a glass in one hand and offered the closed fist of the other.

'Alka Seltzer, Paracetamol and Vitamin C,' he said. 'Then I'll go back down and get you some tea.'

'Don't. Bring. Lawrence,' was all I managed to say.

He came back with two mugs of tea and settled on the end of my bed.

'Oh thank God I don't start work till Monday,' I said. I had finally worn my mother down on the subject of work in the Easter vacation: my marks were getting better and, even more compelling I think, was the money. It was worrying to have her agree, knowing how much she wanted to veto it, to have her confirm how badly we needed the cash.

I couldn't sit up far enough to drink anything, but I cuddled the mug into my neck and sniffed the sweet steam.

'Thanks,' I said. 'How did you know?'

'I've had plenty practice with pick-me-ups,' said Danny. 'Remember?'

'I meant how did you know I'd need it? Did I see you last night when I came in?'

'Oh, dear,' said Danny, the solicitousness beginning to wear off and the *schadenfreude* taking over. 'Can't you remember anything?'

I didn't respond.

'You talk a load of bollocks at the best of times, no offence, but you were in space last night. Are you sure it was only drink?'

'Like what, for instance?' I said. I hadn't thought I could feel any sicker, but cold sweats were flooding me now.

'On and on about ludo, on and *on* and on about the phone

getting cut off. Oh and, by the way, Elvis Presley is well past saving. You should give yourself a break on that one.'

'Did any of it make any sense?' I asked, carefully.

'Not so's you'd notice,' said Danny. 'I was pretty pissed too.'

'Well, I'm never going to drink again,' I said and I meant it. It was obviously far too risky. 'What was your excuse? Trouble in Pameladise?'

'Your mum's a lovely person,' said Danny. 'And your dad's the salt of the earth. How come you're such a complete cow?'

'Skipped a generation,' I said. 'My children'll be poppets.'

Danny didn't answer and we sat in silence for a while.

'So why d'you go out and get plastered?' he said eventually. 'It's not like you.'

'Just all got too much,' I said.

'What did?' said Danny. I chewed my lip and looked at him for a long time before answering. There wasn't much of it that I could tell him and what I could didn't sound like a good enough excuse for this amount of self-destruction. The only worry he could share in was Lawrence, and that led to all kinds of murky waters with the kind of undercurrents that could pull me down, even when I was feeling on top of the world. This morning, going there would be suicide. But it was for Lawrence. I took a deep breath, filling my lungs too deep for the comfort of my churning stomach beneath them.

'Mum's worried about schools,' I said.

'God, I know,' said Danny.

'So I've been meaning to talk to you about the shares. Tesco? IBM? I know we had hoped to keep them long-term. But we did say at the time, fifty-fifty, and if it was just for me I wouldn't even— but there's that funny school, you know, the Steiner school, and it's a thousand pounds a year. So I was thinking maybe . . .' I stopped.

I couldn't tell if Danny was going to hit me, pass out, or just stand up and walk away. I know, I wanted to tell him. I know. It was the share orders that needed her drunk after lunch and the drinking killed her, and you must hate me whenever you think about it, but you need me – or my mum and dad anyway – so you don't think about it and now I'm making you.

'Forget it,' I said. 'I'm sorry.'

'No,' said Danny. 'You're right. It's the obvious thing to do. But your mum did say there was one more school to try.'

'Bellcraig, yeah,' I said.

'So let's keep our fingers crossed,' said Danny.

'And our toes.'

'And our eyes, to be on the safe side.' He wiped his hands down the fronts of his trousers then picked up his tea and took a gulp.

'Are you all right?' I asked him.

'Yeah, just hungover,' he said.

'You drink too much,' I said. I didn't stop to examine the grounds for my superiority on that one this morning.

'I got drunk,' said Danny, 'since you're sweet enough to care, because Pam and me have split up.'

I sucked my breath in hard and clamped my teeth shut. My insides were in no state to withstand my heart leaping.

'Bitch,' I said. 'Not that it's not understandable. I mean . . .'

'Oh, ta very much. Nice assumption. I, for your information, dumped her.'

'Why?' I said. This was so interesting that I took the chance to sit up and swig at my tea while my hangover was distracted.

'I don't know. She's not . . . She wasn't . . .' He blew out his cheeks and gave me a look as though defying me to laugh. I had never felt less like laughing. He spoke again at last. 'She wanted us to get engaged.'

I hooted, cackled, rolled about, couldn't stop myself. 'Engaged?' I gasped. 'Engaged? Not married? Not moving in together? Engaged! You told me she wasn't a prissy little shit. You told me she was a great laugh when you got to know her. Oh Danny, if only you'd said yes. I could have got you a crystal bud vase and a set of hand towels.'

He said nothing, just stood up very calmly, opened the door and stuck his head out. 'Jugsie!' he shouted. 'Janie wants you to come up and bounce on her bed. Bring your recorder with you.'

Chapter 15

25 March 1985

Crossing our fingers and toes for Lawrence didn't work. No surprise there, but who could have predicted what did?

I came in from my first shift at Boots, two days after the hangover, to find my parents sitting side by side like a pair of effigies on the armless sofa in my father's studio, staring with solemn faces at the big picture of Lawrence. I stopped in the doorway and looked from them to it, from it to them.

'Has something happened?' I said, hoping that if something had, it was the kind of thing that could wait while I had a bath. I had the sore feet you only get from standing up on hard floors in smart shoes all day and the fug of a thousand toiletries was in my hair and lungs.

'Not really,' said my mother. 'Bellcraig said no.'

I squeezed in between them and put an arm around each.

'What reason did they give?' I said.

'Oh the usual, in the end,' said my mother. 'All the usual suspects. Resources, disruption, distraction, overworking the teacher, upsetting the children, annoying the parents, overtiring Lawrence...'

'There's someone who hasn't spent enough time with Lawrence,' I said. I sometimes thought there was a spare Lawrence being recharged round the back somewhere and they swapped over when no one was looking. 'Did you tell her overtiring wouldn't be an issue?'

'She was very upset,' said my mother. 'I don't think it was her decision.' The assistant head, without actually saying it, had hinted at a relative in residential care somewhere and had seemed minded to match my mother's fierceness with some courage of her own.

'If only we had the money,' said my father.

'Well,' I said.

'If I hadn't left it so late, if I'd been working for years and had sold something. Or maybe I'm dreaming.'

'Well,' I said again. 'Actually. There's some money you didn't know about.'

'What money?' said my father. 'This isn't like that last time, is it? "Give up your job, Dad." Remember? "I've got it all covered, Dad."'

'Trust me,' I said. 'I wouldn't muck about with Lawrence's school. I wouldn't get your hopes up. I really do think we'll be able to raise enough for Steiner's. Or what's that other place?'

'Montessori,' said my mother. 'Down near Melrose.'

'Yeah, Montessori,' I echoed. 'Aren't they a bit weird?'

'Not compared with Gray Park,' said my father. 'And they're not weird. They're just different.'

'And so – in case you hadn't noticed – is Lawrence,' said my mother.

'They're very strong on art.'

'And so – in case the state of your nail varnish collection hasn't told you – is Lawrence.' They were getting enthusiastic as they talked, then my mother sighed again.

'But it's forty miles away,' she said. 'Not that we can stay here anyway, not for ever. But we certainly couldn't afford to buy a place in Melrose.' Melrose was one of those little Scottish towns that looked as though it'd been picked up by a freak tornado in the Cotswolds and brought north. It had a ruined abbey and Le Creuset in the shops. It had a foxhunt, for God's sake. So I could see what she meant.

'Just don't write anything off,' I said. 'Let me sort things out with Danny and all will be revealed. How much are the Montessori fees anyway?' I asked, but they just shook their heads.

'I wanted to keep this,' said my father, nodding at his

picture. 'But maybe I'll put a price on it at the degree show and see what happens.'

'You will not,' said my mother. 'You can't. I'm probably being silly, but if he has to go to Gray Park we might never see him looking like that again.' I stared at the picture. As a record of Lawrence's childhood, I couldn't quite see its usefulness, since there was nothing in it that could be identified as a central figure, nothing humanoid anywhere at all. It looked as though it might have been made *with* Lawrence – by rolling him in paint and rubbing him against the board – but as a portrait *of* Lawrence, I had to take their word for it. I glanced at my mother out of the corner of my eye and wondered if she was for real.

'Of course you should keep it,' I said stoutly, however. 'I bet when it's finished you wouldn't be able to part with it even if you tried.'

My father turned and looked at me, surprised but not annoyed. 'It is finished,' he said. 'Can't you tell? I wonder what Montessori's upper age-limit is?'

'I'm going to play to my strengths, Dad,' I told him, 'and make a cup of tea.'

Danny and Lawrence burst in through the back door while I was at it, both with new haircuts and a strong whiff of Brylcreem about them, as though I needed more hair-care stink after my day in the stock room.

'Mummy Daddy Mummy Daddy Mummy Daddy,' Lawrence shouted, bustling right through the kitchen at top speed.

'Hello, little brother,' I started to shout after him, but then I thought the better of it. My parents needed the cheering up he always brought with him more than I did. My face must have clouded.

'What is it?' said Danny.

'Bellcraig,' I told him. I was filling the kettle, glad to have something to do that meant I didn't have to look at him. 'Both of them are just sitting through there staring into space. So . . . Danny boy, you've been holding on to those shares as long as possible which is excellent. Very prudent and all that. But it's time. We've got to move.' He was silent and I turned to him at last.

'We've got to sell up,' I said. 'Spring the first year's fees. They can't decide between Steiner's in town or some other arty place down in the Borders . . . What is it?'

He was staring at me, his face pale and his chest lifting and falling rapidly.

'Don't tell me they've dropped,' I said. 'I haven't been great at checking but every time I looked they seemed armour-plated. Have they crashed? Have they?'

Danny didn't answer.

'They can't have!' I said. 'It's the mid-eighties, for God's sake. It's Tesco. Danny, what's wrong?'

Still he said nothing. He was shaking, with a fast thrumming under his skin like a dog in a thunderstorm.

'They've gone,' he said at last, and his voice was shaking too. 'I sold them.'

For a long time I couldn't speak, then I started to piece it all together.

'That was why you looked like you'd been hit with a tree whenever I mentioned them?' I said. 'I thought it was . . . *That* was why?' He nodded. 'Come on, calm down,' I told him. The shivering was worrying me and putting a hand out to him I could feel the heat of a sudden sweat through his clothes.

'But what did you sell them for?' I said. 'Why?'

'Oh Janie,' he groaned. 'Why do you think?'

It was the way he drawled it; the complacency, the acceptance, the bland assumption that I would accept it too. That was what drove away any thoughts of being kind.

'Your hobby,' I said, and he flinched at my tone. 'Your harmless pastime?'

'Come upstairs,' he said, his voice still wobbly but louder, getting determined. 'I want to show you something.' I followed him to his bedroom and waited while he rummaged in the drawers of his desk.

'Look at this.' He gave me a bundle of A4 paper, stapled

together, with the logo of the psychology department promi-
nent in the corner. It was folded open to a page where several
lines of text had been highlighted in bubblegum pink. 'This is
what I'm taking for my long option next year. And I'm going
to write my dissertation on it: The Addictive Personality.
Look at the bits I've marked.'

'... disease model, psychological model and structural
model of addiction will be explored ...' I read. '... looking at
a range of compulsive behaviours including alcoholism, drug
abuse, problem gambling and eating disorders ...'

'See?' said Danny. 'I've accepted that I've got a problem,
and I'm going to put it right.' He smiled. He looked *pleased*.

So I left, slamming out of the room, out of the house,
stalking up the hill to the park, tears leaking out of the corners
of my eyes.

That smile had told me everything. He wasn't going to face
his problem and put it right. He was going to wallow in
anything he could get his hands on that told him his problem
was interesting and spend the rest of his life not only as a
gambler, but as a gambler and a bore. No matter how hard I
tried ... I stopped. How hard had I tried? Had I tried that
hard? I thought he blamed himself, or me, or both of us, for
his mum and so I pussy-footed around, careful not to upset
him, never telling it straight. I knew what I thought, of course,
after all these years watching him at it, listening to his excuses,
but had I ever really given it to him straight?

I stopped short, swerved around the corner, went into the
telephone kiosk and dialled the number for home. Danny
answered.

'Come to the park,' I said. 'Meet me at the swings.'

'Next year,' I began, sitting astride the swing, rocking gently
and facing his profile, 'next year, you're going to sit through
the disease model, the psycho model and the structural model
– whatever the hell that is. So today, will you sit through the
cut-the-crap model just once? Will you give it a go?' He
nodded. I took a deep breath and put my feet flat on the

ground, coming to a rest. 'Do you want to stop?' I said. He nodded again. 'So . . . stop. The End.'

'Simple as that, eh?'

'Yup.'

'Unbelievable,' said Danny. 'You have no sympathy, do you?'

'I have bottomless wells of sympathy. What is it you need it for? Are you poor, hungry, ill, homeless?'

'You can't just not believe in addiction. It's a real thing.'

'Nah,' I said. 'If it was a real thing there wouldn't be half a dozen different models of it. There would just be what it was and its name. Like this.' I knocked the seat of the swing. 'It's a swing-seat.'

'Fucking philosophy course,' said Danny. 'Okay, say there's no such thing as addiction, and I can just stop. How?'

'How? What do you mean, how? You don't gamble.'

'How? I stay away from the track, obviously. I stay out of the bookies. I don't go to the casino. I don't read the sports pages, even though their names are so pretty and many of them are film titles too. Right?'

'Wrong.'

'Well fucking how, then?' he shouted at the top of his voice.

'The same way you don't smoke. And stop shouting.'

'I *don't* smoke.'

'Exactly. Okay, I'll help you out. You don't smoke by . . . not putting cigarettes in your mouth, not lighting them and not breathing in. That's how you don't smoke. You don't "not smoke" by staying away from newsagents and the entrances of supermarkets. Right? You don't not smoke by never going into pubs where they sell fags. So *how* are you going to not gamble?'

'By . . . not filling in betting slips and giving them to bookies with money.'

'Hallelujah. That, in a nutshell, is the cut-the-crap model of how to stop gambling.'

'Cheap trick, Janie. My gambling isn't caused by going to the bookies and giving them my money.'

'Really?'

'You're doing my head in. Okay, my gambling *is* caused by blah-blah blah, cause and effect, logical philosophy, blah-blah-blah. Pain in the arse. But that's not what I mean. I gamble because I . . .'

'You gamble because you . . .'

'I gamble because of my mother?'

'Nope.'

'Didn't think so,' he said. 'Okay, I gamble because . . . ?'

'You gamble because . . . it's your moral code? Civic duty? Out of concern for the struggling bookies? To make me proud of you?'

'Ouch. How about . . . I gamble because it eases tension.'

'So what?'

'What do you mean, so what?'

'I mean so what? Being asleep eases tension, but we all get up every morning.'

'Yeah, but everybody wants to ease tension sometimes.'

'Bingo. You finally said it.'

'What?'

'You said you gamble because you *want to* ease tension. You gamble because you want to.'

'Well, *duh*.'

'But you said you didn't. You asked how are you going to stop gambling, and I told you and you acted like I'd tricked you. But you weren't asking how to stop gambling. You were asking how to stop wanting to.'

Danny rolled his eyes and sighed. 'So . . . ?' he said, in tones of weary patience. 'How am I going to stop wanting to?'

'I have no idea.'

'Cow. What you're saying boils down to "snap out of it".'

'Yeah,' I said. 'And?'

'It's an addiction, Janie. It's an illness.'

'I thought "illness" was just one of the "models".'

'It's a recognized condition,' he said, his voice rising.

'So was satanic possession till someone noticed there was no such thing,' I said.

'But this is a *real* problem,' said Danny.

'Bullshit,' I said. 'Gambling, Danny, is something *you do*. And if your biggest problem is something you *do*, then in my book you don't have any problems.' Then the way he was looking at me, his teeth clenched and everything in his face shut tight against me, finally sent me over the edge.

'Jesus Christ!' I screamed at him. 'You don't know you're born! Imagine if there really was something in your life that you had no control over, imagine if you suddenly found yourself somewhere and you had no idea why and there was no way back and you couldn't do anything about it and you just had to get on with it! Imagine how bloody crazy it would make you to have to listen to someone else who was doing exactly what they felt like doing, because they enjoyed it, and asking for the world's sympathy as well!'

Danny was blinking at me with both hands raised in surrender.

'Woah, woah, woah,' he said. 'Get back in your pram. Are you talking about anyone in particular, Janie? Is there something you need to say?' I could feel myself blushing.

'Imagine,' I said slowly, 'how Lawrence is going to feel at Gray Park. *Then* tell me you've got problems.' Danny put up his hands to ward off my words as though I was hitting him, and the fight went out of me.

'Did Bellcraig give any reason?' he said at last.

'Yeah. What Mum called The Usual Suspects. You know, the—' I stopped and stared at him, through him, remembering.

'Oh, for Christ's sake,' said Danny. 'Upsetting the other kids, upsetting the other parents, spoiling the class photos, all that crap?'

'The Usual Suspects,' I said again, remembering the arm pumping up and down under the optic, filling the whisky glass.

'Bastards,' said Danny.

'Have you got a sports paper?' I said. Danny blushed. 'Oh,

stop messing about, Dan. It's important. Have you got a copy of the *Sporting Life* back at the house?'

'You said I didn't not smoke by avoiding the fag adverts,' said Danny.

'Come on!' I yelled back to him as I sprinted to the entrance of the park.

'What is it?' said Danny, panting along at my side as we thundered down the hill and wheeled around the corner into our street.

'There's a horse called The Usual Suspect,' I told him. 'It's the title of a film.'

We clattered into the kitchen and Danny yanked on the toggle of his backpack, fishing out the folded paper.

'I'm pretty sure there isn't,' he said. 'I don't even remember the film, to tell you the truth, but I'm nearly a hundred per cent sure it isn't the name of a horse.' I ignored him and spread the paper on the draining board. Danny was standing right behind me watching over my shoulder as I read. I twitched a sheet over and started to scan the next page.

'There's a Last Suspect,' said Danny. 'He's a bit lively.' I spun round and clutched his upper arms, shaking him.

'That's it!' I said 'Last Suspect. That is it.' I remembered clearly now; the barman filling his glass at the optic, laughing his head off and saying, 'It was the *last* one you'd *suspect* was going to win,' and everyone groaning. 'Last Suspect.'

'*Is* that the name of a film?' said Danny.

'No.'

Danny snorted, but I shushed him. I needed to think. I needed to check. I got the phone book out of the kitchen junk drawer and looked up the number of Coasters.

'Yes, hello,' I said. 'I was wondering if you could tell me – I might be too early – but can you tell me is Nick Cave booked to come there this summer? He is? Yes, I thought so. No, I'll leave it just now, thanks.'

Danny was staring at me with one eyebrow hooked up and his tongue poked into his cheek.

'So the horse's name wasn't a film after all,' he said. 'And you've finally tracked down the gig of gigs but you're not sure you want a ticket?'

'Ssh,' I whispered. My parents and Lawrence were on their way to the kitchen, so I dragged Danny through into the dining room and up the stairs, not speaking again until my bedroom door was closed behind us.

'What's the most amount of money you've ever put on a horse?' I said.

'A grand,' said Danny.

'A thousand pounds? You are such an idiot. A thousand pounds on a *horse*? That might not *win*? Okay, what's the most amount you're allowed to?'

'Allowed by you?' said Danny. 'None.'

'Ha-ha. Allowed by law.'

'As much as you like. Whatever you can get the bookies to accept.'

'Roughly?'

'Sky's the limit.'

'How much would you say this house is worth?' I said.

He didn't answer, just raised his eyebrows and stared.

'Would you be willing to get a mortgage?'

'What are you doing?' said Danny.

'And bet the whole lot? You put up the money and I pick the race and the horse—'

'I think I could guess the horse, Janie.'

'—and the horse and it's a fifty-fifty split of the winnings. Like the shares.'

'Oh, like the shares!' said Danny. 'Of course. Look how well that's worked out.'

'But here's the deal: if I'm wrong and you end up mortgaged to your eyeballs, I will never tell you what to do again, and I'll work until it's paid off. But if I'm right and you end up rich, you stop gambling.'

'Why would I do that?'

'Out of gratitude.'

'You're nuts,' said Danny. 'That's the wrong way round. You're saying I'm going to have the win of my lifetime and

223

then stop. I'm going to start the world's biggest run of luck and *then* stop? Have you any idea how hard that would be?'

'That's the deal. We win. You stop. Take it or leave it.'

'I'll leave it,' said Danny.

'What?'

'I'm joking,' said Danny. 'But there's one condition. You tell me what the hell's going on.'

'No way,' I said.

'Okay,' said Danny. 'I'll take it anyway. But what am I going to say to the bank?'

Whatever it was, they bought it and he came home the next day with a glossy brochure and a spring in his step.

'How long is it going to take?' I asked him.

'Couple of weeks,' said Danny. 'I have to have a survey done.'

'Plenty time,' I said.

'Yeah?' said Danny. 'When's the race?'

'What do you mean, when's the race? It's this summer's Derby. I thought you knew about horses.'

'You didn't say it was the Derby,' said Danny.

'Yes, I did,' I told him. 'Didn't I?'

'But you said it was Last Suspect,' said Danny.

'I did. It is. What's wrong?'

'Last Suspect's eleven,' Danny said.

'So?'

'The Derby is a race for three year olds.'

'What?'

'The Derby is only for horses that are three years old,' said Danny very slowly. 'Last Suspect is eight years too old to be in it.'

I couldn't, for a minute, even begin to catch up with myself. I was eight years out. Eight *years* out. That made it 1977, for God's sake. I couldn't have had a job in a pub at twelve. Could there be another horse, Usual Suspect, that really *was* in the Derby this year? But Danny would know it. Could it be a baby that no one had heard of yet, that would run in the Derby when it was three? In 1987? I sighed with relief. That was it. And by 1987, I'd be graduated and working and Danny wouldn't need to hock the house.

But hang on. I would be graduated in 1987 and I would be working. So it couldn't have been 1987 when I had the summer job in the Coopers' and the barman filled his glass at the optic . . . and Nick Cave was on at Coasters this year. *This* year. What was going on? I was sure it was Last Suspect.

'I don't understand,' I said. 'How could an eleven-year-old horse be in a race for three-year-olds?'

'It can't,' said Danny. 'Janie, whoever gave you this tip was having you on. You're not safe to be out, pal.'

'What races can eleven-year-old horses be in?' I said.

'You haven't got a clue, have you?' said Danny. 'Christ, I can't believe I listened to you. They can be in tons of different races. Ten a day.'

'But it's one that everyone bets on, office sweepstakes and everything.'

'Must be the National,' said Danny.

'But it can't be. It's definitely a big race in the summertime when we've got summer jobs in pubs and things.'

'So this tip was a horse with a name like a film except not and a race in the summer while you're working in a pub. Are you sure it was a race tip, Janie? Are you sure it wasn't a crossword clue?' He shook his head at me, almost smiling. 'Why couldn't it be in a big race in the springtime?' he said. 'When we've got Easter jobs in pubs and things.'

For a long moment, I thought I was going to throw up, right there on the bottom bunk in Danny's bedroom. It was springtime and I had a day job in Boots and a night job in the Maybury Inn, just like last time when it was springtime and I had a morning job in Gregg's the bakers and a night job in the Coopers' and the manager in the Coopers' liked me so much that I went back in the summer and one night, in the summer, we went to see Nick Cave.

'When is the Grand National?' I said, when the insides of

my cheeks had stopped pouring with water and I knew it was safe to open my mouth.

'Saturday,' said Danny. 'And Last Suspect is entered at fifty-to-one.'

'This Saturday?' I said. 'Well, that's that then. I blew it. Gray Park it is.'

'You didn't blow anything,' said Danny. 'Why is it always down to you?'

I couldn't answer this at once, had to think. 'I feel a sense of responsibility,' I said at last.

'Yeah,' said Danny. 'I've noticed that.'

I almost laughed.

'So,' he went on, 'we've got till Saturday to raise as much as we can with the house as security.'

'You said two weeks,' I reminded him.

'I said a mortgage from the bank took two weeks,' said Danny. 'I've got other options. Right.' He twitched a sheet of paper off his desk and uncapped a pen with his teeth. 'We need to spread it, work out two routes, and decide where to pull the plug.'

'What are you talking about?' I said.

'We need to stick to the counter limits,' he said, 'because if they have to phone for clearance the odds are going to drop. And the odds are going to drop anyway as soon as we start to show, so we get organized and do it all in one day, right? They won't even notice till after the close of business and then it'll be too late. But just in case, we need to decide when to stop spreading it and just bung on everything we've got. If you see it drop to five-to-one and try to place ten grand, say, then they'll phone it in and we'll be at evens before I get a chance to dump mine too.'

'And what do you think we'll get?' I said. Danny was shaking his head.

'Christ, if we had time to organize the mortgage. If we could put the whole lot on at once, five grand tax in advance on a forty thousand bet. It would be . . . the winnings would be two million.'

'So why can't we just do that anyway?' I said. 'With whatever we have got? Why do we have to run around with synchronized watches?'

'Because a forty grand bet would have to be done with a banker's order,' said Danny. 'They're not going to touch that much cash with a bargepole.'

'Why not?' I demanded.

'Because they're going to know it's bent.'

'Why would they—' I began. And stopped.

'There's no way it's clean money where I'm getting it from,' said Danny. 'We need to keep our heads down.'

'Are you really up for it?' I said. *I* was, of course I was, because it was Lawrence for one thing, and because *I* knew. But even with everything I knew about Danny's so-called problem I couldn't quite believe he would go as far as this.

'Why not?' he said. 'I like a bit of a flutter.'

'This isn't a flutter,' I told him, with my fingers crossed to make it true. 'It's a sure thing.'

'Hey!' said Danny. 'Isn't that the name of a film?'

Chapter 16

13 July 1985

'Come on, Janie!' yelled my mother from the front door. 'We're going to be late.'

I bounced Lawrence off my legs with a one and a two and a one, two, three and dumped him onto the couch beside me.

'I'm watching the news!' I yelled back. 'Just coming.'

'How many times have I told you?' shouted my mother. 'Not with Lawrence.' I was with her on this now; I had lost faith in my ability to switch off quick once I remembered what was happening, and he had seen the massacre on Christmas Eve, clapping his hands at first and shouting, 'Bang! Bang!' then growing solemn as the camera juddered and swung and the sound of bullets rose above the shouts of the men and the noise of rocks on riot shields. 'I didn't know it was going to happen,' I had said to my mother, as she stood in front of the screen and shrieked at me to get him out of the room. 'I would never have let him watch that, Mum. We wanted to see the report from Lapland. We were waiting for Santa Claus.' How could I have forgotten that this was going to happen? Same way as I forgot the Brighton bomb.

There was nothing on the news today anyway.

'There's nothing on the news today anyway, is there Lollipop?' I said. 'The Rainbow Warrior's on its way back from the South Pacific. So what, eh? That's not news.'

'Who?' said Lawrence.

'A big boat,' I said. 'A big green peaceful boat and it didn't get sunk.'

'Big boat,' said Lawrence.

'And the concert's starting,' said my mother, coming to lean in the doorway. 'So Danny'll be turning over to the other side.' At that moment Danny appeared with a foil tray of spare ribs and two bottles of imported lager. He dumped the ribs down on the coffee table and handed one of the bottles to Lawrence. I looked questioningly at my mother.

'It's lemonade,' she said. 'We rinsed the bottle out.'

'Big boy juice,' said Lawrence, clinking bottles with Danny and scooting almost horizontal on the couch to try to make his feet reach the coffee table where Danny's were already resting.

'Where do you get spare ribs at one o'clock in the afternoon?' I asked Danny.

'It's caveman food,' said Danny, ripping off a piece with his teeth and snarling theatrically at Lawrence.

'Grrr!' said Lawrence.

'Fine, whatever,' I said. 'Enjoy the show.'

'You're sure you don't mind missing it?' said my mother. I shook my head. 'All right then. Lawrence, you behave yourself and do whatever Danny tells you, okay? And Danny, remember the house limit.'

'What's this, what's this?' I said, my antennae twitching.

'I'm pledging five thousand pounds for Lawrence if Tina Turner blows him a kiss,' said Danny. 'P-ledg-ing. Not B-etting.' He batted his eyelashes at me and gave an innocent smile.

'Okay, well, how about you can pledge the same from me if Bob Geldof says the f-word,' I told him.

My mother tutted, and Danny called me a cheapskate, because that would never happen.

'Oh look, look, it's starting,' said my mother as the camera panned over the crowds in Wembley Stadium, and zoomed in on the Prince of Wales in his striped shirt and double-breasted suit.

'Well, there you go,' I said. 'The world's most eligible bachelor. It's rocking already.'

'Who is that beside him?' said my mother. 'She looks like she's sucking a lemon.' No one would ever be good enough for him, according to my mother.

Lawrence had put his half-gnawed rib down on top of a library book and had begun to boogie (that was the only word for it) very energetically, waving his beer bottle about his head. Danny started hand-jiving.

'Let's go,' said my mother, jingling her car keys. 'That's us off, Jock,' she shouted at the studio door on the way past, and my father had roused himself and got to the window in time to wave as we drew away.

She asked me another few times if I was sure I didn't mind missing it all, but I could tell from the curl at the sides of her mouth and the way she drove leaning slightly forward over the wheel that she was too excited to care, really.

'Have you got the keys?' she said as we pulled away from the lights at the top of Fairmilehead. 'And the map? And the tape measure?'

'And a notebook and the camera,' I said, checking again to put her mind at ease. The keys were still tied together with string and still had on them the estate agent's pink paper tag. We had signed the contract – or rather they had, my parents had – at noon the day before. The house was ours. And in forty minutes my mother and I would put the key in the front door and walk inside. We were half-pretending to ourselves that we were going to measure for curtains, hence the tape and the notebook, but I at least was planning mostly to run about from room to room shouting, 'Whoopee!'

It had taken a lot of careful repetition before we had managed to make my parents understand, of course. We sat them down and told them that Lawrence could go to the Steiner school, or we could move to Melrose for Montessori and buy a house with a studio, or lots of space to make one. When we told them where it came from though they both, physically, blanched and stared at us as if we had suddenly unzipped our human suits and revealed the tentacles within.

'It must seem ... reckless,' Danny had said at last with rather considerable understatement. 'But it was the only way. Janie has been very loyal to me, but the truth is I've got a problem and this was the only way I was ever going to face it. High stakes, though, huh?' They only blinked more.

To be fair, I hadn't planned that part. It just sort of turned out that way. Waiting for the start, standing hugging each other, practically holding each other up, I think, in the middle of the floor in the Corstorphine Ladbroke's, I had been surprised to find that Danny was trembling almost as much as me. Of course, *I* was trembling. It had occurred to me, too late, that absolutely anything could happen. Perhaps the jockey had grown up in the next street to wherever the Mastertons had moved to, and so he hadn't become a jockey after all because his new friend Ludo wasn't interested in playing at horses, and the jockey who was riding today in his place had just had a fight with his girlfriend and was feeling listless. Of course, *I* was nervous. But Danny was pure waxy white, with blue lips. He turned and looked me straight in the eye, as he did these days when I was wearing flats.

'Tell me it's going to work out,' he said. 'Where did you get this tip? Tell me it's going to be all right.'

'I'd love to,' I answered. 'But who knows? Sorry.'

His eyes widened.

'Who knows?' he echoed. 'You said it was a sure thing.'

'There's no such thing as a sure thing,' I said. Danny's mouth dropped open and he gaped at me, as if it was *me*. As if it was me who had problems. As if it was me who was mad.

Suddenly the room around us lifted with an intake of breath and someone said: 'They're off.' I don't know about Danny but I didn't have the nerves for this. I turned for the door and left, dragging him with me. Outside, we stood on the pavement, not moving, not speaking, until the race was over and men were beginning to leave the shop and mooch away.

'Well?' I said at last. 'Someone has to go in and find out.'

'You tricked me,' said Danny. 'You knew I had a problem. It was up to you to be the one who . . .'

'You're right,' I said. 'You left it up to someone else to be the one who.'

'I didn't have a choice!' said Danny.

'Oh yes, I forgot,' I answered. 'You don't have a choice, poor thing, you have a problem.'

'Are you gloating?' he said. 'What's happened to you?'

'Of course I'm not gloating. Shut up,' I said. 'It's just that ... I see right through you.'

'What does that mean?' demanded Danny, but he was looking shifty.

'Look, if you've got a problem that you hate and you wish you didn't have, right? Well, if someone comes along like I did and tells you that you could get rid of it, you don't argue and tell them they're wrong and fight for the right to keep it. You don't argue with someone who's bringing you good news.'

Danny was scowling at me, thinking hard.

'So, since you did argue with me ... I see right through you. You're busted.'

Still he said nothing.

'You know I'm right,' I told him, 'and you don't want to admit it and that's the clincher. You are so busted. If you really wanted to stop gambling, me telling you it was a choice would be the best news of your life.'

He was looking at his feet, but it didn't take long for him to answer.

'Of course,' he said. 'Of course it would.'

'So, if I promise never to laugh at you, never to make you feel silly for not doing it before, if I promise I'll be proud of you, can you just for God's sake stop?'

He waited a long time, then he nodded, and I believed him.

And the day we sat my parents down to tell them the news, when he did finally manage to explain what he was on about, they believed him too. But far from it reassuring them it only rattled them more; he wanted them to be happy that he wasn't an addict any more, headed for the skids, but all they heard was that he had been an addict headed for the skids, and he hadn't told them. It was like me bursting in and shouting, 'Great news, Mum! I'm off the smack.' It took them a while to catch up.

'And how much ... ?' said my father again.

'Well, less than we hoped,' said Danny, not looking at me. I had lost my nerve and dumped eight thousand at thirty-to-one and I had forgotten to pay the tax on one bundle of two grand. 'But enough. You know, plenty.'

'We can't accept half of it,' my mother had said. 'It's yours.'

'Not any more,' Danny had told her. 'We're a syndicate, Janie and me. We're both on the slips. Otherwise we'd have to pay a ton of tax when we split it.'

'So does that mean I can't just give a chunk of it to Mum and Dad either?' I asked him. He shook his head.

So really this house we were on our way to see this Saturday afternoon, both of us with fizzles of excitement making our voices shake when we talked about it, this house was actually mine. But I didn't think about it like that, and we had an accountant on the case now, ferreting out all the different ways I could begin to trickle some of it back to my parents where it belonged.

'There's the school,' said my mother, slowing down as the road swung past the gates to a manor house. You couldn't see much from the road, but we knew from the visit that there were tractor tyres full of sand in the garden and waders hanging from their shoulder straps in the cloakroom so that the kids could paddle up to their waists in the pond at break. And the headmistress had come to my father's degree show and bought a painting to hang in the staffroom. I still thought they were a bit strange, but I could tell Lawrence was going to love it.

She fell quiet as we skirted Melrose and nosed the car up away from the river into the hills, dropping a gear as the engine began to growl. (It was still the Maxi as yet and this hill was no joke.) Slower and slower we climbed up through the trees on either side, past the farm, past the cattleman's cottage, and then with a surge forward like the back end of a humped bridge we came out on top at the gates to the house.

'Sorrowless House,' the estate agent had said, plucking the brochure out of the file.

'Sorrowless House?' my mother had echoed. 'I'll take it.' And she had laughed.

'It's a corruption of Sorrell Lees,' said the estate agent. 'And Sorrell in a house name is like Moss in a house name: code for damp.' But we didn't listen.

My mother inched up the drive, lurching from one side to the other to avoid the pot holes. There were mammoth rhododendrons on either side of us, all of them the bog-standard kind, washed-out purple and straggly with it.

'It's in need of a bit of TLC,' the estate agent had said, frowning at the photograph on the front of the folder, reluctant to let us see it.

'Perfect,' said my mother. 'Pre-scuffed. Lawrence-proof.'

We rolled over the weedy gravel to the front door and stopped. There was a dock about waist height growing out of a crack in the middle of the doorstep. The key, as big and heavy as a panto prop, grated in the lock and then turned with a clunk, making me bump my knuckles.

'And there's an access issue,' the estate agent had said. 'The Roxburgh Hunt has an uncontested right, up the drive and through the yard. Twenty years' worth. Old Miss Mantle was very pro-hunt and it's firmly established now.'

'How exciting,' said my mother. 'My little boy will love to see that.'

Inside the porch, red and white marble tiles stretched back into the gloom of the house and the only light, shafts of blue and yellow full of dust motes, came from the skylight two storeys above. All the shutters were closed.

'Working shutters,' my mother had said as she read the particulars.

'There's no electricity upstairs,' the estate agent had told her. 'Miss Mantle lived on the ground floor ever since the fifties.'

'No electricity upstairs?' I had repeated. That was getting a bit too unspoiled for me.

'Good,' had come from my mother. 'Why do you need electricity upstairs? It destroys family life to have teenagers living in their bedrooms, that's what I say. And anyway there's plenty room downstairs, isn't there?'

'Drawing room, dining room, morning room and library,' the estate agent had said. 'Not including the kitchen and offices and the billiard room, of course.'

We headed straight for the billiard room, of course. Facing due north with soaring windows and nothing above it so we could put in some skylights. It was to be the studio.

'And I'm just going to face facts and put a little armchair and a reading lamp in a corner for me,' said my mother. 'Or I'll never see him.'

We went out the back door, pausing to look in on the downstairs loo, which had a high wooden cistern with a chain, and stank. In the yard, some ancient dried-up bundles of horse dung showed where the Roxburgh Hunt had exercised its right last winter.

'What are we going to do with all of these stables and things?' my mother said. 'Even if we use one for a garage and keep coal in another one. Look at them all. Maybe we've been greedy.' I hugged her. Only my mother would think moving to a half-wired house with one bathroom was too much swank.

'Well, first we're going to clean them out,' I said.

The estate agent had been pretty clear about that.

'Miss Mantle's executors are not undertaking to clear the outbuildings before the sale,' he had said. 'They're in Canada, and it's going to be quite an undertaking.' Then his mask had slipped for a minute. 'She was as mad as a brush and there's a century's dreck in those stables. Rather you than me.'

We pushed open the door of the first one to meet the front wall of a huge stack of grey straw bales with little nest holes and mouse runs channelled into them here and there. The floor was deep with feathers and droppings.

'How did she even get those top bales up there?' I said. 'And why?'

It was winter before we got around to them. We moved in

August after my mother and I had spent a month scouring the floors and rubbing wax into the sun-bleached shutters. You could almost hear the wood gulping. When moving day came, though, we all laughed and cringed to see our Dralon suite and our sets of bunk beds marooned in the enormous rooms. And when we sat to eat at Danny's old table in the middle of the new kitchen, my father would pretend to write a list of things he needed before making the trip to the cupboards at the walls.

'We have to get some new furniture,' my mother said. 'And some rugs. I want to keep the tiles clear so Lawrence can go his trike inside when it's raining, but we need some rugs to deaden the acoustics. It sounds like a factory canteen in here.'

'I said that,' said Danny. 'I told you that.' He had. He had pointed out very reasonably that we would need to keep some furniture in his house in Corstorphine, where the two of us were going to live in the term-time until we graduated, but my mother had insisted that she would buy him new things and take her old junk away to Sorrowless with her. Now it looked as though it would be making its way back again and when you took a good look at it, after twenty years of service and the last four with Lawrence in the frame, it hardly seemed worth hiring a van.

'Well, at least let's not get anything before Mona and David come to visit,' said my father. 'Even they won't want to stay the night rolled in a sleeping bag on the floor. In fact if we hide all the tables and chairs and make them eat standing up we might get away with an hour, start to finish.' It had been a long time since my father bothered to hide how he felt about them. The death knell had been when Auntie Mona had looked at his picture of Lawrence and said:

'I don't suppose you *would* want an actual likeness, would you?'

It had taken my father a minute to work out what she meant and when he did he only turned away without answering, but my mother, overhearing from the kitchen, had spat in Mona's tea. And when Grandpa Jock died and Uncle

David suggested not bringing Lawrence to the funeral 'because it was going to be a difficult enough day for everyone without that', things between the brothers and sister went cold in a way that you just knew would never warm through again.

'That!' my father had said. '"Without that".'

'I don't think he meant Lawrence was "that", Dad,' I told him. 'I think he meant Lawrence coming to the funeral was "that", you know. It's not quite so bad.'

'I can't believe you're sticking up for them,' my father said. 'Where do they get the nerve?'

'They're space aliens,' I told him. 'Don't even let it bother you. They're from Mars. Or they're from Earth and we're from Mars.'

'I know you don't like strong language, Jock,' Danny chipped in. 'But in this case I really think the only thing is to say fuck 'em. I think you should say it ten times tonight before bed and you'll feel better in the morning.'

'You're a good lad,' said my father. 'You're from wherever we're from, Danny boy.'

So there was no incentive to sort things out to impress any visitors. None of Dad's new buddies from the Borders Artists Collective would have noticed if we were all sitting around on orange boxes and the other parents from the school would never admit they cared about the state of people's furniture. When Danny and I came back for Christmas my mother was still trundling dishes along the passageway to the scullery in a pram and they still had the TV remote on a string so they could lob it over from the couch to Lawrence's beanbag but reel it back in if he wouldn't stop flicking.

We were struggling out of Danny's car (after an awkward silent drive not talking about his latest break-up) trying to get all our bags and bundles under control to make one trip of it when Lawrence started shouting from the back door.

'Boots!' he yelled. 'School! Boots on Lolly neck. Boots and trousers.'

'He's regressing,' I said to Danny, waving at Lawrence but

not managing to smile. 'It's that school. He's talking complete mince.'

'He's trying to tell you he went paddling in the waders,' said my mother, scooping him up and bringing him over the wet yard towards us. 'Lawrence, tell Janie properly what happened at school today.'

'Lolly wear boots an trousers right up a neck a go in the water.'

'Fourteen-word sentence,' said my mother, with shining eyes, kissing me and then Danny over Lawrence's head. 'I don't want to hear another word about the school, okay? Welcome home and Merry Christmas. Wait till you see the size of the tree.'

I trailed in after her, wondering who this was. This wasn't my mother. This woman in Hunter wellies and a Down's Syndrome Association oilcloth pinny. This woman not asking me how the trip was and whether I was hungry or warm enough or whether she could carry something. Except, it suddenly occurred to me, looking at her back striding into Sorrowless House with Lawrence riding her hip, this was my mother, finally getting to be who she wanted to be, getting to be who she really was all along.

'What is it?' said Danny. I hadn't realized anything was showing on my face.

'Nothing, just good to be home and it's funny how things turn out . . . That kind of thing. Low blood sugar, probably.'

'Yeah,' said Danny. 'It's just as well we don't know what's coming, eh?'

'Too right,' I said. 'Drive you nuts if you did.'

'So what happened to Kirsty, anyway?' I asked him at last the next morning. 'Since you're obviously not going to tell me unless I make you.' We were standing in the biggest barn, cradling coffees in our hands and appraising the tower block of straw bales. Kirsty had arrived after Laura had left, Laura having popped up just after the departure of the one after Pam, but in the last two weeks of term there had been long phone calls late at night, then a tearful Kirsty on the doorstep looking for Danny when he was out at football practice and then finally silence, and a parcel of returned gifts sent recorded delivery that I had to sign for.

Danny shrugged.

'And Laura for that matter,' I said. 'You never did say what happened to Laura. Why do your girlfriends always leave you, Dan? You can't blame the gee-gees now.'

'Don't say "gee-gees", for God's sake,' said Danny. 'You sound like the treasurer of the golf club. "What's your poison, squire?" I never did blame the gee-gees.'

'I know,' I said. 'It was just my subtle way of getting them into the context so I could check how you're doing.'

'I'm fine,' said Danny. 'You ruined it for me for ever. Thanks.'

'Anytime,' I said.

'And even if you hadn't,' he went on, 'this sodding research project would have knocked all the fun out of it, peering at it under a microscope.'

'I was worried about the project, if I'm honest,' I said.

'Don't be,' said Danny. 'It's perfect displacement. Like those anorexics who're forever baking cakes for people.'

'Like that girl Trisha in your class last year?'

'Yeah, like Trisha. Five stone three. Hardly had the energy to pipe the icing.'

'She should run a catering company if she wants to stay really trim.'

'You're such a cow. It's not about staying trim.'

'And you should specialize in addicts. Be a counsellor. Nothing like telling other people what to do to keep your mind off your own worries. It works for me.'

'Oh yes,' said Danny. 'I've noticed that telling other people what to do works wonders for you.'

'And asking them questions that are none of my business,' I said. 'That can get me through the day as well.' He waited, smiling. 'So why do all your girlfriends leave you?'

'I don't want to tell you,' Danny said. 'It's embarrassing.'

He shifted his feet and looked away from me. I wiped the smile off my face.

'I'm sorry,' I said. 'I was just winding you up. You never seemed that bothered or I wouldn't have . . . sorry.' I waited. He said nothing. 'You *can* tell me, you know.'

He stole a quick glance at me and nodded. 'Okay,' he said, visibly summoning courage. 'It's because my penis is too big.'

I put down my coffee cup and shoved him hard with both hands into the straw bales which puffed out stale dust in a cloud. He lay back, laughing and coughing, wiping at the coffee stain down his anorak and trousers.

'That was hot,' he said. 'You could have scalded me for life.'

'Filthy pig,' I said, sitting down beside him.

'Nosy cow,' he said. 'But since we're on the subject, why have you never had a boyfriend?' I bristled.

'I have. Milton. And boys at school.'

'What boys at school?' said Danny. 'When?' When, was a good question.

'There is someone,' I said. 'You don't know him and it's complicated.'

'How? Is he married? Gay? Do *you* know him? Is he famous and you're just stalking him?'

'I'll get you another coffee,' I replied.

When I came back and edged the barn door open, carefully balancing the mugs, Danny had laid a ladder against the bales and climbed it and was now sitting on the top, looking away from me. He beckoned me up.

'You're not going to believe this,' he said.

I climbed slowly, feeling the ladder bounce gently off the bales every time I lifted my foot from a rung. It didn't feel safe at all; I could hear its rubber feet crackling as they slid about in the straw litter on the floor below.

'Oh, I hate this!' I said. 'Can you hold on to the top?'

But that only made it worse. When Danny leaned over, the whole front of the hay stack shifted, bulging outwards, and when he grabbed the top rung the ladder pivoted slightly and came to rest nearly vertical. I hugged it, stuck.

'Come on, ya chicken,' said Danny. 'It's only ten feet.'

'I really, really hate this,' I said and my voice must have convinced him because he stopped making chicken noises and spoke to me in a firm voice.

'Come on. Six more steps and I'll get you at the top. You've got to see it.'

'How will I get down?' I said, not even trying to sound as though I wasn't petrified.

'I'll get you down,' said Danny. 'Come on, six steps.'

I lifted one foot off the rung, squealing as the ladder slid and settled below me, but I put my instep squarely on the next rung up and again and again and then Danny grabbed me around the upper arms and hauled me onto the bale beside him. The ladder slid away to the side and clattered to the stable floor. I, with no thought to my dignity, hugged the bale with both arms like a fat girl backwards on her pony in a Thelwell print and whimpered. Danny shuffled along until he was right behind me, prised my hands free and pulled me upright, then clamped an arm round my waist so that we were spooned together like a knight and a maiden on a charger.

'Look down there,' he said. I looked.

No wonder the stack of bales had wobbled as we climbed it; it wasn't a stack at all. It was just a wall, one bale thick, with us balanced on the top. On the other side was a heap slightly lower than the top of the bales, jagged and grey. It looked as though a giant cement mixer had poured out its load just as it was setting, and it had hardened there in a great jumbled lump.

'What is it?' I said.

'It's dust sheets,' said Danny. 'And dust.'

I looked closer and saw that he was right. The greyness changed tone here and there and I could see where the corner of one sheet was rucked up away from the one below.

'But what do you think it is underneath?' I said. Danny shrugged. I was torn between the excitement of what it might be and the fear of knowing that I was sitting fifteen feet in the air on a wavering tower of ancient straw with no way of getting down again.

'Something worth hiding,' he said.

'It was a vintage car with a pickled head in *The Silence of the Lambs*,' I said, before I could stop myself.

'Oh great,' said Danny. 'We're stuck up here and now you've had a stroke.'

'What do you mean stuck?' I said. 'You promised you'd get me down.'

'And so I will.' He shuffled away from me again and, digging his feet in between two bales, he began to kick one of them out of place.

'Danny stop it!' I shouted, back to straddling the fat pony again. 'The whole thing's going to collapse. What are you doing?'

After a few minutes of being kicked, while the rest of the wall juddered, one bale finally fell away from its neighbours and landed in the doorway in a cloud of foul-smelling flecks. He started on the next.

'I'm making a ramp,' he said grimly, over his shoulder. 'Wait a minute. Once I've kicked enough of them into a pile you'll just be able to slide down them on your—' Suddenly, one of the bales burst out of its binding with a snap and Danny disappeared ownwards, with a yelp. I started laughing before I could help myself and by the time I found myself falling as well it was too late to do anything about it, except keep laughing and choking on straw dust, and gagging on the stink of mouse, until a bale coming down behind me hit me hard on the back of the neck and shut me up.

Danny was sitting a few feet away, a bit higher than me since he was on top of the beginnings of his ramp. He was scowling.

'That's not how that was supposed to happen,' he said. 'There was no reason for that idea not to work. Are you okay?'

'I am,' I said, getting to my feet and starting to brush myself off before deciding it wasn't worth it. 'And at least we've got the stack down.' Danny stood up and plunged backwards into the mess of straw, launching himself over the exploded bales like a child trying to get beyond the big waves on the beach.

'So?' I said, when he stopped. 'What is it?'

'I don't . . . pthyeaugh!' said Danny, spitting something out. 'I don't know what all of it is, but this bit here's a grand piano.'

'You're kidding!' I said, throwing myself into the heap and galumphing through it and over it like a porpoise.

'I'm not. Steinway. That's the good ones, right?'

'You're kidding!' I said again. 'If you're winding me up I'm going to kill you.' I reached the edge of the pile and tugged at a corner of a tarpaulin. It shifted with a dry crackle and released another cloud of mushroomy grime. Holding my breath and squeezing my eyes half-shut, I rolled it backwards. Underneath was an onyx and gilt ormolu side table with griffin-head feet and acanthus leaves climbing its legs.

'Oh, my God!' said Danny's voice a hillock or two away in the pile.

'What?'

'You should see this. There's this green and yellow table that looks like Fungus the Bogeyman,' said Danny. 'I didn't think furniture could go mouldy.'

'It's meant to be like that,' I shouted back. 'It's called ormolu.' And there was a pair. 'Mum!' I shouted, struggling through the shifting heaps towards the door. 'Mum! Come and see this! MUM!'

It took all day but eventually we uncovered the lot: chaises longues, wing chairs, bulbous Victorian bedroom suites and spindly Georgian drawing-room suites, collector's cabinets with their marquetry springing up like the bristles on a hedgehog, a tiger-skin rug, head softened and gruesome with mould, endless leaves of mahogany table with no legs to be seen anywhere, wine coolers and knife boxes looking like giants' crematorium urns, and Turkey carpets rolled in sacking that made loud scuffling noises when we shifted them.

'I feel bad about the Canadians,' my mother said. 'We

should really tell them. I mean, some of these things must be family heirlooms.'

'Bollocks!' said Danny. 'I mean, nonsense.'

'They weren't interested, Mum.'

We wore her down in the end and then we spent the rest of the Christmas holiday lugging things into the house. Sometime between Boxing Day and New Year we got ourselves a system. We would drag whatever it was along the scullery passage into the laundry room and scrape off the worst of the filth, with scarves tied over our faces like cowboys raiding a mail train. Then we would make an honest assessment of the state of decay. Could it go straight into the house after a polish? Would it need to be sent away for a proper repair? Or was it a goner? Except that, to my mother, nothing was ever a goner.

'I'll learn upholstery,' she would say. 'Maybe if we rub it all over with a cut brazil nut. We can patch that. We can cover it in cushions. We can stand a vase on that bit. Look, this vase. No, the other way round so you can't see the crack. There, that's perfect.'

Even the tiger-skin rug survived, mostly. We cut off its head and paws and burned them in a brazier in the yard, but the rot had travelled so far up its legs and down its neck that by the time we had hacked back into the good dry skin there was only enough left to fling over the back of a sofa to hide the fact that the padding was three-quarters gone and we had packed out the frame with a sleeping bag.

'It's quite comfortable,' said my mother, wriggling her shoulders back against the stripes. 'Now, where do you think?'

Danny kept telling my mother there was no need to be so thrifty, so stingy – we could send the whole lot to the restorers in Edinburgh and get it back gleaming and smelling of beeswax – but she shook her head and said what was the point of that? She might as well get a decorator to fill the house with repro; he was missing the point. I agreed with her, kind of; at least, I understood. I knew that the posh magazines would get there in a few years. 'Shabby chic' would take over the world. 'Elegant decay' would be what everyone was aiming for with their paint distressing and their crackle glaze. My mother was just way ahead of fashion: shabby decay.

Chapter 17

31 December 1985

By Hogmanay the house was nearly full and, although there were still a few silverfish surfacing out of armchairs when you first sat in them, mostly when you looked around you saw the reflection of polished wood and the plummy gleam of new velvet cushions (we had cleaned the little shop in Melrose High Street out of velvet cushions to make up for the sagging springs, but still sitting in some of the chairs was a surprising plummet and for ever afterwards guests had to be warned not to try it with a full glass in their hand). The smell was getting there too. Incense, polish, Shake n' Vac, hot Christmas tree, Glade, burnt-out Hoover motors and mincemeat aren't too bad as long as you keep the windows open, and with every fireplace stoked to make up for the windows the whole house was a giant flue. We had found an enormous woodpile in one of the other stables, only it was so dry after all those years that it went up like kindling and Danny seemed to spend all day barrowing loads of it around the house, with Lawrence trotting after him carefully steering two or three logs in his old pushchair, and my father hurrying after both of them, testing pictures by putting his cheek against the canvas to see that they weren't getting too warm. We had hung the pictures that came out of the stable, portraits and landscapes mostly and so dirty you had to look at them from one side to see what they were. My father said they would be better hanging while he worked round them slowly and cleaned them off.

'Aren't they going to look a bit . . . daft beside yours?' I said.

'Thanks, sweetheart,' said my father. 'Thanks for saying it

that way round.' I don't know if he realized I was just being diplomatic; actually I thought they would make each other look daft, his giant splotches mounted on blocks and these whiskered ancestors that were as much gilded frame as actual paint. 'Anyway, I'm hoping not to be filling the house with mine. I'm hoping somebody might buy them.'

'But I'm wondering,' said my mother later, 'whether it would be better to try to get them into galleries, or whether we could convert one of the outbuildings here. Do you think anyone would trek all the way out here to look at pictures? Would we need to open a tea-shop too? Only Dad's pictures are not really tea-shop pictures, are they? Pass the Blu tack, darling.'

We were getting Lawrence's room ready for the night, even though he was determined to stay up 'for the bells'. I hoped he would make it, or at least that we would manage to wake him, because I had bought fireworks – ever since the Millennium, New Year just didn't seem like New Year to me without fireworks and the rest took no convincing. Danny had strolled down to the farm to check with the farmer that we wouldn't be blasting half his livestock into spontaneous abortions if we set them off and he had come back saying he hoped it was okay but he had invited the farmers up to first-foot us and watch the show. The mum and dad and their daughter who was home from college, he said, looking innocent. I rolled my eyes. Danny had lined up another girl-next-door, then. Fine by me.

I snapped a piece of Blu tack off the sheet and passed it up to my mother, holding up the flashlight so she could see what she was doing.

'I hope this isn't going to go on too much longer,' I said, aware that I sounded grumpy. My mother only laughed. Lawrence had chosen for himself one of the suites of Edwardian bedroom furniture in blackest mahogany. It was quite a sight to see his little face marooned on six feet of bolster in the middle of rolling billows of carving, but the problem was that on the wardrobe, bed head and dressing stand, as well as fleurs-de-lis and pendulous vegetation that might have been roses but looked a lot more like Savoy cabbage, there were gargoyle heads and although they had been the main draw when Lawrence was downstairs in the laundry room holding his mummy's hand shouting 'monster bed', 'monster cupboard', it was a different matter altogether when he was lying alone in his room in the flickering lamplight.

So every evening we Blu-tacked cut-outs of Spot the Dog and Postman Pat over the girning horrors. In the night, as the fire died down, Spot and Pat began to drop off and by the morning some of the gargoyles were revealed again, some were still covered and a few were half-visible, leering from above Pat's peaked cap as the Blu tack was vanquished by the damp. In the morning though, Lawrence was brave again and would shout 'monster drawers' from his bed, laughing, and would go around the room in my mother's arms snatching off the masks and shouting, 'Boo!' My mother said if she made a game of it, he would stop being frightened and we wouldn't have to cover them at all, but I reckoned if she made it too much fun she would be at it for ever, tacking up pictures of David Beckham and Lara Croft for him when he was twenty.

'Is everything okay?' she asked me, rolling and kneading the blob I had passed her and then pressing Spot hard onto the top of the bedpost.

'Of course,' I said. 'What do you mean?'

'You don't mind the Murrays coming? The people from the farm?'

'Of course not,' I said. 'It's good luck to have company at Hogmanay.'

'So you don't mind?' She was standing still in the middle of Lawrence's bed, watching me closely. Light dawned at last.

'You think I mind Danny asking that girl?' I said. 'Mother.'

'I just wondered,' said my mother, stepping down. 'You and he seem very close sometimes.'

'We are very close,' I said. 'He's like my little brother.'

'He's exactly the same age as you,' said my mother. 'Three weeks older.'

'Yeah, but he's ... he's my little brother.'

'He's the same height as you,' said my mother.

'Yeah, but...' I stopped and gave her a big smile. 'No, Mum, I don't mind the farmer's girl coming up to watch the fireworks with the boy I think of as my little brother, okay?' Not that I might not puke if she squeals in girlish terror at the loud bangs and nestles in his manly arms. But it's more likely she'll drive the whole family up here in the tractor and help chop logs for the bonfire, huh? Farmer's girl, after all.'

Bel Murray wasn't the squealing type, though. And I could tell right away she wasn't the tractor-driving type either. She was wearing a white sleeveless Puffa over cashmere and had long legs in white jeans. I was wearing a peacock-blue evening dress out of one of Miss Mantle's trunks as a favour to Lawrence, who loved it, and got a very amused look from her when Danny introduced us. One of the beads fell off the dress when I put my hand out to shake hers and Lawrence shouted, 'I find! I find!' and dropped to all fours to chase it down. This excitement was his favourite thing about the dress, but it didn't do much for my image.

'And what do you do?' said Bel. 'Art?' I could see what she meant.

'Philosophy,' I said.

'Philosophy?' she echoed, and smiled a tiny smile. 'What on earth are you going to do after *that*?' Which, since I'm always going on about the importance of straight talking, should have made me warm to her, but all I thought was that I was glad to see Lawrence bearing down, his chocolatey hands reaching up to her white Puffa for a hello cuddle.

A little later, after everyone had got their drinks, I was standing on my own trying not to look as though I was standing on my own, watching them. My mother was warning Mrs Murray not to sit down too suddenly in the blue armchair; my father was explaining his new series of work to a politely nodding Farmer Murray, and Lawrence was squatting down, happily chatting to one of the dolphin's heads carved into the bottom of the big bookcase, trying to feed it Twiglets. I heard Bel murmur to Danny: 'You're a very interesting family.'

'Oh, they're not my family,' Danny replied. 'We're just friends. But they are interesting, yes.'

You cretin, I thought. You creepy, tail-wagging little cretin. But at midnight he came straight to me to say Happy New Year and kiss me on both cheeks with a mwah, mwah like we always did. Then he turned to Lawrence.

'Happy New Year, Jugsie,' he shouted. 'Big boys' hand-shake or sloppy kiss?' Lawrence was puckering up, chocolate, Twiglets, lemonade dribble and all, and Danny kissed him without a second's hesitation, then held him out to Bel, who did the same.

The question, in Bel Murray's confident voice, swam around in my head for days. My father was doing what he had always longed to, my mother was doing the same, Lawrence was doing wonders at the Montessori, Danny – of course – was doing Bel Murray, but what about me? What was I doing? What was I going to do?

'Oy,' shouted Danny from the stables as I trudged back, head down, hands in pockets, from a walk in the woods. 'Send your mum out for a bit. Mr Hodge is going to walk us through.'

My mother was in the kitchen stirring a copper pan full of marmalade. She had chalked a line on the flagstones and told Lawrence he wasn't allowed any nearer the stove.

'Message from Danny,' I said to her. 'They're going to walk through the . . . what? Sorry, Mum, I wasn't really listening. A Mr Hodge is out there and they're going to walk through something?'

My mother lifted the wooden spoon out of the marmalade and looked around for somewhere to set it down.

'Would you mind?' she said. 'Just keep stirring and make sure Lawrence stays back. I won't be long.' She shoved the spoon into my hand and left. Lawrence took a step towards me. I waved the spoon at him, showering little droplets of marmalade over the floor. He looked down and shuffled his toes back behind the line.

'Hot,' he said, quoting my mother.

'Burning hot,' I said.

'Peel off all your skin and die,' said Lawrence. So maybe Danny had had a hand in the safety lesson too.

My mother came back, flushed and twittering, before the marmalade had boiled, while the spoon was still scraping against gritty sugar on the bottom of the pan. Danny was with her, carrying a folder that he spread on the kitchen table.

'Pretty exciting, eh?' said my mother.

'What are you up to?' I said. 'Who is Mr Hodge anyway?'

'I thought you'd never ask,' said Danny. 'He's a builder. Listen to this.'

I listened but I couldn't believe my ears. In the summer, once we graduated and once Mr Hodge had finished the conversion, Danny was going to start running counselling courses. For addicts. In the stables. Based on cutting-the-crap.

'You're kidding, right?' I said. 'Here? A bunch of drunks and junkies here in the house? Mother, are you crazy? We'll be hounded out of the valley with rotten eggs. We'll be robbed. What about Lawrence?'

'Gamblers,' said Danny. 'Not drunks and junkies. At least to start with.'

'And I'm going to do the catering and look after the books,' said my mother. 'And your dad says if any of them are interested in art therapy, he could help with that. Dad's painting's much more art therapy than country gallery, after all.'

'You're all nuts,' I told them. 'You can't just set this kind of thing up like a cake stall. You need qualifications.'

'I'm a recovered compulsive gambler, son of an alcoholic, and a chartered psychologist,' said Danny. 'Or I will be by the end of June.'

'Yeah, but...' I said. But what? But he was wee Danny

Conway, and the cut-the-crap method wasn't a method, it was just me having a go at him because he didn't know he was born. And my mother couldn't cook toast.

'The cut-the-crap method isn't a method,' I said. 'It was just me having a go. And it was the big bet that cracked you. Wait a minute; you're not suggesting we do *that*?'

'The big bet persuaded me to give in,' said Danny. 'But it was the cut-the-crap method that worked.'

'I wish it had a different name,' said my mother.

'It doesn't have any name,' I shouted. 'It doesn't exist.'

'But it worked,' said Danny.

'That's not the point,' I began, but they both laughed.

'Oh Janie, that philosophy course,' said my mother. 'Of *course* that's the point.'

'You might as well wave crystals over them,' I said. 'You can't use things you don't understand.'

'I don't really understand aeroplanes,' said my mother. 'But Lawrence got to see Disneyland at half-term anyway.'

'You're all nuts,' I said again.

'But the thing is, Janie,' said my mother, 'that won't matter because so are they.' Even I had to laugh at this and from that moment on the prospective clientele were known as 'Danny's Nutters', by all of us, including Lawrence – which was obviously going to end in red faces and refunds.

'Anyway what are you going to do with your life that's so worthwhile?' said Danny. And I stopped laughing.

Except, I reminded myself, sitting in Danny's house mid-week, trying to concentrate on the television and ignore the sounds of him and Bel floating down from upstairs, I was doing something, or at least I had. I made all those phone calls, I had averted disasters, I was like a millionaire philanthropist or a carrier of typhoid: just by existing I was doing plenty. On the screen the crowds were screaming their appreciation and waving pictures of the astronauts and the American anchor-woman, her voice trembling but her hair rigid, was saying something about mankind and the firmament and America which I hoped for her sake was a quotation.

I had averted disasters like the one that was just about to not happen tonight. And so I was glad to be watching on my own. This way, when I popped the cork on my half-bottle of champagne and drank a toast to myself, I wouldn't need to explain it to anyone. The countdown had begun.

I turned up the sound to drown out the cabaret from upstairs. They had moved quickly and for the last week or two Bel had been very much in evidence. Like termites. But Danny seemed happy enough. The count was down to ten now, everyone chanting together, Danny and Bel panting along with them in the background, seven, six, five. I untwisted the wire around the champagne cork. It was up and off. I watched it inching upwards away from the puff of dust on the launch pad then nudged the cork with my thumbs. It couldn't have been properly chilled: the cork shot out and hit the ceiling and there was a yelp from the room above. I glanced towards it.

So I wasn't looking at the screen when it happened. I only heard the bellow from the crowd, and when I did look back there was nothing but blue sky and a plume of pale grey smoke. The shuttle was gone.

The phone rang under my hand and I lifted it. It was my mother. I could hear Lawrence bawling in the background and my father shushing him.

'Are you watching the Challenger launch?' she said.

'Yup,' I answered. I couldn't trust myself to say any more.

'That poor woman,' said my mother. 'Her poor family. Lawrence is—'

'I can hear him,' I said.

'Is Danny there?' said my mother.

'No,' I said.

Danny threw open the door, scowling, in his dressing gown.

'What the fuck is it?' he said.

'Yes, *Mum*,' I said pointedly into the telephone. 'That's him now. I'll have to go.'

'Well?' said Danny, once I had hung up.

'Is everything all right?' drawled Bel from upstairs. 'Can I help?'

'The shuttle blew up,' I said.

'The what? Oh, right. In America.'

'I was watching it on the telly. Lawrence was watching it on the telly.'

'You banged on the floor with a broom to tell me that?'

'It was a cork.'

'So the shuttle blew up,' said Danny. 'What do you expect *me* to do about it?'

'Nothing,' I said, and I stared at him, thinking. I had told them about the Challenger. And they had sent back a postcard saying they knew already. 'I don't expect you or anyone else to do anything, Dan. The days of me leaving stuff to other people ended tonight.'

'Well, great,' said Danny. 'I'm very glad we cleared that up.'

'Will I come down?' called Bel in her amused voice. 'What's going on?'

'Oh for God's sake,' I said, 'can you not just peel her off the sheets and get rid of her?'

Danny looked at me, highly amused and very close to saying something, but in the end he just reached out and mussed my hair with one hand. I jerked my head away from him. I've always hated people rumpling my hair.

'Stop it,' I said. 'You need both hands for your dressing gown.'

'Trust us' they had told me, and I had. I should have known, really. When I used to turn to Ludo in the cinema when the adverts were on and ask him had he locked the car, he would answer yes, and I would relax. Then he would add 'I'm sure I did' and it would nag at me right through the film. Nobody says they're sure unless they're not. 'Trust us' was like that. Nobody told you to trust them unless you shouldn't. Like that message that started springing up on church noticeboards and bumper stickers telling us all that there was hope. Everyone knew what that meant. If you asked a doctor how bad it was and he told you there was hope you'd know exactly what he was saying.

Trust them? Not any more. I was here to save Elvis, not to tell answering machines that he needed a saviour then sit back trustingly to watch the show. That's what I'm going to do, Bel, I thought to myself, and I even know where I'm going to start. I went upstairs to my bedroom and switched on my PC, waiting while the cogs churned and the screen wheezed itself into life, dreaming of Windows. When the yellow cursor was blinking at me in the top-left corner of the screen like a lighthouse at the edge of a moonlit sea, I started typing. 'Dear Mr Rushdie' I began.

I was still struggling with the first draft when the front door shut behind Bel at last and Danny came sprinting upstairs to knock at my door.

'Sorry about earlier,' he said. 'You okay?'

'Fine,' I said, 'just busy.'

'Yeah, right,' said Danny. 'I was meaning to speak to you about that.' I waited. 'Actually it was Bel who got me thinking. She was asking me what you're going to do after graduation and I couldn't answer her. So . . . I'm wondering if you'd be interested in helping me,' he went on.

'Helping you do what?'

'Helping me out, working for me. At the clinic.'

'Gosh, Danny, I'm just so flattered I don't know what to say,' I said with my hands clasped under my chin. 'I've dreamed of being a part of your empire and now my dreams have come true. And I'm touched to the heart to know how much Bel cares. Tell her that from me.'

'What exactly is your problem?' he said and left.

It took a good few rewrites and even then when I read it over it still seemed like a threat so, if I sent it off to him via his publishers, he would never see it. Some matronly secretary who thought he needed looking after and a good haircut would put a match to it in her wastepaper basket and tell no one. I needed to find out his home address and send it there. Therefore, I needed a private detective to get the address for me. And while I was at it I was going to try to slip unnoticed past a prime chance for Sod's Law to catch me. Every time I had tried to find Ludo since I came back to go round again, something had stopped me. So tomorrow, while I was sorting out Mr Rushdie, I was just going to casually float the idea of finding Ludo too. In short, I was going to do the equivalent of happening to mention the lump in my armpit while the doctor was writing out the prescription for the verruca ointment, and everyone knew that it was much less likely to be cancer if you only happened to mention it while you were seeing to your verruca.

I blew off Secular Ethics the next afternoon and made my way from the university down through the backstreets to Fountainbridge, where, amongst the launderettes and swirling litter, KJB Enquiries – picked at random from the Yellow Pages – was to be found. I never made it.

On the corner of Grove Street and Upper Grove Place, I thought I heard my name and turned. There was someone standing back-aways on the other side of the road looking towards me. He wasn't moving and wasn't standing out in the middle of the pavement, but he wasn't exactly hiding. He was behind a lamp-post almost leaning against the wall of the building in a way that, if the lamp-post had been a bus stop, would have made perfect sense. I glanced around to see if there was someone else who might have spoken. There was no one. Only this man standing beside a lamp-post as though it was a bus stop. Faint memories stirred. He was wearing a tan overcoat with a scarf under the neck and the kind of grey shoes you get in Littlewoods, that the kind of men who shop in Littlewoods think you can wear with suit trousers. Far from dapper then, but the memory that stirred was of men in pinstripes, with sunglasses, smiling at me. (Had they even worn sunglasses or was I making that up?) I turned away, with a pulse knocking in my throat, telling myself it was my imagination. But I heard it again, clearer this time.

'Miss Lawson?'

I started to move, purposefully, but without running.

Whatever they had in mind sending one man on his own to waylay me in the street instead of two to knock on my door, I wanted no part of it.

'Have it your own way,' the man shouted after me. 'I'll send you an email.'

I stopped dead, and felt my memory shuffle and fall into place. Before I had even turned around again I knew. I didn't need to see him look at me with his head on one side, not quite smiling. I remembered perfectly. I walked slowly towards him.

'You'll send me an email?' I said. 'Running short of postcards at last?'

'Pilchard,' said the man and put out his hand. 'Got time for a cuppa?'

I nodded.

'Frappuccino at Starbucks?' he said, and I couldn't help a grin spreading over my face.

'There's a Martin's the bakers with a coffee shop round the corner,' I said. He tucked my arm into his like he was my long-lost uncle and we set off.

'I thought you'd forgotten me for a minute there,' he said, as we sat down in the sweet steam of Martin's back room with our thick cups of instant and iced buns.

'Hardly. That was a pretty unforgettable day. I was on my way out the door to go to Ludo's house and there you were. I felt afterwards as if you'd hypnotized me.'

'Ludo's house?' said Pilchard. 'I don't know anything about any Ludo.' He was heaping brown sugar into his cup, and once he had stirred it in, he put the saucer on top to keep it hot and cut his bun into four pieces. He took a long time selecting which quarter to start with. 'I'm talking about the day of the Royal Jilting,' he said.

'Oh yeah,' I said. 'That was the same day. So . . . what are you doing here this time?' I tried for an air of innocence but I don't think it came off.

'Dunno,' said Pilchard. He had half-finished his bun and lifted the saucer off the top of his coffee cup, shaking the

257

drips of condensation off it while he took his first sip. Now he fished inside his overcoat and took out a small brown envelope. He waved it at me. Inside was a postcard, typed: 'Go and see Janie Lawson (Edinburgh). Tell her.'

'I got that yesterday,' he said.

'You *got* it?' I stared at him. 'I thought you *sent* them.'

He shook his head and laughed. 'No, I just do what I'm told, same as you.' I read the postcard again.

'What is it you're supposed to tell me?'

'I'm not sure,' he said slowly. 'They keep me up-to-date with you and I've done this kind of thing before and so basically what I think they want to get through to you is that you shouldn't do anything until you're told. You should just ... you know.'

'Trust them.'

'Exactly.' He looked up at me, with a sudden spark of interest. 'Were you going to do something?'

'I was, as it happens,' I said. 'And they've got a nerve, after Challenger.'

'I know,' said Pilchard. 'Awful, wasn't it? But look at this.'

He fished in his pocket again and drew out a small piece of newspaper which he held at arm's length and peered at down his nose. '"A nuclear power plant near the town of Chernobyl in the Ukraine has been forced to close after failing routine safety checks",' he said. 'There's a chance, you see, that letting the shuttle explode was ... a sprat to catch a mackerel.'

'A sprat ... ?' I was speechless. 'That's barbaric.'

'I agree,' said Pilchard, and he slid the newspaper cutting towards me to let me see for myself. 'It's only a personal theory of my own, you understand. But it's funny how often it seems to turn out that way. A small thing goes wrong and then a huge thing goes right. I've noticed a pattern.' He looked rather proud. 'So what were you planning today?'

'Salman Rushdie,' I said, trying not to sound sheepish.

He frowned at me with his mouth stuck out in a little rosette shape.

'Oh no, no, no,' he said. 'They wouldn't like that. Not at all

258

they wouldn't. A little personal thing like that. Far too handy to have up their sleeve.'

'Salman Rushdie's a sprat?' I said. Pilchard nodded slowly with his eyes closed as though confirming that the patient had slipped away. Then he seemed to shake it off and smiled at me, with the light of devilment back in his eyes.

'Salman Rushdie,' he said. 'Oh dear, oh dear, oh dear. You've already buggered the monarchy for them, if you'll pardon the expression. No wonder they sent me.'

My head was fizzing with questions.

'It seems heartless down here at our level,' said Pilchard, 'but it's a case of keeping the boat steady and making sure you're ready for the big ones. It's a question of . . . choosing your battles.'

I nodded. 'I believe in that,' I said. 'I always have.'

'And as I say, it's only a theory of mine. But I can tell you they weren't pleased about Dennis Nilsen. They never worked out who did that.' His voice was odd, all of a sudden, hard with triumph, and it made me wonder.

'Was it you?' I said. He looked startled and shook his head.

'Was it you?' he said to me.

'No way,' I said. 'It happened five years before I got here.'

'I would have been gobsmacked if it *had* been you,' said Pilchard after a pause. 'You're not exactly covert, are you? With your placards and your fifty-to-one shots.' I thought about getting offended but in the end I just shrugged.

'So,' he went on, 'there must be a lone wolf somewhere.'

'How d'you mean?'

'One of us that they don't know about,' said Pilchard.

'One of us?' I said, faintly. 'Another round-again?' I had finally caught up. I had thought it was me. Then I thought it was me and him. Then I thought it was me and him and them. And now I had finally caught up: it was them and me and him and all the rest of us.

'Yes,' said Pilchard. 'One of us. I call us second chancers.'

'How many of us are there?' I asked.

'No idea,' said Pilchard. 'I know there's you and me and

there was the woman who came to welcome me when I came back and there was another bloke that I had to go and speak to like I'm speaking to you, so that's what? Four, five?'

'Where are they?' I said. 'The woman and the bloke.'

'Oh, dead,' said Pilchard and, seeing my face, he hurriedly added: 'I mean, just dead. The woman was in her eighties when I met her and that was twenty years ago.'

'And the bloke?'

'Yes, well,' said Pilchard. 'He didn't adjust. I happened to see his picture in the *Evening Standard*. He went under a tube train.'

'They threw him under a train because he didn't adjust?' I said. I took a quick look at the doorway through to the front shop. I reckoned I could get most of the way to the street before Pilchard squeezed out from behind the table. He wasn't a slim man.

'No, no, no,' he said. 'He threw himself. Never got his head round it. Missed his wife and she didn't want to know when he tried again. Spent too much time with his head in a book trying to figure the ins and outs.'

I gave an embarrassed kind of laugh and Pilchard nodded.

'Yes, I was worried about the philosophy degree,' he said. 'But – don't take this the wrong way – it doesn't seem to have had much impact.'

Questions were firing around my head like pinballs, so fast and with so many jostling behind them I could hardly catch one and ask it before it was gone. 'So, it's not a good idea to try to make it the same? But you said they hate it when things go different. How does that—?'

'It's confusing, isn't it?' said Pilchard. 'It gets better though, in time.'

'How long have you been here?' I said. 'I mean when did you come back from and everything?'

'Nineteen ninety-nine,' said Pilchard. 'Back to 1960. You?'

'Two thousand and two.'

He whistled and looked impressed. 'So what happened with Y2K?' he said. I gave a chortle of laughter.

'Nothing!' I told him. 'Total overreaction. A few cans of beans might have gone off in a warehouse somewhere. But absolutely nothing happened.'

'So,' said Pilchard, nodding thoughtfully. 'They got it sorted.' I tried not to look like I was thinking he was crazy, and then when I thought about it some more I realized he might have a point and I nodded back.

'So Pilchard,' I said.

He beamed at me. 'I wondered how long it would take before you asked,' he said.

'What are we all doing here?'

He waited a moment, but before he even started to speak I knew what he was going to say.

'Dunno. I've got a theory, though. And you might be able to confirm it. You want to hear?' He didn't wait for me to answer this. 'I'll go and get us another coffee and what? A sandwich? A sandwich. And then I'll tell you what I think and you can say if you agree.'

He brought me a hard cob with grated cheddar and onion on it and I tried to look grateful. I must have failed.

'Roll on Pret a Manger, huh?' he said. I laughed. He didn't look the Pret a Manger type. I would have thought the overlap between Pret a Manger customers and men in grey slip-ons was pretty slight. 'What do you miss?' he said.

'The Internet.'

'I never got into the Internet much,' said Pilchard. 'I will this time, mind, but I can't say as I miss it exactly. With me it's fleece. I lived in fleece. And hot chicken from Tesco.'

'Australian people,' I said. 'I miss all the Australians.'

'Easyjet.'

'I don't miss Easyjet,' I told him.

'*Buffy the Vampire Slayer*,' said Pilchard. 'I know, I know, but I saw it one Friday tea-time when the snooker finished early and I got hooked.'

'Sounds like quite a life,' I said, not really laughing at him, thinking about him sitting in his fleece, eating his hot chicken and watching *Buffy*. Something told me he wouldn't have had a dilemma about finding his wife again when he got back. Something told me one of the bonuses for Pilchard would be all those engine numbers to rewrite in his book. 'Anyway, tell me your theory.'

He took a bite of sandwich and chewed steadily, breathing in and out hard through his nose, then he washed down the mouthful with a slurp of coffee and began.

'I think round-agains, second chancers, come back to fix things,' he said.

I had been holding my breath and now I let it out in a long hiss. 'Well, duh,' I said before I could stop myself.

Pilchard chuckled. 'I haven't heard that for years,' he said. 'It's soooo years since I heard that.'

'Oh God, Pilchard, please,' I said. 'Don't do slacker slang.' It was like watching your dad dancing to Abba.

'Yes, but listen,' he said. 'I think we come back to fix something in particular, and it's something right at the end of what we know. So for me, coming back on New Year's Eve 1999, I've always thought it was the Millennium bug, and the woman who greeted me, she came back from six days after the fire in Vienna. *Six days*. And that boy who threw himself under the tube train? That was a week after Martin Luther King was assassinated, and it said in the paper that he had a picture of King in his wallet, and his suicide note said he couldn't face an unknown future.' Pilchard ended on a triumphant note and waited, I think, for me to start marvelling.

'I've got no idea what you're talking about,' I said. 'I'm not saying you're wrong. I just don't understand.'

'Okay, listen,' said Pilchard. 'The boy who threw himself under a train came back to save Martin Luther King, and he failed and so he killed himself. And we know he must have come back from just around then, because that's why his future was unknown.'

'Everyone's future is unknown,' I said.

'Except ours,' said Pilchard. 'But haven't you ever thought about when you catch up with yourself again? I mean, you get used to it, knowing what's happening. It must be strange when it stops.'

This had never occurred to me before. Probably I had never faced the thought that I *would* just keep going and catch up with myself, but now that I did let the idea in, I could see why someone might not be able to face it.

'But—' I began.

'Hang on,' said Pilchard. 'Let me finish. So he came back for King and failed. I think I came back to stop the Millennium bug from putting us all into meltdown. And the woman – what was her name? It was all so long ago – but she came back from six days after the Vienna fire.'

'Yeah, what Vienna fire?' I said. 'That was before my time.'

'No,' said Pilchard. 'That was 1973. But she did the job. You don't remember it because it didn't happen. Like you don't remember everything falling apart on the 1st of January 2000. That's great news for me, I can tell you. Takes some of the pressure off.'

I stirred my spoon round and round the dregs in my cup, testing it all out, seeing if it made sense.

'So can you confirm my theory?' said Pilchard.

I pressed my fingertips into my eye sockets, trying to make my thoughts order themselves.

'I'm still a bit confused,' I said. 'How can anything bad ever happen if there are all these round-agains who could stop it? I don't mean this to sound like a criticism, Pilchard, but if I'd been here when Kennedy died, say, I just know I wouldn't have been able to keep my mouth shut. I'd have tried to tell someone.'

'I know you would,' said Pilchard. 'And where do you think it would have got you? That's the point. We come back from *just after* something, so that when we have to blow cover we're not going to be useful for very long and even if they crack us, it won't do them much good.'

'Them,' I said. 'The guys in the suits with the sunglasses?'

'Sunglasses?' said Pilchard.

'Oh right. Yeah, I thought maybe I was making that up. So

let me get this straight. You're saying we come back, we lie low, we wait for the thing we're here for to come around, and then we go for it. And then the spooks in suits try to use us for their own ends but they fail because we've just about outlived our usefulness.'

'It makes sense,' said Pilchard. 'After I told Hull everything I knew, they asked me if there was anything else I could think of. And I said no, and they said what about the two towers. And all I could think of was the Tolkein book, which is what I told them and then they went quiet. How about you? Did they ask you about something you'd never heard of?'

'Yes!' I said. 'The tank. They asked me what I knew about the tank.'

'What tank?'

'I don't know. I think your theory might be right.'

'And is there anything that happened just before you came back that would be worth the trip?' said Pilchard. 'When exactly was it?'

'March 2002.'

'Was there something? In February, January?'

'No,' I said slowly. 'What about the year before, though?'

'Late 2001?'

'September,' I said. 'That seems like a long time compared with Vienna and Martin Luther King.'

'It's not an exact science,' said Pilchard. 'I wouldn't imagine, anyway. Can't be.'

'Well, if we can stretch it to September then yes. Certainly there was.'

'Don't tell me,' said Pilchard. 'It's best if I don't know.'

I could see what he meant. If he had known what the tank was I wouldn't have wanted the details either. I half-wished he hadn't told me as much as he had.

'Pilchard, you know what's bothering me? I'm not being modest, but I'm not exactly qualified for this. I mean, if I'd known I was coming . . .'

'Ah well,' said Pilchard. 'Better luck next time.'

'Sorry?'

'With paying attention. Practice makes perfect. Bill Gates is seven hundred and fifty, you know.'

'Are you telling me we can go round more than once? More than twice, I mean?'

He looked to both sides as though checking for eavesdroppers – a bit late now, I thought – and then leaned in towards me across the table. I'm joking,' he whispered. Then he sat up and laughed.

'I'd be immensely grateful if you wouldn't do that,' I said, trying to frown, but laughing in spite of myself. 'It's hard enough keeping a hold of it all. But to get back to my point: there must be a thousand people who would have been more use than me. Why not one of them?'

'Dunno,' said Pilchard, and he had no theory about this one.

Out of the corner of my eye I could see a figure hovering, and when I turned to look I noticed the empty shop and the chairs on the tables around us.

'That's us closing,' said the girl. She had an anorak on over her uniform and was unpinning her cap. Involuntarily, I found myself gripping the edge of the vinyl seat with both hands, starting to breathe rapidly, the room suddenly spinning.

'Yes, and I better go,' said Pilchard. 'I've a long journey.'

'No!' I blurted. 'You can't. We've hardly started.'

He was easing himself out of the booth, putting on his scarf, and another of the bakery girls was by the door, holding it open for us in that way that looks almost polite but is really just a sign that they're going to lock it after you. I hurried after Pilchard out into the street.

'Can you leave me a number?' I said.

He shook his head. 'They wouldn't like it,' he told me. 'They would go bananas if they knew how long we'd talked this afternoon. Best not.'

'But what am I going to do?' I said. 'My whole plan was I was going to try to do things, save . . . people, and now you're saying not to.'

'What about this clinic?' said Pilchard. 'While you're waiting. I do voluntary work myself.'

'That's just crazy,' I said. 'I definitely want to stick around to help pick up the pieces, but as for it working? Danny was a fluke.'

'Well, I don't think I can agree with you there,' said Pilchard. 'I remember something about something, oh years ago now. It was probably on *Richard and Judy.*'

'I never watched *Richard and Judy.*'

'Oh, I loved it,' said Pilchard. 'Judy especially. There's a woman for you. Anyway, it was some American thing and it didn't sound a kick in the pants off your approach.'

'It's not an approach!' I said. 'I was just having a go at Danny.'

'You'll be fine,' said Pilchard. He stuck out his hand to shake.

'Wait,' I said. 'There was something else.' I stuck my own hands behind my back, thinking childishly that if I didn't shake he wouldn't leave. 'Something else I was supposed to fix.'

'No, Janie,' said Pilchard, and his voice was hard, pulsing through me. 'You need to get that straight. There's nothing here for you to fix and you can't get back to where there is.' I could feel myself begin to cry, but it wasn't his words, more his voice, reverberating through me like a bell. I struggled against it.

'Ludo!' I only just managed to grab the word and spit it out before it disappeared.

'You are so stubborn,' said Pilchard, but his voice was gentle again.

'He's my . . . You can laugh if you want,' I said. 'But do you believe in soulmates?'

'Oh, yes,' said Pilchard, solemnly. 'I most certainly do.'

'So?'

'Listen to your heart.'

'What does that mean?' I said. 'Listen to my heart. What are you saying?'

'Follow your heart for once and see where you end up. Switch your brain off.'

'And then what?'

'Just . . . let it happen,' said Pilchard, waving vaguely. 'Work in Danny's clinic. Get ready for the job when the time comes. Someone will be in touch.' He was walking away from me backwards and every nerve in my body wanted to run after him.

'You can't just leave!' I screamed at him. Two men passing on the other side of the street glanced up, interested, and once they had had a good look at us they gave Pilchard a warning glare.

'Think about me at the Millennium,' he said. 'Keep your fingers crossed.' He was still backing away. If I just grabbed hold of him and didn't let go, what could he do? Would he prise my hands off? Would he wrestle himself out of my grasp and fight me? He turned the corner and was gone.

Chapter 18

11 February 1990

'How do you pick up that glass on the table?' I asked.

The man looked at the glass, then at me and then back at the glass. I waited. He turned and stared out of the window at the dabs of snow dropping softly straight down. I went over to the window and closed the blind. The snow wasn't lying, each flake striking the cobbles of the yard and disappearing into dampness.

I sat down again.

'Describe how you would pick up that glass,' I said. The man drummed his fingers on the wooden arms of his chair. I waited.

'Okay, I'll tell you,' I said at last. This guy was one of the smouldering ones – his air of grievance was as clear as if he stamped his feet and howled – and it was a type that always unsettled me. If he snapped, and no one had yet, but if this one did, he would feel instantly and permanently justified. He was like one of those men who truly believe that knocking their wife's teeth in can be explained by telling the judge she nagged him.

'There's no need,' he said, in a voice of wounded exhaustion. 'I've heard it.'

'Good,' I said, with a smile. 'Recap for me then, will you?'

'Reach out, put my hand round it, lift my arm,' he muttered.

'And how do you not—' I began.

'Don't reach out, don't put my hand round it, don't lift my arm,' he said, loudly. He was beginning to whip himself into a temper. If anyone ever gave what he was feeling a name –

Therapy Rage – he would give up trying to control it completely.

'So how do you not gamble?' I said. 'Or – if you can't miss out a step – how do you gamble? And then, how do you not gamble?'

'I've had enough of this,' he said.

'Okay,' I answered. I stood up and went to sit behind my desk. 'Do you want to wait a while and see if you change your mind or do you want to leave? Because if you're leaving I better call you a cab now, in case that snow starts to lie.'

'Bitch,' said the man.

'I know it feels hard,' I told him. 'But it's like flicking a switch that's really stiff. Once it's flicked, things look different.'

'Call me the taxi.'

'Of course,' I told him, and dialled the number. 'And will you do one thing for me?'

'No,' said the man, staring over my shoulder with his mouth set in a line.

I had to work hard not to laugh.

'Okay, well here's what I was going to ask you, just in case you change your mind. Next time you go to the casino, when you sit down at the table, ask yourself what would happen if gambling was illegal and there was a cop standing behind you and if you put your chips down he would cuff you and throw you in jail for the night? Ask yourself what you would do then.'

I had snagged his interest.

'I'd—' he began.

I held up my hand.

'I don't want an answer,' I said. 'I want you to ask yourself the question next time you're sitting down. Do that for me. And if you want to tell me how it went, you know where we are. Jen?' I said into the receiver as the ringing stopped. 'It's Janie. Any chance of a cab to catch the two o'clock?' I covered the receiver. 'You better pack,' I told the man. 'There's not much time.'

This thought experiment had worked in the past. Belinda, after her fourth failed day-course, had worked it out for herself and come flying back to tell us. 'And I thought, if there was a cop there and I was going into the cells for the night, right? I wouldn't do it, right? Like I had a choice, right? And if I had a choice when the cop was there, I had a choice when the cop wasn't there, right? So I was free to choose. So I chose. I bought my wee boy a pair of jeans.' But Belinda was as bright as a button and she had a fully functioning guilt-gland. I didn't hold out as much hope for this character, and I think he knew it.

'Bitch,' he said again as he left the room.

'At your service,' I called after him.

'But that's okay,' Danny would always say. 'I really think some of them only stop because they hate you so much and they can't stand you looking down on them all. And you do look down on them, Janie. You really are a complete cow. No sympathy. But it's good – you're like my secret weapon.'

'At least when they crack it and I say I'm proud of them, it means something,' I said. 'When you say you're proud of them they think so what, you were proud of them anyway. Every tot gets a lollipop.'

'Somebody's got to look out for their self-esteem,' said Danny. 'You'd have them all slashing their wrists if I wasn't here.'

'Yeah, well, some people are right to have low self-esteem,' I would say. 'Some people suck.'

And so we went on. We weren't making any money, but it kept us off the streets, and when it worked I really *was* proud of them, and of Danny, and even of myself. And Lawrence loved them. He could stand just about anything except pity – that cloying, hair ruffling, oh-what-a-tragedy pity that some people (women, mostly) switched on like a lightbulb when they saw him coming – and the great thing about compulsive gamblers is that they're so sorry for themselves they haven't any pity left over for anyone else. Most of them really thought that not being able to stay away from the dog track was a greater burden than Down's Syndrome anyway, and they treated Lawrence like a lucky little tyke who would never know all their troubles. He lapped it up.

I finished writing up my notes on the Therapy Rage guy and let myself out, locking the office door behind me. In the warm corner of the kitchen, Lawrence, Danny and my mother were sitting in a row staring at the television screen, where an unchanging shot of a dusty African road was staring back at them.

'Have I missed anything?' I said.

'Princess Fergie reading a poem,' said Danny. So, no, not really.'

'What's she doing there?' I asked.

'No show without Punch,' said my mother, always a bit down on the Duchess for some reason. She suspects her of hanging on with an eye to the succession, and I suppose she's got a point.

'How is he?' Danny said, without taking his eyes from the screen.

'Packing,' I told him. 'You better go and say goodbye.'

Danny glanced at his watch.

'Don't worry,' I said. 'It'll be hours yet. Probably.'

'I don't want to miss him,' said Danny. 'Come and get me if anything happens.' He stood at the doorway watching the television for another minute and then ran off down the scullery passage towards the yard. I squeezed myself into the space he left, still warm, and put my arm around Lawrence.

'Budge up, Fatso,' I said. 'Aren't you bored yet?'

'I can't believe it,' said my mother. 'I said I'd watch it with him and I thought he'd get sick of waiting in ten minutes, but here we still are.'

Lawrence continued to sit and look at the screen, his ANC flag at the ready in his fist.

'You're not normal, Lollipop,' I told him.

'Duh,' said Lawrence, which cracked me up.

'I wonder when they'll give him your card?' said my

mother. Lawrence's class had made a welcome home card so outsize and so thick with poster paint it had to be sent in a box. We watched in silence for a while and then heard Danny come jogging back along the corridor.

'Anything?'

'Nope,' said Lawrence. My father must have heard the commotion from his studio; we heard his footsteps and then he stuck his head round the door.

'Any sign of Nelson?' he said.

We all shook our heads.

'Any sign of lunch?'

My mother waved at the fridge and my father withdrew his head again. Danny lifted Lawrence out of his place in the middle of the couch and sat down with him on his knee.

'But no farting,' he said. 'Listen, Janie, Colin's going to stay on after all.'

'Oh joy,' I couldn't help but say.

'Don't worry, he's not going to do any more sessions. He's just going to hang out. Maybe chop some logs, walk in the woods.' I turned and gave Danny a hard look past Lawrence's flag. 'The guy lives in a bedsit in Easter Road,' said Danny. 'I can't just chuck him out because he's having a bit of a struggle.'

'He called me a bitch,' I said. 'Five times in one hour.'

'Were you being one?' said Danny.

'That's a bad thing to call you,' said Lawrence. 'He's a bad man. Is he the man with the picture of the lady on his tummy?'

'That's the one,' I said. 'A real prince.'

'I like him,' said Lawrence. 'He's a nice man. I want a picture of a lady on my tummy.'

The front bell clanged and we heard the door scrape open.

'Oh Lord,' said my mother. 'That'll be Frances, Danny. I'd better make some lunch.' Danny played it very cool, just sat still with Lawrence in his lap and watched the screen, but I could see him running his tongue around his teeth, getting ready for a kiss. Frances was based in Aberdeen, a doctor on the acute children's ward and so when she made it down to spend time with Danny it was usually for at least forty-eight hours, and this time it was to be five whole days.

'Frances,' said Lawrence, waving his flag. 'I want a picture of Frances on my tummy.'

The kitchen door opened and there she was, snowflakes settling on her cloud of black hair, waist still managing to look nipped in even under a Barbour jacket.

'What are you all doing?' she asked, dumping her bags and coming over to kiss the top of Danny's head. I stood up to let her sit beside him.

'Waiting for Nelson Mandela,' I said.

'He's really late,' said Lawrence.

'Yeah,' said Danny, 'and it's not like he needed any more of a build-up.'

Frances sniffed. 'Well, it'll be on the news later anyway, won't it?' she said. 'Who wants to come for a walk in the snow?' Lawrence gave her a piercing look and turned to face the screen again. I stared at Danny for what must have been a full thirty seconds but he, although his cheeks reddened, didn't catch my eye. Frances waited, then gave an awkward little half-laugh and went off to say hello to my father.

Five whole days. Frances baked a lemon layer cake for my mother, took Lawrence to the trampoline centre, bought one of my father's sketches, and emerged every morning down the short flight of stairs from Danny's corner of the house to meet me on the landing, looking artfully dishevelled and very smug. Or maybe I was imagining it. I wasn't, however, imagining her sickening attempts to get chummy with me.

'I should be sensible and cut mine off too,' she said on the landing on the third morning, ruffling her curls and studying my razor-crop, which always looked like a guinea-pig pelt until after my shower, no two hairs going in the same direction.

'Yeah, who'd have curly hair?' I agreed. 'You either chop it off or you turn into a narcissistic bore trying to look like

273

Andie MacDowell.' I shrugged in sisterly resignation and left her there blinking.

'Do you think it's serious?' my mother asked me as we watched them strolling off down the drive for a drink that evening. 'I'd love to see Danny happy.'

'He's only twenty-four, Mum,' I said. 'He's got a lot of rosy-cheeked lasses in Barbour jackets to get through yet before he's ready to settle down.'

'And what about you?' she said, still staring out of the window. My mother always broached difficult topics when we were side by side, looking straight ahead. 'I worry about you, Janie. All you do is work. Where are you ever going to meet someone nice?'

'I'm only twenty-four too, Mum,' I said. 'There's plenty time.'

'But if you wanted a family . . .' said my mother.

'Mother, there is plenty of time,' I said firmly. My mother heaved a sigh. 'Okay,' I went on. 'I promise if I'm still single when I'm thirty, I'll go to an evening class.'

'Oh, Janie, please don't leave it until you're thirty,' said my mother.

'For God's sake, Mum, you didn't have Lawrence until you were nearly forty.'

'And I wouldn't change him for the world,' said my mother. 'But still. And anyway, who are you going to meet at an evening class when you're in your thirties?' She chewed her lip for a while before she spoke again. 'I know this sounds mean,' she said. I couldn't wait for this; my mother just didn't *do* mean. 'But don't leave it until all the good ones are taken. When you're thirty-five—'

'How time flies,' I said. 'I was thirty, ten seconds ago.'

'When you're thirty-five all the men will either be toy-boys, or they'll have failed once already, or they'll be the ones that no one else wanted.'

'Maybe one of them will be my soulmate,' I said. 'Maybe one of them is out there right now waiting for me and only me. And we could have met at school or at university or last year or next year or in ten years' time and it won't make any difference. The minute we *do* meet, we'll know.'

My mother was shaking her head.

'Are you sure you're not just being stubborn?' she said.

'What do you mean?'

'So long as you're sure,' she said and, giving me a squeeze, she left me.

I came back into my bedroom after a shower the morning after Frances had left to find Danny sitting on the edge of my bed.

'I'm bored,' he said.

'Well, dump her then,' I answered.

'Oh ha ha,' said Danny. 'Can I get under your covers? It's freezing in here.' I nodded and he burrowed under the heap of blankets and duvets on the bed.

'It doesn't matter how warm I am when I wake up,' I said, 'by the time I've got to the bathroom it's worn off and I have to have the shower so hot, I'm getting thread veins in between my shoulder-blades. Shut your eyes till I get my knickers on.'

Danny clamped his hand over his eyes while I shuffled off my dressing gown and hurried into bra, pants, tights, and vest before the warmth of the shower was all undone.

'Okay,' I said.

'What are thread veins?' said Danny.

'Little purple—'

'I don't really care,' he said. 'God, I'd hate to be a girl. This house *is* beyond a joke, though. Why don't we ask your mum about proper heating again?' I had pulled on a cord skirt and a thick jersey and was now getting extra socks and a pair of boots on before my feet cooled down.

'Because,' I said, mimicking my mother, '"the upstairs floorboards have never been disturbed and they're all complete and the skirting boards too and it would cost a fortune not to damage them and our money has to last Lawrence's lifetime and it's much more healthy and we never get colds and we can always lay a fire." Why don't you move out?'

'Why don't *you* move out?' said Danny. 'Anyway, that's not what I wanted to talk about. I'm bored at work.' I groaned. This would take a while, so I pulled my boots off again and got into the bottom of the bed, leaning against the footboard, wiggling my toes into a warm patch under Danny's leg.

'Why aren't you bored?' he said.

'It's a question of attitude,' I told him. 'You call it boredom, I call it contentment. Make the most of it while you've got it, cos it won't last.'

'But how can you be contented?' said Danny. 'It drives me nuts. You're twenty-four and you act like you're forty-five.'

'Forty seven,' I told him. He laughed and kicked me.

'You never have a boyfriend,' he said. 'Why is that? It drives me nuts.'

'And I'm supposed to be the bossy one,' I said. 'You haven't met the love of your life yet; neither have I. You're filling in the time with a cast of thousands, I'm not. We're just different.'

'Okay so you're waiting to meet the love of your life,' said Danny, sounding for him rather sour.

'And you *haven't* met yours yet, have you?' I asked, just checking. 'It's not Frances?'

'Well, it's not Frances,' he said, and paused as if he was going to say more. Then he scowled again. 'How the hell do you expect to meet him anyway, when you never meet anyone?'

This was a bit too close to the bone. 'I got some good advice from someone who knows about these things,' I said. 'They told me to just let it happen. Just follow my heart.'

'So why didn't you?' said Danny.

'I did,' I told him. 'I followed my heart. It didn't lead anywhere.'

'Oh pass the sick bag,' said Danny. 'Enough with the extended metaphor already.' I hated it when he did New York Jewish, and when he was right. 'And – getting back to the subject – I'm bored at work. You fobbed me off last summer.

You said let's talk about it in the winter. Well, look at your breath in front of your face. It's winter. Let's talk.'

I didn't see the point in having the same conversation again, but he had asked for it so I started the litany.

'We can't have drunks and junkies in the house. Or even near the house. We'd never get planning permission for the accommodation, we'd need medical staff, we'd need security staff, we'd have to know what we were doing . . .'

'Speak for yourself,' said Danny. 'I know exactly what I'm doing. And I've got to change something. Jeez, Janie, how can you be so . . . bovine?'

I kicked him this time, and he caught hold of my foot and started to tickle it. At this moment my mother, still holding her lantern in the gloom of the February morning, peered around my door.

'Janie?' she said. Then: 'Danny? Oh! I'm sorry, I didn't mean to— I mean—'

'It's okay, Mum,' I said. 'We're having a meeting.'

'This house is beyond a joke in the winter, Moira,' said Danny. My mother giggled at him.

'But you're learning,' she said. 'Jock and I hardly notice the cold once we're tucked up at night.' There was a silence long enough for the clock downstairs to chime five of its seven chimes and, if possible, the cold got even colder. My mother cleared her throat and withdrew.

He was right about me, of course. It was only because I knew the time would come when I had to turn my back on all of this – Sorrowless and Danny and my family – and do the job (as Pilchard put it) that I was content to wallow in it now. Still, the imagery bothered me.

'Mum?' I said, at coffee time that day. 'If I was an animal, what kind of animal would I be?' She looked at me for a minute or two.

'A cat,' she said at last. I blew her a kiss. 'A nice big tabby cat, curled on a chair in a warm kitchen with milk on its whiskers.' Oh, I thought. 'And Lawrence would be a . . . badger. Or maybe a groundhog.' So much for mother-love.

So it was partly pride that got me thinking in the end. And once I got started it didn't take me long. I went to tell Danny and found him propped up in bed reading by candlelight, in a skiing jacket, knitted mittens and a Nepalese hat with pigtails.

'I've had an idea,' I said.

'Don't untuck the blankets, for God's sake,' he said, as I began to haul them away from the footboard to get in opposite him. 'Just get in at the top. I won't jump you.'

'I think we should write a book.'

A slow smile spread over Danny's face as he thought about it and by the time he spoke his eyes were shining. 'Perfect,' he said. 'And not just for gamblers. If we don't need to have them in the house, we can do drunks and junkies and bulimics and anorexics and smokers and philanderers—'

'Philanderers?' I said.

'It's the latest thing,' he said. 'Sex addiction. Earle *et al*? I photocopied a review and left it on your desk.'

'Jesus,' I said, and then regathered my thoughts. 'Plus self-help tapes. Tapes are going to be huge – you can make a different one for every kind of loser.'

Danny whistled. 'So anyone in the world who's struggling with problems could have your voice in their ear calling them names. How can it fail?'

I met my mother on the stairs making my way back to my room. She tried not to look interested.

'Another meeting,' I told her. 'We've got big plans, Mum.'

'For work?' said my mother. I nodded. 'Will it mean more catering?' she said, trying to look enthusiastic.

'No,' I said, staunchly. 'We're moving in a very different direction.'

'But you'll be keeping the men?' she said. 'Won't you? We'd never stay on top of the garden without the men.'

We kept the men. As Danny and I sat in his office the day before the Big Meeting in London, one of them could be heard trundling up and down the drive on the mower with the roller attachment, giving the gravel the first flattening of spring.

'Are you going to visit the Queen?' Lawrence had asked, when he first heard about the Big Meeting in London.

'Practically, Lollipop,' I told him. In fact, I was going to visit the commissioning editor at Spender and Gerard and every time I thought about it my stomach dropped six inches and flapped, like a careless mountaineer losing his footing and swinging from his rope. I still thought the whole thing was a fluke.

'But it can't be,' said Danny. 'If it was just a fluke it would have fallen apart as soon as we tried to . . . do that thing you always say is so important.'

'Reduce it to first principles,' I said.

'Right. But it didn't fall apart. It kept making more and more sense, and every new place we tried to apply it, it worked. So, when you're in the meeting—'

'Yeah, remind me why it's me going to this meeting again.'

'Because I'm too chicken and I said so before you,' said Danny. 'When you're in the meeting, if they ask about your experience in the field, what are you going to say back?'

'I'm going to describe the clinic and say that we've tried out the method extensively in the area of compulsive gambling, which offers an excellent testing ground because there is no physical dimension to the . . .' I gritted my teeth and spat the next word 'addiction . . .'

'Well done,' said Danny.

'. . . so the psychological element is laid bare. I'm going to say that we have had excellent – I've said excellent twice now – extremely promising results in sessions with disordered eaters, and I'm not going to say it was one fat girl from Melrose who babysits my little brother, and we're in the middle of very useful discussions with a trained psychologist in Los Angeles who works with . . . I can't say it.'

'You've got to,' said Danny. 'They need to hear it. They'll probably want to put it on the cover in big red letters.'

'Okay, who works with sex addicts. Bollocks, bollocks, bollocks!'

'I wouldn't finish off with three bollockses,' said Danny.

'But otherwise, that sounds pretty good. So, Miss Lawson, very briefly if you will, can you describe the proposed book?'

'No I, can't.' I said. 'April Fool!' Danny ignored me. 'You don't think it's significant?' I asked. 'Them setting up the meeting for the first of April?'

He cleared his throat and spoke in a clear voice.

'The book is called *The Golden Shovel* because it offers a new way to kick addiction by shovelling away all the – pardon me – bullshit that surrounds it. That's an important keystone. There are three sections to the book: defining addiction, dismantling myths and then, most importantly, practical exercises. Now stop arsing about and give the chapter headings.'

'I can't say important keystone. Okay: Shakes and Cravings, A Lot of What you Fancy, and Poor Me and Everyone like Me. Then, what is it . . . Free Will is Powerful, Choosing is a Choice, and Please, Somebody Help Me Lift this Matchstick off my Legs Before it Crushes Me. These chapter titles sound worse every time, you know.'

'They were your idea. I said they sounded like articles in *Take a Break* and you shouted me down.'

'Yeah, but I'm starting to doubt myself. I think they might be too far ahead of their time.'

'You call that self-doubt?' said Danny. 'Come on. You're nearly there. Four chapters of exercises.'

'A Night in the Cells, Will I Put My Head in the Blender or Not, That was So Hellish I Think I'll Do it Again, and finally Getting over Yourself and Staying There. I quite like the last one.'

'You would,' said Danny. 'Right, you're ready. Give them hell.'

I gave them hell. And they loved it. They loved the title, loved the chapter headings, particularly loved the sex addiction.

'What about nicotine?' said the marketing director, lighting up for the fifth time since we'd begun. 'Will there be a separate chapter on smoking?'

'It doesn't merit one,' I said. 'It's what we call – Danny and I – it's what we call a No-Brainer.' He looked at me with interest.

'It stinks, it makes you stink, it kills you. No brain required.' They tittered cravenly.

'It *is* addictive,' said the marketing director. 'Nicotine is physically addictive.'

'Oh yes,' I agreed. 'It is unpleasant while you're getting it out of your system.'

'So?' he said.

'Well, basically, diddums,' I told him. 'Try pancreatic cancer for a week and see if you'd swap back.'

They lapped it up. So much so that I thought I had better make sure they understood.

'You do understand, don't you,' I said, 'that our stance – the apparent lack of sympathy – is not just because we're nasty people and we get off on sneering? It really is a . . . a . . .' Jesus H. Christ, I was going to have to say it '. . . an important keystone in the programme. Anyone who is serious about getting over an addiction has to dismantle the myths. And the myth of "poor me, I can't help it, I'm so powerless" is the strongest one of all. We have to hold to it pretty hard to get through that.'

'No, no, no,' said the commissioning editor. 'We love all that stuff. We'd hate you to tone it down. It's very now. Very Thatcher.'

I blinked. Had he really just said that?

'Well,' I said, carefully, trying to wrest a compliment out of it. 'Self-help *is* rather Thatcherite, I suppose, in essence.'

'Hmm,' said the editor. 'But this one especially. It's the tone. That wonderful bossiness. That air of effortless command. Pure Thatcher. How did you hit on it?'

'Yes, how did you and your partner devise that persona? It's priceless.'

All the way back to the hotel, I tried not to think about

that, walking down Portobello Road, desperate for distraction, instead of taking the tube. I even bought an *Evening Standard* to concentrate on, but the headlines didn't make any sense. 'Mermaids found in the Thames'? 'Skating rink proposed for Albert Hall'? I glanced at the dateline and remembered. It was April Fool's Day, of course. Then I stopped walking and read the date again. It was the 1st of April 1990. It was my wedding day.

I don't know how long I stood there, feet rooted, head spinning, while the memories of the first time around engulfed me: standing in the foyer of the registry office, with my father in a hired kilt and Ludo's sister Katie in the bridesmaid's dress I had let her choose herself, feeling the beginning of a cold sweat and holding my arms away from my sides like a peg doll; arriving at the reception and noticing how much dowdier it looked in the grey afternoon of early spring than it had on the lamp-lit winter's evening when we had seen it first and made the booking; sitting in the ladies' loos with my girlfriends and a bottle of claret, singing *Copacabana* and trying to ignore the fact that I would have to go back out sometime and dance with Uncle David; and most of all for some reason, I could remember as clear and familiar as the feeling of Lawrence's hand in mine, the touch of the dress as I put it over my head, the cold satin and the rough netting underskirt, the strange tug of the boned bodice as my mother buttoned it up behind. I looked down at myself, expecting to see it there, and then lifted my head again.

A man was marching along in front of me, going in the same direction, weaving on and off the pavement, outside the parked cars and then inside again, dodging past the slower walkers. His hair was streaming out behind him and his jacket, velvet or corduroy, was flapping at each stride, flashing the seat of his trousers and falling again. The hair was too long, and the clothes were different, but there wasn't a shadow of a doubt. It was Ludo.

Chapter 19

1 April 1990

'Ludo!' I broke into a run. 'Ludo?'

People around me gave bored glances, but the man kept walking.

'Ludo? Ludo Masterton?' I reached him and he turned.

His face was tanned, his hair longer than he used to wear it, and he was slimmer too, firmer, fitter-looking, and in better clothes. The jacket *was* velvet, which was a bit much, especially with a T-shirt underneath, but overall he looked fantastic.

'You look—' I began, but nipped it off in time. 'Hi.'

He smiled politely and then looked over my shoulder and shifted from foot to foot.

'You obviously don't remember me,' I said. I was trying not to stare too hungrily, reminding myself I had no right to throw my arms around him and squeeze him, jumping up and down. I stuck out my hand. 'Janie Lawson.' And it's our wedding day and I've found you. I knew my eyes were shiny and I made a huge effort to get a grip.

'Sorry,' said Ludo. 'I'm afraid I don't.' He had an English accent. I'm afrayed I dewnt. I laughed and he smiled back at me.

'We met at a party,' I said. 'In Edinburgh. And you gave me your number, but I lost it. And don't worry about not remembering – you were pretty far gone.' Ludo was looking at me with about four layers of expression in his eyes. He was always good at layering. There was politeness on top; Margrite Masterton's upbringing had seen to that. There was amusement, which was Ludo's trademark mood in his younger days;

there was a glimmer of panic, which was only to be expected – he had just been borne down upon by a strange woman in the street shouting his name – but there was also a faint but unmistakable look of interest. Of course there was; I smiled wider.

'I was born in Edinburgh,' said the strange English accent coming out of Ludo's mouth, 'but I left when I was a kid. Not to say we couldn't have met at a party, you understand, but I'm pretty sure I wouldn't have been drunk.'

'Well, then I must be mistaken,' I said. 'I mean, it must have been somewhere else.' I could hardly keep my heels on the ground, so strong was the urge to lean my head against his shoulder and put my arms around his neck. I knew that if I rested my head on his shoulder my mouth would be just at the place where there was a soft hollow between his scratchy stubble and scratchy chest. I looked down at the ground.

'Who knows?' said Ludo's voice, in the accent. 'So, I gave you my number?'

When I looked up, he was smiling broadly at me, only the look of interest and a bit of the panic left. I nodded.

'Are you busy?' he said, looking around him. 'Now, I mean. Do you have time for a drink?' I followed him back to the Portobello Road and into a dark pub, one of those London pubs that seems to have nothing at all to recommend it, not good beer, edible food, comfortable seats or clean toilets, but which is always packed. I subsided into a chair, one of two empty ones opposite a couple on a banquette and sharing the same table. Ludo went to the bar.

'So,' he said, clinking his pint glass against my wine glass. 'Jane, you said?'

'Janie.' The wine was disgusting.

'You don't like "Jane"?'

'It's not my name,' I said. 'It says Janie on my birth certificate; I'm not sure why.'

'Wacky parents,' said Ludo. 'Lucky you.'

I thought about putting him right, but then realized that here, now, this time, he wasn't wrong.

'And what do you do?' he said. He seemed genuinely interested, like how men aren't ever supposed to be. He sounded as though he actually wanted to know. 'Not just so we can work out where it was we met,' he went on, confirming this. 'Just generally. What do you do? Tell me about yourself.'

'Well,' I said, 'I'm from Edinburgh, like you, and I'm a . . . I suppose you'd call it a therapist. I run an addiction centre.' Ludo made the stunned face that people make when they hear this and then he did what people do if they hear this when they have a drink in their hand: he put his glass down. I picked my glass up and clinked his again.

'Don't worry,' I said. 'It's an addiction centre for compulsive gamblers.'

'I bet that's fun,' he answered. I actually managed to laugh at this for the first time in years. He could do no wrong. I took another huge slug of the disgusting wine and beamed at him.

'So you're a psychologist?' he said.

'Sort of,' I answered. 'Believe it or not, I actually did a philosophy degree, but I swerved.' He nodded and looked thoughtful.

'I did psychology,' he said. Talk about irony, I thought, staring at him. He was staring back at me. Then I wondered what he was thinking to make him be looking at me like that.

'You must think I'm an untrained quack meddling in your field,' I said, taking a guess. He shook his head, seeming to come to his senses. 'But I work with a proper psychologist,' I went on. 'And he's the boss.'

'Your husband?' said Ludo.

I tried not to look shocked. 'No,' I said, 'I'm not married.' I wanted to say that if I had been married I wouldn't have been running after boys I remembered from parties, but I knew if I said that I would sound like a little girl from the sticks out of her depths in big bad London, which was too near the truth. Ludo shrugged as though to indicate that this was good news

285

but it wouldn't have been the end of the world. I hoped he was just playing it cool.

'How about you?' I said. Then blurted: 'What do you do for a living, I mean?'

'Oh, banking,' said Ludo. 'Snore. Don't ask. And where do you live now? Still Edinburgh? I haven't been back for years.' Banking, I thought. From philosophy to banking? I wondered what had happened and why the family had moved and how I could find out.

'No, not now,' I said. 'Actually, how embarrassing is this? But I still live with my mum and dad and Lawrence. Pretty uncool, huh?' Ludo's eyes flashed.

'Who's Lawrence?' he said.

'Oh, my little brother,' I reassured him. Ludo put down his glass and wiped his mouth as though he had misjudged the act of taking a pull and slopped his chin.

'You've got a little brother?' he said.

'Yeah,' I said. 'He's eight. He's lovely. But really I only live there because the treatment centre is on site. We live in this crazy big old house in the middle of nowhere and the centre is in the old stables. I really do need to think about moving out though. It's getting ridiculous.' Already I was planning a move to London, of course. I would move in with Ludo and look after the writing and marketing side of things, leaving the clinic to Danny; Danny, who for some reason I hadn't really mentioned yet. Why had I not just said two brothers? Or maybe I would move in with Ludo and start having babies straight after the wedding, let Danny have the whole thing. Ludo was draining his glass and I felt my face begin to fall. But instead of telling me it had been lovely to see me again, he reached over and took one of my hands in both of his, turning it, caressing the inside of my wrist with the tips of his fingers.

'Do you have time for another?'

I nodded, and he went back to the bar, leaving me to drink the dregs of my wine, shudder at the taste of it and stare into space. It was just as Pilchard had told me it would be. I had just waited for it to happen and now it was happening. I could hear Pilchard's voice, airy but urgent too, telling me to follow my heart. I had and it had led me right back to Ludo, just like before. Except different and better. I could see Pilchard's face in front me, looking at me with that watchful look. I blinked. Pilchard was sitting at the next table, looking at me with his watchful look.

'Quite a coincidence,' he said, speaking loud across the noisy space that divided us. 'I live over the road. This is my local.' I laughed. Nothing would surprise me today, and nothing could shake this feeling I had, spreading in me like the heat of gulped brandy, that finally, finally, finally I was on my way home. I didn't believe Pilchard, of course, not for a minute; but if they had tipped him off and he wanted to be on the spot to witness me finding Ludo again, I wasn't going to complain. He wasn't smiling back, though. He came and sat in Ludo's chair and stared, solemn-faced, waiting.

'What?' I said at last.

'Just this,' said Pilchard. 'Why shouldn't you have a little brother? Why would the news that you have a little brother make someone choke on his beer?' He reached over and squeezed my shoulder then stood and, struggling a bit in the crowd, he left the bar. Ludo had to pass right by him, hunching his shoulders to keep the two glasses steady as he threaded his way back to me. He smiled at me again as he sat down, but the smile wavered.

'Something up?' he asked.

'Ludo?' I said. I couldn't think of any other way to put it. 'Why shouldn't I have a little brother?'

He frowned at me, politely enquiring.

'I just mentioned Lawrence and you spluttered as if you were surprised. There's only one explanation I can think of for that, but I wonder if you've got another one.'

He gave a little sigh and looked off to one side. That was what finally convinced me. That sigh and the looking away to the side with such elaborate, such ostentatious, patience; that was no part of getting to know someone on a first drink, that was a sigh from deep inside a marriage. Ludo spread his hands and gave me a sheepish grin.

'Don't drink that wine,' he said. 'Let's go somewhere and get some champagne. After all it's a special occasion, isn't it? It's our anniversary, kind of, wouldn't you say?'

We didn't speak while elbowing our way out of the pub and waiting to be shown to a table in a dark little bar down the street with candles and a old man playing the piano.

'I just want to make it clear, right at the start,' I told him, when we had clinked glasses and taken our first swallow, 'that I don't blame you. I made a mess of it and I don't blame you in the slightest for trying to make sure I didn't do the same again.'

'That's extraordinarily magnanimous of you, Janie,' said Ludo. 'I must admit when I saw you today my only impulse was to flee, but I'm glad now I didn't. It's really good to see you again.'

'You too,' I said. 'You seem very different. Not just the accent, although I must say "Oh my God" about the accent.' Ludo frowned. 'Sorry,' I exclaimed. 'There's nothing wrong with it. It's just a surprise. Anyway, you seem . . . different.'

'You seem exactly the same,' said Ludo. I think I must have frowned at that. 'In a good way,' he added and smiled.

The champagne was delicious and we finished the bottle and ordered more as we poured out to each other the first morning, school again, trying to work it out, giving up, trying again, Ludo's move to London, to a house in Chelsea and a car with a driver.

'Don't tell me you resisted temptation.'

'No, only it was 1985 before I came up with a winner.'

'Nineteen eighty-five?' Ludo streamed with laughter. 'I had my first million within six months. That's why we moved. You mean you just stayed there in Tyler's Acre Avenue, trotting along to school every day for four years?' I managed to laugh back. It did sound pathetic now. 'And you did a philosophy degree,' he said poking me in the chest across the table. 'After all you said to me about it.'

'I thought it would help. You know, with this.'

'And? Did it?'

'No,' I said, laughing. 'How about you? What do you think this is?'

'Who cares?' said Ludo, filling my glass. I laughed again and sipped my champagne. The other tables were beginning to drop away, in that way they do, until only the face across from you, your hands and his hands and the candles in between have any clarity, as though your little table alone is in a patch of glass warmed with a breath and everything else is misty.

'It really is lovely to see you,' he said again, reaching over the table and cupping my cheek in his hand. I rested my head against his palm and smiled at him.

'I'm sorry,' I said, meaning for everything, for all the things I had done that only Ludo knew, for everything I wasn't sure I had done because it might have been him who did it to me. That didn't matter anymore. He took a deep breath, and I thought that if he could just say sorry to me for everything he had done that only I knew and everything he might not have done because I did it to him, if only whose fault it was didn't matter, maybe our future could start right here.

'I forgive you,' said Ludo. He took his hand away as I moved my head to take a sip of champagne.

But that was fine. If it really was me, if everything that had gone wrong in our lives was my fault, then I was glad this new, improved Ludo had the guts to tell me. Pilchard's face suddenly floated in front of me again and I looked around the room wondering if he was here again for real, watching me.

'What are you looking for?' said Ludo.

'Nothing,' I told him. Pilchard wasn't there. 'Hey, I know you've never met Pilchard,' I said, 'but did you get the phone number in Hull? Did you get postcards?'

Ludo was shaking his head.

'Well, did you meet the other guys?' I asked. 'The guys in

the suits who pretend to be Jehovah's Witnesses? Really? None of them? You must be way more subtle than me at doing whatever you've done.'

Ludo said nothing.

'What have you done anyway?' I asked.

'What are you talking about, Janie?' he asked. 'I'm not used to the feeling that I'm missing something. Don't you just love knowing what's going on all the time?'

'I'm talking about that thing we used to say. Remember? Elvis? We used to joke about it.' Ludo snorted with laughter and inhaled some champagne.

'Go back and save Elvis,' he said, coughing and laughing. 'I had forgotten about that.'

'So?' I said, waiting. 'What did you try to put right, since you've been back? I stopped the royal wedding.'

His jaw dropped open. 'You did?' he said. 'Why?'

It was my turn for blank gazing. 'What do you mean, why? And I . . . Well actually, that's all I did directly. I was going to send a letter about Fred and Rose West but the Nilsen one back-fired and after that I just phoned the number and told them instead. Chernobyl, Tiananmen Square . . . What about you?'

'Who are Fred and Rose West?' said Ludo. I thought for a moment he was teasing, like Pilchard with Bill Gates, then a stranger thought struck me. If he didn't know about the Wests maybe he hadn't come back from the same corner of the multiverse as me.

'Ludo, what do you know about the Rainbow Warrior?'

He gave me an odd look and answered in the same careful tone that I had just used to him. 'It didn't get sunk this time. Why do you ask?' My shoulders, which I hadn't realized until that moment had crept up around my ears, dropped down again.

'And AIDS?' I said.

'Yeah, disgusting disease, pamphlets, condoms. What exactly are you asking me?'

I chewed my lip, trying not to say what was threatening to burst out of me.

'What is it?' said Ludo, at last. 'God, you're exactly the same.'

'Didn't you even think about maybe tipping off Salman Rushdie?' I couldn't help it. 'And you live right here in London. Terrence Higgins lived in London. You could have gone round and told him.'

'Rushdie didn't happen,' said Ludo, which was true. 'And nobody would have believed about AIDS before it took off. Nobody would have listened. They still don't.' This was true too. And to give him his due, he was squirming.

'That's hardly the point,' I said. 'Would you really just wait and read in the papers again about all the bodies coming out of Cromwell Road and not even feel a bit bad that you did nothing to stop it?'

'I don't know anything about Cromwell Road,' he said. Fair enough. I had forgotten some pretty huge disasters too; I had forgotten what year the Falklands was. But that wasn't the point. Making a packet of money was one thing, and I had no room to talk. Making a packet of money and trying to avoid the woman who had ruined your life, well that was understandable too. But doing nothing, absolutely nothing, so that Pilchard didn't even know he was here and the suits didn't get a whiff of him, that was something else.

I did like this new Ludo, bits of him anyway. I liked the carelessness and the confidence. And when you love someone, I'm sure it's their essence you love, not anything on the surface. So with Essence of Ludo to love and a top-coat of New Ludo to like and admire, I should be happy. The 1st of April 1990 should, once again, be the happiest day of my life. I should shut up and let it be so. And yet. And yet.

'It's the Wests' house,' I said.

'Who?'

This couldn't be right. I remembered Ludo reading it out to me, as we sat up in bed one Sunday morning and me pleading with him to shut up. We even argued about it. He called me an escapist and I called him a ghoul. He couldn't have forgotten.

But he really didn't seem to know. There was only one possible explanation for that.

'Before,' I began. 'When I said I stopped the royal wedding, you seemed surprised.'

'I am,' said Ludo. 'You obviously think I haven't done enough "good works" but at least I haven't done any gratuitous meddling like that.'

'And you have no idea who Fred and Rosemary West are? Or what happened at the house in Cromwell Road?' Ludo was bobbing his head from side to side in time with my talking trying to hurry me along. 'I don't see how you could have forgotten all that if you were around when it happened.' I took a deep breath. 'You went back to 1981, same as me, right?' I paused and heaved another deep breath. 'But where did you start from?' I asked.

'Same as you,' said Ludo. 'Today. Our wedding day.'

I took a steadying sip from my glass, then folded my hands in my lap, clenched my jaw and tried to ignore the rolling in the pit of my stomach.

'You came back from our wedding day?' I said.

'Why?' said Ludo, with his eyes very round. 'Didn't you?'

'Can I ask you something?' I said, trying to stay calm. 'What is it you think I was apologizing for? When I said I knew I had made a mess of it— If you don't know anything about what happened when we were married . . . what did you think I was referring to?'

Ludo shrugged. 'I said I thought it was magnanimous,' he said mulishly, not quite meeting my eye. I looked around the room; it was all back now. Our little bubble of shining eyes and candlelight had popped.

'Can I ask you something else?' I said.

Ludo shrugged again as if to say I could please myself.

'Did you not even think about coming to find me? After you lost me on our wedding day, did you not want to get me back again?'

'It's not like it never occurred to me,' said Ludo. 'But somehow it just didn't work out that way.'

I would not cry. I had spent nine years thinking about him and yearning for him, wanting only to get the chance to put it right, and he had come back from our wedding day, *from our wedding day*, and not given me a second thought. I would not cry. He seemed careless, I had thought, and I was spot on. He was without a care in the world. Me, Salman, Elvis; none of us mattered a damn.

'So, what's with all this?' I waved around at the flitting waiters.

'I couldn't resist it,' said Ludo. 'It seemed meant. Today of all days.'

'After all these years? Just because of the date on the calendar you suddenly want to start again?'

'I don't know about "starting",' said Ludo. 'I mean, you live in Scotland and I live here, but I did think maybe an interlude.'

'An interlude?' I had calmed down now. Actually I had gone down much further than calm, but Ludo couldn't read it, misjudged it completely.

'An after-dinner interlude,' he said, with that coy grin I had always hated so much. 'It is our wedding night after all.'

'And I bet we aren't a stone's throw from your house,' I said. 'How convenient, how very handy.'

'Well, that might be awkward,' said Ludo. 'But aren't you booked into a hotel?'

I couldn't look at him. Not at his face anyway, but I stared at his hands, at his left hand in particular, specifically at the third finger of his left hand, at an indented band of skin, rubbed smooth. I pointed to it.

'When did you take your ring off?' I said.

'Hah, well, yes,' said Ludo. 'At the bar when I was getting the first drinks. There are limits.'

I started to put on my coat.

'Oh come off it, Janie,' drawled Ludo. 'When did you turn into such a prig?'

I hurried towards the door, determined not to cry where he could see me.

'We're outside the rules, you and me,' he called after me. 'Surely you can see that.'

All the way home on the train, I kept thinking the same thought over and over again. My husband didn't even want to be married to me on my wedding day. And I kept hearing his voice telling me why. Except it had turned into all their voices, all six of them – five publishers and Ludo – and it wasn't just 'pure Thatcher' any more and 'exactly the same'; it wasn't the tone they were talking about either, the persona. Ludo and the chorus of publishers were all saying the same thing: 'You are the spitting image of Mrs Thatcher, Janie, and you always have been. If you stood side by side no one could tell you apart.' Your husband never loved you, I told myself. Your publishers think you're a vaudeville turn, a dominatrix. Danny thinks you're a cow. At that my eyes finally overflowed and tears started splashing down. The only person who loves me is Lawrence, I thought, and Lawrence loves everyone. And my parents, and they've got to. Danny thinks I'm a cow.

And now with the tears came barking sobs that I couldn't stop and couldn't turn into silent weeping no matter how I tried. I have never cried for so long in my life. Normally, there's a physical limit, no matter how destroyed you are, but this time whenever I thought I had stopped and sat up to blow my nose it was as though some supply tank somewhere inside me tipped up with the movement and refilled the reservoirs, like a steam iron, like a baby doll. I put my head against the train window and howled.

Then, without knowing I had fallen asleep, I suddenly awoke with the feeling of dried tears, or worse, puckering the side of my face and a man in striped trousers, with a watch chain across his waistcoat, looking at me in concern. He cleared his throat.

'Murray Mint, miss?' he said. I shook my head. He wouldn't be offering me mints if he knew me.

It was midnight before I got back. I crept into the house and up to my room shivering in the chill, then I crawled into bed and began to cry again, hoarsely and painfully, but still somehow pumping out the tears. My husband hated me, even on our wedding day. Danny thought I was a cow. The clients loathed me and the only reason they ever came back was that they loved Danny more than they hated me. Everybody loved Danny. My parents loved Danny out of choice and they only loved me because they were my parents and it was the law. Everyone loved Danny even though he was a gambler and a womanizer and a pain in the neck, and everyone hated me even though all I ever tried to do was help people and save people and . . .

I woke up at six and lay on my back, sniffing and thinking, then I padded through the house in my tights, my feet wooden with cold, knocked on his door and sidled in. Only the pom-pom on the top of his hat was showing above the blankets, but he spoke at once.

'How'd it go?' he said.

'Great,' I croaked. 'Also . . .'

'What?' he said struggling up out of the mountain of covers and trying to focus on me.

'Remember once you asked me about boyfriends and I said there was someone but it was complicated?'

'What?' said Danny. He took off his hat and scratched his head, then dropped back onto his pillows.

'Doesn't matter. It wasn't complicated actually; it was dead simple. Can I ask you a question?'

I came and sat on the edge of the bed. He didn't answer for so long that I thought he was asleep, but eventually he said: 'What is it?'

'Do I remind you of Mrs Thatcher?'

'Yeah, why?' said Danny. I started crying again, silently.

He opened an eye and watched me weep for a bit.

'What's wrong?' he said, at last. 'Hadn't it ever occurred to you? I always thought she was your role model.' The tears were pouring fast now. 'Obviously not. Sorry. I mean,' he cleared his throat and propped himself up on his elbows, 'I always thought she was your role model for social interaction.

You know how she always knows best and you always know best? Not in terms of her being a raging fascist and you not. Which is quite a significant factor, so really, when you take that into account, no, you're nothing like each other. My final answer is no.'

'But what about if you *do* know best?' I said. 'What if you can't help it because you just do?'

'It doesn't bother me,' said Danny. 'I think it's funny, but has someone said something?'

I let the tears continue to fall, but I tried over and over again to wipe my nose with the heel of my hand. The skin between my nostrils was broken from blowing so much and every time I wiped it a needle of pain made my eyes water even more. Eventually, I could speak again.

'You know at work? Our method? It *is* ours, isn't it? It's not just me? I mean, you say all the same things I do, don't you? About facing it and taking control of things and how everyone's responsible for themselves. Don't you?'

'Yeah,' said Danny, but there was a 'but' coming. I saved him the trouble of working out how to put it.

'But you're kind. And I'm not. You're a friend and I'm a complete cow. And that's why everyone loves you and everyone hates me.'

'Everyone doesn't hate you,' said Danny. 'It's just some people aren't ready to hear things just the way you tend to put them.'

'In cow-language, you mean?'

'Well, yes.'

My nose was beginning to bleed, nipping so badly that I couldn't wipe it again, so I sniffed really hard instead and it honked in my throat and hurt me where I was all swollen from sobbing, which made me cry more.

'Can I ask you another question?' I said. I was wallowing in it now, but I couldn't stop myself. 'Elvis Presley, right? If he was still alive, out of his head on pills and booze and I came along and tried to help him, the way I try to help people, do you think it would work?'

'Elvis Presley?' said Danny. 'Surrounded by his yes-men? I don't think he'd go for straight-talking, no. What *is* it?'

'I didn't know,' I wailed. 'I really didn't know.'

'You didn't know what?' said Danny.

'And now you're saying I wouldn't even be any good to Elvis, if he was still alive. And everyone hates me and everyone loves you.'

Danny sat up in bed and rubbed his face.

'Two things,' he said. 'Sorry, three. One: if *everyone* loves me – here comes one of those logical arguments you like so much – if everyone loves me, that includes you, and you've got a bloody funny way of showing it. Two: everyone doesn't hate you, if I'm someone, because I certainly don't. But if I'm chopped liver, which I get the distinct impression I am, then maybe you're right.'

'What's the third thing?' I said.

'And shut up about Elvis fucking Presley. That's not the third thing, that's just an aside. Three: if you really think you're being a cow and you don't want to be one, then stop. Problem solved. And if it's hard, do it anyway. And if it hurts, try cancer for a week and see which hurts more.'

'How long have you been waiting for the chance to say that?' I asked him.

'I haven't been,' said Danny. 'I'm a nice person that people love.'

'Are you nearly finished?'

'Hardly started.' We sat glaring at each other for a minute, both of us breathing hard. I was slowly beginning to digest those logical arguments he had fired at me. It was harder to follow them when someone else was dishing them out.

'Can I ask you one last question?' I said. He nodded. 'You know how you always break up with your girlfriends?'

A grin spread over his face.

'Is it always the same reason?'

'Yes,' he said. 'Every time. Every girl.'

'What's wrong with them?' I said. 'What was wrong with Frances, for instance?'

'Well, Frances wasn't always quite bossy enough,' said Danny. I started smiling too. 'She didn't keep enough pointless secrets. She went days without interfering sometimes. She had this annoying idea that I should do what *I* wanted instead of what *she* wanted. She just wasn't the girl for me.'

'I'm sorry,' I said.

'So you should be,' said Danny. He held the blankets up. 'Get in.'

I had just slid under the blankets when my mother put her head round and peered into the room.

'Danny? Have you seen Janie? She's back but she's not in her— Oh, you're there, sweetheart. Another meeting?'

'Em, no actually, Mum,' I said. 'So if you wouldn't mind?'

My mother yelped. 'Oh! Sorry! Carry on! Oh goody, goody, goody. I must go and tell Dad.'

'What a family you are,' said Danny when she had shut the door. 'Lawrence is the only one of the lot—'

There was a loud knock and my mother's voice came again.

'I'm not coming in!' she called. 'Only, I was wondering *what* exactly to tell him.'

'Tell him we're engaged,' shouted Danny. We listened to my mother's feet thumping gently along the passageway in her slippers, then Danny kissed me.

'Ouch,' I said. 'My nose is cut from blowing it.'

'Right in the middle bit?' said Danny, wincing. 'So it makes your eyes nip?'

'Really bad,' I said. 'It even hurts when I'm talking.'

'So shut up.'

'And kissing.'

'Fine by me,' said Danny. 'You're covered in snot and you didn't brush your teeth last night, did you?'

'Can we just lie here?' I said.

'Well, I said I'd take Lawrence swimming later,' said Danny. 'But we can just lie here for now.'

Chapter 20

26 July 2001

I turned over my diary to a fresh page and, noticing the date, my heart banged in my chest, so hard, with such a thump, that my fingertips tingled. Old people try to warn you; they tell you that the time begins to flash by, decades gone like seasons, weeks passed while you pop to the shops. Then there's the impossible but irrefutable fact that time, squeezing and stretching, makes you crawl towards relief and good news like an ant across a desert, all-clears from the hospital just dots in the distance, but you hurtle towards the appointments you dread like Benny Hill going downhill in a bathtub. Well, I was fifty-seven now all told, looking thirty-six of course, and it was summer 2001, which meant that the event I had been dreading since Pilchard told me what I was here for was sucking me towards it quick enough to give me whiplash. Most days, these days, I just felt sick.

There was a knock at the door and I swept my diary away.

'It's only me,' said Joey, entering.

'Only you?' I echoed. 'Is that all?' She gave a weary sigh and then spoke loudly.

'Behold! It is I – Josephine.'

'That's more like it,' I said. We had talked about Joey's self-esteem issues before, many times.

'Ready?' I said, when she had folded herself into the chair opposite me and tucked in her elbows and heels. 'Tell me about . . . oh, let's say, Thursday.'

'You would,' said Joey. 'You're psychic.' She flicked through a shorthand notebook she had ready on her lap and then cleared her throat. 'Cornflakes, banana, digestive biscuit, soup, buttered roll, apple, lamb chop, peas, courgettes, boiled potatoes, watermelon. Three teas, two coffees, milk in the cornflakes and a glass of wine.'

'Anything else?' I said.

'Four Mars Bars, Jumbo Twix or so, family pack of microwave popcorn – toffee flavour – and six Senokot.'

'That's pretty good, then,' I said. 'That's five servings of fruit and veg, I think, and popcorn instead of crisps, and laxatives instead of your toothbrush down your throat. That's good going. Well done. Now, when did you have the Mars Bars? Talk me through the build-up.'

'I will,' said Joey. 'But can I just ask something? How would you describe me? If someone who had never met me asked you what I looked like, what would you say?'

'Why?' I asked.

'Because I just asked your husband the same thing in our session and he said if he had to describe me in three words they would be: blonde, brown-eyed, pretty.'

'And what did you say?' I asked her.

'Fat, ugly, spotty,' said Joey.

'I would say – this is the God's honest truth – I would say you were fat, blonde and pretty. In that order. That's what I'd say. That would be the best way to pick you out of a crowd.'

'Your husband's full of shit, isn't he?' said Joey. 'And you can't be fat *and* pretty.'

'He was just being a guy,' I said. 'I bet there's at least one fat girl you think is pretty. Go on, name one.'

'Fergie?'

'There you go,' I said. 'Princess Fergie. Fat, *ginger* and pretty, for God's sake.'

'Yeah, but that's different,' said Joey. 'She doesn't need to be skinny. She's going to be the queen.' I must have looked sceptical, because she went on: 'Don't you think so? I mean Chuckles must be fifty. No one's going to marry him now.'

'We're wandering off the point a bit here,' I said, trying to sound stern and squashing the thought that if he did die alone we'd know whose fault it was. 'What weight do you think you would have to be to get: blonde, fat, and pretty?'

Joey giggled. 'Fourteen stone, maybe.'

'How about blonde, pretty and fat?'

'Eleven? Eleven and a half?'

'So let's see if we can get you started. Talk me through the junk. You ready? I'm going to be shovelling, mind. I'm not going to swallow any crap.'

'I'm not going to serve any crap,' said Joey.

'Glad to hear it,' I told her. 'In that case maybe you could explain what you mean by "a Twix *or so*"?'

I went to meet Danny in the kitchen for lunch, although I didn't think I could eat anything after an hour of Joey's binges. 'Why didn't you tell Joey Paton she was fat?' I said, once he had put down the bread knife and was laying slices into the grill pan. 'Just one for me. I'm not hungry.'

'So that you'd have something to bond over,' said Danny. 'I knew she'd run to you to check.'

'Well, it's an honour to be a fly in your tangled web,' I said. 'Very clever. Don't put any cheese on mine.'

'You okay?' said Danny, looking up at me from his squat in front of the cooker and searching my face.

'Fine,' I said. 'Just not hungry.'

'You want to talk about it?' asked Danny. He never believed me when I said I was fine, unless I really was.

I had always known it was coming, of course, but I had managed for a while to put it out of my mind. First there was the wedding to plan, and then the book to write, and the book tour, and the sequel, and the expansion, and the sister clinics to visit, and the column to produce week in and week out, and all of a sudden here we were.

My mother kept asking about grandchildren in the way that mothers do, so subtly that you can't even tell them to stop it.

'Oh well, who knows where we'll all be a year from now,' she would say, when Danny and I were thrashing out who would go to Toronto and who would stay here for the audit.

'What do you mean, Moira?' Danny would ask her. 'We're not thinking of moving. Are you thinking of moving? Where are you thinking of going?'

'Goodness me, no,' my mother would answer, pinkly. 'We're not moving.'

'She meant, maybe this time next year we'll have a baby,' I would say to Danny later when we were back at home.

He would roll his eyes and mutter something about women, then smile and say: 'Well, who knows? Maybe this time next year we will.'

But we didn't. And the next time my mother broached the subject – 'Don't you think sometimes, Janie, you try to do too much? Don't you think you should slow down?' – I would know exactly what she meant and I would wish I had some news for her, but I never did.

'I don't do any more than Danny,' I would answer. 'I certainly don't do any more than Dad. And he's sixty.'

I had finally warmed up enough to risk moving away from the stove without my fingers turning white and I went to get glasses while Danny tiled the slices of bread with slabs of cheese. My stomach lurched at the sight of them.

'Is Dad stopping too?' I asked him.

'He said to give him a shout,' said Danny. 'And your mum and Lawrence should be back any minute.'

I stacked five glasses in the crook of my arm and picked up the big water jug.

Danny put his arms around me and hooked his chin over my shoulder as I stood at the sink waiting for the water to run cold.

'Can I just point out in case you decide you do need to talk after all that I am a chartered psychologist and a very good listener and I love you.'

'I love you too,' I said, but I didn't really hear him.

I had expected a baby to come along. I had half-expected to come back from our honeymoon with morning sickness. Certainly I had never done anything to prevent it. But the years went by and all we had to show for them was a shelf of co-authored books and a rating in the *Scotsman*'s top 100 Power Couples. And the nearer it got to the time when I might have to go when they sent for me, the harder I found it to think about going the extra mile to make it happen. What if we trotted along to a fertility clinic and ended up with the sickly triplets I had imagined for Ludo and me all those years ago and then, come September, I disappeared in a puff of smoke, or worse, *was* disappeared into a government bunker somewhere and Danny just got left with them? He was still an attractive man, wearing better than me (bastard), and he drew women to him like flies, like a man who has co-written a bestselling book about why men have no excuse for being unfaithful. For, as we had expected, shovelling through the shit of sex addiction was our real breakthrough. Anyway, the way I saw things, he'd find it a lot easier to get started on someone else without three spindly orphans in tow.

I heard the rumble of my mother's car coming up the roughest bit of the drive, and the horn gave out a series of blasts on a hip-hop beat as it careered around into the yard, the wheels just clipping the grass at the edge of the gravel.

'I can't believe she lets Lawrence drive it,' I said, watching for them through the window. 'He's a maniac.'

'Yeah,' said Danny, 'and then she's got the nerve to look tense with *me*.' This was true; my mother braced her brake-foot against the carpet in the passenger seat, checked over her shoulder for you on motorways and peered across at the speedo when she noticed a camera coming, but she sat like the Dalai Lama beside Lawrence whomping up and down the drive.

They appeared around the corner of the washhouse, and I screamed.

'Lolly's had a buzz cut!' I shouted back to Danny, making for the scullery passage door to meet them coming in. When I got there, Lawrence was posing, trying to look cool, pouting and poking his Raybans further up his nose, but he broke into giggles when he saw my face.

'What have you done?' I said to him, turning him around to look at it from all angles. 'Mother, how could you let him?'

'I know,' said my mother. 'Look.' She fished in her handbag and brought out a long, black, silky plait, bound with Sellotape at the root-end. 'Only I can't work out if it's a lovely keepsake or just creepy.'

'Hmm,' I said. 'I know what you mean. You could always weave it into a bracelet.' We both considered the idea briefly and shuddered. In the kitchen, Danny looked at the haircut from all angles with a serious expression on his face.

'Well?' said Lawrence at last.

'You look exactly like Captain Picard,' said Danny. Lawrence blushed with pleasure and put his shades back on.

'Take over the bridge, Mr Conway,' he said. 'I'm going to show Dad.'

My father came back with him, slightly dazed as he always was when plucked away from his canvas and tumbled back into the world with the third dimension.

'What did you do with the hair?' he asked my mother and she waved the plait at him.

'Can I have it?' said my father. 'I might be able to use it.' My mother all but threw it at him and went to wash her hands.

I couldn't keep my eyes off Lawrence over the lunch table. Danny had been kind; in fact, my brother had a head like a football and a chin that was at least a double, so it was hard to imagine anyone looking less like Jean-Luc Picard. And these days, I hated anything to change.

'The only one in the family not to have hair like a Brillo,' I said, mournfully. 'What a waste.'

'Yeah but Janie,' said Lawrence, through a mouthful of cheese on toast. 'I was going bald.'

I gawped at him.

'Don't be ridiculous, Loll,' I said, and I knew my voice was shaky. 'You're only twenty. You can't be going bald.'

'I was bald when I was twenty,' said my father. 'Only that

was before *Star Trek* so I combed it over and looked like a pillock instead.'

'Before *Star Trek*?' echoed Lawrence, sounding troubled. His world's philosophy started from the idea that in the beginning was the Enterprise, and 'before *Star Trek*' was a concept beyond him.

'Well, before *Next Gen*,' said my mother, but Lawrence just shook his head to bat away such nonsense and took another bite of his toast. My mother smiled ruefully across at me. Only a day or two before we had been looking at photographs of me when I was a child and trying to answer Lawrence's tearful demands to know where he was in them, why we had left him at home.

'It was before you were born, darling,' said my mother.

'I wanted to go to see all those flowers,' said Lawrence stubbornly, scowling at the three of us standing in the tulip fields.

'But you weren't here,' said my mother. 'It was before you were born. You know how babies get born, don't you?' she said, cajoling him. She was smiling, but she couldn't meet my eye; she must have been thinking the same as me, which was that maybe if we had a baby to show him and we could get him to remember all the time before it came along, maybe then the idea would click.

I raised my slice of dry toast to my lips, but put it down again. Babies took nine months and it was July and after that came August and then it would be September. And anyway, I told myself, trying to make it hurt because pain is so much easier to take than dread, you'll never have a baby. You're pushing forty. Your little brother is going bald.

And maybe it was the cruel side-light from the kitchen window, my father's hard morning of concentration in front of the canvas, the way my mother scraped her Brillo-pad hair off her face with kirby-grips and didn't bother with make-up day to day, but suddenly, sitting there, they looked old. With a sickening thud I wondered, if Lawrence couldn't get his head round *before*, what he was going to make of *after*. And what, if I was leaving, Danny's next wife and all their children would make of Lawrence in their lives. Danny himself I didn't doubt for a second, but what had I been thinking? I couldn't go without telling him where and why.

I caught his arm as we were ferrying dishes along to the scullery.

'I do want to talk to you,' I blurted out. 'You know how you're always asking me to? At least, I don't want to. But I think I should.' Danny looked at me consideringly.

'Talk as in talk?' he said.

'Talk as in really talk,' I answered.

'Will we go away for the weekend?' he said. 'We could leave after Group tomorrow and go somewhere quiet.' Men are not like us, as lesser self-help books than *The Golden Shovel* never tire of telling. No woman in the world would respond to what I had just said by suggesting we start talking about it the following evening after driving to a hotel. A woman would be badgering for at least a hint, right now, and would be feverishly planning how to cancel all other engagements and get the dirt in one lavish splurge.

'Nah,' I said. 'I want to watch the Wimbledon final.' Danny rolled his eyes. He still didn't believe me that Goran was going to do it, even though he was through to the semi. 'But let's talk tonight.'

We faced each other across the table at home, after supper, plates cleared, dishwasher whirring and sloshing in the background and a bottle of good red wine between us waiting. Danny wiggled his eyebrows at the wine.

'So it's not a Tesco's claret moment?' he said.

'I'm just going to tell you,' I said. 'And the chance of you believing me is nil. But hear me out, okay?' I opened the knife drawer in the table and took out the envelopes bundled together with an elastic band. 'Have a look,' I told him.

'Hey! I remember these,' said Danny. 'I remember these from years ago. So, I'm finally getting to read them.' He leafed them all without speaking, looked up at me briefly, then flicked through them again.

'C?'

'Chernobyl. It's some place in the Ukraine, with a nuclear power station.'

'What massacre?'

'Tiananmen Square in China. It was averted. Now listen and try not to interrupt.'

That wasn't a problem; Danny's mouth dropped open and stayed hanging open until long after I had stopped. I reached over the table and tapped him under the chin with my knuckle, like we used to do when Lawrence was a baby to teach him to keep his tongue in and breathe through his nose. Then we just sat there looking at each other until the dishwasher, beginning its rinse cycle with a whoosh, made us both jump.

'I'm not kidding,' I said. 'I'm not lying to you.'

'I know,' said Danny, and I let out a hissing sigh of relief. 'I love you,' he went on. 'Nothing can change that.'

'I had to tell you before September,' I said. 'I don't know what's going to happen and I didn't want you to think I had just walked out. Promise me if I don't come back you'll tell my parents and Lawrence that I love them and make it okay. Promise. And promise me you'll always take care of Lawrence for me. I know it sounds impossible and you don't believe it, but promise anyway?'

Danny was stroking my hand.

'It doesn't sound impossible,' he said in a gentle voice. 'It sounds absolutely classic. The only bit that's hard to swallow is you keeping it quiet for so long.' I relaxed into his voice before I had really heard what he was saying. Hang on, I thought. Me keeping it quiet is the bit that's hard to swallow? Danny was still stroking my hand. 'But we're going to get you better,' he said. 'And everything is going to be fine.'

'Ah,' I said. 'Right. I'm with you. Yes, I can see why you'd think what you're thinking. But consider this for a minute. What about Last Suspect? What about these postcards? You remember them coming.'

'Janie, I was so out of my tree when we put that bet on Last

Suspect, everything you did seemed normal enough to me. But obviously, something as extravagant as that, something so grandiose – just like those shares you made us buy, remember? And when you said those men were threatening you, and then you said they were bailiffs, and your mum said later they were Jehovah's Witnesses?'

'And the postcards?'

'Yep, you've had this for a long time. But we can tackle it. It's a disease.'

'Gosh, it's just like the old days,' I said. 'Now *I've* got a disease. Does mine have a name?'

'You've got Munchausen's Syndrome, Janie my darling.'

I tried to speak very calmly. 'Munchausen's Syndrome,' I said. 'My dad is a respected artist, my mum has got her houseful of disintegrating heirlooms. We're millionaires, or we would have been if we hadn't spent it all on the clinic. Is that how it usually works? Do Munchausen's people usually make their grandiose plans come true? Is *that* classic?' Danny's face clouded for a moment and then he shrugged it away.

'That might make it harder to get you out the other end,' he said. 'But maybe not. Maybe having a reality that's not so bad means it'll be easier to give up on all the fantasies. We'll get you there.'

'What are you suggesting?' I said. 'Are you going to put me in an asylum? Like it's 1830? Or are you just going to cure me yourself?'

'I don't know what I'm going to do,' said Danny. 'It's not my area. I'll take advice.'

I was beginning to feel like the woman in *The Stepford Wives*. Was it Ali McGraw? It was that other one who's nearly Ali McGraw. This couldn't be happening.

'This is exactly why I never told anyone,' I said. 'I knew I would sound mad. And once you've decided someone's mad, you can just sit there with that oily smirk on your face being oh-so patient and oh-so caring and not listening to a word.'

'I am listening,' said Danny. 'I see how frightening it must be. But remember what you said to me? Way way back. You

308

said if I wasn't just looking for an excuse to gamble I would be happy to hear that stopping was in my control. Well, it's the same deal here. If you're not hooked on all the drama, wouldn't you rather think it was just some frayed wires in your head?'

'Of course,' I said. 'Of course I'd rather have a nice understandable condition with a name and a cure.'

'Well, there you are then,' said Danny, patiently. 'Why are you getting annoyed?'

'Because it's not true,' I told him. 'Of course I'd rather not have to go and tell them about the terrorists and be put in an oubliette while they work out what to do with me. I'm sick with nerves. But I can't make it go away by saying I don't believe it.'

'Don't upset yourself,' said Danny. 'You're not going anywhere.'

'I'm going wherever they tell me whenever they ask,' I said to him.

'Right,' he said. 'To stop the planes flying into the skyscrapers and killing all those people.'

'And if you have me sectioned before they call and I can't get away, then . . .'

Then what?'

'Then you'll be responsible for thousands of deaths. And as soon as I get out I'll divorce you.' He took his hand away from mine then.

'Don't make me into the enemy here, Janie,' he said.

'Well, don't be one,' I answered. We said nothing for a while.

'Okay,' said Danny. 'How about this? I'll start doing a bit of reading, and making a few calls, and on September the 12th you start dealing with this, agreed?'

'If I'm here,' I said.

He nodded, kind, patient. 'But in the meantime,' he said. 'I don't think you should see clients.'

I couldn't help laughing a dry little laugh. 'Okay,' I said. 'Whatever. Fine by me.'

We spat and shook.

'So,' I said. 'You're not much of a psychologist, then, are you? Don't you think you should have noticed that your wife was psychotic?'

'It's not a psychosis.'

'Still, I would keep it quiet, Danny. Don't put it on your CV.' He blew a raspberry at me, trying to lighten the mood, but his eyes were strained. Poor bloke; I could almost have felt sorry for him if it hadn't been that what he was going through was a gnat to a boulder when you put it next to what I was going through. We finished the wine and went to bed, perfectly friendly, but when we put the light out I lay awake staring up into the dark. I suppose I had assumed I would be able to make him believe me, because of Last Suspect and Goran and things like that. I really hadn't thought through how unhinged it would all sound to someone who hadn't actually been there and seen it: Chernobyl and Princess Diana and everything. And I certainly hadn't thought how very neatly all my experiences could be turned into a list of symptoms and given a name. I thought about the boy who had thrown himself under a tube train. Hadn't Pilchard said he had tried to find his wife and talk to her? But he had also said the last straw was when he worked round again to where he'd come in. This September had been blocking out everything beyond it for me and I'd hardly thought of that.

'Try to sleep,' said Danny, softly. 'Everything's going to be all right.'

'I was just thinking,' I said, 'that I don't know what's going to happen on the night in March. March the 5th 2002: that's when it started.'

'What do you think will happen?' said Danny, turning onto his side and putting his arm across me.

I put my hands on his arm and lifted one knee to let him put his leg underneath.

'I don't know. Maybe nothing. Maybe I'll disappear. Maybe I'll still be here but I won't remember anything about all of this.'

'That would be good,' said Danny. 'That's what I'm hoping for.' He circled his hand slowly on my stomach in the way that usually soothes me to sleep.

'Don't,' I said. 'Sorry. It's making me dizzy.' He stopped. 'I could make you believe,' I said. 'When they call me, I could ask them if you could come too. They'll probably say no, but I could ask.'

'Don't worry about it now,' said Danny. 'Try to sleep.'

I couldn't have got through much of this: the thumping dread, the near blackouts every time I stood up too fast, nothing to do all day and Danny treating me with such tender concern that I wanted to punch him. I know he said something to my parents too, because my mother came round and filled my freezer with casseroles, as though Munchausen's might be driven off by her bacon and cashew nut medleys and her cornflour pudding pies. Lucky then, in a way, that it was less than a week until the call came.

'Miss Lawson?' said the voice on the phone. It was Sunday morning, Danny was out at football practice and I was still in my dressing gown.

'No,' I said, thinking it was a cold caller.

'I beg your pardon, Mrs Conway,' said the voice. 'I assumed you'd have kept your own name.'

'Who is this, please?' I said, although I was becoming sure I knew.

'We'll pick you up tomorrow,' said the voice. 'We'll send a car.' I took a long, steady breath in, filling my lungs to the bottom, telling myself I wasn't going to be sick.

'Can I ask something?' I said. 'Can my husband come with me?'

'I'm afraid that won't be possible,' said the voice.

I spent the day at my parents' house.

I sat in my father's studio and watched him standing rock-still with his brush in his hands.

'Aren't you bored?' he asked me. I shook my head, but he

frowned before he looked away and he kept glancing back at me again. I knew I was distracting him.

'Dad,' I said, standing up and coming towards him. 'I love you and I'm so proud of you I could burst.' Even after all we had been through, after how far we'd come from Tyler's Acre Avenue and Limtec, my father's eyes flashed a warning. 'Loopy Talk' they said and he gulped. I kissed him and left him in peace at last.

I sat in the garden with my mother, too sick to stay beside her on the swing-seat, so I lay on the grass and looked up at the sky through the branches of the sycamores, listening to the birds and to Mr Murray cutting silage down the hill.

'I'm going away, Mum,' I said.

'I know, darling,' said my mother. 'Danny told us all about it.'

'I don't know when I'll be back.'

'We'll visit.'

'I'm sorry,' I said.

'What for?' said my mother, peering down at me over the side of the swing. 'For having the Munchkins?' I laughed. 'Think about it, Janie darling. Look at me. I always wanted to live in a great big house and have antiques and that's not all.' I waited. 'I only went out with your father because he said he was an artist and I was impressed.'

'But that's not why you married him.'

'No, but what I'm saying is, it's obvious where you got this from. *I'm* sorry. *I'm* the one who should be sorry.'

'I forgive you,' I said, dryly, and she poked me with her toe.

'That's still not all,' she said, not looking at me this time. 'There's something worse than that. It's a disease, Danny says. My daughter is suffering from a serious mental disorder. But you know what?' I waited. 'I'm glad you got it and changed everything for us. Do you hear me? I'm actually glad. What kind of mother is that?' I knelt up and looked at her lying in the swing, with her hands clapped against her cheeks in horror. She squeezed her eyes shut, hiding from my gaze, then made herself open them again.

'I wouldn't be glad if it was horrible for you,' she said. 'If it was cancer. I'm not that bad. But I think – from what Danny told me – I think it sounds like fun.'

I put my arms around her neck, laughing, and we hugged.

'I love you,' I told her. 'You're right – you're miles worse than me – but I love you.'

I sat beside Lawrence on the couch in the kitchen and watched three episodes of *Deep Space Nine*.

'Don't you ever wonder if they miss their families when they join the Starfleet, Lolly?' I asked him. Lawrence turned to look at me.

'Captain Sisko misses Jake,' he said.

'Exactly,' I said. 'But he's still happy that Jake's doing what he wants to do. And it doesn't mean that Jake doesn't love his dad, just because he moved away, does it?'

'Nope,' said Lawrence, his attention back on the episode again.

'I mean, you love *your* Dad, and Mum and Danny and me, but if you could go and work on the Enterprise, you would go.'

Lawrence laughed. 'It's on the telly,' he said. 'Not on the real world.' I paused and wondered whether to press on.

'And if I ever went away and didn't see you anymore, it wouldn't mean I didn't love you to bits.' He turned to me again.

'Commander Worf must get lonely, missing all the other Klingons,' he said. 'I might go if I could share a cabin with Commander Worf.' I lifted my arm and Lawrence launched himself sideways and crash-landed for a cuddle.

'I spoke to the family today,' I said to Danny, lying in the dark that night. 'Tried to, anyway.'

'They just want you well,' he said. 'Same as me.'

'You don't have a shadow of a doubt that you're right, do you?' I said.

'For once,' said Danny. 'How d'you like taking it instead of dishing it out?'

I hugged him hard.

'But say – just say – you're wrong,' I insisted, 'you would understand, wouldn't you? You wouldn't think I didn't love you just because I went away. Not with thousands of lives at stake.'

'Ssh-ssh,' said Danny.

'Anyway, I might come back. They might let me come back.'

'Hush,' said Danny. 'Go to sleep.'

The car came at lunchtime the next day; Danny was at work. A big black car, very clean, with a driver in a uniform. He took me to East Fortune airfield where a disconcertingly small plane was waiting with its engine running, and another man, in a different uniform, was standing at the bottom of the steps. He ushered me up them and followed me, shutting us both in. I put myself into one of the dozen or so seats, did up my belt and closed my eyes.

I never get travel sick, but I could forgive myself this time for the cold sweats and the need to gulp my breaths down. Just after take-off, trying to distract myself, I began to work on the window-blind to roll it up, but the steward rose from his seat behind me and asked me to stop.

'My instructions were that the blinds should stay down, ma'am,' he said.

'What if I was to peek round the side when you've gone for a pee?' I asked him. 'Are you licensed to kill?' He didn't smile.

So it was impossible to tell where we were going. No sunshine filtered through the blinds to tell me even the direction; the only clue I had was how long it took us to get there, which was two hours. I looked at my watch as we landed.

'Not the UK, then,' I said. 'Unless we came by Orkney to confuse me.'

I couldn't really account for what was making me feel skittish enough to give back-chat to these firm-jawed minions; maybe I was beyond fear now (although if I was it was only

my mind that knew it and not my body) or maybe it was
because the whole thing seemed just slightly bogus, slightly
low-budget TV drama, and I was hamming it up to match.
Certainly, after unfolding myself and walking down the steps
again behind the gold-braided jacket, when I recognized my
welcome party, I whooped with genuine delight. It was the
teeth from all those years ago in Tyler's Acre Avenue. I would
have known him anywhere. *He* had a few more expression
lines and a better suit, but *they* were the same as ever, even
brighter if anything and maybe a bit bigger as the gums had
receded under constant flossing.

'Miss Lawson,' he said.

'Great to see you,' I said. 'How've you been?'

He didn't answer, but pointed me towards a car parked on
clipped grass just to the side of the runway. I walked towards
it slowly, looking all around. There were no other planes and
only a featureless corrugated block of a building, with no signs
in any language. The car had no numberplate either and it was
no surprise, when I got in and the door closed on me, to find
that the windows were blacked out.

The drive wasn't long, no more than twenty minutes, and
for all I knew we might have been circling the runway and
then driven into the corrugated building I had seen when I
stepped off the plane. When the car came to rest and the door
opened we were inside an unloading bay with a high concrete
platform for lorries to back towards and an automatic door
just closing on the daylight behind us. I stood and looked
enquiringly at the teeth. He ushered me towards the back of
the space, away from the entrance, where a door stood open.
Now my bravado began to desert me. I walked towards the
door, through it, and down the passageway beyond. I was, I
soon realized, walking literally down. We were descending, as
gradually as a wheelchair ramp, the temperature dropping as
we went and our footsteps, the teeth's tipped heels and my
sandal soles, changing, muting, deadening as we moved down,
and down, and down. It can only have been a few minutes
until we reached the bottom, but it seemed as long as the flight

315

and the drive combined. The teeth moved in front of me and, after giving a soft, courteous knock, he opened a door and stood aside for me to enter.

'Miss Lawson, sir,' he said. I clenched my jaw and walked in.

'Janie,' said Pilchard. 'Please sit down.'

Chapter 21

I was all right for a second, and then Pilchard leapt out of his chair and put an arm around me, just as the grey began to close in from the sides.

'Put your head down,' he said. 'I'll get you a glass of water.'

'Wha—?' I said. 'How can you be here? With them. How is this . . . What's going on?'

'Listen,' said Pilchard, 'and I'll tell you.'

'But they work for the government,' I said. 'So how can *you* be here?'

'They work for me,' said Pilchard.

I tried to figure it out.

'But I posted the letter,' I said. 'All those years ago. About Dennis Nilsen. It was addressed to the Home Secretary and I posted it and they brought it back to my house.'

'I intercepted it,' said Pilchard.

'How? I put it right in the post box,' I said. 'How could you intercept it? That's not possible.'

He smiled at me with his head on one side, fondly almost. 'You think that's the impossible part?' he said, which was a good point.

'But if you're all in it together,' I said, 'why do I even have to be here? Who is it I'm going to tell about Septemb—'

Pilchard was shaking his head as if in wonder.

'What?' I demanded.

'How can you be so dim?' he said loudly. 'How can a person who is so bright be so dim? It's been driving me crazy. I mean, don't get me wrong, it's come in very handy, but even so I've felt like shaking you more than once.'

'What do you mean?' I said. Pilchard threw his chair back

317

from the desk and started pacing to and fro across the room, shouting. 'What were their names?' he said. 'Either their real names or the names on the passports. What were the flight numbers? Where were the flights going? What time did they take off? Hmm?' He put his hands flat down on the desk and glared at me. I shrugged. 'What qualifications do you have for this so important job you've willingly believed you've been picked for? Hmm?' I said nothing. 'Don't you think if this "job" was actually going to be given to someone it would be someone who knew the ropes?'

'Someone who knew the ropes?' I said. 'How the hell does someone get to know these ropes?'

He ignored me, kept ranting. 'Enniskillen,' he thundered. 'The London bombs, the Brighton bomb, Mrs Gandhi, the *Herald of Free Enterprise*. You didn't remember any of them.'

'And the Christmas Eve massac—' I said, not even trying to defend myself, but Pilchard cut me off.

'The Christmas Eve massacre, Janie,' he bellowed, 'didn't happen before.'

'It didn't happen?' I said. 'Well, you can hardly blame me for not remembering then, can you?'

'No, no,' said Pilchard. He was making a visible effort to calm down, but as soon as he started to speak again his voice rose. 'But I *can* blame you for not realizing that if twenty-four striking miners had been gunned down, on Christmas Eve, by soldiers in police uniforms, it wouldn't be something you'd *forget*!'

'Right,' I said. 'I get the message. I'm not here to stop 9/11.'

'Duh,' said Pilchard.

'But it is going to be stopped, isn't it?' I said.

He waved a hand dismissively.

'Of course,' he said. 'It won't happen.'

'So why *am* I here?' I said.

'Listen and I'll explain everything,' said Pilchard.

'No, I don't mean that,' I told him. 'I mean, yes of course, I want to know that too, but I mean why am I *here*. Today, in this ... whatever this place is.'

'Because I knew if we didn't go through with the performance you would lift the phone and start meddling. I haven't forgotten how close you got after Challenger. Tell the truth, now. If no one had contacted you, you would have gone it alone.'

'Of course I would,' I said. 'Especially after Challenger.' Then an unpleasant thought occurred to me. 'Pilchard. It's only July. Are you going to keep me here until September?'

'You still don't know me at all, do you?' Pilchard said. 'Of course I'm not going to *keep* you here. When have I ever done anything bad to you?'

'Well, I've been pretty frightened once or twice,' I said.

'I had to stop you meddling,' said Pilchard. 'I've never known anyone like you for meddling.' I thought about Ludo, keeping his head down and taking care of number one and concluded that maybe Pilchard had a point. Another one.

'I only wanted to make things work out,' I said. 'That's not so bad, is it?'

'It's understandable,' Pilchard said, concedingly. 'But making things work out is my job.' He spoke quite without a trace of ego, but with great conviction.

'Okay,' I began. I was trying to turn the mass of darting ideas in my head, flitting like fish, into one sensible question. 'Why did you make me think I was here for 9/11?'

'Something for you to focus on,' said Pilchard. 'Because it was near the time you came in. That was a nice touch, don't you think? But it was just a coincidence really. Although . . . Will I tell you?' He studied me for a while, then sniffed decisively. 'Yes, why not, I think I will. Remind me to tell you something.'

'So if that was a coincidence,' I said slowly, 'what am I really here for?'

'Oh Janie, Janie, Janie, Jane, Jane,' said Pilchard. 'Wouldn't you feel better if you worked it out for yourself? Hmm? If you actually did something with all that philosophy for once?'

I waited, not even trying. And eventually Pilchard began to speak again.

'That night, the night you left, what had you just decided to do?'

'Leave my husband,' I said.

Pilchard slapped his hand across his eyes and groaned. 'Wrong,' he said. 'What was the last thing you thought before you went to sleep?'

'I thought ... I was wondering about IVF,' I said.

Pilchard gave an exaggerated wink and clicked one side of his mouth at me. 'As loyal as you were to that worm,' he said, 'I knew that so long as it was just you and him there was every chance that you would leave him in the end. And I wouldn't have had to bring you back at all. I don't do it lightly, you know. And once you'd left *him* there was every chance you'd end up where I wanted you. Friends Reunited, you know. Very useful indeed. But you would never leave him once you had a baby, would you? You'd never have broken up a family.'

'Probably not,' I said. 'But what does that have to do with anything?'

'Come on, Janie,' said Pilchard. 'Use your brain. When did I come to see you?'

'When I stopped the royal wedding,' I said. 'And again when I was going to get Salman Rushdie's address and then again in London...' I wound down into silence.

'You're getting it, aren't you? At last.'

'I was on my way out the door to see Ludo,' I said. 'And the second time, I was going to ask the private detective to find me Ludo's address. You were stopping me seeing Ludo! But why?'

'Now the other end,' said Pilchard. 'Think about the day you went back to. What did you do differently?'

'My father lost his—'

Pilchard was shaking his head. 'The day,' he said. 'That very day. I don't like waste. I sent you back just to the very day you had to start over.'

I stared at him and then at the floor, thinking.

'I got thrown out of history.'

'Physics,' said Pilchard.

'Was it? Okay. I bitched up my auntie to my mum.'

Pilchard was shaking his head. 'Does this ring a bell?' he said. 'Hi, Janie,' he was speaking in a high-pitched voice. 'Hi, Danny.' His voice had got even higher. 'It's good to see you.'

'Yes,' I said. 'That was different. Last time, the first time, I was really mean to that annoying little Danny Conway.' Pilchard was nodding.

'On the 5th of March 1981 you told him not to speak to you again,' he said.

'It was that day?'

Pilchard was still nodding.

'And Danny – in case you haven't noticed – is averse to rejection. Even if you *had* tracked him down after you'd left Ludo, he might not have forgiven you. Yes, Danny is about as averse to rejection as you are averse to seeing what is in front of your stubborn face.' He was working himself up again. 'Fourteen years, it took you. Fourteen years living in the same house, and I finally had to let you meet that useless worm again before the penny dropped.'

'I knew you didn't just happen to be there in London that day,' I said.

Pilchard raised his hands to heaven. 'No flies on you,' he said.

I giggled. 'So you wanted me and Danny together,' I said. 'That's very kind of you, Pilchard. I have been very happy. Even though he now thinks I'm deranged.'

'It'll pass,' said Pilchard.

'And I do see that it was best to take me back to before I ever hurt him. I do see that. But . . . why? What's so important about us?'

'It's not you,' said Pilchard. 'You're not important at all.'

'Well shucks,' I said.

'It's your daughter. Yours and Danny's. She's very impor-tant. She's absolutely crucial.'

'My daughter?' I said. 'You mean we're going to have a baby, Danny and me?'

'Despite your best efforts to scupper everything by hanging around for fourteen years,' said Pilchard. 'You should listen to your mother sometimes.'

'When?' I said. 'Do you know when she's coming?'

'How are you feeling?' said Pilchard.

'Stop changing the subject and tell me when she's coming.'

'How are you feeling?' said Pilchard again.

'I'm feeling – Gee, Pilch, I can't really say why, but I'm feeling a bit overwhelmed. Or no, I don't want to overreact here, let's say I'm feeling nonplussed. I'm feeling rather nonplussed. And sick, like I better hold onto something in case I fall over.'

'Not to worry,' said Pilchard. 'It goes away after the first few months, usually.'

The world swayed around me like brandy up the sides of a swirled glass and then resettled with a click into a different place. I put my hands over the zip of my jeans. Pilchard was smiling at me. I smiled back.

'My daughter?' I said.

'At last,' said Pilchard.

'What is it she does?' I said, and while I was asking a thought occurred to me. 'In fact, how can it be that she does anything if it doesn't matter when she's born? If you wanted her before now, but now will do . . . she wouldn't be the same person. Every month she would be a completely different person. Have you not realized that, Pilchard?'

'Have I not realized that?' he echoed. 'Please, Janie, take my word for it, you don't need to be on the lookout in case I miss a trick.' I blushed. 'I've had a good look,' he went on, 'and it doesn't seem to matter when she comes. So long as she does.'

'You've had a good look at what?' I said.

'Everything,' he said. 'From a broad perspective.' He sounded modest again, just as he had when he'd said it was his job to fix things. I stared at him.

'Are you God, Pilchard?' I asked. He made a sound halfway between a sniff and a laugh.

'I'm not God,' he told me. 'But we go to the same gym.'

'So . . .' I said. 'From your broad perspective, what is it she does? Is that what you wanted to tell me?'

'Not a chance,' said Pilchard. 'Don't even ask. She's going to have a normal childhood.'

'Does that mean you're going to let me go home to Danny?' I said.

'Of course,' said Pilchard. 'Don't you know me by now? Danny's wife will return to him and tell him the happy news.' My smile widened for a moment as I imagined the scene, then it faded.

'That was an unusual way to put it,' I said. 'Danny's wife?' Pilchard said nothing.

'Am *I* going home?' I said.

'Yes,' said Pilchard. '*You are.*'

I looked at him closely, trying to read his expression, but there didn't seem to be any grey area in what he had just said, so I left it.

'That's why it's today that I'm here, then,' I said. 'Mission accomplished? Time for debriefing?' Pilchard nodded.

'Although,' he said, 'if you really had been going to stop the terrorists, it would have been better to start today, better not to have life set up as a permanent emergency. That's something you have actually learned.'

'I have?' I said.

'You seem to have,' said Pilchard. 'If you want to save some clapped-out drunk of a cabaret artiste in Vegas, for instance? Just for instance, mind. It's better to work through a really good treatment with him than to break down the bathroom door and try to unblock his windpipe. That's the way I do things. Unspectacular but always effective.'

'And you really are going to stop the planes flying into the towers?' I said. 'You promise?'

'It's not going to happen,' said Pilchard. 'It's already dealt with. No last-minute heroes required.'

'What did you do? Was this the thing you decided you would tell me?' Pilchard clicked his fingers, remembering.

'Yes. Well, sort of. What I did was, as I say, unspectacular. I amplified the intelligence.'

'That certainly wouldn't make much of a spectacle,' I agreed.

'And President Gore is a great listener,' said Pilchard.

'So, don't be *too* modest,' I said to him. 'You did that. The election.'

'I didn't,' said Pilchard. 'That just went the other way on its own. Probably because there weren't so many angry women turning Republican.'

'Right,' I said. 'Because of no Monica Lewinsky. So you did *that.*'

'No,' said Pilchard, holding up one finger like a choirmaster. 'And this is what I wanted to tell you. You did that.' I blinked at him.

'I really didn't,' I said. 'I think I would know.'

Pilchard opened a drawer in his desk and drew something out. It was a plastic folder with a photograph inside. He handed it to me.

'I've been looking forward to this,' he said.

It was a portrait of Bill Clinton, head and shoulders, with a bookcase behind him and a desk in front, crossed miniature flags and an inkwell. He was wearing his usual expression, looking straight at the camera and smiling with his chin high and his curranty little eyes flooded with wisdom and pride.

I looked up at Pilchard, eyebrows raised.

'What?' I said.

'Look behind him.' I looked and shrugged. Pilchard leaned over the desk and tapped his finger against the photograph. I looked closer. On the shelf just behind Clinton's head was a copy of *The Golden Shovel.* It was half-hidden and most people wouldn't have known it was there, but the cover of your own book on a shelf is like the roof of your own car in a packed car park. There was no doubt about it.

'Good job, Agent Lawson,' said Pilchard. 'Well saved.'

I gazed at it as long as I thought I could without looking conceited, then I spoke again.

'There is one thing that's bothering me.'

'Now's the time to ask,' said Pilchard.

'Why did Ludo come back?'

A frown crossed Pilchard's face. 'That was a mistake,' he said. 'It's a very delicate procedure. And two people lying side by side in the dark, touching even . . .'

'You're kidding,' I said. 'He just got swept up and came along for the ride?'

Pilchard shrugged. Something was nagging at me, though.

'Wait a minute,' I said. 'Ludo didn't come back from the same night as me. He came back from our wedding day.'

'No,' said Pilchard, breathing out heavily. 'He didn't. He was lying to you when he said that.'

'Why?' I asked.

'Because he's a worm,' said Pilchard. 'He plays games and he doesn't care how much they hurt people. I can't tell you how it's irritated me, watching him prosper.'

'He was lying?' I said. 'Just to hurt me?'

'Just for laughs,' said Pilchard. 'The worm.'

'Strike him down, then. Smite him. I won't tell.'

Pilchard smiled and then rubbed his hands over his face. 'I don't know about you,' he said, 'but I'm exhausted. I think we should call it a day.'

'Hear, hear,' I said. 'I'm exhausted for two, remember.' We grinned at each other.

'And that's another reason for you not going back home tonight,' said Pilchard. 'It's seven thirty now. I think you should have some supper, and sleep here. We can make you very comfortable then we'll get you home in the morning.' I was already shaking my head.

'I'll – thanks – but I'll just go home, I think. I can sleep late tomorrow.'

'I really think it would be best if you rested first,' said Pilchard. He was looking at me with a frank, open gaze and even when I stared hard at him it didn't change, but still.

'I don't trust you,' I said.

'Explain,' said Pilchard.

'You told me that you would only give "jobs" to someone who knew the ropes, and I asked how someone would get to know the ropes and you didn't answer. And you said two people lying side-by-side in the dark can make things tricky and now you don't want me to go home and lie beside Danny. And you said yourself the thing I came to do is done.'

'I told you you were going home,' said Pilchard. 'I gave you my word.'

'You said "Danny's wife" was going home,' I corrected. 'Is "Ludo's wife" still back there too, where none of this ever happened? I'm not asking if some version of Janie Lawson in some version of the multiverse is going home, Pilch. I'm talking about *me*.'

'Multiverse!' said Pilchard with a curl of his lip. 'Those physics nerds haven't got a bloody clue. Where else would you go but home? Hmm?'

'How old is Bill Gates?' I asked.

'Mid-forties? Fifty?' said Pilchard, looking very innocent. 'Janie, I gave you my word.'

'Have I actually got a choice?' I said.

'No,' said Pilchard. 'You have no choice. Trust me.'

Awake. Darkness. My head feels heavy, far too heavy to lift, but I roll it from side to side on the sheet underneath me. I can hear someone else breathing. I'm certainly not in the room down the concrete passage where I lay down after supper last night. I reach out my hand, for Danny, for Ludo. It flails against something hard and makes a rapping sound. The person breathing snorts and resettles and I realize, when the rhythm of their breath breaks, that they are not alone. There are three of us in here. What did I rap my hand on?

I reach out again more carefully and feel a railing, and another, and another. Not metal, though – it feels like painted wood – and so I think probably not a hospital or a prison. I reach out very tentatively to the other side as well. More railings. I'm in a cage. I'm in a very homemade-feeling cage,